THE TREASURE OF HIDDEN VALLEY

By

WILLIS GEORGE EMERSON

First published in 1915

British Library Cataloguing-in-Publication Data
A catalogue record for this book is available
from the British Library

DEDICATED
TO

THE MEMORY OF MY FATHER

REVEREND STEPHEN LAFAYETTE EMERSON

(The Flockmaster of this story)

CONTENTS

WILLIS GEORGE EMERSON

Willis George Emerson was born in 1856, and spent his early education at Knox College, Illinois, USA. He later attended *Northern Ohio University*, after which he was admitted to the bar in 1886. Emerson quickly lost interest in the legal profession however, and moved to Kansas where he became heavily involved in politics; actively campaigning on behalf of the Republican Party in both the 1888 and 1900 elections. Emerson is best known as a prominent American novelist though, and is famed for his evocative tales of the Mid-West. Among his better-known novels are *Buell Hampton* (1902), *The Builders* (1906), *Smoky God vs. Voyage in the Inner World* (1908), *The Treasure of Hidden Valley* (1915) and *The Man Who Discovered Himself* (1919). *Smoky God vs. Voyage in the Inner World* is particularly notable for its unusual plotline; the protagonist discovers an Eden like civilisation in in the centre of the earth, where a scientifically advanced race of long-lived giants is discovered worshipping a 'smoky God' – the interior sun. This was the first literary work to bring Emerson widespread acclaim. A man of many talents and interests, Emerson also worked as a newspaperman, lawyer, politician and promoter, forming the North American Copper Company in Wyoming. Emerson is also credited with founding the town of Grand Encampment, a municipality in Carbon County, Wyoming. With Emerson's Copper Company based there, it became a booming centre of copper mining and smelting. A sixteen-mile tramway was built to carry copper ore from the mountains into the town for smelting; a tramway which was, at the time, the longest in the world. He died on 11 December, 1918.

Sons of the rugged, rock-ribbed hills,
Far from the gaudy show
Of Fashion's world-its shams and frills
Brothers of rain and snow:
Kith of the crags and the forest pines,
Kin of the herd and flock;
Wise in the lore of Nature signs
Writ in the grass and rock.

Beings of lithe and lusty limb,
Breathing the broad, new life,
Chanting the forest's primal hymn
Free from the world's crude strife.
Your witching lure my being thrills,
O rugged sons! O rugged hills!

CHAPTER I.

AT THE PARTING OF THE WAYS

IT was a dear, crisp October morning. There was a shrill whistle of a locomotive, and then a westbound passenger train dashed into the depot of an Iowa town. A young man descended the car steps with an armful of luggage. He deposited his parcels on the platform, and half expectantly looked about him.

Just then there was a "honk! honk!" from a huge automobile as it came to a palpitating halt, and a familiar voice called out: "Hello, Roderick, old man!" And a moment later Roderick Warfield was shaking hands with his boon friend of former college days, Whitley Adams. Both were in their early twenties, stalwart, well set up, clean-cut young fellows.

Whitley's face was all aglow in the happiness of reunion. But Roderick, after the first cordial greeting, wore a graver look. He listened quietly while his comrade rambled on.

"Mighty glad to receive your wire last night at the club. But what brings you home so unexpectedly? We've been hearing all sorts of glowing stories—about your being in the thick of affairs in little old New York and rolling in the shekels to beat the band."

"Fairy tales," was the laconic reply, accompanied by a look that was compounded of a sigh and a wistful smile.

"How's that?" asked young Adams, glancing up into the other's face and for the first time noticing its serious expression. "Don't tell me you've struck a financial snag thus early in your Stock Exchange career."

"Several financial snags—and struck 'em pretty badly too, I'm afraid."

"Whew!" exclaimed Adams.

"Oh, I'm not down and out," laughed Roderick, half amused at the look of utter discomfiture on his companion's countenance. "Not by a long chalk! I'm in on several good deals, and six months from date will be standing on velvet. That is to say," he added, somewhat dubiously, "if Uncle Allen opens up his money bags to tide me over meanwhile."

"A pretty big 'if,' eh?" For the moment there was sympathetic sobriety in the youth's tone, but he quickly regained his cheerfulness. "However, he'll come through probably all right, Rod, dear boy. It's the older fellows' privilege, isn't it? My good dad has had the same experience, as you will no doubt have guessed. There, let me see; how long have you been away? Eight months! Gee! However, I have just gotten home myself. My old man was a bit furious at my tardiness in coming and the geometrical increase of my expense account. To do Los Angeles and San Francisco thoroughly, you know, runs into a pot of money. But now everything is fixed up after a fashion with no evidence in sight of further squalls." He laughed the laugh of an overgrown boy laboring under the delusion that because he has finished a collegiate course he is a "man."

"Of course," he continued with a swagger, "we chaps who put in four long years at college should not be expected to settle down without having some sort of a valedictory fling."

"There has not been much of a fling in my case," protested Warfield. "I tackled life seriously in New York from the start."

"But got a tumble all the same," grinned Adams. "However, there's no use in pulling a long face—at least not until your Uncle Allen has been interviewed and judiciously put through his paces. Come now, let us get your things aboard."

The conversation was halted while the young owner of the big 60 H. P. car helped his chauffeur to stow away the luggage. "To the club," he called out as he seated himself in the tonneau with his boyhood friend—college chum and classmate.

"Not this morning!" exclaimed Roderick, shaking his

head as he looked frankly and a bit nervously into the eyes of Whitley Adams. "No club for me until I have squared things up on the hill."

"Oh, well, just as you say; if it's as bad as that, why of course—" He broke off and did not finish the sentence, but directed the chauffeur to the residence of Allen Miller, the banker.

They rode a little way in silence and then Whitley Adams observed: "You've made a muddle of things, no doubt," and he turned with a knowing look and a smile toward Roderick, who in turn flushed, as though hit.

"No doubt," he concurred curtly.

"Then when shall I see you?" asked Whitley as the auto slowed down at the approach to the stately Miller home.

"I'll 'phone you," replied Roderick. "Think I can arrange to be at the club this evening."

"Very well," said his friend, and a minute later he had whirled away leaving a cloud of dust in the trail of the machine.

Roderick Warfield met with a motherly reception at the hands of his Aunt Lois, Mrs. Allen Miller. The greetings over and a score of solicitous questions by his Aunt Lois answered, he went to his room for a bath and a change of clothes. Then without further delay he presented himself at the bank, and in a few moments was closeted in the president's private room with his uncle and guardian, Allen Miller.

The first friendly greetings were soon followed by the banker skidding from social to business considerations. "Yes," said Allen Miller, "I am glad to see you, Roderick, mighty glad. But what do you mean by writing a day ahead that a good big sum is required immediately, this without mention of securities or explanation of any kind?" He held up in his hand a letter that ran to just a few niggardly lines. "This apology for a business communication only reached me by last night's mail."

The kindly look of greeting had changed to one that was fairly flinty in its hardness. "What am I to expect from such a demand? A bunch of unpaid accounts, I suppose." As he uttered this last

13

sentence, there was a wicked twang in his voice—a suggestion of the snarl of an angry wolf ready for a fierce encounter. It at least proved him a financier.

A flush of resentment stole over Roderick's brow. His look was more than half-defiant. On his side it showed at once that there would be no cringing for the favor he had come to ask.

But he controlled himself, and spoke with perfect calm.

"My obligations are not necessarily disgraceful ones, as your manner and tone, Uncle, might imply. As for any detailed explanation by letter, I thought it best to come and put the whole business before you personally."

"And the nature of the business?" asked the banker in a dry harsh voice.

"I am in a big deal and have to find my *pro rata* contribution immediately."

"A speculative deal?" rasped the old man.

"Yes; I suppose it would be called speculative, but it is gilt-edged all the same. I have all the papers here, and will show them to you." He plunged a hand into the breast pocket of his coat and produced a neatly folded little bundle of documents.

"Stop," exclaimed the banker. "You need not even undo that piece of tape until you have answered my questions. A speculative deal, you admit."

"Be it so."

"A mining deal, may I ask?"

Roderick's face showed some confusion. But he faced the issue promptly and squarely.

"Yes, sir, a mining deal."

The banker's eyes fairly glittered with steely wrathfulness.

"As I expected. By gad, it seems to run in the blood! Did I not warn you, when you insisted on risking your meagre capital of two thousand dollars in New York instead of settling down with what would have been a comfortable nest egg here, that if you ever touched mining it would be your ruin? Did I not tell you your father's story, how the lure of prospecting possessed him, how he could never throw it off, how it doomed him to a life of hardship and poverty, and how it would have left you, his child, a pauper but for an insurance policy which it was his one redeeming act of prudence in carrying?"

"Please do not speak like that of my father," protested Roderick, drawing himself up with proud

The banker's manner softened; a kindlier glow came into his eyes.

"Well, boy, you know I loved your father. If your father had only followed my path he would have shared my prosperity. But it was not to be. He lost all he ever made in mining, and now you are flinging the little provision his death secured for you into the same bottomless pool. And this despite all my warnings, despite my stern injunctions so long as it was my right as your guardian to enjoin. The whole thing disgusts me more than words can tell."

Into the banker's voice the old bitterness, if not the anger, had returned. He rose and restlessly paced the room. A silence followed that was oppressive. Roderick Warfield's mind was in the future; he was wondering what would happen should his uncle remain obdurate. The older man's mind was in the past; he was recalling events of the long ago.

Roderick Warfield's father and Allen Miller had as young men braved perils together in an unsuccessful overland trip when the great California gold rush in the early fifties occurred. At that time they were only boys in their 'teens. Years afterward they married sisters and settled down in their Iowa homes—or tried to settle down in Warfield's case, for in his wanderings he had been smitten with the gold fever and he remained a mining nomad to the end of his days. Allen Miller had never been blessed with a child, and it was not until late in their married life that any addition came to the Warfield family. This was the beginning of Roderick Warfield's career, but cost the mother's life. Ten years later John Warfield died and his young son Roderick was given a home with Mr. and Mrs. Allen Miller, the banker accepting the guardianship of his old friend's only child.

The boy's inheritance was limited to a few thousand dollars of life insurance, which in the hands of anyone but Allen Miller would have fallen far short of putting him through college. However, that was not only accomplished, but at the close of a fairly brilliant college career the young man had found himself possessed of a round couple of thousand dollars. Among his college friends had been the son of a well-to-do New York broker, and it was on this friend's advice that Roderick had at the outset of his business life adventured the maelstrom of Gotham instead of accepting the placid backwaters of his Iowan home town. Hence the young man's present difficulties and precarious future, and his uncle's bitterness of spirit because all his past efforts on Roderick's account had proved of such little avail.

At last the banker resumed his chair. The tightly closed lips showed that his mind was made up to a definite line of action. Roderick awaited the decision in silence—it was not in his nature to plead a cause at the cost of losing his own self-respect He had already returned the unopened bundle of mining papers to the inner pocket of his coat.

"As for any advance to meet speculative mining commitments," began the man of finance, "I do not even desire to know the amount you have had in mind. That is a proposition I cannot even entertain—on principle and for your own ultimate good, young man."

"Then I lose all the money I have put in to date."

"Better a present loss than hopeless future entanglements. Your personal obligations? As you have been using all available funds for speculation, I presume you are not free from some debts."

"Less than a thousand dollars all told."

"Well, you have, I believe, $285.75 standing to your personal credit in this bank—the remnant of your patrimony."

"I did not know I had so much," remarked Roderick with a faint smile.

"All the better, perhaps," replied the banker, also smiling grimly. "The amount would have doubtless been swallowed up with the rest of your money. As matters stand, some payment can be made to account of your obligations and arrangements entered into for the gradual liquidation of the outstanding balance." Young Warfield winced. The banker continued: "This may involve some personal humiliation for you. But again it is against my principles to pay any man's debts. Anyone who deliberately incurs a liability should have the highly beneficial experience of earning the money to liquidate it I propose to give you the chance to do so."

Roderick raised his eyebrows in some surprise. "In New York?" he enquired.

"No, sir," replied Allen Miller rather brusquely and evidently nettled at the very audacity of the question. "Not in New York, but right here—in Keokuk. Calm your impatience, please. Just listen to the proposals I have to make—they have been carefully thought out by me and by your Aunt Lois as well. In the first place, despite your rather reckless and improvident start in life, I am prepared to make you assistant cashier of this bank at a good salary." Again Roderick evinced amazement. He was quite nonplussed at his uncle's changed demeanor. The conciliatory manner and kindly tone disarmed him. But could he ever come to renounce his New York ambitions for humdrum existence in the old river town of Keokuk? He knew the answer in his heart. The thing was impossible.

"And if you are diligent," continued the banker, "prove capable and make good, you may expect in time to be rewarded with a liberal block of stock in the bank. Come now, what do you say to this part of my programme?" urged the speaker as Roderick hesitated.

The young man's mind was already made up. The offer was not even worth considering. And yet, he must not offend his guardian. It was true, Allen Miller's guardianship days were past, but still in his rapid mental calculations Roderick thought of his stanch old stand-by, Uncle Allen Miller, as "Guardian." He lighted a cigar to gain time for the framing of a diplomatic answer.

"Well," said the banker, with a rising inflection, "does it require any time to consider the generous offer I make?"

Roderick pulled a long breath at his cigar and blew rings of smoke toward the ceiling, and said: "Your offer, Uncle, is princely, but I hardly feel that I should accept until I have thought it all over from different points of view and have the whole question of my future plans fully considered. What are the other items on your programme?"

"They should be rather counted as conditions," replied the banker drily. "The conditions on which the offer I have just made are based."

"And they are what?"

"You must quit speculation, give up all expensive habits, marry and settle down." The words were spoken with all the definiteness of an ultimatum.

Again Roderick winced. He might have been led to all or at least some of these things. But to be driven, and by such rough horse-breaking methods—. never! no, never. He managed to restrain himself, however, and replied quietly: "My dear uncle, the idea of marrying for some years yet, to tell you the truth, has never entered my head. Of course," he went on lightly, "there is a young lady over at Galesburg, Stella Rain, where my Knox college days were spent, the 'college widow,' in a way a very lovely sort and in whom I have been rather interested for some two years, but—"

"That will do, young man," interrupted Allen Miller, sharply and severely. "Never mind your society flyers—these lady friends of yours in Galesburg. Your Aunt Lois and myself have already selected your future wife."

He laughed hoarsely, and the laugh sounded brutal even to his own ears. Allen Miller realized uncomfortably that he had been premature and scored against himself.

"Oh, is that so?" ejaculated Roderick in delicate irony. A pink flush had stolen into his cheeks.

The old banker hesitated in making reply. He grew hot and red and wondered if he had begun his match-making too abruptly—the very thing about which his good wife Lois had cautioned him. In truth, despite the harsh methods often imposed on him by his profession as a banker, a kinder heart than Allen Miller's never beat. But in this new rôle he was out of his element and readily confused. Finally after clearing his throat several times, he replied: "Yes, Roderick, in a way, your Aunt Lois and I have picked out the girl we want you to marry. Her father's wealth is equal to mine and some day perhaps—well, you can't tell—I'll not live always and, provided you don't disobey me, you may inherit under my will a control of the stock of this banking house, and so be at the head of an important and growing financial institution."

Roderick instead of being fifty-four and calculating, was only twenty-four and indifferent to wealth, and the red blood of his generous youth revolted at the mercenary methods suggested by his uncle regarding this unknown girl's financial prospects. And then, too, the inducement thrown out that under conditions of obedience he might inherit the fortune of his uncle, was, he interpreted, nothing short of an attempt to bribe and deprive him of his liberty. He flushed with indignation and anger. Yet with a strong effort he still controlled his feelings, and presently asked: "Who is the fair lady?"

"The daughter of an old friend of mine. They live only a short distance down the river. Their home is at Quincy, Illinois. Mighty fine old family, I can tell you. Am sure you'll like her immensely."

"Am I to understand," asked Roderick rather caustically, "that the young lady acquiesces and enters graciously into your plans?"

"Well, I can't say that!" replied Allen Miller, rubbing his chin. "But your Aunt Lois and I have talked over the possible alliance in all its lights."

"With the young lady's family, I presume?"

"No, not even that. But we are perfectly certain that we have only to speak the word to put the business through all right."

"Business!"—Roderick repeated the word with bitter emphasis.

"Yes, sir, business," retorted Allen Miller, with some warmth. "To my mind matrimony is one of the most important deals in life—perhaps *the* most important."

"If the money is right," laughed the young man contemptuously. "But don't you think that before another word is said about such a matter I should have the chance of seeing the young lady and the young lady a chance of seeing me?"

The humor of the situation had brought a pleasant smile to his face. The banker looked relieved.

"Wait now, my boy," he replied musingly. "Do you remember when you were a little chap, perhaps twelve or thirteen years old, going with your Aunt Lois and myself to St. Louis on the Diamond Joe boat line?"

"Yes, I remember it perfectly."

"Well, then," continued Allen Miller, "you perhaps haven't forgotten a lady and gentleman with a little tot of a girl only five or six years old, who joined us at Quincy. You engaged in a regular boyish love affair at first sight with that little girl. Well, she is the one—a mighty fine young lady now—just passed eighteen and her father is rated away up in the financial world."

For the moment Roderick's indignation over the cold-blooded, cut-and-dried, matrimonial proposition was arrested, and he did not even notice the renewed reference to finance. He had become pensive and retrospective.

"How very long ago," he mused more to himself than to his Uncle Allen—"How very long ago since that trip down the river. Yes, I remember well the little blue-eyed, black-curly-headed chick of a girl. It was my first steamboat ride and of course it was a holiday and a fairyland affair to my boyish fancy."

He drew in a long breath and looked out through the window at the snow which was now falling, as if many chapters of the world's history had been written in his own life since that far away yet well remembered trip. He fell silent for a spell.

Allen Miller chuckled to himself. At last his scheme was working. All his life he had been a success with men and affairs, and his self-confidence was great. He rubbed his hands together and smiled, while he humored Roderick's silence. He would tell his wife Lois of his progress. Presently he said: "She is an only child, Roderick, and I think her father could qualify for better than a quarter of a million."

This time the reiterated money recommendation jarred unpleasantly on Roderick's nerves and revived his antagonism. He hastily arose from his chair and walked back and forth across the room. Presently he halted before his uncle and with forced deliberation—for his anger was keyed to a high tension—said: "I am pleased, Uncle, to know the young lady is not a party to this shameful piece of attempted barter and sale business. When I marry, if ever, it shall be someone as regards whom wealth will count as of least importance. True love loathes avarice and greed. I require no further time to consider your proposals. I flatly reject your offer of a position in the bank, and shall leave Keokuk tomorrow. I prefer hewing out my own destiny and while doing so retaining my freedom and my self-respect. This is my decision, and it is an irrevocable one."

The ebullition of pent-up feelings had come so suddenly and unexpectedly that Allen Miller was momentarily overwhelmed. He had arisen and was noticeably agitated. His face was very white, and there was a look in his eyes that Roderick Warfield had never seen before.

"Young man," he said, and his voice was husky and trembling with suppressed rage—"you shall never have a dollar of my fortune unless you marry as I direct I will give you until tomorrow to agree to my plans. If you do not desire to accept my offer without change or modification in any shape, then take the balance of your money in the bank and go your way. I wash my hands of you and your affairs. Go and play football with the world or let the world play football with you, and see how it feels to be the 'pigskin' in life's game."

With these words the old man swung a chair round to the fireplace, dropped into it, and began vigorously and viciously pounding at a lump of coal. There was an interval of silence. At last Roderick spoke; his voice was firm and low.

"There will not be the slightest use, Uncle, in reopening this question tomorrow. My mind, as I have said, is already made up—unalterably." The last word was uttered with an emphasis that rang finality.

The banker flung down the poker, and rose to his feet. His look was equally determined, equally final, equally unalterable.

"All right," he snapped. "Then we'll get through the banking business now."

He touched a push-button by the side of the mantel. During the brief interval before a clerk responded to the summons, not another word was spoken.

"Bring me the exact figure of Mr. Warfield's credit balance," he said to his subordinate, "and cash for the amount. He will sign a check to close the account."

Five minutes later Roderick had the little wad of bills in his pocket, and was ready to depart Uncle and nephew were again alone.

"There is one other matter," said the banker with cold formality. "There is a paper in my possession which was entrusted to my keeping by your father just before he died. I was to deliver it to you at my discretion after you had attained your majority, but in any case on your reaching the age of twenty-five. I will exercise my discretion, and hand over the paper to you now."

He advanced to a safe that stood open at one side of the room, unlocked a little drawer, and returned to the fireplace with a long linen envelope in his hand. A big red splash of wax showed that it had been carefully sealed.

"This is yours," said the banker shortly, handing it over to the young man.

The latter was greatly agitated. A message from his dead father! What could it mean? But he mastered his emotions and quietly bestowed the packet in his breast pocket—beside the papers connected with the mining deal.

"I'll read this later," he said. And then he extended his hand. There was yearning affection in his eyes, in the tremor of his voice: "Uncle, we surely will part as friends."

"You can regain my friendship only by doing my will. I have nothing more to say. Good-by."

And without taking the proffered hand, Allen Miller turned away, leaning an elbow on the mantelshelf. His attitude showed that the interview was at an end.

Without another word Roderick Warfield left the room. Outside the soft snow was falling in feathery silence. At a street corner the young man hesitated. He glanced up the road that led to his old home—Allen Miller's stately mansion on the hill. Then he took the other turning.

"I guess I'll sleep at the Club to-night," he murmured to himself. "I can bid Aunt Lois good-by in the morning."

CHAPTER II.

A MESSAGE FROM THE GRAVE

ALLEN MILLER, the rich banker, was alone—alone in the president's room at his bank, and feeling alone in the fullest sense of the word now that Roderick Warfield had gone, the youth he had reared and loved and cherished as his own child, now turned out of doors by the old man's deliberate act.

For full an hour he walked slowly back and forth the whole length of the apartment But at last he halted once again before the open grate where some slumbering chunks of coal were burning indifferently. He pushed them together with the iron poker, and a bright blaze sprung up.

Looking deep into the fire his thoughts went back to his boyhood days and he saw John Warfield, his chum of many years. He thought of their experience in the terrible massacre in the Sierra Madre Mountains in the region of Bridger Peak, of a lost trail, of hunger and thirst and weary tramps over mountain and down precipitous canyons, of abrupt gashes that cut the rocky gorges, of great bubbling springs and torrents of mountain streams, of a narrow valley between high mountains—a valley without a discoverable outlet—of a beautiful waterway that traversed this valley and lost itself in the sides of an abrupt mountain, and of the exhausting hardships in getting back to civilization.

Then Allen Miller, the flint-hearted financier, the stoic, the man of taciturn habits, did a strange thing. Standing there before the blazing fire, leaning against the mantel, he put his handkerchief to his eyes and his frame was convulsed with a sob. Presently he turned away from the open grate and muttered aloud: "Yes, John Warfield, I loved you and I love your boy, Roderick. Some day he shall have all I've got. But he is self-willed—a regular outlaw—and I must wake him up to the demands of a bread-winner, put the bits into his mouth and make him bridle-wise. Gad! He's a dynamo, but I love him;" and he half smiled, while his eyes were yet red and his voice husky.

"Ah, John," he mused as he looked again into the fire, "you might have been alive today to help me break this young colt to the plough, if you had only taken my advice and given up the search for that gold mine in the mountains. Thank God for the compact of secrecy between us—the secret shall die with me. The years, John, you spent in trying to re-dis-cover the vault of wealth—and what a will-o'-the-wisp it proved to be—and then the accident. But now I shall be firm—firm as a rock—and Roderick, the reckless would-be plunger, shall at last feel the iron hand of his old guardian beneath the silken glove of my foolish kindness. He's got to be subdued and broken, even if I have to let him live on husks for a while. Firm, firm—that's the only thing to be."

As he muttered the last words, Allen Miller shut his square jaws together with an ugly snap that plainly told the stern policy he had resolved on and would henceforth determinedly pursue. He put on his great fur-lined cloak, and silently went out into the evening shadows and thick maze of descending snow-flakes.

Meanwhile Roderick Warfield had reached his club, engaged a bedroom, and got a cheerful fire alight for companionship as well as comfort. He had telephoned to Whitley Adams to dine with him, but for two hours he would be by himself and undisturbed. He wanted a little time to think. And then there was the letter from his father. He had settled himself in an easy chair before the fire, the sealed envelope was in his hand, and the strange solemn feeling had descended upon him that he was going to hear his dead father speak to him again.

There was in the silence that enveloped him the pulsing

sensation of a mysterious presence. The ordeal now to be faced came as a climax to the stormy interview he had just passed through. He had reached a parting of the ways, and dimly realized that something was going to happen that would guide him as to the path he should follow. The letter seemed a message from another world. Unknown to himself the supreme moment that had now arrived was a moment of transfiguration—the youth became a man—old things passed away.

With grave deliberation he broke the seal. Inside the folds of a long and closely written letter was a second cover with somewhat bulky contents. This he laid for the meantime on a little table by his side. Then he set himself to a perusal of the letter. It ran as follows:

"My dear Son:—

"This is for you to read when you have come to man's estate—when you are no longer a thoughtless boy, but a thoughtful man. With this letter you will find your mother's picture and a ring of pure gold which I placed upon her finger the day I married her—gold with a special sentiment attached to it, for I took it from the earth myself—also a few letters—love letters written by her to me and a tress of her hair. I am sure you will honor her memory by noble deeds. I loved her dearly.

"I was younger at the time than you are now, Roderick, my son. Your Uncle Allen Miller—about my own age—and myself planned a trip to California. It was at the time of the great gold excitement in that far off land.

"The Overland Train of some two score of ox teams that we were with traveled but slowly; frequently not more than eight or ten miles a day. I remembered we had crossed the south fork of the Platte River and had traveled some two days on westward into the mountains and were near a place called Bridger Peak. It must have been about midnight when our camp was startled with the most terrific and unearthly yells ever heard by mortals. It was a band of murderous Indians, and in less time than it takes to describe the scene of devastation, all of our stock was stampeded; our wagons looted and then set on fire. Following this a general massacre began. Your Uncle Allen and myself, both of us mere boys in our 'teens, alert and active, managed to make our escape in the darkness. Being fleet of foot we ran along the mountain side, following an opening but keeping close to a dense forest of pine trees. In this way we saved our lives. I afterwards learned that every other member of the party was killed.

"We were each equipped with two revolvers and a bowie knife and perhaps jointly had one hundred rounds of cartridges. A couple of pounds of jerked beef and a half a loaf of bread constituted our provisions. Fortunately, Allen Miller carried with him a flint and steel, so that we were enabled to sustain ourselves with cooked food of game we killed during the weary days that followed.

"With this letter I enclose a map, roughly drawn, but I am sure it will help you find the lost canyon where flows a beautiful stream of water, and where your Uncle Allen and myself discovered an amazing quantity of gold—placer gold. It is in a valley, and the sandbar of gold is about a mile up stream from where the torrent of rapid water loses itself at the lower end of the valley—seemingly flowing into the abrupt side of a mountain. At the place where we found the gold, I remember, there was a sandbar next to the mountain brook, then a gorge or pocket like an old channel of a creek bed, and it was here in this old sandbar of a channel that the nuggets of gold were found—so

27

plentiful indeed, that notwithstanding we loaded ourselves with them to the limit of our strength, yet our 'takings' could scarcely be missed from this phenomenal sandbar of riches. We brought all we could possibly carry away with us in two bags which we made from extra clothing. Unfortunately we lost our way and could not find an opening from the valley, because the waters of the stream disappeared, as I have described, and we were compelled, after many unsuccessful attempts to find a water grade opening, to retrace our steps and climb out by the same precipitous trail that we had followed in going down into this strange valley.

"We wandered in the mountains as far south as a place now known as Hahn's Peak, and then eastward, circling in every direction for many miles in extent. After tramping in an unknown wilderness for forty-seven days we finally came to the hut of a mountaineer, and were overjoyed to learn it was on a branch of the Overland trail Not long after this we fell in with a returning caravan of ox team freighters and after many weeks of tedious travel arrived at St. Joseph, Mo., footsore and weary, but still in possession of our gold. A little later we reached our home near Keokuk, Iowa, and to our great joy learned that our treasure was worth many thousands of dollars. Your Uncle Allen Miller's half was the beginning of his fortune. An oath of secrecy exists between your Uncle Allen Miller and myself that neither shall divulge during our lifetime that which I am now writing to you, but in thus communicating my story to you, my own flesh and blood, I do not feel that I am violating my promise, because the information will not come to you until years after my death.

"Since your mother's death, I have made seven trips into the Rocky Mountain region hunting most diligently for

THE TREASURE OF HIDDEN VALLEY

an odd-shaped valley where abrupt mountains wall it in, seemingly on every side, and where we found the fabulously rich sandbar of gold.

"But I have not succeeded in locating the exact place, not even finding the lost stream—or rather the spot where the waters disappeared out of sight at the base of a high mountain range. On my last trip, made less than one year ago, I met with a most serious accident that has permanently crippled me and will probably hasten my taking off. On the map I have made many notes while lying here ill and confined to my room, and they will give you my ideas of the location where the treasure may be found. To you, my beloved son, Roderick, I entrust this map. Study it well and if, as I believe, you have inherited my adventurous spirit, you will never rest until you find this lost valley and its treasure box of phenomenal wealth. In Rawlins, Wyoming, you will find an old frontiersman by the name of Jim Rankin. He has two cronies, or partners, Tom Sun and Boney Earnest. These three men rendered me great assistance. If you find the lost mine, reward them liberally.

"I have communicated to no one, not even your good Uncle Allen Miller, that I have decided on leaving this letter, and the information which it contains is for your eyes alone to peruse long after my mortal body has crumbled to dust In imparting this information I do so feeling sure that your Uncle Allen will never make any effort to relocate the treasure, so that it is quite right and proper the secret should descend to you.

"My pen drags a little—I am weary and quite exhausted with the effort of writing. I now find myself wondering whether this legacy—a legacy telling you of a lost gold mine that may be found somewhere in the fastnesses of the

29

mountains of Wyoming—will prove a blessing to you or a disquieting evil. I shall die hoping that it will prove to your good and that your efforts in seeking this lost mine will be rewarded.

"With tenderest love and affection,

"Your father,

"John Warfield."

When Roderick reached the end of the letter, he remained for a long time still holding it in his hands and gazing fixedly into the glowing embers. He was seeing visions—visions of a Wyoming gold mine that would bring him unbounded wealth. At last he broke from his reveries, and examined the other package. It was unsealed. The first paper to come forth proved to be the map to which his father had referred—it was a pencil drawing with numerous marginal notes that would require close examination. For the present he laid the document on the table. Then reverently and tenderly he examined the little bunch of love letters tied together by a ribbon, the tress of hair placed between two protecting pieces of cardboard, and the plain hoop of gold wrapped carefully in several folds of tissue paper. Lastly he gazed upon the photograph of his mother—the mother he had never seen, the mother who had given her life so that he might live. There were tears in his eyes as he gently kissed the sweet girlish countenance.

With thought of her and memories of the old boyhood days again he fell into a musing mood. Time sped unnoticed, and it was only the chiming of a church clock outside that aroused him to the fact that the dinner hour had arrived and that Whitley Adams would be waiting for him downstairs. He carefully placed all the papers in a writing desk that stood in a corner of the room, locked it, and put the key in his pocket. Then he descended to meet his friend.

"Nothing doing, I can see," exclaimed Whitley the moment he saw Roderick's grave face.

"You've got it right," he answered quietly. "The big 'if' you feared this morning turned out to be an uncompromising 'no.' Uncle Allen and I have said good-by."

"No wonder you are looking so glum."

"Not glum, old fellow. I never felt more tranquilly happy in my life. But naturally I may seem a bit serious. I have to cut out old things in my life, take up new lines."

"I suppose it's back to New York for you."

"No. Everything goes by the board there. I have to cut my losses and quit."

"What a cruel sacrifice!"

"Or what a happy release," smiled Roderick. "There is something calling me elsewhere—a call I cannot resist—a call I believe that beckons me to success."

"Where?"

"Well, we won't say anything about that at present I'll write you later on when the outlook becomes clearer. Meanwhile we'll dine, and I'm going to put up a little business proposition to you. I want you to buy my half share in the *Black Swan*."

"Guess that can be fixed up all right," replied Whitley, as they moved toward the dining room. And, dull care laid aside, the two old college chums gave themselves up to a pleasant evening—the last they would spend together for many a long day, as both realized.

By eleven o'clock next morning Roderick Warfield had adjusted his financial affairs. He had received cash for his half interest in the *Black Swan,* a river pleasure launch which he and Whitley Adams had owned in common for several years. He had written one letter, to New York surrendering his holding in the mining syndicate, and other letters to his three or four creditors enclosing bank drafts for one-half of his indebtedness and requesting six months' time for the payment of the balance.

With less than a hundred dollars left he was cheerfully prepared to face the world.

Then had come the most painful episode of the whole visit— the parting from Aunt Lois, the woman of gentle ways and kindly heart who had always loved him like a mother, who loved him still, and who tearfully pleaded with him to submit even at this eleventh hour to his uncle's will and come back to his room in the old home. But the adieus had been spoken, resolutely though tenderly, and now Whitley Adams in his big motor car had whisked Roderick and his belongings back to the railway depot.

He had barely time to check his trunk to Burlington and swing onto the moving train. "So long," he shouted to his friend. "Good luck," responded Whitley as he waved farewell. And Roderick Warfield was being borne out into the big new world of venture and endeavor.

Would he succeed in cuffing the ears of chance and conquer, or would heartless fate play football with him and make him indeed the "pig-skin" as his uncle had prophesied in the coming events of his destiny—a destiny that was carrying him away among strangers and to unfamiliar scenes? As the train rushed along his mind was full of his father's letter and his blood tingled with excitement over the secret that had come to him from the darkness of the very grave. The primal man within him was crying out with mad impatience to be in the thick of the fierce struggle for the golden spoil.

A witchery was thrumming in his heart—the witchery of the West; and instead of struggling against the impulse, he was actually encouraging it to lead him blindly on toward an unsolved mystery of the hills. He was lifted up into the heights, his soul filled with exalted thoughts and hopes.

Then came whisperings in a softer strain—gentle whisperings that brought with them memories of happy college days and the name of Stella Rain. It was perhaps nothing more nor less than the crude brutality with which his uncle had pressed his meretricious matrimonial scheme that caused Roderick now to think so longingly and so fondly of the charming little "college widow" who had been the object of his youthful aspirations.

All at once he came to a resolution. Yes; he would spend at least one day on the old campus grounds at Knox College. The call of the hills was singing in his heart, the luring irresistible call. But before responding to it he would once again press the hand and peep into the eyes of Stella Rain.

CHAPTER III.

FINANCIAL WOLVES

ON the very day following Roderick Warfield's departure from Keokuk there appeared in one of the morning newspapers an item of intelligence that greatly surprised and shocked the banker, Allen Miller. It announced the death of the wife of his old friend General John Holden, of Quincy, Illinois, and with the ghoulish instincts of latter-day journalism laid bare a story of financial disaster that had, at least indirectly, led to the lady's lamented demise. It set forth how some years before the General had invested practically the whole of his fortune in a western smelter company, how the minority stockholders had been frozen out by a gang of financial sharps in Pennsylvania, and how Mrs. Holden's already enfeebled health had been unable to withstand the blow of swift and sudden family ruin. The General, however, was bearing his sad bereavement and his monetary losses with the courage and fortitude that had characterized his military career, and had announced his intention of retiring to a lonely spot among the mountains of Wyoming where his daughter, the beautiful and accomplished Gail Holden, owned a half section of land which had been gifted to her in early infancy by an unde, a prominent business man in San Francisco. Allen Miller was sincerely grieved over the misfortunes that had so cruelly smitten a life-long friend. But what momentarily stunned him was the thought that Gail Holden was the very girl designated, in mind at least, by himself and his wife as a desirable match for Roderick. And because the latter had not at once fallen in with these matrimonial plans, there had been the bitter quarrel, the stinging words of rebuke that could never be recalled, and the departure of the young man, as he had told his aunt, to places where they would never hear of him unless and until he had made his own fortune in the world.

As the newspaper dropped from his hands, the old banker uttered a great groan—he had sacrificed the boy, whom in his heart he had cherished, and still cherished, as a son, for a visionary scheme that had already vanished into nothingness like a fragile iridescent soap-bubble. For obviously Gail Holden, her only possessions an impoverished father and a few acres of rocky soil, was no longer eligible as the bride of a future bank president and leader in the financial world. The one crumb of consolation for Allen Miller was that he had never mentioned her name to Roderick—that when the sponge of time came to efface the quarrel the whole incident could be consigned to oblivion without any humiliating admission on his side. For financial foresight was the very essence of his faith in himself, his hold over Roderick, and his reputation in the business world.

The afternoon mail brought detailed news of General Holden's speculative venture and downfall. Allen Miller's correspondent was a lawyer friend in Quincy, who wrote in strict confidence but with a free and sharply pointed pen. It appeared that Holden's initial investment had been on a sound basis. He had held bonds that were underlying securities on a big smelting plant in Wyoming, in the very district where his daughter's patch of range lands was situated. It was during a visit to the little ranch that the general's attention had been drawn to the great possibilities of a local smelter, and he had been the main one to finance the proposition and render the erection of the plant possible. At this stage a group of eastern capitalists had been attracted to the region, and there had come to be mooted a big consolidation of several companies, an electric lighting plant, an aerial tramway, a valuable producing copper mine and several other different concerns that were closely associated with the smelting enterprise.

In the days that followed a Pennsylvanian financier with a lightning rod education, by the name of W. B. Grady had visited Holden at his Quincy home, partaken of his hospitality, and persuaded him to exchange his underlying bonds for stock in a re-organized and consolidated company.

By reputation this man Grady was already well known to Allen Miller as one belonging to the new school of unscrupulous stock manipulators that has grown up, developed, flourished and waxed fat under the blighting influence and domination of the Well Known Oil crowd. This new school of financiers is composed of financial degenerates, where the words "honor," "fair dealing" or the "square deal" have all been effectually expunged—marked off from their business vocabulary and by them regarded as obsolete terms. Grady was still a comparatively young man, of attractive manners and commanding presence, with the rapacity, however, of a wolf and the cunning of a fox. He stood fully six feet, and his hair, once black as a raven's, was now streaked with premature gray which was in no way traceable to early piety. But to have mentioned his name even in a remote comparison to such a respectable bird as the raven rendered an apology due to the raven. It was more consistent with the eternal truth and fitness of things to substitute the term "vulture"—to designate him "a financial vulture," that detestable bird of prey whose chief occupation is feasting on carrion and all things where the life has been squeezed out by the financial octopus, known as "the system."

It developed, according to Banker Miller's correspondent, that no sooner had General Holden given up his underlying bonds of the smelter company and accepted stock, than foreclosure proceedings were instituted in the U. S. District Court, and the whole business closed out and sold and grabbed by Grady and a small coterie of financial pirates no better than himself. And all this was done many hundreds of miles away from the home of the unsuspecting old general, who until it was too late remained wholly ignorant and unadvised of the true character of the suave and pleasant appearing Mr. Grady whose promises were innumerable, yet whose every promise was based upon a despicable prevarication.

And thus it was when the affairs of General Holden were fairly threshed out, that Allen Miller discovered his old friend had been the prey of a financial vampire, one skilled in sharp practice and whose artful cunning technically protected him from being arrested and convicted of looting the victim of his fortune. Holden had fallen into the hands of a highwayman as vicious as any stage robber that ever infested the highways of the frontier. The evidence of the fellow's rascality was most apparent; indeed, he was in a way caught redhanded with the goods as surely as ever a sheep-killing dog was found with wool on its teeth.

To the credit of Allen Miller, he never hesitated or wavered in his generosity to anyone he counted as a true and worthy friend. That very evening Mrs. Miller departed for Quincy, to offer in person more discreetly than a letter could offer any financial assistance that might be required to meet present emergencies, and at the same time convey sympathy to the husband and daughter in their sad bereavement.

"Lois, my dear," the banker had said to his wife, "remain a few days with them if necessary. Make them comfortable, no matter what the expense. If they had means they wouldn't need us, but now—well, no difference about the why and wherefore—you just go and comfort and help them materially and substantially."

It was in such a deed as this that the true nobility of Allen Miller's character shone forth like a star of the brightest magnitude—a star guaranteeing forgiveness of all his blunders and stupid attempts to curb the impulsive and proud spirit of Roderick War-field Yet sympathy for Gail and her father in no way condoned their poverty to his judgment as a man of finance or reinstated the girl as an eligible match for the young man. He would have been glad of tidings of Roderick—to have him home again and the offensive matrimonial condition he had attached to his offer of an appointment in the bank finally eliminated.

But there was no news, and meanwhile his wife had returned from her mission, to report that the Holdens, while sincerely grateful, had declined all offers of assistance. As Mrs. Miller described, it was the girl herself who had declared, with the light of quiet self-reliance in her eyes, that by working the ranch in Wyoming as she proposed to work it there would be ample provision for her father's little luxuries and her own simple needs.

So Allen Miller put Gail Holden out of mind. But he had many secret heartaches over his rupture with Roderick, and every little stack of mail matter laid upon his desk was eagerly turned over in the hope that at last the wanderer's whereabouts would be disclosed.

CHAPTER IV.

THE COLLEGE WIDOW

STELLA RAIN belonged to one of the first families of Galesburg. Their beautiful home, an old style Southern mansion, painted white with green shutters, was just across from the college campus ground. It was the usual fate of seniors about to pass out of Knox College to be in love, avowedly or secretly, with this fair "college widow." She was petite of form and face, and had a beautiful smile that radiated cheerfulness to the scores of college boys. There was a merry-come-on twinkle in her eyes that set the hearts of the young farmer lad students and the city chaps as well, in tumultuous riot. Beneath it all she was kind of heart, and it was this innate consideration for others that caused her to introduce all the new boys and the old ones too, as they came to college year after year, to Galesburg's fairest girls. She was ready to fit in anywhere—a true "college widow" in the broadest sense of the term. Her parents were wealthy and she had no greater ambition than to be a queen among the college boys. Those who knew her best said that she would live and die a spinster because of her inability to select someone from among the hundreds of her admirers. Others said she had had a serious affair of the heart when quite young. But that was several years before Roderick Warfield had come upon the scene and been in due course smitten by her charms. How badly smitten he only now fully realized when, after nearly a year of absence, he found himself once again tête-à-tête with her in the old familiar drawing-room of her home.

There had been an hour of pleasant desultory conversation, the exchange of reminiscences and of little sympathetic confidences, a subtly growing tension in the situation which she had somewhat abruptly broken by going to the piano and dashing off a brilliant Hungarian rhapsody.

"And so you are determined to go West?" she inquired as she rose to select from the cabinet another sheet of music.

"Yes," replied Roderick, "I'm going far West. I am going after a fortune."

"How courageous you are," she replied, glancing at him over her shoulder with merry, twinkling eyes, as if she were proud of his ambition.

"Stella," said Roderick, as she returned to the piano, where he was now standing.

"Yes?" said she, looking up encouragingly.

"Why; you see, Stella—you don't mind me telling you—well, Stella, if I find the lost gold mine—"

"If you find what?" she exclaimed.

"Oh, I mean," said Roderick in confusion, "I mean if I find a fortune. Don't you know, if I get rich out in that western country—"

"And I hope and believe you will," broke in Stella, vivaciously.

"Yes—I say, if I do succeed, may I come back for you—yes, marry you, and will you go out there with me to live?"

"Oh, Roderick, are you jesting now? You are just one of these mischievous college boys trying to touch the heart of the little college widow." She laughed gaily at him, as if full of disbelief.

"No," protested Roderick, "I am sincere."

Stella Rain looked at him a moment in admiration. He was tall and strong—a veritable athlete. His face was oval and yet there was a square-jawed effect in its moulding. His eyes were dark and luminous and frank, and wore a look of matureness, of determined purpose, she had never seen there before. Finally she asked: "Do you know, Roderick, how old I am?"

As Roderick looked at her he saw there was plaintive regret in her dark sincere eyes. There was no merry-come-on in them now; at last she was serious.

"Why, no," said Roderick, "I don't know how old you are and I don't care. I only know that you appeal to me more than any other woman I have ever met, and all the boys like, you, and I love you, and I want you for my wife."

"Sit down here by my side," said Stella. "Let me talk to you in great frankness."

Roderick seated himself by her side and reaching over took one of her hands in his. He fondled it with appreciation—it was small, delicate and tapering.

"Roderick," she said, "my heart was given to a college boy when I was only eighteen years old. He went away to his home in an eastern state, and then he forgot me and married the girl he had gone to school with as a little boy—during the red apple period of their lives. It pleased his family better and perhaps it was better; and it will not please your family, Roderick, if you marry me."

"My family be hanged," said Roderick with emphasis. "I have just had a quarrel with my uncle, Allen Miller, and I am alone in the world. I have no family. If you become my wife, why, we'll—. we'll be a family to ourselves."

Stella smiled sadly and said: "You enthusiastic boy. How old are you, Roderick?"

"I am twenty-four and getting older every day." They both laughed and Stella sighed and said: "Oh, dear, how the years are running against us—I mean running against me. No, no," she said, half to herself, "it never can be—it is impossible."

"What," said Roderick, rising to his feet, and at the same moment she also stood before him—"What's impossible? Is it impossible for you to love me?"

"No, not that," said Stella, and he noticed tears in her eyes. "No, Roderick," and she stood before him holding both his hands in hers—"Listen," she said, "listen!"

"I am all attention," said Roderick.

"I will tell you how it will all end—we will never marry."

"Well, I say we shall marry," said Roderick. "If you will have me—if you love me—for I love you better than all else on earth."

He started to take her in his arms and she raised her hand remonstratingly, and said: "Wait! Here is what I mean," and she looked up at him helplessly. "I mean,"—she was speaking slowly—"I mean that you believe today, this hour, this minute that you want me for your wife."

"I certainly do," insisted Roderick, emphatically.

"Yes, but wait—wait until I finish. I will promise to be your wife, Roderick—yes, I will promise—if you come for me I will marry you. But, oh, Roderick,"—and there were tears this time in her voice as well as in her eyes—"You will never come back— you will meet others not so old as I am, for I am very, very old, and tonight I feel that I would give worlds and worlds if they were mine to give, were I young once again. Of course, in your youthful generosity you don't know what the disparagement of age means between husband and wife, when the husband is younger. A man may be a score of years older than a woman and all will be well—if they grow old together. It is God's way. But if a woman is eight or ten years older than her husband, it is all different. No, Roderick, don't take me in your arms, don't even kiss me until I bid you good-by when you start for that gold' mine of yours"—and as she said this she tried to laugh in her old way.

"You seem to think," said Roderick in a half-vexed, determined tone, "that I don't know my own mind—that I do not know my own heart. Why, do you know, Stella, I have never loved any other girl nor ever had even a love affair?"

She looked at him quickly and said: "Roderick, that's just the trouble—you do not know—you cannot make a comparison, nor you won't know until the other girl comes along. And then, then," she said wearily, "I shall be weighed in the balance and found wanting, because—oh, Roderick, I am so old, and I am so sorry—" and she turned away and hid her face in her hands. "I believe in you and I could love you with all my strength and soul. I am willing—listen Roderick," she put up her hands protectingly, "don't be impatient—I am willing to believe that you will be constant—that you will come back—I am willing to promise to be your wife."

"You make me the happiest man in the world," exclaimed Roderick, crushing her to him with a sense of possession.

"But there is one promise I am going to ask you to make," she said.

"Yes, yes," said he, "I will promise anything."

"Well, it is this: If the other girl should come along, don't fail to follow the inclination of your heart, for I could not be your wife and believe that the image of another woman was kept sacredly hidden away in the deep recesses of your soul. Do you understand?" There was something in her words—something in the way she spoke them—something in the thought, that struck Roderick as love itself, and it pleased him, because love is unselfish. Then he remembered that as yet he was penniless—it stung him. However, the world was before him and he must carve out a future and a fortune. It might take years, and in the meantime what of Stella Rain, who was even now deploring her many years? She would be getting older, and her chances, perhaps, for finding a home and settling down with a husband would be less and less.

But he knew there was no such thought of selfishness on her part—her very unselfishness appealed to him strongly and added a touch of chivalry to his determination.

Stella Rain sank into a cushioned chair and rested her chin upon one hand while, reaching to the piano keys with the other, she thrummed them softly. Roderick walked back and forth slowly before her in deep meditation. At last he paused and said: "I love you, I will prove I am worthy. There is no time to lose. The hour grows late. I have but an hour to reach my hotel, get my luggage and go to the depot I am going West tonight I will come for you within one year, provided I make my fortune; and I firmly believe in my destiny. If not—if I do not come—I will release you from your betrothal, if it is your wish that I do so."

Stella Rain laughed more naturally, and the old "come-on" twinkling was in her eyes again as she said: "Roderick, I don't want to be released, because I love you very, very much. It is not that—it's because—well, no difference—if you come, Roderick," and she raised her hand to him from the piano—"if you come, and still want me to be your wife, I will go with you and live in the mountains or the remotest corner of the earth."

He took her hand in both his own and kissed it tenderly. "Very well, Stella,—you make it plain to me. But you shall see—you shall see," and he looked squarely into her beautiful eyes.

"Yes," she said, rising to her feet, "we shall see, Roderick, we shall see. And do you know," the twinkling was now gone from her eyes once more and she became serious again—"do you know, Roderick, it is the dearest hope of my life that you will come? But I shall love you just as much as I do now, Roderick, if for any cause—for whatever reason—you do not come. Do you understand?"

"But," interposed Roderick, "we are betrothed, are we not?"

She looked at him and said, smiling half sadly: "Surely, Roderick, we are betrothed."

He put his big strong hands up to her cheeks, lifted her face to his and kissed her reverently. Then with a hasty good-by he turned and was gone.

As Roderick hurried across the old campus he felt the elation of a gladiator. Of course, he would win in life's battle, and would return for Stella Rain, the dearest girl in all the world. The stars were twinkling bright, the moon in the heavens was in the last quarter—bright moon and stars, fit companions for him in his all-conquering spirit of optimism.

CHAPTER V.

_____

WESTWARD HO!

AS the train rumbled along carrying Roderick back to Burlington, he was lost in reverie and exultation. He was making plans for a mighty future, into which now a romance of love was interwoven as well as the romance of a mysterious gold mine awaiting rediscovery in some hidden valley among rugged mountains. Yes; he would lose no further time in starting out for Wyoming. The winning of the one treasure meant the winning of the other—the making of both his own. As he dreamed of wealth unbounded, there was always singing in his heart the name of Stella Rain.

Next day he was aboard a westbound train, booked for Rawlins, Wyoming, where, as his father's letter had directed, he was likely to find the old frontiersman, Jim Rankin; perhaps also the other "cronies" referred to by name, Tom Sun and Boney Earnest At Omaha a young westerner boarded the train, and took a seat in the Pullman car opposite to Roderick. In easy western style the two fell into conversation, and Roderick soon learned that the newcomer's name was Grant Jones, that he was a newspaper man by calling and resided in Dillon, Wyoming, right in the midst of the rich copper mines.

"We are just over the mountain," explained Jones, "from the town of Encampment, where the big smelter is located."

As the train sped along and they became better acquainted, Grant Jones pointed out to Roderick a dignified gentleman with glasses and a gray mustache occupying a seat well to the front of the car, and told him that this particular individual was no other than the "Boss of Montana"—Senator "Fence Everything" Greed. Jones laughed heartily at the name.

"Of course, he is the U. S. Senator from Montana," continued Jones, soberly, "and his name is F. E. Greed. His enemies out in Montana will be highly pleased at the new name I have given him—'Fence Everything,' because he has fenced in over 150,000 acres of Government land, it is claimed, and run the actual home-settlers out of his fenced enclosures while his immense herds of cattle trampled under foot and ate up the poor evicted people's crops. Oh, he's some 'boss,' all right, all right."

"Why," exclaimed Roderick, "that's lawlessness."

Grant Jones turned and looked at Roderick and said: "The rich are never lawless, especially United States Senators—not out in Montana. Why, bless your heart, they say the superintendent of his ranch is on the payroll down at Washington at $1800 a year.

"Likewise the superintendent of the electric lighting plant which Senator Greed owns, as well as the superintendent of his big general store, are said to be on the government payroll.

"It has also been charged that his son was on the public payroll while at college. Oh, no, it is not lawless; it is just a dignified form of graft. Of course," Jones went on with arched eyebrows, "I remember one case where a homesteader shot one of the Senator's fatted cattle—fine stock, blooded, you know. It was perhaps worth $100. Of course the man was arrested, had a 'fair trial' and is now doing time in the penitentiary. In the meantime, his wife and little children have been sent back East to her people. You see," said Jones, smiling, "this small rancher, both poor in purse and without influence, was foolish enough to lose his temper because five or six hundred head of Senator Greed's cattle were driven by his cowboys over the rancher's land and the cattle incidentally, as they went along, ate up his crops. Little thing to get angry about, wasn't it?" and Jones laughed sarcastically.

"Well, don't the state conventions pass resolutions denouncing their U. S. Senator for such cold-blooded tyrannizing methods?"

"If the state of Montana," replied Grant Jones, "should ever hold a state convention of its representative people—the bone and sinew of its sovereign citizens, why, they would not only retire Senator Greed to private life, but they would consign him to the warmer regions."

"You surprise me," replied Roderick. "I supposed that every state held conventions—delegates you know, from each county."

"They think they do," said Jones, winking one eye, "but they are only ratification meetings. The 'Boss,'"he continued, nodding his head towards Senator Greed, "has his faithful lieutenants in each precinct of every county. His henchmen select the alleged delegates and when they all get together in a so-called state convention they are by pre-arrangement program men. The slate is fixed up by the 'Boss' and is duly ratified without a hitch. Therefore instead of being a convention representing the people it is a great big farce—a ratification picnic where 'plums' are dealt out and the ears of any who become fractious duly cuffed."

At Grand Island in the afternoon, during a stop while engines were changed, Roderick left the train and stretched his legs by walking up and down the depot platform. Here he saw Grant Jones in a new rôle. Notwithstanding Jones was in rough western garb—khaki Norfolk coat, trousers to match, and leather leggings—yet he was the center of attraction for a bevy of young ladies. Two of these in particular were remarkable for their beauty; both had the same burnished golden hair and large brown eyes; they were almost identical in height and figure, petite and graceful, dressed alike, so that anyone at a first glance would have recognized them to be not only sisters but doubtless twins.

When the train was about ready to start, these two girls bade adieu to their numerous friends and permitted Grant Jones with all the gallantry of a Beau Brummel to assist them onto the car.

Later Grant Jones took great pains to assure Roderick that it was a pleasure to introduce him to the Misses Barbara and Dorothy Shields—"'Two of our' mountain wild flowers," Grant said, laughing pleasantly, "who reside with their people way over south in the Wyoming hills, not far from Encampment, on one of the biggest cattle ranges in the state."

Roderick, already captivated by the whole-souled, frank manner of Grant Jones, now found himself much interested in the beautiful twin sisters as well. Hour followed hour in bright and sprightly conversation, and soon the tenderfoot who had been inclined to condole with himself as a lonely stranger among strangers was feeling quite at home in the great western world of hospitable welcome and good comradeship.

At an early hour next morning Grant Jones, the Shields girls and a dozen other people left the train at the little town of Walcott. They extended hearty invitations for Roderick to come over to southern Wyoming to see the country, its great mines and the big smelter. "If you pay us a visit," said Grant Jones, laughing, "I'll promise you a fine big personal in the *Dillon Doublejack*, of which mighty organ of public opinion I have the honor to be editor."

Roderick, with a bow of due reverence for his editorial majesty and a bright smile for the sisters, promised that he likely would make the trip before very long. Then he swung himself onto the already moving train and continued his westward journey to Rawlins.

CHAPTER VI.

RODERICK MEETS JIM RANKIN

IT was seven o'clock the same morning when Roderick left the train at Rawlins.

The raw, cold wind was blowing a terrific gale, the streets were deserted save for a few half drunken stragglers who had been making a night of it, going the rounds of saloons and gambling dens.

A bright-faced lad took charge of the mail bags, threw them into a push cart and started rumbling away up the street. Warfield followed and coming up with him inquired for a hotel.

"Right over there is the Ferris House," said the young fellow, nodding his head in the direction indicated.

As Roderick approached the hotel he met a grizzled keen-eyed frontiersman who saluted him with a friendly "Hello, partner, you be a stranger in these yere parts, I'm assoomin'."

"Yes, I just arrived on this morning's train."

"Waal, my handle is Jim Rankin. Been prospectin' the range hereabouts nigh thirty years; uster be sheriff of this yere county when people wuz hostile a plenty—have the best livery stable today in Wyomin', and always glad to see strangers loiterin' 'round and help 'em to git their bearin's if I can be of service— you bet I am."

Thus early had Roderick encountered his father's old friend. He was delighted, but for the present kept his own counsel. A more fitting time and place must be found to tell the reason of his coming.

"Thank you," he contented himself with saying as he

accepted the frontiersman's hand of welcome; "glad to meet you, Mr. Rankin."

"Here, boy," shouted the latter to an attache of the hotel, "take care of this yere baggage; it belongs to this yere gentleman, a dangnation good friend uv mine. He'll be back soon fur breakfast. Come on, stranger, let's go over to Wren's. I'm as dry as a fish."

Roderick smiled and turning about, accompanied his new discovery down the street to Wren's. As they walked along Rankin said: "Here's my barn and here's the alley. We'll turn in here and get into Wren's by the back door. I never pester the front door. Lots uv fellers git a heap careless with their artillery on front steps that are docile 'nuff inside." As they passed through a back gate, Jim Rankin, the typical old-time westerner, pushed his hat well back on his head, fished out of his pocket a pouch of "fine cut" tobacco, and stowing away a large wad in his mouth began masticating rapidly, like an automobile on the low gear. Between vigorous "chaws" he observed that the sun would be up in a "minute" and then the wind would go down. "Strange but true as gospel," he chuckled—perhaps at his superior knowledge of the West—"when the sun comes up the wind goes down."

He expectorated a huge pit-tew of tobacco juice at an old ash barrel, wiped his iron gray mustache with the back of his hand, pushed open the back door of the saloon and invited Roderick to enter.

A fire was burning briskly in a round sheet iron stove, and a half dozen wooden-backed chairs were distributed about a round-topped table covered with a green cloth.

Rankin touched a press button, and when a white-aproned waiter responded and stood with a silent look of inquiry on his face the frontiersman cleared his throat and said: "A dry Martini fur me; what pizen do you nominate, partner?"

"Same," was Roderick's rather abbreviated reply as he took in the surroundings with a furtive glance.

As soon as the waiter retired to fill the orders, Roderick's new found friend pulled a coal scuttle close to his chair to serve as a receptacle for his tobacco expectorations, and began: "You see, speakin' wide open like, I know all these yere fellers—know 'em like a book. Out at the bar in front is a lot uv booze-fightin' sheep herders makin' things gay and genial, mixin' up with a lot uv discharged railroad men. Been makin' some big shipments uv sheep east, lately, and when they get tumultuous like with a whole night's jag of red liquor under their belt, they forgit about the true artickle uv manhood and I cut 'em out. Hope they'll get away afore the cattle men come in from over north, otherwise there'll be plenty uv ugly shootin'. Last year we made seven new graves back there," and he jerked his thumb over his shoulder, "seven graves as a result uv a lot uv sheep herders and cow punchers tryin' to do the perlite thing here at Wren's parlors the same night They got to shootin' in a onrestrained fashion and a heap careless. You bet if I wuz sheriff uv this yere county agin I'd see to it that law and order had the long end uv the stick—though I must allow they did git hostile and hang Big Nose George when I wuz in office," he added after a pause. Then he chuckled quietly to himself, for the moment lost in retrospection.

Presently the waiter brought in the drinks and when he retired Rankin got up very cautiously, tried the door to see if it was tightly shut. Coming back to the table and seating himself he lifted his glass, but before drinking said: "Say, pard, I don't want to be too presumin', but what's your handle?"

Roderick felt that the proper moment had arrived, and went straight to his story.

"My name is Roderick Warfield. I am the son of John Warfield with whom I believe you had some acquaintance a number of years ago. My father is dead, as you doubtless may have heard—died some fourteen years since. He left a letter for me which only recently came into my possession, and in the letter he spoke of three men—Jim Rankin, Tom Sun and Boney Earnest."

As Roderick was speaking, the frontiersman reverently returned his cocktail to the table.

"Geewhillikins!" he exclaimed, "you the son uv John Warfield!

Well, I'll be jiggered. This just nachurly gits on my wind. Shake, young man." And Jim Rankin gave Roderick's hand the clinch of a vise; "I'm a mighty sight more than delighted to see you, and you can count on my advice and help, every day in the week and Sundays thrown in. As you're a stranger in these parts, I'm assoomin' you'll need it a plenty, you bet. Gee, but I'm as glad to see you as I'd be to see a brother. Let's drink to the memory uv your good father."

He again lifted his cocktail and Roderick joined him by picking up a side glass of water.

"What?" asked Rankin, "not drinkin' yer cocktail? What's squirmin' in yer vitals?"

"I drink nothing stronger than water," replied Roderick, looking his father's old friend squarely in the eyes. Thus early in their association he was glad to settle this issue once and for all time.

"Shake again," said Rankin, after tossing off his drink at a single swallow and setting down his empty glass, "you sure 'nuff are the son uv John Warfield. Wuz with him off and on fur many a year and he never drank spirits under no circumstances. You bet I wuz just nachurly so dangnation flabbergasted at meetin' yer I got plumb locoed and sure did fergit. Boney and Tom and me often speak uv him to this day, and they'll be dangnation glad to see you."

"So you're all three still in the ring?" queried Roderick with a smile.

"Bet yer life," replied Rankin sturdily. "Why, Tom Sun and Boney Earnest and me have been chums fur nigh on to thirty years. They're the best scouts that ever hunted in the hills. They're the chaps who put up my name at the convenshun, got me nominated and then elected me sheriff of this yere county over twenty-five years ago. Gosh but I'm certainly glad to see yer and that's my attitood." He smiled broadly.

"Now, Warfield," he continued, "what yer out here fur? But first, hold on a minute afore yer prognosticate yer answer. Just shove that 'tother cocktail over this way—dangnation afeerd you'll spill it; no use letting it go to waste."

"I've come," replied Roderick, smiling and pushing the cocktail across to Jim Rankin, "to grow up with the country. A young fellow when he gets through college days has got to get out and do something, and some way I've drifted out to Wyoming to try and make a start. I have lots of good health, but precious little money."

Jim Rankin drank the remaining cocktail, pulled his chair a little closer to Roderick's and spoke in a stage whisper: "You know, I'm assoomin', what yer father was huntin' fur when he got hurt?"

Roderick flushed slightly and remained silent for a moment. Was it possible that his father's old friend, Jim Rankin, knew of the lost mine? Finally he replied: "Well, yes, I know in a general way."

"Don't speak too dangnation loud," enjoined Rankin. "Come on and we'll hike out uv this and go into one uv the back stalls uv my livery stable. This's no place to talk about sich things—even walls have ears."

As they went out again by the back door the morning sun was looking at them from the rim of the eastern hills. Side by side and in silence they walked along the alley to the street, then turned and went into a big barn-like building bearing a signboard inscribed: "Rankin's Livery, Feed and Sale Stable."

Although there was not a soul in sight, Rankin led his new acquaintance far back to the rear of the building. As they passed, a dozen or more horses whinnied, impatient for their morning feed.

Cautiously and without a word being spoken they went into an empty stall in a far corner, and there in a deep whisper, Rankin said: "I know the hull shootin' match about that 'ere lost gold mine, but Tom and Boney don't—they've been peevish, good and plenty, two or three different times thinkin' I know'd suthin' they didn't. Not a blamed thing does anybody know but me, you bet I went with your father on three different trips, but we didn't quite locate the place. I believe it's on Jack Creek or Cow Creek—maybe furder over—don't know which, somewhere this side or t'other side of Encampment River. You kin bet big money I kin help a heap—a mighty lot But say nothin' to nobody—specially to these soopercilious high-steppin' chaps 'round here—not a dangnation word—keep it mum. This is a razzle-dazzle just 'tween you an' me, young man."

A silence followed, and the two stood there looking at each other. Presently Roderick said: "I believe I'll go over to the hotel and get some breakfast; this western air gives one a ravenous appetite."

Then they both laughed a little as if anxious to relieve an embarrassing situation, and went out to the street together. Jim knew in his heart he had been outclassed; he had shown his whole hand, the other not one single card.

"All right," Rankin finally said, as if an invitation had been extended to him. "All right, I'll jist loiter along with yer over to'rd the hotel."

"At another time," observed Roderick, "we will talk further about my father's errand into this western country."

"That's the dope that sure 'nuff suits me, Mr. War-field," replied Rankin. "Whatever you say goes. Yer can unbosom yerself to me any time to the limit. I've got a dozen good mining deals to talk to you about; they're dandies—a fortune in every one uv 'em—'a bird in every shell,' I might say," and Rankin laughed heartily at his happy comparison. "Remember one thing, Warfield,"—he stopped and took hold of the lapel of Roderick's coat, and again spoke in a whisper—"this yere town is full uv 'hot air' merchants. Don't have nuthin' to do with 'em—stand pat with me and I'll see by the great horn spoon the worst you get will be the best uv everythin' we tackle. Well, so long until after breakfast; I'll see you later." And with this Rankin turned and walked briskly back to his stables, whistling a melody from the "Irish Washerwoman" as he went along.

Arriving at his stables he lighted a fire in a drumshaped stove, threw his cud of tobacco away and said: "Hell, I wish this young Warfield had money. I've got a copper prospect within three mile uv this here town that'll knock the spots out uv the Ferris-Haggerty mine all holler. Geewhillikins, it'll jist nachurally make all the best mines in Wyomin' look like small-sized Shetland ponies at a Perch'ron draft horse show. You bet that's what I've got."

After feeding his horses he came back to the livery barn office, now quite warm and comfortable, pulled up an old broken backed chair, sat down and lit his pipe. After a few puffs he muttered half aloud: "Expect I'm the only man in Wyomin' who remembers all the early hist'ry and traditions about that cussed lost mine. I've hunted the hills high and low, north, south, east and west, and dang my buttons if I can imagine where them blamed nuggets came from. And my failure used to make me at times a plenty hostile and peevish. John Warfield brought three of 'em out with him on his last trip. He gave Tom one, Boney one and me one."

Thrusting his hand into his pocket Rankin produced a native nugget of gold, worn smooth and shiny, and looked at it long in silent meditation. It was a fine specimen of almost pure gold, and was worth perhaps five and twenty dollars.

Presently the old frontiersman brought his fist down with a startling thump on his knee and said aloud: "I'll be blankety-blanked if I don't believe in that dangnation fairy story yet. You bet I do, and I'll help John Warfield's boy find it, by the great horn spoon I will, if it takes every horse in the stable."

Jim Rankin relit his pipe, smoked vigorously and thought. The power of silence was strong upon him. The restless spirit of the fortune hunter was again surging in his blood and awaking slumbering half-forgotten hopes—yes, tugging at his heart-strings and calling to him to forsake all else and flee to the hills.

Rankin was a character, a representative of the advance band of sturdy trail-blazers of the West—tender-hearted as a child, generous to a fault, ready to divide his last crust with a friend, yet quick to resent an injury, and stubborn as a bullock when roused to self-defense. There was nothing cunning about him, nothing of greed and avarice, no spirit of envy for the possession of things for the things' sake. But for him there was real joy in the mad pursuit of things unattainable—a joy that enthralled and enthused him with the fervor of eternal youth. His was the simple life of the hills, loving his few chums and turning his back on all whom he disliked or mistrusted.

Other men and greater men there may be, but it was men of Jim Rankin's type that could build, and did build, monuments among the wild western waste of heat-blistered plains and gaunt rock-ribbed mountains, men who braved the wilderness and there laid the first foundation stones of a splendid civilization— splendid, yet even now only in its first beginnings, a civilization that means happy homes and smiling fields where before all was barrenness and desolation.

CHAPTER VII.

GETTING ACQUAINTED

RODERICK spent a few days in Rawlins, improving his acquaintance with Jim Rankin and making a general survey of the situation. The ex-sheriff proved to be a veritable repository of local information, and Roderick soon knew a little about everyone and everything in the district. He learned that Tom Sun, one of his father's old associates, had from small beginnings come to be the largest sheep owner in the state; he was rich and prosperous. With Boney Earnest, however, the other friend mentioned in the letter, the case was different. Boney had stuck for years to prospecting and desultory mining without achieving any substantial success, but had eventually become a blast furnace man in the big smelting plant at Encampment. There he had worked his way up to a foreman's position, and with his practical knowledge of all the ores in the region was the real brains of the establishment, as Jim Rankin forcibly declared. He had a large family which absorbed all his earnings and always kept him on the ragged edge of necessity.

Rankin himself was not too well fixed—just making a more or less precarious subsistence out of his stage line and livery stable business. But he had several big mining deals in hand or at least in prospect, one or other of which was "dead sure to turn up trumps some day." The "some day" appeared to be indefinitely postponed, but meanwhile Jim had the happiness of living in the genial sunshiny atmosphere of hope. And the coming of Roderick had changed this mellowed sunshine into positive radiance, rekindling all the old fires of enthusiasm in the heart of the old-time prospector. With Roderick the first surge of eager impetuosity had now settled down into quiet determination. But old Jim Rankin's blood was at fever-heat in his eagerness to find the hidden valley. When alone with Roderick he could talk of nothing else.

Roderick, however, had shrewdly and cautiously summed up the measure of his usefulness. Jim Rankin had not the necessary capital to finance a systematic search among the mountain fastnesses where nature so jealously guarded her secret. Nor could he leave his horses and his livery business for any long period, however glibly he might talk about "going out and finding the blamed place." As for any precise knowledge of where the quest should be commenced, he had none. He had shared in the frequent attempts and failures of Roderick's father, and after a lapse of some fifteen or sixteen years had even a slimmer chance now than then of hitting the spot. So, all things duly considered, Roderick had adhered to his original resolution of playing a lone hand. Not even to Rankin did he show his father's letter and map; their relations were simply an understanding that the old frontiersman would help Roderick out to the best of his power whenever opportunity offered and in all possible ways, and that for services rendered there would be liberal recompense should golden dreams come to be realized.

Another reason weighed with Roderick in holding to a policy of reticence. Despite Jim's own frequent cautions to "keep mum—say nothing to nobody," he himself was not the best hand at keeping a secret, especially after a few cocktails had lubricated his natural loquacity. At such moments, under the mildly stimulating influence, Jim dearly loved to hint at mysterious knowledge locked up in his breast. And in a mining camp vague hints are liable to become finger posts and signboards—the very rocks and trees seem to be possessed of ears. So young Warfield was at least erring on the safe side in keeping his own counsel and giving no unnecessary confidences anywhere.

There was nothing to be gained by remaining longer at

Rawlins. Roderick's slender finances rendered it imperative that he should find work of some kind—work that would enable him to save a sufficient stake for the prospecting venture, or give him the chance to search out the proper moneyed partner who would be ready to share in the undertaking. And since he had to work it would be well that his work should, if possible, be on the range, where while earning his maintenance and husbanding his resources, he could at the same time be spying out the land and gaining invaluable experience. So he had on several occasions discussed with Jim Rankin the chances of finding a temporary job on one of the big cattle ranches, and after one of these conversations had come his decision to move at once from Rawlins. His first "voyage of discovery" would be to Encampment, the busy smelter town. He remembered the cordial invitation extended to him by Grant Jones, the newspaper man, and felt sure he would run across him there. From the first he had felt strongly drawn to this buoyant young spirit of the West, and mingled with his desire for such comradeship was just a little longing, maybe, to glimpse again the fair smiling faces of the twin sisters—"mountain wild flowers" as Grant Jones had so happily described Barbara and Dorothy Shields.

So one fine morning Roderick found himself seated beside Jim Rankin on the driver's seat of an old-fashioned Concord stage coach. With a crack of Jim's whip, the six frisky horses, as was their wont at the beginning of a journey, started off at a gallop down the street. Five or six passengers were stowed away in the coach. But these were nothing to Jim Rankin and Roderick Warfield. They could converse on their own affairs during the long day's drive. The old frontiersman was, as usual, in talkative mood.

"By gunnies," he exclaimed sotto-voce, as they wheeled along, "we'll find that pesky lost gold mine, don't you forget it. I know pretty dangnation near its location now. You bet I do and I'll unbosom myself and take you to it—jist you and me. I'm thinkin' a heap these yere days, you bet I am."

Along in the afternoon they crossed over Jack Creek, an important stream of water flowing from the west into the North Platte River. Jim Rankin stopped the stage coach and pointed out to our hero the "deadline" between the cattle and sheep range. "All this yere territory," said Jim, "lying north uv Jack Creek is nachure's sheep pasture and all lyin' south uv Jack is cattle range."

"It's well known," he went on, "where them blamed pesky sheep feed and graze, by gunnies, vegetation don't grow agin successful for several years. The sheep not only nachurlly eat the grass down to its roots, but their sharp hoofs cut the earth into fine pulp fields uv dust. Jack Creek is the dividin' line—the 'dead line.'.rdquo;

"What do you mean by the 'dead line'." asked Roderick.

"The 'dead line,'"replied old Jim as he clucked to his horses and swung his long whip at the off-leader—"the 'dead line' is where by the great horn spoon the sheep can't go any furder south and the cattle darsn't come any furder north, or when they do, Hell's a-pop-pin'.rdquo;

"What happens?"

"What happens?" repeated the frontiersman as he expectorated a huge pit-tew of tobacco juice at a cactus that stood near the roadway. "Why, by gunnies, hundreds uv ondefensible sheep have been actooally clubbed to death in a single night by raidin' cowboys and the sheep-herders shot to death while sleepin' in their camp wagons: and their cookin' outfit, which is usually in one end uv the wagon, as well as the camp wagons, burned to conceal evidence of these dastardly murders. Oh, they sure do make things gay and genial like."

"Astonishing! The cowboys must be a pretty wicked lot," interrogated Roderick.

"Well, it's about six uv one and half a dozen uv the other. You see these pesky sheep herders and the cowboys are all torn off the same piece uv cloth. Many a range rider has been picked from his hoss by these sheep men hidden away in these here rocky cliffs which overlook the valley. They sure 'nuff get tumultuous."

"But what about the law?" inquired Roderick. "Does it afford no protection?"

Jim laughed derisively, pushed his hat far back and replied: "Everybody that does any killin' in these here parts sure does it in self-defense." He chuckled at his superior knowledge of the West. "Leastways, that's what the evidence brings out afore the courts. However, Tom Sun says the fussin' is about over with. Last year more'n twenty cattle men were sentenced to the pen'tentiary up in the Big Horn country. Sort uv an offset fur about a score uv sheep men that's been killed by the cow punchers while tendin' their flocks on the range. You bet they've been mixin' things up with artil'ry a heap."

"I clearly perceive," said Roderick, "that your sympathies are with the cattle men."

Jim Rankin turned quickly and with his piercing black eyes glared at Roderick as if he would rebuke him for his presumption.

"Young man, don't be assoomin'. I ain't got no sympathy fur neither one uv 'em. I don't believe in murder and I don't believe very much in the pen'tentiary. 'Course when I was sheriff, I had to do some shootin' but my shootin' wuz all within the law. No, I don't care a cuss one way or 'tother. There are lots uv good fellers ridin' range. Expect yer will be ridin' before long. Think I can help yer get a job on the Shields ranch; if I can't Grant Jones can. And ther's lots uv mighty good sheep-herders too. My old pal, Tom Sun, is the biggest sheep-man in this whole dang-nation country and he's square, he is. So you see I ain't got no preference, 'tho' I do say the hull kit and bilin' uv 'em could be improved. Yes, I'm nootral. Put that in yer pipe and smoke it, fur it goes dangnation long ways in this man's country to be nootral, and don't git to furgit'n it."

It was late in the afternoon when they neared the little town of Encampment. Old Jim Rankin began to cluck to his horses and swing his whip gently and finally more pronouncedly.

If it is the invariable habit of stage drivers at the point of departure to start off their horses in a full swinging gallop, it is an equally inviolable rule, when they approach the point of arrival, that they come in with a whoop and a hooray. These laws are just as immutable as ringing the bell or blowing the locomotive whistle when leaving or nearing a station. So when Jim Rankin cracked his whip, all six horses leaned forward in their collars, wheeled up the main street in a swinging gallop, and stopped abruptly in front of the little hotel.

As Roderick climbed down from the driver's seat he was greeted with a hearty "Hello, Warfield, welcome to our city." The speaker was none other than Grant Jones himself, for his newspaper instincts always brought him, when in town, to meet the stage.

The two young men shook hands with all the cordiality of old friends.

"If you cannot get a room here at the hotel, you can bunk with me," continued Grant. "I have a little shack down towards the smelter."

Roderick laughed and said: "Suppose, then, we don't look for a room. I'll be mighty pleased to carry my baggage to your shack now."

"All right, that's a go," said Grant; and together they started down the street.

Grant Jones' bachelor home consisted of a single room—a hastily improvised shack, as he had correctly called it, that had cost no very large sum to build. It was decorated with many trophies of college life and of the chase. Various college pennants were on the walls, innumerable pipes, some rusty antiquated firearms, besides a brace of pistols which Jim Rankin had given to Grant, supposed to be the identical flint-locks carried by Big Nose George, a desperado of the early days.

"You see," explained Grant as he welcomed his guest, "this is my Encampment residence. I have another shack over at Dillon where I edit my paper, the *Dillon Doublejack*. I spend part of my time in one place and part in the other. My business is in Dillon but social attractions—Dorothy Shields, you may have already guessed—are over this way." And he blushed red as he laughingly made the confession.

"And talking of the Shields, by the way," resumed Grant. "I want to tell you I took the liberty of mentioning your name to the old man. He is badly in need of some more hands on the ranch—young fellows who can ride and are reliable."

Roderick was all alert.

"The very thing I'm looking for," he said eagerly. "Would he give me a place, do you think?"

"I'm certain of it. In fact I promised to bring you over to the ranch as soon as you turned up at Encampment."

"Mighty kind of you, old fellow," remarked Roderick, gratefully and with growing familiarity.

"Well, you can take that bed over there," said the host. "This one is mine. You'll excuse the humble stretchers, I know. Then after you have opened your grip and made yourself a little at home, we'll take a stroll. I fancy that a good big porterhouse won't come amiss after your long day's drive. We've got some pretty good restaurants in the town. I suppose you've already discovered that a properly cooked juicy Wyoming steak is hard to beat, eh, you pampered New Yorker?"

Roderick laughed as he threw open his valise and arranged his brushes and other toilet appurtenances on the small table that stood at the head of the narrow iron stretcher.

A little later, when night had fallen, the young men went out into the main street to dine and look over the town. It was right at the edge of the valley with mountains rising in a semi-circle to south and west, a typical mountain settlement.

"You see everything is wide open," said Grant, as he escorted Roderick along the streets, arm linked in arm. For they had just discovered that they belonged to the same college fraternity—Kappa Gamma Delta, so the bonds of friendship had been drawn tighter still.

"You have a great town here," observed Roderick.

"We have about 1200 to 1500 people and 18 saloons!" laughed

the other. "And every saloon has a gambling lay-out—anything from roulette to stud-poker. Over yonder is Brig Young's place. Here is Southpaw's Bazaar. The Red Dog is a little farther along; the Golden Eagle is one of the largest gambling houses in the town. We'll have our supper first, and then I'll take you over to Brig Young's and introduce you."

As they turned across the street they met a man coming toward them. He was straight and tall, rather handsome, but a gray mustache made him seem older than his years.

"Hello, here is Mr. Grady. Mr. Grady, I want to introduce you to a newcomer. This is Mr. Roderick Warfield."

"Glad to meet you, Mr. Warfield," said Grady in a smooth voice and with an oleaginous smile. To Roderick the face seemed a sinister one; instinctively he felt a dislike for the man.

"Your town is quite up-to-date, with all its brilliant electric lights," he observed with a polite effort at conversation.

"Yes," replied Grady, "but it is the monthly pay roll of my big smelting company that supports the whole place."

There was a pomposity in the remark and the look that accompanied it which added to Roderick's feelings of repulsion.

"Oh, I don't know," interposed Grant Jones, in a laughing way. "We have about five hundred prospectors up in the hills who may not yet be producers, but their monthly expenditures run up into pretty big figures."

"Of course, that amounts to something; but think of my pay roll," replied Grady, boastingly. "Almost a thousand men on my pay roll. We have the biggest copper mine in the Rocky Mountain region, Mr. War-field. Come down some day and see the smelter," he added as he extended his hand in farewell greeting, with a leer rather than a smile on his face. "I'll give you a pass."

"Thank you," said Roderick coldly. And the two friends resumed their walk toward Brig Young's saloon.

"I don't mind telling you," remarked Grant, "that Grady is the most pompous, arrogant and all-round hated man in this mining camp."

"He looks the part," replied Roderick, and they both laughed.

A minute later they were seated in a cosy little restaurant. Ample justice was done to the succulent Wyoming porterhouse, and cigars were lighted over the cups of fragrant coffee that completed the meal. Then the young men resumed their peregrinations pursuant to the programme of visiting Brig Young's place, certified by Grant Jones to be one of the sights of the town.

The saloon proved to be an immense room with a bar in the corner near the entrance. Roulette tables, faro lay-outs and a dozen poker tables surrounded with feverish players were all running full blast, while half a hundred men were standing around waiting to take the place of any player who went broke or for any reason dropped out of the game.

"I guess nearly all the gambling is done here, isn't it?" asked Roderick.

"Not by a big sight. There are eighteen joints of this kind, and they are all running wide open and doing business all the time."

"When do they close?" inquired Roderick.

"They never close," replied Grant. "Brig Young boasts that he threw the key away when this place opened, and the door has never been locked since."

As they spoke their attention was attracted to one corner of the gaming room. Seven players were grouped around a table, in the centre of which was stacked a pile of several thousand dollars in gold pieces. Grant and Roderick strolled over.

A score of miners and cowboys were standing around watching the game. One of them said to Grant Jones: "It's a jack pot and they're dealing for openers."

Finally someone opened the pot for $500. "It's an all-fired juicy pot and I wouldn't think of openin' it for less." Tom Lester was the player's name, as Grant whispered to Roderick.

"I'll stay," said One-Eyed Joe.

"So will I," said another.

The players were quickly assisted with cards—four refused

to come in, and the other three, having thrown their discards into the deck, sat facing each other ready for the final struggle in determining the ownership of the big pot before them. It was a neck and neck proposition. First one would see and raise and then another would see and go better. Finally, the showdown came, and it created consternation when it was discovered that there were five aces in sight.

Instantly Tom Lester jerked his Colt's revolver from his belt and laid it carefully down on top of his three aces and said: "Steady, boys, don't move a muscle or a hand until I talk." The onlookers pushed back and quickly enlarged the circle.

"Sit perfectly still, gentlemen," said Tom Lester, quietly and in a low tone of voice, with his cocked revolver in front of him. "I'm not makin' any accusations or loud talk—I'm not accusin' anybody in particular of anything. Keep perfectly cool an' hear a cool determined man talk. Far be it from me to accuse anyone of crooked dealin' or holdin' high cards up their sleeves."

As he spoke he looked at One-Eyed Joe who had both a reputation at card skin games and a record of several notches on his gun handle.

"I want to say," Lester continued, "that I recognize in the game we're playin' every man is a perfect gentleman and it's not Tom Lester who suspicions any impure motives or crooked work.

"We will now order a new deck of cards," said Tom while fire was flashing out of his steel gray eyes. "We will play this game to a finish, by God, and the honest winner will take the stakes. But I will say here and now so there may be no misunderstandin' and without further notice, that if a fifth ace shows up again around this table, I'll shoot his other eye out." And he looked straight at One-Eyed Joe, who never quivered or moved a muscle.

"This ends my remarks concernin' the rules. How d'ye like 'em, Joe?"

"Me?" said Joe, looking up in a surprised way with his one eye. "I'm 'lowin' you have made yer position plain—so dangnation plain that even a blind man kin see the pint."

The new deck was brought and the game went on in silence. After a few deals the pot was again opened, and was in due course won by a player who had taken no part in the previous mix-up, without a word falling from the lips of either Tom Lester or One-Eyed Joe.

Roderick and Grant moved away.

"Great guns," exclaimed the former. "But that's a rare glimpse of western life."

"Oh, there are incidents like that every night," replied Grant, "and shooting too at times. Have a drink?" he added as they approached the bar.

"Yes, I will have a great big lemonade."

"Well," laughed Grant, "I'll surprise both you and my stomach by taking the same."

As they sipped their drinks, Grant's face became a little serious as he said: "I'm mighty glad you have come. You seem to be of my own kind. Lots of good boys out here, but they are a little rough and many of them are rather careless. Guess I am getting a little careless myself. There are just two men in these mountains who have a good influence over the boys. One is Major Buell Hampton. Everybody trusts him. By the way, I must introduce you to him. He is one of the grandest men I have ever met" As Grant said this he brought his fist down decisively on the bar.

"The other is the Reverend Stephen Grannon," he went on, "the travelling horseback preacher—carries saddle bags, and all that. Why, do you know, the boys are so respectful to Reverend Grannon that they hire a man to go up and down the street ringing a bell, and they close up all their places for an hour every time he comes to town. He preaches mostly in the big tent you perhaps saw further up the street, at other times in the little church. The boys are mighty respectful to him, and all because they know he goes about doing good. If anyone falls ill, Reverend Grannon is the first to offer help. He visits the poor and cheers them with a spirit of hope. He never leaves town without going into every saloon and shaking hands with the barkeepers, giving them the same kind of advice but not in the same way—the same advice that we used to get when we stood around our mother's knee before we had learned the sorrows of the big world."

For a moment Grant was serious. Then looking up at Roderick, he laughed and said: "We all have to think of those old days once in a while, don't we?"

Roderick nodded gravely.

"Now I come to think of it," said Grant, "the present moment's a very good time. We'll go down and call on one of Nature's noblemen. He is somewhat of an enigma. You cannot tell how old he is by looking at him. He may have seen fifty years or a hundred and fifty—the Lord only knows, for nobody in this camp has any idea. But you will meet a magnificent character. Come along. I'm going to present you to my friend, Major Buell Hampton, about whom I've just been speaking. I guess we'll catch him at home."

CHAPTER VIII.

A PHILOSOPHER AMONG THE MOUNTAINS

AS THE two young men walked down the brilliantly lighted main street of Encampment, Grant Jones explained that the water had been dammed several miles up the south fork of the Encampment river and conducted in a California red-wood pipe down to the smelter plant for power purposes; and that the town of Encampment was lighted at a less cost per capita than any other town in the world. It simply cost nothing, so to speak.

Grant had pointed out several residences of local celebrities, but at last a familiar name drew Roderick's special attention—the name of one of his father's old friends.

"This is Boney Earnest's home," Grant was remarking. "He is the fellow who stands in front of the furnaces at the smelter in a sleeveless shirt and with a red bandana around his neck. They have a family of ten children, every one of them as bright as a new silver dollar. Oh, we have lots of children here and by the way a good public school. You see that log house just beyond? That is where Boney Earnest used to live when he first came into camp—before his brood was quite so numerous. It now belongs to Major Buell Hampton. It is not much to look at, but just wait until you get inside."

"Then this Major Hampton, I presume, has furnished it up in great shape?"

"No, nothing but rough benches, a table, some chairs and a few shelves full of books. What I mean is that Major Hampton's personality is there and that beats all the rich furniture and all the bric-à-brac on earth. As a college man you will appreciate him."

Without ceremony Grant rapped vigorously at the door and received a loud response to "come in." At the far end of a room that was perhaps 40 feet long by 20 feet in width was an open fireplace in which huge logs of wood were burning. Here Major Hampton was standing with his back to the fire and his hands crossed behind him.

As his visitors entered, the Major said in courtly welcome: "Mr. Grant Jones, I am glad to see you." And he advanced with hand extended.

"Major, let me introduce you to a newcomer, Roderick Warfield. We belong to the same 'frat.'.rdquo;

"Mr. Warfield," responded the Major, shaking the visitor's hand, "I welcome you not only to the camp but to my humble dwelling."

He led them forward and provided chairs in front of the open fire. On the center table was a humidor filled with tobacco and beside it lay several pipes.

"Mr. Warfield," observed the Major, speaking with a marked southern accent, "I am indeed pleased, suh, to meet anyone who is a friend of Mr. Jones. I have found him a most delightful companion and I hope you will make free to call on me often. Interested in mining, I presume?"

"Well," replied Roderick, "interested, yes, in a way. But tentative arrangements have been made for me to join the cowboy brigade. I am to ride the range if Mr. Shields is pleased with me, as our friend here seems to think he will be. He is looking for some more cowboys and my name has been mentioned to him."

"Yes," concurred Grant, "Mr. Shields needs some more cowboys very badly, and as Warfield is accustomed to riding, I'm quite sure he'll fill the bill."

"Personally," observed the Major, "I am very much interested in mining. It has a great charm for me. The taking out of wealth from the bosom of the earth—wealth that has never been tainted by commercialism—appeals to me very much."

"Then I presume you are doing some mining yourself."

"No," replied the Major. "If I had capital, doubtless I would be in the mining business. But my profession, if I may term it so, is that of a hunter. These hills and mountains are pretty full of game, and I manage to find two or three deer a week. My friend and next door neighbor, Mr. Boney Earnest, and his family consisting of a wife and ten children, have been very considerate of me and I have undertaken the responsibility of furnishing the meat for their table. Are you fond of venison, Mr. Warfield?"

"I must confess," said Roderick, "I have never tasted venison."

"Finest meat in the world," responded the Major. "Of course," he went on, "I aim to sell about one deer a week, which brings me a fair compensation. It enables me to buy tobacco and ammunition," and he laughed good naturedly at his limited wants.

"One would suppose," interjected Grant Jones, "that the Boney Earnest family must be provided with phenomenal appetites if they eat the meat of two deer each week. But if you knew the Major's practice of supplying not less than a dozen poor families with venison because they are needy, you would understand why he does not have a greater income from the sale of these antlered trophies of the hills."

The Major waved the compliment aside and lit his pipe. As he threw his head well back after the pipe was going, Roderick was impressed that Major Buell Hampton most certainly was an exceptional specimen of manhood. He was over six feet tall, splendidly proportioned, and perhaps weighed considerably more than two hundred pounds.

There were little things here and there that gave an insight into the character of the man. Hanging on the wall was a broad-brimmed slouch hat of the southern planter style. Around his neck the Major wore a heavy gold watch guard with many a link. To those who knew him best, as Roderick came subsequently to learn, this chain was symbolical of his endless kindnesses to the poor—notwithstanding his own poverty, of such as he had he freely gave; like the chain his charities seemed linked together without a beginning—without an end. His well-brushed shoes and puttees, his neatly arranged Windsor tie, denoted the old school of refinement and good breeding.

His long dark hair and flowing mustaches were well streaked with gray. His forehead was knotted, his nose was large but well formed, while the tangled lines of his face were deep cut and noticeable. From under heavily thatched eyebrows the eyes beamed forth the rare tenderness and gentle consideration for others which his conversation suggested. Long before the evening's visit was over, a conviction was fixed in Roderick's heart that here indeed was a king among men—one on whom God had set His seal of greatness.

In later days, when both had become well acquainted, Roderick sometimes discovered moments when this strange man was in deep meditation—when his eyes seemed resting far away on some mysterious past or inscrutable future. And Roderick would wonder whether it was a dark cloud of memory or anxiety for what was to come that obscured and momentarily dimmed the radiance of this great soul. It was in such moments that Major Buell Hampton became patriarchal in appearance; and an observer might well have exclaimed: "Here is one over whom a hundred winters or even countless centuries have blown their fiercest chilling winds." But when Buell Hampton had turned again to things of the present, his face was lit up with his usual inspiring smile of preparedness to consider the simplest questions of the poorest among the poor of his acquaintances—a transfiguration indescribable, as if the magic work of some ancient alchemist had pushed the years away, transforming the centenarian into a comparatively young man who had seen, perhaps, not more than half a century. He was, indeed, changeable as a chameleon. But in all phases he looked, in the broadest sense of the word, the humanitarian.

As the three men sat that night around the fire and gazed into the leaping flames and glowing embers, there had been a momentary lull in the conversation, broken at last by the Major.

"I hope we shall become great friends, Mr. War-field," he said.

"But to be friends we must be acquainted, and in order to be really acquainted with a man I must know his views on politics, religion, social questions, and the economic problems of the age in which we live."

He waved his hand at the bookshelves well filled with volumes whose worn bindings showed that they were there for reading and not for show. Long rows of periodicals, even stacks of newspapers, indicated close attention to the current questions of the day.

"Rather a large order," replied Roderick, smiling. "It would take a long time to test out a man in such a thorough way."

The Major paid no heed to the comment. Still fixedly regarding the bookshelves, he continued: "You see my library, while not extensive, represents my possessions. Each day is a link in life's chain, and I endeavor to keep pace with the latest thought and the latest steps in the world's progress."

Then he turned round suddenly and asked the direct question: "By the way, Mr. Warfield, are you a married man?"

Roderick blushed the blush of a young bachelor and confessed that he was not.

"Whom God hath joined let no man put asunder," laughed Grant Jones. "The good Lord has not joined me to anyone yet, but I am hoping He will."

"Grant, you are a boy," laughed the Major. "You always will be a boy. You are quick to discover the ridiculous; and yet," went on the Major reflectively, "I have seen my friend Jones in serious mood at times. But I like him whether he is frivolous or serious. When you boys speak of marriage as something that is arranged by a Divine power, you are certainly laboring under one of the many delusions of this world."

Roderick remembered his compact with Stella Rain, the pretty little college widow. For a moment his mind was back at the campus grounds in old Galesburg. Presently he said: "I beg your pardon, Major, but would you mind giving me your ideas of an ideal marriage?"

"An ideal marriage," repeated the Major, smiling, as he knocked the ashes from his meerschaum. "Well, an ideal marriage is a something the young girl dreams about, a something the engaged girl believes she has found, and a something the married woman knows never existed."

He looked deep into the open grate as if re-reading a half forgotten chapter in his own life. Presently refilling and lighting his pipe he turned to Roderick and said: "When people enter into marriage—a purely civil institution—a man agrees to bring in the raw products—the meat, the flour, the corn, the fuel; and the woman agrees to manufacture the goods into usable condition. The husband agrees to provide a home—the wife agrees to take care of it and keep it habitable. In one respect marriage is slavery," continued the Major, "slavery in the sense that each mutually sentences himself or herself to a life of servitude, each serving the other in, faithfully carrying out, when health permits, their contract or agreement of partnership. Therefore marriages are made on earth—not in heaven. There is nothing divine about them. They are, as I have said, purely a civil institution."

The speaker paused. His listeners, deeply interested, were reluctant by any interruption to break the flow of thought. They waited patiently, and presently the Major resumed: "Since the laws of all civilized nations recognize the validity of a partnership contract, they should also furnish an honorable method of nullifying and cancelling it when either party willfully breaks the marriage agreement of partnership by act of omission or commission. Individuals belonging to those isolated cases 'Whom God hath joined'—if perchance there are any—of course have no objections to complying with the formalities of the institutions of marriage; they are really mated and so the divorce court has no terrors for them. It is only from among the great rank and file of the other class whom 'God hath *not* joined' that the unhappy victims are found hovering around the divorce courts, claiming that the partnership contract has been violated and broken and the erring one has proven a false and faithless partner.

"In most instances, I believe, and it is the saddest part of it all, the complainant is usually justified. And it is certainly a most wise, necessary, and humane law that enables an injured wife or husband to terminate a distasteful or repulsive union. Only in this way can the standard of humanity be raised by peopling the earth with natural love-begotten children, free from the effects of unfavorable pre-natal influences which not infrequently warp and twist the unborn into embryonic imbeciles or moral perverts with degenerate tendencies.

"Society as well as posterity is indebted fully as much to the civil institution of divorce as it is to the civil institution of marriage. Oh, yes, I well know, pious-faced church folks walk about throughout the land with dubs to bludgeon those of my belief without going to the trouble of submitting these vital questions to an unprejudiced court of inquiry."

The Major smiled, and said: "I see you young men are interested in my diatribe, or my sermon—call it which you will—so I'll go on. Well, the churches that are nearest to the crudeness of antiquity, superstition, and ignorance are the ones most unyielding and denunciatory to the institution of divorce. The more progressive the church or the community and the more enlightened the human race becomes, the less objectionable and the more desirable is an adequate system of divorce laws—laws that enable an injured wife or husband to refuse to stultify their conscience and every instinct of decency by bringing children into the world that are not welcome. A womanly woman covets motherhood—desires children—love offerings with which to people the earth—babes that are not handicapped with parental hatreds, regrets, or disgust. Marriage is not a flippant holiday affair but a most serious one, freighted not alone with grave responsibilities to the mutual happiness of both parties to the civil contract, but doubly so to the offspring resultant from the union. But I guess that is about enough of my philosophy for one evening, isn't it?" he concluded, with a little laugh that was not devoid of bitterness—it might have been the bitterness of personal reminiscence, or bitterness toward a blind and misguided world in general, or perhaps both combined.

Grant Jones turning to Roderick said: "Well, what do you think of the Major's theory?"

"I fear," said Roderick in a serious tone, "that it is not a theory but an actual condition."

"Bravo," said the Major as he arose from his chair and advanced to Roderick, extending his hand. "All truth," said he, "in time will be uncovered, truth that today is hidden beneath the débris of formalities, ignorance, and superstition."

"But why, Major," asked Grant, "are there so many divorces? Do not contracting parties know their own minds? Now it seems impossible to conceive of my ever wanting a divorce from a certain little lady I know," he added with a pleasant laugh—the care-free, confiding laugh of a boy.

"My dear Jones," said the Major, "the supposed reasons for divorce are legion—the actual reasons are perhaps few. However it is not for me to say that all the alleged reasons are not potent and sufficient. When we hear two people maligning each other in or out of the court we are prone to believe both are telling the truth. Truth is the underlying foundation of respect, respect begets friendship, and friendship sometimes is followed by the more tender passion we call love. A man meets a woman," the Major went on, thoughtfully, "whom he knows is not what the world calls virtuous. He may fall in love with her and may marry her and be happy with her. But if a man loves a woman he believes to be virtuous and then finds she is not—it is secretly regarded by him as the unforgivable sin and is doubtless the unspoken and unwritten allegation in many a divorce paper."

He mused for a moment, then went on: "Sometime there will be a single standard of morals for the sexes, but as yet we are not far enough away from the brutality of our ancestors. Yes, it is infinitely better," he added, rising from his chair, "that a home should be broken into a thousand fragments through the kindly assistance of a divorce court rather than it should only exist as a family battle ground." The tone of his voice showed that the talk was at an end, and he bade his visitors a courteous good-night, with the cordial addition: "Come again."

"It was great," remarked Roderick, as the young men wended their homeward way. "What a wealth of new thought a fellow can bring away from such a conversation!"

"Just as I told you," replied Grant "But the Major opens his inmost heart like that only to his chosen friends."

"Then I'm mighty glad to be enrolled among the number," said Roderick. "Makes a chap feel rather shy of matrimony though, doesn't it?"

"Not on your life. True love can never change—can never wrong itself. When you feel that way toward a girl, Warfield, and know that the girl is of the same mind, go and get the license—no possible mistake can be made."

Grant Jones was thinking of Dorothy Shields, and his face was aglow. To Roderick had come thought of Stella Rain, and he felt depressed. Was there no mistake in his love affair?—this was the uneasy question that was beginning to call for an answer. And yet he had never met a girl whom he would prefer to the dainty, sweet, unselfish, brave little "college widow" of Galesburg.

CHAPTER IX.

THE HIDDEN VALLEY

WITHIN a few days of Roderick's advent into the camp he was duly added to the cowboy list on the ranch of the wealthy cattleman, Mr. Shields, whose property was located a few miles east from the little mining town and near the banks of the Platte River. A commodious and handsome home stood apart from the cattle corral and bunk house lodgings for the cowboy helpers. There were perhaps twenty cowboys in Mr. Shields' employment. His vast herds of cattle ranged in the adjoining hills and mountain canyons that rimmed the eastern edge of the valley.

Grant Jones had proved his friendship in the strongest sort of an introduction, and was really responsible for Roderick securing a job so quickly. But it was not many days before Roderick discovered that Doro-try Shields was perhaps the principal reason why Grant rode over to the ranch so often, ostensibly to visit him.

During the first month Roderick did not leave the ranch but daily familiarized himself with horse and saddle. He had always been a good rider, but here he learned the difference between a trained steed and an unbroken mustang. Many were his falls and many his bruises, but finally he came to be quite at home on the back of the fiercest bucking broncho.

One Saturday evening he concluded to look up Grant Jones and perhaps have another evening with Major Buell Hampton. So he saddled a pony and started. But at the edge of town he met his friend riding toward the country. They drew rein, and Grant announced, as Roderick had already divined, that he was

78

just starting for the Shields home. They finally agreed to call on Major Buell Hampton for half an hour and then ride out to the ranch together.

As they approached Major Hampton's place they found him mounting his horse, having made ready for the hills.

"How is this, Major?" asked Grant Jones. "Is it not rather late in the afternoon for you to be starting away with your trusty rifle?"

"Well," replied the Major, after saluting his callers most cordially, "yes, it is late. But I know where there is a deer lick, and as I am liable to lose my reputation as a hunter if I do not bring in a couple more venisons before long, why I propose to be on the ground with the first streak of daylight tomorrow morning."

He glanced at the afternoon sun and said: "I think I can reach the deer lick soon after sun-down. I shall remain over night and be ready for the deer when they first begin stirring. They usually frequent the lick I intend visiting."

The Major seemed impatient to be gone and soon his horse was cantering along carrying him into the hills, while Roderick and Grant were riding leisurely through the lowlands of the valley road toward the Shields ranch.

All through the afternoon Buell Hampton skirted numerous rocky banks and crags and climbed far up into the mountain country, then down abrupt hill-sides only to mount again to still higher elevations. He was following a dim trail with which he showed himself familiar and that led several miles away to Spirit River Falls.

Near these falls was the deer lick. For three consecutive trips the hunter had been unsuccessful. He had witnessed fully a dozen deer disappear along the trail that led down to the river's bank, but none of them had returned. It was a mystery. He did not understand where the deer could have gone. There was no ford or riffle in the river and the waters were too deep to admit belief of the deer finding a crossing. He wondered what was the solution.

This was the real reason why he had left home late that

afternoon, determined, when night came on, to tether his horse in the woods far away from the deer lick, make camp and be ready the following morning for the first appearance of some fine buck as he came to slake his thirst. If he did not get that buck he would at least find the trail—indeed on the present occasion it was less the venison he was after than the solving of the mystery.

Arriving at his destination, the improvised camp was leisurely made and his horse given a generous feed of oats. After this he lighted a fire, and soon a steaming cup of coffee helped him to relish the bread and cold meat with which he had come provided.

After smoking several pipes of tobacco and building a big log fire for the night—for the season was far advanced and there was plenty of snow around—Buell Hampton lay down in his blankets and was soon fast asleep, indifferent to the blinking stars or to the rhythmic stirring of clashing leafless limbs fanned into motion by the night winds.

With the first breaking of dawn the Major was stirring. After refreshing himself with hot coffee and glancing at the cartridges in his rifle, he stole silently along under the overhanging foliage toward the deer lick.

The watcher had hardly taken a position near an old fallen tree when five deer came timidly along the trail, sniffing the air in a half suspicious fashion.

Lifting his rifle to his shoulder the hunter took deliberate aim and fired. A young buck leaped high in the air, wheeled about from the trail and plunged madly toward his enemy. But it was the stimulated madness of death. The noble animal fell to its knees—then partially raised itself with one last mighty effort only to fall back again full length, vanquished in the uneven battle with man. The Major's hunting knife quickly severed the jugular vein and the animal was thoroughly bled. A little later this first trophy of the chase had been dressed and gambreled with the dexterity of a stock yard butcher and hung high on the limb of a near by tree.

The four remaining deer, when the Major fired, had rushed

frantically down the trail bordered with dense underbrush and young trees that led over the brow of the embankment and on down to the river. The hunter now started in pursuit, following the trail to the water's edge. But there were no deer to be seen.

Looking closely he noted that the tracks turned directly to the left toward the waterfall.

The bank was very abrupt, but by hugging it closely and stepping sometimes on stones in the water, while pushing the overhanging and tangled brushwood aside, he succeeded in making some headway. To his surprise the narrow trail gave evidence of much use, as the tracks were indeed numerous. But where, he asked himself, could it possibly lead? However, he was determined to persevere and solve the mystery of where the deer had gone and thus escaped him on the previous occasions.

Presently he had traversed the short distance to the great cataract tumbling over the shelf of rock almost two hundred feet above. Here he found himself under the drooping limbs of a mammoth tree that grew so close to the waterfall that the splashing spray enveloped him like a cold shower. Following on, to his astonishment he reached a point behind the waterfall where he discovered a large cavern with lofty arched roof, like an immense hall in some ancient ruined castle.

While the light was imperfect yet the morning sun, which at that hour shone directly on the cascade, illuminated up the cavern sufficiently for the Major to see into it for quite a little distance. It seemed to recede directly into the mountain. The explorer cautiously advanced, and soon was interested at another discovery. A stream fully fifteen feet wide and perhaps two feet deep flowed directly out of the heart of the mountain along the center of the grotto, to mingle its waters with those of Spirit River at the falls.

Major Hampton paused to consider this remarkable discovery. He now remembered that the volume of Spirit River had always impressed him as being larger below the noted Spirit River Falls than above, and here was the solution. The falls marked the junction of two bodies of water. Where this hidden river came from he had no idea. Apparently its source was some great spring situated far back in the mountain's interior.

The Major was tensioned to a high key, and determined to investigate further. Making his way slowly and carefully along the low stone shelf above the river, he found that the light did not penetrate more than about three hundred feet. Looking closely he found there was an abundance of deer sign, which greatly mystified him.

Retracing his steps to the waterfall, the Major once more crept along the path next to the abrupt river bank, and, climbing up the embankment, regained the deer trail where he had shot the young buck. He seated himself on an old fallen tree. Here on former occasions Major Hampton had waited many an hour for the coming of deer and indulged in day-dreaming how to relieve the ills of humanity, how to lighten the burdens of the poor and oppressed. Now, however, he was roused to action, and was no longer wrapped in the power of silence and the contemplation of abstract subjects. His brain and his heart were throbbing with the excitement of adventure and discovery.

After full an hour's thought his decision was reached and a course of action planned. First of all he proceeded to gather a supply of dry brush and branches, tying them into three torch-like bundles with stout cord, a supply of which he invariably carried in his pockets. Then he inspected his match box to make sure the matches were in good condition. Finally picking up his gun, pulling his hunting belt a little tighter, examining his hatchet and knife to see if they were safe in his belt scabbard, he again set forth along the deer trail, down to the river. Overcoming the same obstacles as before, he soon found himself in the grotto behind the waterfall.

Lighting one of his torches the Major started on a tour of further discovery. His course again led him over the comparatively smooth ledge of rock that served as a low bank for the waters of the hidden stream. But now he was able to advance beyond the point previously gained. After a while his torch burned low and he lighted another. The subterranean passage he was traversing narrowed at times until there was scarcely more than room to walk along the brink of the noisy waters, and again it would widen out like some great colosseum. The walls and high ceilings were fantastically enchanting, while the light from his torch made strange shadows, played many tricks on his nerves, and startled him with optical illusions. Figures of stalactites and rows of basaltic columns reflected the flare of the brand held aloft, and sometimes the explorer fancied himself in a vault hung with tapestries of brilliant sparkling crystals.

Finally the third and last torch was almost burned down to the hand hold and the Major began to awaken to a keen sense of his difficult position, and its possible dangers. When attempting to change the stub of burning brushwood from one hand to the other and at the same time not drop his rifle, the remnants of the torch fell from his grasp into the rapid flowing waters and he was left in utter darkness. Apprehension came upon him—an eerie feeling of helplessness. True, there was a box of matches in the pocket of his hunting coat, but these would afford but feeble guidance in a place where at any step there might be a pitfall.

Major Hampton was a philosopher, but this was a new experience, startling and unique. Everything around was pitch dark. He seemed to be enveloped in a smothering black robe. Presently above the murmur and swish of running water he could hear his heart beating. He mentally figured that he must have reached a distance of not less than three miles from Spirit River Falls. The pathway had proved fairly smooth walking, but unknown dangers were ahead, while a return trip in Stygian darkness would be an ordeal fraught with much risk.

Stooping over the low bank he thrust his hand into the current to make sure of its course. The water was only a little below the flat ledge of rock on which he was standing, and was cold as the waters of a mountain spring. It occurred to him that he had been thirsty for a long time although in his excitement he had not been conscious of this. So he lay down flat and thrust his face into the cool grateful water.

Rising again to his feet he felt greatly refreshed, his nerve restored, and he had just about concluded to retrace his steps when his eyes, by this time somewhat accustomed to the darkness, discovered in an upstream direction, a tiny speck of light He blinked and then questioningly rubbed his eyes. But still the speck did not disappear. It seemed no larger than a silver half dollar. It might be a ray of light filtering through some crevice, indicating a tunnel perhaps that would afford means of escape.

Using his gun as a staff wherewith to feel his way and keeping as far as possible from the water's edge, Major Hampton moved slowly upstream toward the guiding spot of radiance. In a little while he became convinced it was the light of day shining in through an opening. The speck grew larger and larger as he slowly moved forward.

Every once in a while he would stop and turn his face in the opposite direction, remaining in this position for a few moments and then quickly turning round again to satisfy himself that he was under no illusion. But the luminous disc was really growing larger—it appeared now to be as big as a saucer. His heart throbbed with hope and his judgment approved that the advance should be continued.

Yes, the light was increasing, and looking down he fancied he could almost see the butt of his gun which was being used as a walking stick. Presently his feet could indistinctly be seen, and then the rocky pavement over which he was so cautiously shuffling his way.

Ten minutes later the mouth of a tunnel was reached, and he was safe once more, bathed in God's own sunshine, his eyes still dazzled after the Cimmerian blackness from which he had emerged. He had traversed the entire length of the subterranean cave or river channel, and had reached the opposite side of a high mountain. Perhaps the distance through was only about three and a half miles. Trees and underbrush grew in profusion about the mouth of the tunnel into which the hidden river flowed. There was less snow than on the other side of the barrier. Deer sign were everywhere, and he followed a zig-zag deer path out into an open narrow valley.

The Major's heart now leaped with the exultation of accomplishment. Brushing the light covering of snow away, he seated himself on the bank of the stream which could not, now that he looked upon it in the open day, be dignified by calling it a river. Along the edges of the watercourse were fringes of ice but in the center the rapid flow was unobstructed.

It was only a big mountain brook, but one perhaps that had never been seen before by the eyes of man. The exploration and the excitement together had greatly fatigued Buell Hampton, and he was beginning to be conscious of physical exhaustion and the need of food notwithstanding the sustaining stimulus of being a discoverer in one of Nature's jealously guarded wonderlands.

After resting a short time he started to walk farther into the valley and forage along the stream. The hunter was on the lookout for grouse but succeeded in shooting only a young sage hen. This was quickly dressed and broiled, the forked stick that served as a spit being skilfully turned in the blaze of a fire of twigs and brushwood. The repast was a modest one, but the wayfarer felt greatly refreshed, and now stepped briskly on, following the water channel toward its fountain head.

It was indeed a beautiful valley—an ideal one—very little snow and the deer so plentiful that at a distance they might be mistaken for flocks of grazing sheep. The valley appeared to be exceedingly fertile in season. It was a veritable park, and so far as the explorer could at present determine was completely surrounded by high snow-capped mountains which were steep enough to be called precipices. He soon came to a dyke that ran across the valley at right angles to the stream. It was of porphyry formation, rising to a height of from three to four feet, and reaching right across the narrow valley from foothill to foothill. When Major Hampton climbed upon this dyke he noticed that the swiftly flowing brook had cut an opening through it as evenly almost as if the work had been chiseled by man. He was anxious to know whether the valley would lead to an opening from among the mountains, and after a brief halt pushed hurriedly on.

But an hour later he had retraced his steps and was again seated on the bench-like dyke of porphyry. He had made a complete circuit of this strange "nest" or gash in the vastness of the Rocky Mountain Range and was convinced there was no opening. The brook had its rise in a number of mammoth springs high up on the mountain foothills at the upper end of the valley, where it was also fed by several waterfalls that dropped from the dizzy cliffs far above.

The valley was perhaps three miles long east and west and not over one-half mile wide north and south. The contour of the mountain sides to the south conformed to the contour on the north, justifying the reasonable conjecture that an earthquake or violent volcanic upheaval must have torn the mountains apart in prehistoric times. It was evidently in all truth a hidden valley—not on the map of the U. S. Survey—a veritable new land.

"To think," mused the Major, aloud, "that I have discovered a new possession. What an asylum for the weary! Surely the day has been full of startling surprises."

He was seated on the dyke almost at the very edge of the brock where the waters were singing their song of peaceful content. He let his glance again sweep the valley with the satisfied look of one conscious of some unanalyzed good fortune.

There was no snow on the porphyry dyke where he rested. It was moss-covered in many places with the coating of countless centuries. Most likely no human foot but his had ever pressed the sod of this sequestered nook among the mighty mountains. The very thought was uplifting—inspiring. Pulling his hunter's hatchet from its sheath he said aloud: "I christen thee 'Hidden Valley,'"and struck the porphyry rock a vigorous blow, so vigorous indeed that it chipped off a goodly piece.

Major Buell Hampton paused, astonished. He looked and

then he looked again. He picked up the chipped off piece of rock and gazed long and earnestly at it, then rubbed his eyes in amazement. It was literally gleaming with pure gold.

Immediately the hatchet again came into play. Piece after piece was broken open and all proved to be alike—rich specimens fit for the cabinet of a collector. The drab moss-covered dyke really contained the wealth of a King Solomon's mine. It was true—true, though almost unbelievable. Yet in this moment of overwhelming triumph Buell Hampton saw not with the eyes of avarice and greed for personal gain, but rather with the vision of the humanitarian. Unlimited wealth had always been for him a ravishing dream, but he had longed for it, passionately, yearningly, not as a means to supply pleasures for himself but to assuage the miseries of a suffering world.

He was not skilled in judging rock carrying values of precious metals, but in this instance the merest novice could hardly be mistaken. Hastily breaking as much of the golden ore as he could carry in his huge coat pockets and taking one last sweeping survey over the valley, the Major started on his return trip to Spirit River Falls. Arriving at the point where the waters of the brook disappeared in the natural tunnel of the "Hidden River," the name he mentally gave to the romantic stream, he gathered some torch material and then started on the return trip. Two hours later he emerged from behind the turbulent waters at Spirit River Falls. In the waning afternoon he regained his camp. After watering his patient horse, giving it another feed of oats and apologizing with many a gentle caressing pat for his long absence and seeming neglect, the Major set out for home, the dressed deer strapped on behind his saddle, with the deer skin rolled around the venison as a protection.

Early the following morning Buell Hampton visited an assay office, carrying with him an ore sack containing nine pounds and a half of ore. The Major felt certain it was ore—gold ore, almost pure gold—but was almost afraid of his own convictions. The discovery was really too good to be true.

The assayer tossed the sack of gold onto a table where other samples were awaiting his skill and said: "All right, Major, come in sometime tomorrow."

"It's important," replied the Major, "that you assay it at once. It is high grade; I wish to sell."

"Oh, ho!" replied the assayer with elevated eyebrows. Possibly he was like many another who encouraged the "high-graders" in their nefarious thefts from their employers when they were trusted to work on a rich property.

"Why, Major Hampton, I didn't know you were one of 'em— one of us," and he finished with a leer and a laugh. "Bet I can tell what mine it came from," he went on as he leisurely untied the ore sacks.

"I will remain right here," replied Major Hampton firmly, without yielding to the assayer's offensive hilarity, "until you have my samples assayed and make me an offer."

By this time the sack of rock had been emptied into an ore pan and the astonishment depicted on the assayer's countenance would have beggared description. The sight of the ore staggered him into silence. Other work was pushed hurriedly aside and before very long the fire test was in process of being made. When finally finished the "button" weighed at the rate of $114.67 per pound, and the assayer, still half bewildered, handed over a check for almost eleven hundred dollars.

"I say," he almost shouted, "I say, Major Hampton, where in hell did that ore come from? Surely not from any of the producing mines about here?"

"It seems to be a producer, all right," replied the Major, as he folded the check and placed it in his pocketbook.

CHAPTER X.

THE FAIR RIDER OF THE RANGE

WHEN Buell Hampton left the assayer's office he felt a chilliness in the air that caused him to cast his eyes upwards. There had been bright sunshine early that morning, but now the whole sky was overcast with a dull monotonous gray pall. Not a breath of wind was stirring; there was just a cold stillness in the air that told its own tale to those experienced in the weather signs of the mountains.

"Snow," muttered the Major, emphatically. "It has been long in coming this winter, but we'll have a big fall by night."

The season indeed had been exceptionally mild. There had been one or two flurries of snow, but each had been followed by warm days and the light fall had speedily melted, at least in the open valley. High up, the mountains had their white garb of winter, but even at these elevations there had been no violent storms.

Buell Hampton, however, realized that the lingering autumn was now gone, and that soon the whole region would be in the rigorous grip of the Snow King. Henceforth for some months to come would be chill winds, protracted and frequently recurring downfalls of snow, great high-banked snowdrifts in the canyons, and later on the mighty snowslides that sheared timber-clad mountain slopes as if with a giant's knife and occasionally brought death and destruction to some remote mining camp. For the present the Major's hunting expeditions were at an end. But as he glanced at the heavy canopy of snow-laden cloud he also knew that days must elapse, weeks perhaps, before he could revisit the hidden valley high up in the mountains. For yet another winter tide Nature would hold her treasure safe from despoiling hands.

Buell Hampton faced the situation with characteristic philosophy. All through the afternoon he mused on his good fortune. He was glad to have brought down even only a thousand dollars from the golden storehouse, for this money would ensure comfort during the inclement season for a good few humble homes. Meanwhile, like a banker with reserves of bullion safely locked up in his vault, he could plan out the future and see how the treasure was to be placed to best advantage. In Buell Hampton's case the field of investment was among the poor and struggling, and the only dividends he cared for were increased percentages of human happiness. The coming of winter only delayed the good work he had in mind, but even now the consciousness of power to perform brought great joy to his heart. Alone in his home he paced the big room, only pausing at times to throw another log on the fire or gaze awhile into the glowing embers, day-dreaming, unspeakably happy in his day-dreams.

Meanwhile, in anticipation of the coming snowstorm, young Warfield was riding the range and gathering cattle and yearlings that had strayed away from the herd. As he was surmounting a rather steep foothill across the valleys to the westward between the two Encampment rivers, he was startled at hearing the patter of a horse's hoofs. Quickly looking up he saw a young woman on horseback dashing swiftly along and swinging a lariat. She wore a divided brown skirt, wide sombrero, fringed gauntlets, and sat her horse with graceful ease and confidence. She was coming down the mountainside at right angles to his course.

Bringing his pony quickly to a standstill Roderick watched the spirited horse-woman as she let go her lariat at an escaping yearling that evidently had broken out of some corral The lariat went straight to its mark, and almost at the same moment he heard her voice as she spoke to her steed, quickly but in soft melodious tones: "That will do, Fleetfoot. Whoa!" Instantly the well-trained horse threw himself well back on his haunches and veered to the left. The fleeing yearling was caught around one of its front feet and thrown as neatly as the most expert cowboy on the range could have done it.

"By George," said Roderick to himself, "what a fine piece of work." He watched with admiring eyes as the young lady sat her horse in an attitude of waiting. Presently a cowboy rode up, and relieving her of the catch started the yearling back, evidently toward the corral. Turning about, the horsewoman started her horse at a canter directly toward him, and Roderick fell to wondering what sort of a discovery he had made.

A moment later she brought her horse to a standstill and acknowledged his salutation as he lifted his sombrero. He saw the red blood glowing under the soft tan of her cheeks, and as their eyes met he was fairly dazzled by her beauty. He recognized at a glance the western type of girl, frank and fearless, accustomed to the full and health-giving freedom of life in the open, yet accomplished and domesticated, equally at home in the most tastefully adorned drawing room as here on horseback among the mountains.

"I beg pardon," he said in a stammering way, "but can I be of any service?"

At his words she pulled her pony to a standstill and said: "In what way, pray?"—and there was a mischievous smile at Roderick's obvious embarrassment.

"Why, I saw you lariating a yearling."

"Oh," she said, throwing back her head and laughing softly, "that was a long time ago. It is doubtless in the corral by now."

As she spoke, Roderick dismounted. He was capable now of assimilating details, and noted the silken dark Egyptian locks that fell in fluffy waves over her temples in a most bewitching manner, and the eyes that shone with the deep dark blue of the sapphire. His gaze must have betrayed his admiration, for, courteously waving her hand, she touched with her spurs the flanks of her mount and bounded away across the hills. Roderick was left standing in wonderment.

"Who the dickens can she be?" he soliloquized. "I've been riding the range for a good many weeks, but this is the first time I've spotted this mountain beauty."

Throwing himself onto his horse, he started down toward the south fork of the Encampment river and on to the westward the Shields ranch, wondering as he rode along who this strange girl of the hills could be. Once or twice he thought of Stella Rain and he manfully endeavored to keep his mind concentrated on the one to whom he was betrothed, running over in memory her last letter, reckoning the time that must elapse before the next one would arrive, recalling the tender incidents of their parting now two months ago. But his efforts were in vain. Always there kept recurring the vision of loveliness he had encountered on the range, and the mystery that surrounded the fair rider's identity. Once again since Major Buell Hampton's long diatribe on love and matrimony, he was vaguely conscious that his impetuous love-making on that memorable evening at Galesburg might have been a mistake, and that the little "college widow" in her unselfishness had spoken words of wisdom when she had counselled him to wait awhile—until he really did know his own mind—until he had really tried out his own heart, yes, until—Great heavens, he found himself recalling her very words, spoken with tears in her soft pretty eyes: "That's just the trouble, Roderick. You do not know—you cannot make a comparison, nor you won't know until the other girl comes along."

Had the other girl at last come? But at the disloyal thought he spurred his horse to a gallop, and as he did so the first snowflakes of the coming storm fluttered cold and damp against his flushed cheeks. At last he thought of other things; he was wondering now, as he glanced around into the thickening atmosphere, whether all the stray mavericks were at last safe in the winter pastures and corrals.

CHAPTER XI.

WINTER PASSES

THAT night the big snow storm did indeed come, and when Roderick woke up next morning it was to find mountain and valley covered with a vast bedspread of immaculate white and the soft snowflakes still descending like a feathery down. The storm did not catch Mr. Shields unprepared; his vast herds were safe and snug in their winter quarters.

The break in the weather marked the end of Roderick's range riding for the season. He was now a stock feeder and engaged in patching up the corrals and otherwise playing his part of a ranch hand. And with this stay-at-home life he found himself thinking more and more of the real mission that had brought him into this land of mountains. Nearly every night when his work was finished, he studied a certain map of the hills—the inheritance left him by his father. On this map were noted "Sheep Mountain," "Bennet Peak," "Hahn's Peak" and several other prominent landmarks. From his own acquaintance with the country Roderick now knew that the lost valley was quite a distance to the south and west from the Shields ranch.

Thus the wintry days wore on, and with their passing Roderick became more and more firm in his determination to be ready, when the snow was gone in the spring, to take up his father's unfinished task of finding again the sandbar abounding with nuggets of gold. Indeed in his life of isolation it gradually came about that he thought of little else by day and dreamed of nothing else at night. Sometimes in the solitude of his room he smiled at his loneliness. What a change from the old college days—from the stir and excitement of New York. During the winter he had been invited to a score of gatherings, dances, and parties, but somehow he had become taciturn and had declined all invitations.

Then, with stern self-control he had succeeded in putting out of mind the mysterious beauty of the range. Love at first sight!— he had laughed down such silliness, and rooted out of his heart the base treason that had even for a fleeting moment permitted such a thought. Yes, there was nothing but firmest loyalty in his mind for Stella Rain, who was waiting for him so faithfully and patiently, and whose letters cheered him and filled him with greater determination than ever to find the lost mine.

His labors on the ranch were arduous but his health was excellent. At college he had been an athlete—now he was a rugged, bronzed-faced son of the hills. His only recreations were laying plans for the future and writing letters to Stella.

Not infrequently his mind wandered back to Keokuk, the old river town, and his heart grew regretful that he had quarreled with his Unde Allen Miller, and his thoughts were tender of his Aunt Lois. Once he wrote a letter to Whitley Adams, then tore it up in a dissatisfied way, returning to the determination to make his fortune before communicating with his old friends.

And so the winter passed, and spring had come again.

It was one morning in early May, just after he had finished his chores, when to his surprise Grant Jones shouted to him through the corral fence: "Hello, old man, how is ranching agreeing with you, anyway?"

"Fine," responded Roderick, "fine and dandy." He let himself through the gate of the corral and shook hands with Grant. "Come up to the bunk house; seems mighty good to see you."

"Thanks," responded Grant, as they walked along. "Do you know, Warfield, I have been shut up over on the other side of the range ever since that first big snow-storm? I paddled out on snowshoes only once during the winter, and then walked over the tops of trees. Plenty of places up on the Sierra Madre," continued

Grant, nodding his head to the westward, "where the snow is still twenty to thirty feet deep. If a fellow had ever broken through, why, of course, he would have been lost until the spring."

"Terrible to think about," said Roderick.

"Oh, that's not all," said Grant with his old exuberant laugh. "It would have been so devilish long from a fellow's passing until his obituary came to be written. That is what gets on my nerves when I'm out on snowshoes. Of course the columns of the *Doublejack* are always open to write-ups on dead unfortunates, but it likes to have 'em as near as possible to the actual date of demise. Then it's live news."

"Sounds rather grewsome," said Roderick, smiling at Grant's oddity of expression.

Arriving at the bunk house, they were soon seated around a big stove where a brisk fire was burning, for the air without was still sharp and the wind cutting and cold.

"I can offer you a pipe and some mighty fine tobacco," said Roderick, pushing a tray toward him carrying a jar of tobacco and half-a-dozen cob pipes.

"Smells good," commented Grant, as he accepted and began to fill one of the pipes.

"Well, tell me something about yourself, Grant. I supposed the attraction over here at the ranch was quite enough to make you brave snowstorms and snow-slides and thirty-foot snowdrifts."

"Warfield," said Grant, half seriously, between puffs at his pipe, "that is what I want to talk with you about. The inducement is sufficient for all you suggest. She is a wonder. Without any question, Dorothy Shields is the sweetest girl that ever lived."

"Hold on," smiled Roderick. "There may be others in the different parts of the world."

"Is that so?" ejaculated Grant with a rising inflection, while his countenance suggested an interrogation point.

"No, I have no confessions to make," rejoined Roderick, as he struck a match to light his pipe.

"Well, that's just what is troubling me," said Grant, still

serious. "I was just wondering if anyone else had been browsing on my range over here at the Shields ranch while I have been penned up like a groundhog, getting out my weekly edition of the *Dillon Doublejock*, sometimes only fifty papers at an issue. Think of it!" And they both laughed at the ludicrous meagerness of such a circulation.

"But never mind," continued Grant, reflectively, "I will run my subscriptions up to three or four hundred in sixty days when the snow is off the ground."

"Yes, that is all very well, old man. But when will the snow be off? I am considerably interested myself, for I want to do some prospecting."

"Hang your prospecting," said Grant, "or when the snow will go either. You haven't answered my question."

"Oh, as to whether anyone has been browsing on your range?" exclaimed Roderick. "I must confess I do not know. They have had dances and parties and all that sort of thing but—I really don't know, I have not felt in the mood and declined to attend. How do you find the little queen of your heart? Has she forgotten you?"

"No-o," responded Grant, slowly. "But dam it all, I can't talk very well before the whole family. I am an out-door man. You give me the hills as a background and those millions of wild flowers that color our valleys along in July like Joseph's coat, and it makes me bubble over with poetry and I can talk to beat a phonograph monologist." This was said in a jovial, joking tone, but beneath it all Roderick knew there was much serious truth.

"How is it, Grant? Are you pretty badly hit?"

"Right square between the eyes, old man. Why, do you know, sitting over in that rocky gorge of Dillon canyon in the little town of Dillon, writing editorials for the Double jack month after month and no one to read my paper, I have had time to think it all over, and I have made up my mind to come here to the Shields ranch and tell Dorothy it is my firm conviction that she is the greatest woman on top of the earth, and that life to me without her is simply—well, I don't have words to describe the pitiful loneliness of it all without her."

Roderick leaned back in his chair and laughed hilariously at his friend.

"This is no joking matter," said Grant. "I'm a goner."

Just then there came a knock at the door and Roderick hastily arose to bid welcome to the caller. To the surprise of both the visitor proved to be Major Buell Hampton.

Major Hampton exchanged cordial greetings and expressed his great pleasure at finding his two young friends together. Accepting the invitation to be seated, he drew his meerschaum from his pocket and proceeded to fill from a tobacco pouch made of deer skin.

"My dear Mr. Jones and' Mr. Warfield," he began, "where have you been all through the winter?"

"For myself, right here doing chores about twelve hours per day," answered Roderick.

"As for me," said Grant, "I have been way over 'yonder' editing the *Dillon Doublejack*. I have fully a score of subscribers who would have been heartbroken if I had missed a single issue. I snow-shoed in to Encampment once, but your castle was locked and nobody seemed to know where you had gone, Major."

Jones had again laughed good-naturedly over the limited circulation of his paper. Major Hampton smiled, while Roderick observed that there was nothing like living in a literary atmosphere.

"If your circulation is small your persistence is certainly commendable," observed the Major, looking benignly at Jones but not offering to explain his absence from Encampment when Jones had called. "I have just paid my respects," he went on, "to Mr. and Mrs. Shields and their lovely daughters, and learned that you were also visiting these hospitable people. My errand contemplated calling upon Mr. Warfield as well. I almost feel I have been neglected. The latchstring hangs on the outside of my door for Mr. War-field as well as for you, Mr. Jones."

"Many thanks," observed Roderick.

"Your compliment is not unappreciated," said Grant. "When do you return to Encampment?"

"Immediately after luncheon," replied the Major.

"Very well, I will go along with you," said Grant. "I came over on my skis."

"It will be a pleasure for me to extend the hospitality of the comfortable riding sled that brought me over," responded the Major with Chesterfieldian politeness. "Jim Rankin is one of the safest drivers in the country and he has a fine spirited team, while the sledding is simply magnificent."

"Although the jingle of sleigh-bells always makes me homesick," remarked Roderick, "I'd feel mighty pleased to return with you."

"It will be your own fault, Mr. Warfield, if you do not accompany us. I have just been talking to Mr. Shields, and he says you are the most remarkable individual he has ever had on his ranch—a regular hermit They never see you up at the house, and you have not been away from the ranch for months, while the young ladies, Miss Barbara and Miss Dorothy, think it perfectly horrid—to use their own expression—that you never leave your quarters here or spend an evening with the family."

"Roderick," observed Grant, "I never thought you were a stuck-up prig before, but now I know you for what you are. But there must be an end to such exclusiveness. Let someone else do the chores. Get ready and come on back to Encampment with us, and we'll have a royal evening together at the Major's home."

"Excellent idea," responded the Major. "I have some great secrets to impart—but I am not sure I will tell you one of them," he added with a good-natured smile. The others laughed at his excess of caution.

"Very well," said Roderick, "if Mr. Shields can spare me for a few days I'll accept your invitation."

At this moment the door was opened unceremoniously and in walked the two Miss Shields. The men hastily arose and laid aside their pipes.

"We are here as messengers," said Miss Dorothy, smiling. "You, Mr. Warfield, are to come up to the house and have dinner with us as well as the Major and Grant."

"Glorious," said Grant, smiling broadly. "Roderick, did you hear that? She calls you Mr. Warfield and she calls me Grant. Splendid, splendid!"

"I know somebody that will have their ears cuffed in a moment," observed Miss Dorothy.

"Again I ejaculate splendid!" said Grant in great hilarity, as if daring her.

"It is a mystery to me," observed the Major, "how two such charming young ladies can remain so unappreciated."

"Why, Major," protested Barbara, "we are not unappreciated. Everybody thinks we are just fine."

"Major," observed Grant with great solemnity, "this is an opportunity I have long wanted." He cleared his throat, winked at Roderick, made a sweeping glance at the young ladies and observed: "I wanted to express my admiration, yes, I might say my affection for—"

Dorothy's face was growing pink. She divined Grant's ardent feelings although he had spoken not one word of love to her. Lightly springing to his side, she playfully but firmly placed her hands over his mouth and turned whatever else he had to say into incoherency.

This ended Grant's declaration. Even Major Buell Hampton smiled and Roderick inquired: "Grant, what are you mumbling about?"

Dorothy dropped her hand.

"Oh, just trying to tell her to keep me muzzled forever," Grant smiled, and Dorothy's cheeks were red with blushes.

With this final sally all started for the big ranch house where they found that a sumptuous meal had been prepared.

During the repast Barbara learned of the proposed reunion of the three friends at Encampment, and insisted that her father should give a few days' vacation to Mr. Warfield. The favor was quickly granted, and an hour later Jim Rankin brought up his bob-sled and prancing team, and to the merry sound of the sleigh-bells Major Buell Hampton and the two young men sped away for Encampment.

It was arranged that Roderick and Grant should have an hour or two to themselves and then call later in the evening on the Major.

Roderick was half irritated to find no letter at the post office from Stella Rain. In point of fact, during the past two months, he had been noticing longer and longer gaps in her correspondence. Sometimes he felt his vanity touched and was inclined to be either angry or humiliated. But at other times he just vaguely wondered whether his loved one was drifting away from him.

CHAPTER XII.

THE MAJOR'S FIND

WHEN Grant Jones and Roderick arrived at the Major's home that evening they found other visitors already installed before the cheerful blaze of the open hearth. These were Tom Sun, owner of more sheep than any other man in the state; Boney Earnest, the blast furnace man in the big smelting plant; and Jim Rankin, who had joined his two old cronies after unharnessing the horses from the sleigh.

Cordial introductions and greetings were exchanged. Although Roderick had shaken hands before with Boney Earnest, this was their first meeting in a social way. And it was the very first time he had encountered Tom Sun. Therefore the fortuitous gathering of his father's three old friends came to him as a pleasant surprise. He was glad of the chance to get better acquainted.

While the company were settling themselves in chairs around the fireplace, Jim Rankin seized the moment for a private confabulation with Roderick. He drew the young man into a corner and addressed him in a mysterious whisper: "By gunnies, Mr. War-field, it sure is powerful good to have yer back agin. It's seemed a tarnation long winter. But you bet I've been keepin' my mind on things—our big secret—you know."

Roderick nodded and Rankin went on: "I've been prognosticatin' out this here way and then that way on a dozen trips after our onderstandin', searchin' like fur that business; but dang my buttons it's pesterin' hard to locate and don't you forgit it. Excuse us, gentlemen, we are talkin' about certain private

101

matters but we don't mean ter be impolite. I'm 'lowin' it's the biggest secret in these diggin's—ain't that right, Roderick?"

Rankin laughed good-humoredly at his own remarks as he took out his tobacco pouch of fine cut and stowed away a huge cud. "You bet yer life," he continued between vigorous chews, "somebody is nachurlly going to be a heap flustrated 'round here one of these days, leastways that's what we're assoomin'."

"Say, Jim," observed Tom Sun, "what are you talkin' about anyway? Boney, I think Jim is just as crazy as ever."

"I reckon that's no lie," responded Boney, good-naturedly. "Always was as crazy as a March hare with a bone in its throat."

"Say, look here you fellows, yer gittin' tumultuous," exclaimed Rankin, "you're interferin'. Say, Major Hampton, I'm not a dangnation bit peevish or nuthin' like that, but do you know who are the four biggest and most ponderous liars in the state of Wyoming?" The Major looked up in surprise but did not reply. "Waal," said Rankin, expectorating toward the burning logs in the open hearth and proceeding to answer his own question, "Boney Earnest is sure one uv 'em, I am one uv 'em, and Tom Sun is 'tother two." Rankin guffawed loudly. This brought forth quite an expression of merriment The only reply from Tom Sun was that his thirty odd years of association with Jim Rankin and Boney Earnest was quite enough to make a prince of liars of anyone.

Presently the Major said: "Gentlemen, after taking a strict inventory I find there are six men in the world for whom I entertain an especial interest. Of course, my mission in life in a general way is in behalf of humanity, but there are six who have come to be closer to me than all the rest Five of them are before me. Of the other I will not speak at this time. I invited you here this evening because you represent in a large measure the things that I stand for. The snow will soon be going, spring is approaching and great things will happen during the next year—far greater than you dream of. You are friends of mine and I have decided under certain restrictions to share with you an important secret."

Thereupon he pointed to some little sacks, until now unnoticed, that lay on the center table. "Untie these sacks and empty the contents onto the table if you will, Mr. Warfield." Roderick complied.

Each sack held about a hatful of broken rock, and to the amazement of the Major's guests Roderick emptied out on the table the richest gold ores that any of them had ever beheld. They were porphyry and white quartz, shot full of pure gold and stringers of gold. Indeed the pieces of quartz were seemingly held together with purest wire gold.

The natural query that was in the heart of everyone was soon given voice by Jim Rankin. After scanning the remarkable exhibit he turned to Major Buell Hampton and exclaimed: "Gosh 'lmighty, Major, where did this here come from?"

"A most natural question but one which I am not inclined to answer at this time," said the Major, smiling benignly. "Gentlemen, it is my intention that everyone present shall share with me in a substantial way in the remarkable discovery, the evidence of which is lying before you. There are five of you and I enjoin upon each the most solemn pledge of secrecy, even as regards the little you have yet learned of the great secret which I possess."

They all gave their pledges, and the Major went on: "There is enough of these remarkably rich ores for everyone. But should the slightest evidence come to me that anyone of you gentlemen has been so thoughtless, or held the pledge you have just made so lightly, that you have shared with any outsider the information so far given, his name will assuredly be eliminated from this pact. Therefore, it is not only a question of honor but a question of self-interest, and I feel sure the former carries with it more potency with each of you than the latter."

In the meantime Roderick was closely examining the samples of gold. Instinctively he had put his hand to the inside pocket of his coat and felt for his father's map. He was wondering whether

Buell Hampton had come into possession of the identical piece of knowledge he himself was searching for. Presently Jim Rankin whispered in his ear: "By gunnies, Warfield, I guess the Major has beat us to it."

But Roderick shook his head reassuringly. He remembered that his father's find was placer gold—water-worn nuggets taken from a sandbar in some old channel, as the sample in Jim Rankin's own possession showed. The ores he was now holding were of quite a different class—they had been broken from the living rock.

After the specimens had been returned to the sample sacks and the excitement had quieted a little, Major Hampton threw his head back in his own princely way, as he sat in his easy chair before the fire and observed: "Money may be a blessing or it may be a curse. Personally I shall regret the discovery if a single dollar of this wealth, which it is in my power to bring to the light of day, should ever bring sorrow to humanity. It is my opinion that the richest man in the world should not possess more than a quarter of a million dollars at most, and even that amount is liable to make a very poor citizen out of an otherwise good man. Unnecessary wealth merely stimulates to abnormal or wicked extravagance. It is also self-evident that a more equal distribution of wealth would obtain if millionaires were unknown, and greater happiness would naturally follow."

"Yes, but the world requires 'spenders' as well as getters,'"laughed Tom Sun. "Otherwise we would all be dying of sheer weariness of each other."

"Surely, there are arguments on both sides," assented the Major. "It is a difficult problem. I was merely contending that a community of comparatively poor people who earn their bread by the sweat of their brow—tilling the soil and possessed of high ideals of good citizenship—such people beyond question afford the greatest example of contentment, morality and happiness. Great wealth is the cause of some of our worst types of degeneracy. However," he concluded, knocking the ashes from his pipe, "it is not my purpose this evening to sermonize. Nor do I intend at present to say anything more about the rich gold discovery I have made except to reiterate my assurance that at the proper time all you gentlemen will be called on to share in the enterprise and in its profits. Now I believe some of you"—and he looked at Jim Rankin, Tom Sun and Boney Earnest as he spoke—"have another engagement tonight. It was only at my special request, Mr. Warfield, that they remained to meet you and Mr. Jones."

"And we're much obliged to you, Major," said Boney Earnest, arising and glancing at his watch. "Hope old John Warfield's boy and I will get still better acquainted. But I've got to be going now. You see my wife insisted that I bring the folks back early so that she might have a visit with Mr. Rankin and Mr. Sun."

Tom Sun shook hands cordially.

"Glad to have met you, Mr. Warfield," he said, "for your father's sake as well as your own. I trust we'll meet often. Good-night, Mr. Jones."

Rankin whispered something to Roderick, but Roderick did not catch the words, and when he attempted to inquire the old fellow merely nodded his head and said aloud: "You bet your life; I'm assoomin' this is jist 'tween me and you." Roderick smiled at this oddity, as the man of mystery followed his friends from the room.

When the door closed and Roderick and Grant were alone with the Major, pipes were again lighted, and a spell of silence fell upon the group—the enjoyable silence of quiet companionship. The Major showed no disposition to re-open the subject of the rich gold discovery, nor did Roderick feel inclined to press for further information. As he mused, however, he became more firmly convinced than before that his secret was still his own— that Buell Hampton, in this rugged mountain region with its many undiscovered storehouses of wealth, had tumbled on a different gold-bearing spot to that located by Uncle Allen Miller and his father. Some day, perhaps, he would show the Major the letter and the map. But to do this now might seem like begging the favor of further confidences, so until these were volunteered Roderick must pursue his own lonesome trail. The mere sight of the gold, however, had quickened his pulse beats. To resume the humdrum life at the ranch seemed intolerable. He longed to be out on the hills with his favorite pony Badger, searching every nook and corner for the hidden treasure.

Presently Buell Hampton arose and laid his pipe aside, and going to a curtained corner of the room returned with his violin. And long into the night, with only a fitful light from the burning logs in the open fireplace, the Major played for his young friends. It seemed his repertoire was without beginning and without end. As he played his moods underwent many changes. Now he was gay and happy, at another moment sad and wistful. He passed from sweet low measures into wild, thrilling abandonment. Now he was drawing divine harmony from the strings by dainty caresses, again he was almost brutally compelling them to render forth the fierce passion of music that was surging in his own soul. The performance held the listeners spellbound—left them for the moment speechless when at last the player dropped into a chair. The instrument was laid across his knees; he was still fondling it with gentle touches and taps from his long slender fingers.

"You love your violin, Major," Roderick at last managed to articulate.

"Yes," came the low-spoken fervent reply, "every crease, crevice and string of the dear old Cremona that was given me more than half a century ago."

"I wish," said Grant, "that I could express my appreciation of the wonderful entertainment you have given us tonight."

"You are very complimentary," replied the Major, bestirring himself. He rose, laid the violin on the table, and brightened up the fire with additional fuel.

"But I'm afraid we must be going," added Grant. "It is getting late."

"Well, I have a message for you young gentlemen," said the Major. "You are invited to attend one of the most distinguished soirees ever given in the Platte River Valley. Mr. and Mrs. Shields mentioned this today, and made me the special messenger to extend the invitation to you both."

"Splendid," exclaimed Grant. "When does this come off?"

"Two weeks from this evening," replied the Major. "And we will have a comparative newcomer to the valley to grace the occasion. She has been here through the late fall and winter, but has been too busy nursing her sick and bereaved old father to go out into society."

"General Holden's daughter?" queried Grant.

"The same. And Gail Holden is certainly a most beautiful young lady. Have you seen her, Mr. War-field?"

"Not that I'm aware of," replied Roderick.

"A most noble young woman, too," continued the Major. "They are Illinois people. The mother died last year under sad circumstances—all the family fortune swept away. But the girl chanced to own these Wyoming acres in her own right, so she brought her father here, and has started a little cattle ranch, going in for pedigreed dairy stock and likely to do well too, make no mistake. You should just see her swing a lariat," the speaker added with a ring of admiration in his tone.

Roderick started. Great Scott! could this be the fair horsewoman he had encountered on the mountain side just before the coming of the big snow. But a vigorous slap on his shoulder administered by Grant broke him from reverie.

"Why don't you say something, old fellow? Isn't this glorious news? Are you not delighted at the opportunity of tripping the light fantastic toe with a beauty from Illinois as well as our own home-grown Wyoming belles?"

"Well," replied Roderick slowly, "I have not been attending any of these affairs, although I may do so in this instance."

"Miss Barbara Shields," said the Major, "especially requested me to tell you, Mr. Warfield, that she positively insists on your being present."

"Ho, ho!" laughed Grant. "So you've made a hit in that quarter, eh, Roderick? Well, better a prospective brother-in-law than a dangerous rival. Dorothy's mine, and don't you forget it."

Grant's boyish hilarity was contagious, his gay audacity amusing. Even the Major laughed heartily. But Roderick was blushing furiously. A moment before he had been thinking of one fair charmer. And now here was another being thrown at him, so to speak, although in jest and not in earnest. Barbara Shields—he had never dared to think of her as within his reach even had not loyalty bound his affections elsewhere. But the complications seemed certainly to be thickening.

"Come along, old chap," said Grant, as they gained the roadway. "We'll have a look through the town, just to see if there's any news about."

The Bazaar was a popular resort. The proprietor was known as "Southpaw." Doubtless he had another name but it was not known in the mining camp. Even his bank account was carried in the name of "Southpaw."

When Roderick and Grant entered the saloon they found a motley crowd at the bar and in the gaming room, fully twenty cowboys with their broad-rimmed sombreros, wearing hairy chaps, decorated with fancy belts and red handkerchiefs carelessly tied about their necks. Evidently one of them had just won at the wheel and they were celebrating.

The brilliant lights and the commingling of half a hundred miners and many cowboys presented a spectacular appearance that was both novel and interesting. Just behind them came shuffling into the room a short, stout, heavily-built man with a scowling face covered with a short growth of black whiskers. His eyes were small and squinty, his forehead low and his chin protruding.

Roderick and Grant were standing at the end of the bar, waiting for lemonades they had ordered. Roderick's attention was attracted by the uncouth newcomer.

"Grant, who is that gorilla-looking chap?" he asked.

Grant half turned with a sweeping glance and then looking

back at Roderick, replied: "That is Bud Bledsoe. He is a sort of sleuth for Grady, the manager of the smelting plant, the man I introduced you to, remember, the first day you came to Encampment."

"I remember Grady all right," nodded Roderick.

"Well, many people believe he keeps Bledsoe around him to do his dirty work. A while ago there was a grave suspicion that this chap committed a terrible crime, doubtless inspired by Grady, but it is not known positively and of course Grady is all-powerful and nothing was said about it outright."

In the meantime Bud Bledsoe walked into the back part of the room, and finding a vacant seat at a gaming table bought a stack of chips and was soon busy over his cards. Presently the two friends, having lighted fresh cigars, left the saloon.

Grant looked into two or three other places, but finding there was "nothing doing," no news of any kind stirring, at last turned for home. Entering the familiar old bachelor shack, Roderick too felt at home, and it was not long before a cheerful fire was kindled and going. Grant was leaning an elbow on the mantel above and talking to Roderick of the pleasure he anticipated at the coming dance over at the Shields place.

"I wonder what Miss Barbara meant when she sent that special message to you, Roderick? Have you a ground wire of some kind with the young lady and are you on more intimate relations than I have been led to believe?"

Grant smiled broadly at Roderick as he asked the question.

"Search me," replied Roderick. "I have never spoken to her excepting in the presence of other people."

"I presume you know," Grant went on, "that she is the object of Carlisle's affections and he gets awfully jealous if anyone pays court to her?"

"And who's Carlisle?" asked Roderick, looking up quickly.

"Oh, he is the great lawyer," replied Grant "W. Henry Carlisle. Have you never heard of the feud between Carlisle and Attorney Bragdon?"

"No," said Roderick. "Both names are new to me."

"Oh, I supposed everybody knew about their forensic battles. You see, W. Henry Carlisle is the attorney for the Smelter and Ben Bragdon is without doubt the most eloquent young lawyer that ever stood before a jury in southern Wyoming. These two fellows are usually against each other in all big lawsuits in these parts of the country, and you should see the courthouse fill up when there is a jury trial."

Roderick did not seem especially interested, and throwing his cigar stub into the open fire, he filled his pipe. "Now, I'll have a real smoke," he observed as he pressed a glowing firestick from the hearth down on the tobacco.

"Grady and Carlisle are together in all financial ventures," Grant continued.

"Don't look as if you are very fond of this man Grady," commented Roderick.

"Fond of him?" ejaculated Grant in disgust; "he is the most obnoxious creature in the district. He treats everybody who is working for him as if they were dogs. He has this bruiser, Bud Bledsoe, as a sort of bodyguard and this W. Henry Carlisle as a legal protector, so he attempts to walk rough shod over everybody—indifferent and insolent. Oh, let's not talk about Grady. I become indecently indignant whenever I think of his outrages against some of the poor fellows in this camp."

"All right," said Roderick, jovially looking up; "let us talk about the dance and especially Miss Dorothy."

"That's the text," said Grant, "Dorothy—Dorothy Shields-Jones. Won't that make a corker of a name though? If I tell you a secret will you promise it shall be sacred?"

"Certainly," replied Roderick.

"Well," said Grant, reddening, "while I was over there at the *Dillon Doublejack* office, isolated from the world, surrounded with mountains and snow—nothing but snow and snowbanks and high mountains in every direction, why, I played job printer and set up some cards with a name thereon—can't you guess?"

"Impossible," said Roderick, smiling broadly.

"Well, Mrs. Dorothy Shields-Jones," he repeated slowly, then laughed uproariously at the confession.

"Let me see one of the cards," asked Roderick.

"Oh, no, I only kept the proof I pulled before pieing the type, and that I have since torn up. But just wait That girl's destiny is marked out for her," continued Grant, enthusiastically, "and believe me, Warfield, I shall make her life a happy one."

"Hope you've convinced her of that, old man?"

"Convinced her! Why I haven't had the courage yet to say a word," replied Grant, somewhat shamefacedly. "I'm going to rely on you to speak up for me when the critical moment arrives."

"It was rather premature, certainly, to print the lady's double-barreled-name visiting card," laughed Roderick. "But there, you know I'm with you and for you all the time." And he extended the hand of brotherly comradeship.

"And about you and Barbara?" ventured Grant, tentatively. "I've heard your name mentioned in connection with hers several times."

"Oh, forget all that rot," responded Roderick, flushing slightly. He had never mentioned the "college widow" to his friend, and felt that he was sailing under false colors. "It will be a long time before I can think of such matters," he went on, turning toward his accustomed stretcher. "Let's get to bed. It has been a long day, and I for one am tired."

A few minutes later lights were out.

When they got up next morning, they found that a letter had been pushed under the door. Warfield picked it up and read the scrawled inscription. It was addressed to Grant.

"Gee," said Grant as he took the letter from Roderick, "this town is forging ahead mighty fast. Free delivery. Who in the demnition bowwows do you suppose could have done this?"

Opening the envelope he spread the letter on the table, and both bent above it to read its contents. There was just a couple of lines, in printed characters.

Words had been cut out of a newspaper apparently, and stuck on the white sheet of paper. They read as follows:

"Tell your friend to let Barbara alone or his hide will be shot full of holes."

Grant and Roderick stood looking at each other, speechless with amazement. Barbara was the only written word.

"What can be the meaning of this?" inquired Roderick.

"Beyond me," replied Grant. "Evidently others besides myself have come to think you are interested in Barbara Shields. Possibly the young lady has been saying nice things about you, and somebody is jealous."

"Rank foolishness," exclaimed Roderick hotly. Then he laughed, as he added: "However, if the young lady interested me before she becomes all the more interesting now. But let the incident drop. We shall see what we shall see."

They walked up the street to a restaurant and breakfasted.

"It might be," remarked Grant, referring back to the strange letter, "that Attorney Carlisle, who they say is daffy over Barbara Shields, has had that sleuth of Grady's, Bud Bledsoe, fix up this letter to sort of scare you off."

Grant laughed good-humoredly as he said this.

"Scare me off like hell," said Roderick in disgust. "I am not easily scared with anonymous letters. Only cowards write that sort of stuff."

They arose from the table and turned down the street towards the smelting plant It was necessary to keep well on the sidewalks and away from the mud in the roadway, for the weather was turning warm and snow was melting very fast.

"There will be no sleighs and sleigh-bells at the Shields' entertainment," observed Grant. "This snow in the lowlands will all be gone in a day or two."

They paused on a street corner and noticed five logging outfits swinging slowly down the street, then turn into the back yard of

Buell Hampton's home and begin unloading.

"What do you suppose Major Hampton can want with all those logs?" asked Grant.

"Let us make a morning call on the Major," suggested Roderick.

"Right you are," assented Grant.

The Major extended his usual hearty welcome. He had evidently been busy at his writing table.

"We came down," said Grant, "to get a job cutting wood."

The Major looked out of the window at the great stack of logs and smiled. "No, young gentlemen," he said, "those logs are not for firewood but to build an addition to my humble home. You see, I have a small kitchen curtained off in the rear, and back of that I intend putting in an extra room. I expect to have ample use for this additional accommodation, but just at this time perhaps will not explain its purposes. Won't you be seated?"

They pulled up chairs before the fire, which was smouldering low, for in the moderated condition of the weather a larger fire was not needed.

"Only for a moment, Major. We do not wish to take you from your work, whatever it may be. I will confess," Grant went on, smiling, "that we were curious to know about the logs, and decided we would look in on you and satisfy our curiosity; and then, too, we have the pleasure of saying hello."

"Very kind of you, very kind, I am sure," responded the Major; and turning to Roderick he inquired when he expected to return to the Shields ranch.

"I am going out this afternoon," replied Roderick. "By the way, Major, do you expect to be at the Shields' entertainment?"

"No, it is hardly probable. I am very busy and then, too, I am far past the years when such functions interest. Nevertheless, I can well understand how two young gentlemen like yourselves will thoroughly enjoy an entertainment given by such hospitable people as the Shields."

Soon after they took their leave and walked up the street. Grant made arrangements to start directly after luncheon for Dillon,

113

where copy had to be got ready for the next issue of his paper.

As Roderick rode slowly across the valley that afternoon, his mind dwelt on the rich gold discovery made by Buell Hampton, and he evolved plans for getting promptly to serious prospecting work on his own account. Sometimes too he caught himself thinking of the strange girl of the hills who could throw a lasso so cleanly and cleverly; he wondered if their paths would ever cross again.

CHAPTER XIV.

THE EVENING PARTY

THE night of the big fiesta at the Shields ranch had arrived, and the invited guests had gathered from far and near. And what a bevy of pretty girls and gay young fellows they were! Even the cowboys on this occasion were faultless Beau Brummels; chaps, belts, and other frontier regalia were laid aside in favor of the starched shirtfront and dress clothes of the fashionable East. The entertainment was to consist of dancing and song, with a sumptuous supper about the midnight hour.

Roderick of course was there—"by command" of the fair daughter of the house, Barbara Shields. At the entrance to the reception hall the twin sisters gave him cordial welcome, and gaily rallied him on having at last emerged from his anchorite cell. On passing into the crowded room, young Warfield had one of the greatest surprises of his life.

"Hello, Roderick, old scout, how are you anyway?"

Someone had slapped him on the shoulder, and on turning round he found himself face to face with Whitley Adams.

"Whitley, old man!" he gasped in sheer astonishment.

Then followed hand-shaking such as only two old college chums can engage in after a long separation.

"How did it all happen?" inquired Roderick, when the first flush of meeting was over.

"Tell you later," said Whitley. "Gee, old man, I ought to beat you up for not letting me know all this time where you were."

"Well, I have been so confoundedly busy," was the half-apologetic reply.

115

"And so have I myself. I am taking a post-graduate course just now in being busy. You would never guess what a man of affairs I've come to be."

"You certainly surprise me," laughed Roderick drily.

"Oh, but I'm going to take your breath away. Since you've gone, I've become quite chummy with your Uncle Allen."

"You don't say?"

"Yes, siree. I think he took to me first of all in the hope that through me he would get news of the lost prodigal—the son of his adoption whose absence he is never tired of deploring."

"Poor old uncle," murmured Roderick, affectionately and regretfully.

"Oh, he takes all the blame to himself for having driven you away from home. But here—let's get into this quiet corner, man. You haven't yet heard half my news."

The two chums were soon installed on a seat conveniently masked—for other purposes, no doubt—by pot plants and flowers.

"And how's dear Aunt Lois?" asked Roderick, as they settled themselves.

"Oh, dear Aunt Lois can wait," replied Whitley.

"She's all right—don't look a day older since I remember her. It is *I* who am the topic of importance—*I*"—and he tapped his chest in the fervency of his egoism.

"Well, fire away," laughed Roderick.

Whitley rambled on: "Well, I was just going to tell you how your uncle and I have been pulling along together fine. After stopping me in the street two or three times to ask me whether I had yet got news of you, he ended in offering me a position in the bank."

"Gee whizz!"

"Oh, don't look so demed superior. Why, man alive. I'm a born banker—a born man of affairs! So at least your uncle tells me in the intervals of asking after you."

"Yes, you've certainly taken my breath away. But how come you to be in Encampment, Whitley?"

"On business, of course—important business, you bet, or I wouldn't have been spared from the office. Oh, I'll tell *you*— you're a member of the firm, or will be some day, which is all the same thing. There's a fellow here, W. B. Grady, wanting a big loan on some smelter bonds."

"I know the man. But I thought he was rolling in money."

"Oh, it's just the fellows who are rolling in money who need ready money worst," smiled the embryonic banker with a shrewd twinkle in his eyes. "He's a big speculator on the outside, make no mistake, even though he may be a staid and stolid business man here. Well, he needs hard cash just at present, and the proposed loan came the way of our bank. Your uncle jumped at it."

"Security must be pretty good," laughed Roderick.

"No doubt. But there's another reason this time for your uncle's financial alacrity. Seems an old friend of his was swindled out of the identical block of bonds offered by this same Grady, and your uncle sees a possible chance some day of getting them out of his clutches and restoring them to where they properly belong."

"But all that's contrary to one of Uncle Allen's most cherished principles—that friendship and business don't mix. I've heard him utter that formula a score of times."

"Well, cherished principles or no cherished principles, he seems downright determined this time to let friendship play a hand. He tells me—oh, I'm quite in his confidence, you see—that it's a matter of personal pride for him to try and win back his fortune for this old friend, General Holden—that's the name."

"Holden?—Holden?" murmured Roderick. He seemed to have heard the name before, but could not for the moment locate its owner.

"Yes, General Holden. He's ranching up here for the present— or rather his daughter is. They say she's a stunning girl, and my lawyer friend Ben Bragdon has promised to introduce me. Oh, though I'm a man of affairs, old chap, I've an eye for a pretty girl too, all the time. And I'm told she's a top-notcher in the beauty line, this Gail Holden."

"Gail Holden!" Roderick repeated the name out loud, as he started erect in his seat. He knew who the father was now—the daughter was no other than the mysterious rider of the range.

Whitley's face wore a quizzical look.

"Hello! you know her then, old chap?"

"I never met her—at least I have never been introduced to her."

"That's good hearing. Then we'll start level tonight. Of course I'll cut you out in the long run if she proves to be just my style."

"Go ahead," smiled Roderick. He had already recovered his self-possession. "But you haven't informed me yet how you come to know Ben Bragdon, our cleverest young lawyer here, I've been told, and likely enough to get the Republican nomination for state senator."

"Oh, simple enough. I've come up to investigate one technical point in regard to those smelter bonds. Well, Ben Bragdon, your political big gun, happens to be your uncle's legal adviser in Wyoming."

"Which reminds me," interposed Roderick earnestly, "that you are not to give away my whereabout, Whitley—just yet."

"A bit rough on the old uncle not to tell him where you are—or at least let him know that you are safe and well. He loves you dearly, Rod, my boy."

"And I love him—yes, I'll admit it, I love him dearly, and Aunt Lois too. But this is a matter of personal pride, Whitley. You spoke a moment ago of Uncle Allen's personal pride. Well, I've got mine too, and that day of my last visit to Keokuk, when he told me that not one dollar of his fortune would ever be mine unless I agreed to certain abominable conditions he chose to lay down, I on my side resolved that I would show him I could win a fortune from the world by my own unaided efforts. And that's what I'm going to do, Whitley; make no mistake. I don't want him to butt in and interfere in any way. I am going to play this game absolutely alone, and luckily my name gives no clue to the lawyer Ben Bragdon or anyone else here of my relationship with the rich banker of Keokuk, Allen Miller."

"Of course, Rod, whatever you say goes. But all the same there can be no harm in my relieving your uncle's mind by at least telling him that I've heard from you—that you are in good health, and all that sort of thing. But you bet I won't let out where you are or what you are doing. Oh, I'll go up in the old chap's estimation by holding on tight to such a secret. To be absolutely immovable when it would be a breach of confidence to be otherwise is part of a successful young banker's moral make-up, you understand."

Roderick laughed, his obduracy broken down by the other's gay insistence.

"All right, old fellow, we'll let it go at that But as to my being in Wyoming, remember dead secrecy's the word. Shake hands on that; my faith in such a talented and discreet young banker is implicit. But now we must join the others or they'll be thinking us rather rude."

"That—or the dear girls may be fretting out their hearts on my account. A rich young banker from Iowa doesn't blow into Encampment every day, you know." And Whitley Adams laughed with all the buoyant pride of youth, good looks, good health, and good spirits. "Come along, dear boy," he went on, linking his hand in Roderick's arm. "We'll find Lawyer Bragdon, get our introductions, and start fair with the beauteous chatelaine of the cattle range."

Roderick had heard about Ben Bragdon from Grant Jones, but had not as yet happened to meet the brilliant young attorney who was fast becoming a political factor in the state of Wyoming. So it fell to the chance visitor to the town, Whitley Adams, to make these two townsmen acquainted. Bragdon shook Roderick's hand with all the cordiality and geniality of a born "mixer" and far-seeing politician. But Whitley cut out all talk and unblushingly demanded that he and his friend should be presented without further delay to General Holden's daughter.

They found her in company with Barbara Shields who, her duties of receiving over, was now mingling with her guests.

"Miss Holden, let me present you to Mr. Roderick Warfield."

The introducer was Ben Bragdon.

"One of papa's favorite boys," added Barbara kindly, "and one of our best riders on the range."

"As I happen to know," said Gail Holden; and with a frank smile of recognition she extended her hand. "We have already met in the hills."

Roderick was blushing. "Yes," he laughed nervously. "I was stupid enough to offer to help you with a young steer. But I didn't know then I was addressing such a famous horsewoman and expert with the lariat."

Gail Holden smiled, pleasedly but composedly. She possessed that peculiar modesty of dignified reserve which challenges the respect of men.

"Oh, you would have no doubt done a great deal better than I did," she replied graciously.

But Whitley Adams had administered a kick to Roderick's heel, and was now pushing him aside with a muttered: "You never told me you had this flying start, you cunning dog. But it's my turn now." And he placed himself before Miss Holden, and was duly presented by Bragdon.

A moment later Whitley was engaging Gail in a sprightly conversation. Roderick turned to Barbara, only to find her appropriated by Ben Bragdon. And Barbara seemed mightily pleased with the young lawyer's attentions—she was smiling, and her eyes were sparkling, as she listened to some anecdote he was telling. Roderick began to feel kind of lonesome. If there was going to be anyone "shot full of holes" because of attentions to the fair Miss Barbara, he was evidently not the man. He had said to Grant Jones that any association of his name with hers was "rank foolishness," and humbly felt now the absolute truthfulness of the remark. He began to look around for Grant— he felt he was no ladies' man, that he was out of his element in such a gathering. There were many strange faces; he knew only a few of those present.

But his roving glance again lighted and lingered on Gail

Holden. Yes, she was beautiful, indeed, both in features and in figure. Tall, willowy, stately, obviously an athlete, with a North of Ireland suggestion in her dark fluffy hair and sapphire blue eyes and pink-rose cheeks. He had seen her riding the range, a study in brown serge with a big sombrero on her head, and he saw her now in the daintiest of evening costumes, a deep collar of old lace around her fair rounded neck, a few sprigs of lily of the valley in her corsage, a filigree silver buckle at the belt that embraced her lissom form. And as he gazed on this beauty of the hills, this splendid type of womanhood, there came back to him in memory the wistful little face—yes, by comparison the somewhat worn and faded face—of the "college widow" to whom his troth was plighted, for whom he had been fighting and was fighting now the battle of life, the prize of true love he was going to take back proudly to Uncle Allen Miller along with the fortune he was to win with his own brain and hands.

"By gad, it's more than three weeks since Stella wrote to me," he said to himself, angrily. Somehow he was glad to feel angry—relieved in mind to find even a meagre pitiful excuse for the disloyal comparison that had forced itself upon his mind.

But at this moment the music struck up, there was a general movement, and he found himself next to Dorothy Shields. Whitley had already sailed away with Miss Holden.

"Where is Grant?" asked Roderick.

"Not yet arrived," replied Dorothy. "He warned me that he would be late."

"Then perhaps I may have the privilege of the first waltz, as his best friend."

"Or for your own sake," she laughed, as she placed her hand on his shoulder.

Soon they were in the mazy whirl. When the dance was ended Dorothy, taking his arm, indicated that she wished him to meet some people in another part of the room. After one or two introductions to young ladies, she turned to a rather heavy set, affable-looking gentleman and said: "Mr. Warfield, permit me to introduce you to Mr. Carlisle—Mr. Carlisle, Mr. Warfield."

The men shook hands and looked into each other's eyes. Roderick remembered this was the attorney of the smelting plant, and Carlisle remembered this was the young gentleman of whom the Shields sisters had so often spoken in complimentary terms. W. Henry Carlisle was a man perhaps forty years old. He was not only learned in the law, but one could not talk with him long without knowing he was purposeful and determined and in any sort of a contest worthy of his foeman's steel.

Later Roderick danced with Barbara, and when he had handed her over to the next claimant on her card was again accosted by Ben Bragdon. He had liked the young attorney from the first, and together they retired for a cigarette in the smoking room.

"I saw you were introduced to that fellow Carlisle," began Bragdon.

"Yes," replied Roderick, smiling, for he already knew of the professional feud between the two men.

"Well, let me say something to you," Bragdon continued. "You look to me like a man that is worth while, and I take the opportunity of telling you to let him alone. Carlisle is no good. Outside of law business and the law courts I would not speak to him if he were the last man on earth."

"Why," said Roderick, "you are pronounced in your views to say the least."

Bragdon turned to Roderick and for a moment was silent. Then he asked: "What are you, a Republican or a Democrat?"

"Why, I am a Republican."

"Shake," said Bragdon, and they clasped hands without Roderick hardly understanding why. "Let me tell you something else," Bragdon went on. "Carlisle claims to be a Republican but I believe he is a Democrat. He don't look like a Republican to me. He looks like a regular secessionist Democrat and there is going to be a contest this fall for the nomination for state senator. W B. Grady and the whole smelting outfit are going to back this man Carlisle and I am going to beat him. And say—old man—"

he smiled at Roderick when he said this and slapped him on the shoulder familiarly—"I want you on my side."

"Well," said Roderick, half embarrassed and hesitatingly, "I guess I am getting into politics pretty lively among other things. I don't see at this moment why I should not be on your side."

"Well, come and see me at my office over at Encampment and we will talk this matter over." And so it was agreed.

Just then they heard singing, so they threw their cigarettes away and went back to the ballroom. A quartet of voices accompanied on the piano by Gail Holden were giving a selection from the Bohemian Girl. Whitley Adams was hovering near Miss Holden, and insisted on turning the music At the close of the number Whitley requested that Mr. Warfield should sing. Everyone joined in the invitation; it was a surprise to his western friends that he was musical. Reluctantly Roderick complied, and proving himself possessed of a splendid baritone voice, delighted everyone by singing "Forgotten" and one or two other old-time melodies. Among many others, Dorothy, Barbara, and Grant Jones, who had now put in an appearance, overwhelmed him with congratulations. Gail Holden, too, who had been his accompanist, quietly but none the less warmly, complimented him.

Then Gail herself was prevailed upon to sing. As she resumed her seat at the piano, she glanced at Roderick.

"Do you know 'The Rosary'." she asked in a low voice unheard by the others.

"One of my favorites," he answered.

"Then will you help me with a second?" she added, as she spread open the sheet of music.

"I'll be honored," he responded, taking his place by her side.

Her rich contralto voice swelled forth like the sweeping fullness of a distant church organ, and Roderick softly and sweetly blended his tones with hers. Under the player's magic touch the piano with its deep resonant chords added to the perfect harmony of the two voices. The interpretation was wonderful;

the listeners were spellbound, and there followed an interval of tense stillness after the last whispered notes had died away.

As Gail rose and stood before him, she looked into Roderick's eyes. Her cheeks were flushed, she was enveloped in the mystery of song, carried away by music's subtle power. Roderick too was exalted.

"Superb," he murmured ecstatically.

"Thanks to you," she replied in a low voice and with a little bow.

Then the buzz of congratulations was all around them. During that brief moment, even in the crowded ballroom they had been alone—soul had spoken to soul. But now the tension was relaxed. Gail was laughing merrily. Whitley Adams was punching Roderick in the ribs.

"Say, old man, that's taking another mean advantage."

"What do you mean?" asked Roderick, recovering his composure.

"Singing duets like that isn't toeing the line. The start was to be a fair one, but you're laps ahead already." Whitley was looking with comical dolefulness in the direction of Gail Holden.

"Oh, I catch your drift," laughed Roderick. "Well, you brought the trouble on yourself, my boy. It was you who gave me away by declaring I could sing."

"Which shows the folly of paying a false compliment," retorted Whitley. "However, I'm going to get another dance anyhow."

He made a step toward Gail, but Roderick laid a detaining hand on his shoulder.

"Not just yet; the next is mine." And with audacity that amazed himself Roderick advanced to Gail, bowed, and offered his arm. The soft strains of a dreamy waltz had just begun.

Without a word she accepted his invitation, and together they floated away among the maze of dancers.

"Well, that's going some," murmured Whitley, as he glanced around in quest of consolation. Dorothy Shields appeared to be monopolized by Grant Jones, but the two lawyers, Eragdon and Carlisle, were glowering at each other, as if in defiance as to which should carry off Barbara. So Whitley solved the problem by sailing in and appropriating her for himself. He was happy, she seemed pleased, and the rivals, turning away from each other, had the cold consolation that neither had profited by the other's momentary hesitation.

After the first few rounds Roderick opened a conversation with his partner. He felicitated her upon her playing and singing. She thanked him and said: "Most heartily can I return the compliment." He bowed his acknowledgment.

"You must come to Conchshell ranch and call on my father. He will be glad to meet you—has been an invalid all the winter, but I'm thankful he is better now."

"I'll be honored and delighted to make his acquaintance," replied Roderick.

"Then perhaps we can have some more singing together," she went on.

"Which will be a great pleasure to me," he interjected fervently.

"And to me," she said, smiling.

Whether listening or speaking there was something infinitely charming about Gail Holden. When conversing her beautiful teeth reminded one of a cupid's mouth full of pearls.

"It has been some time," explained Roderick, "since I was over your way."

For a moment their eyes met and she mischievously replied;

"Oh, yes. Next time, I'll not only sing for you, but if you wish I will teach you how to throw the lariat."

"I don't presume," replied Roderick banteringly, "you will guarantee what I might catch even if I turned out to be an expert?"

"That," Gail quickly rejoined, "rests entirely with your own cleverness."

Just then it was announced from the dining room that the tables with the evening collation were spread, and as Roderick was about to offer his arm to Miss Holden, Barbara came hurriedly up, flushed and saying: "Oh, Gail, here is Mr. Carlisle who wants to take you to supper. And Mr. Warfield, you are to escort me."

She smiled triumphantly up into his face as she took his arm.

As they walked away together and Barbara was vivaciously talking to him, he wondered what it all meant Everybody seemed to be playing at cross purposes. Again he thought of the letter of warning pushed under Grant Jones' door and mentally speculated how it would all end.

CHAPTER XV.

BRONCHO-BUSTING

IT WAS the morning following the big entertainment at the Shields ranch when Roderick and two other cowboy companions began the work of breaking some outlaw horses to the saddle. The corral where they were confined was a quarter of a mile away from the bunk house.

Grant Jones had remained overnight, ostensibly to pay Roderick a visit during the succeeding day. He was still sound asleep when Roderick arose at an early hour and started for the corral. Whitley Adams had also been detained at the ranch house as a guest. He had invited himself to the broncho-busting spectacle, and was waiting on the veranda for Roderick as the latter strolled by.

An unbroken horse may or may not be an outlaw. If he takes kindly to the bridle and saddle and, after the first flush of scared excitement is over with, settles down and becomes bridle-wise then he is not an outlaw. On the other hand when put to the test if he begins to rear up—thump down on his forefeet—buck and twist like a corkscrew and continues jumping sideways and up and down, bucking and rearing until possibly he falls over backward, endangering the life of his rider and continues in this ungovernable fashion until finally he is given up as unbreakable, why, then the horse is an outlaw. He feels that he has conquered man, and the next attempt to break him to the saddle will be fraught with still greater viciousness.

Bull-dogging a wild Texas steer is nothing compared with the skill necessary to conquer an outlaw pony.

Nearly all cowboy riders, take to broncho-busting naturally and good-naturedly, and they usually find an especial delight in assuring the Easterner that they have never found anything that wears hair they cannot ride. Of course, this is more or less of a cowboy expression and possibly borders on vanity. However, as a class, they are not usually inclined to boast.

Very excellent progress had been made in the work of breaking the bronchos to the saddle. It was along about eleven o'clock when Roderick had just made his last mount upon what seemed to be one of the most docile ponies in the corral. He was a three-year-old and had been given the name of Firefly. The wranglers or helpers had no sooner loosened the blindfold than Roderick realized he was on the hurricane deck of a pony that would probably give him trouble. When Firefly felt the weight of Roderick upon his back, apparently he was stunned to such an extent that he was filled with indecision as to what he should do and began trembling and settling as if he might go to his knees. Roderick touched his flank with a sharp spur and then, with all the suddenness of a flash of lightning from a clear sky, rider and horse became the agitated center of a whirling cloud of dust. The horse seemingly would stop just long enough in his corkscrew whirls to jump high in the air and light on his forefeet with his head nearly on the ground and then with instantaneous quickness rear almost upright Whitley Adams was terribly scared at the scene. The struggle lasted perhaps a couple of minutes, and then Roderick was whirled over the head of the pony and with a shrill neigh Firefly dashed across the corral and leaping broke through a six foot fence and galloped away over the open prairie. The two wranglers and Whitley hastened to Roderick's side. He had been stunned but only temporarily and not seriously injured, as it proved.

"Oh, that's all right," he said presently as he rubbed his eyes.

"Are you hurt?" Whitley inquired. Roderick slowly rose to his feet with Whitley's assistance and stretching himself looked about as if a bit dazed. "No, no," he replied, "I am not hurt but that infernal horse has my riding saddle."

"You had better learn to ride a rocking horse before trying to ride an outlaw, Warfield," said Scotty Meisch, one of the new cowpunchers, sneeringly.

Roderick whirled on him. "I'll take you on for a contest most any day, if you think you are so good and I am so poor as all that," he said. "Come on, what do you say?"

"Well, I ride in the Frontier Day's celebration that comes on in July at our local fair," the cowboy said. "Guess if you want to ride in a real contest with me you'd better enter your name and we'll see how long you last."

"Very well, I'll just do that for once and show you a little something about real roughriding," said Roderick; "and Firefly will be one of the outlaws."

Turning he limped off towards the bunk house with Whitley.

Whitley was greatly relieved that Roderick, although he had wrenched the tendons of his leg, had no broken bones. A couple of other cowboys mounted their ponies, and with lariats started off across the prairie to capture the outlaw and bring back the saddle. Whitley was assured that they were breaking horses all the time and now and then the boys got hold of an outlaw but no one was ever very seriously injured.

Reaching the lounging room of the bunk house, they learned that Grant was up and dressed. He had evidently gone up to the ranch house and at that very moment was doubtless basking in the smiles of Miss Dorothy.

The college chums, pipes alight, soon got to talking of old times.

"By the way," remarked Whitley between puffs, "last month I was back at the class reunion at Galesburg and called on Stella Rain."

Roderick reddened and Whitley went blandly on: "Mighty fine girl—I mean Stella. Finest college widow ever. I did not know you were the lucky dog, though?"

"What do you mean by my being the lucky dog?"

"Oh, you were always smitten in that quarter—everyone

knew that. And now those tell-tale flushes on your face, together with what Stella said, makes it all clear. Congratulations, old man," said Whitley, laughing good-naturedly at Roderick's discomfiture.

As their hands met, Roderick said: "I don't know, old chap, whether congratulations are in order or not. She don't write as often as she used to. It don't argue very well for me."

"Man alive," said Whitley, "what do you want with a college widow or a battalion of college widows when you are among such girls as you have out here? Great Scott, don't you realize that these girls are the greatest ever? Grant Jones shows his good sense; he seems to have roped Miss Dorothy for sure. At first I thought I had your measure last night, when you were talking to Miss Barbara Shields—for the moment I had forgotten about Stella. Then you switched off and cut me out with the fair singer. Say, if somebody don't capture Miss Gail Holden—"

He paused, puffed awhile, then resumed meditatively: "Why, old man, down in Keokuk Gail Holden wouldn't last a month. Someone would pick her up in a jiffy."

"Provided," said Roderick, and looked steadily at Whitley.

"Oh, yes, of course, provided he could win her."

"These western girls, I judge," said Roderick slowly—"understand I am not speaking from experience—are pretty hard to win. There is a freedom in the very atmosphere of the West that thrills a fellow's nerves and suggests the widest sort of independence. And our range girls are pronouncedly independent, unless I have them sized up wrong. Tell me," he continued, "how you feel about Miss Holden?"

"Oh," replied Whitley, "I knew ahead that she was a stunning girl, and after that first waltz I felt withered all in a heap. But when I saw and heard you singing together at the piano, I realized what was bound to come. Oh, you needn't blush so furiously. You've got to forget a certain party down at Galesburg. As for me, I've got to fly at humbler game. Guess I'll have another look around."

He laughed somewhat wistfully, as he rose and knocked the

ashes from the bowl of his pipe.

Roderick had not interrupted; he was becoming accustomed to others deciding for him his matrimonial affairs. He was musing over the complications that seemed to be crowding into his life.

"You see I retire from the contest," Whitley went on, his smile broadening, "and I hope you'll recognize the devoted loyalty of a friend. But now those Shields girls—one or other of them—both are equally charming."

"You can't cut Grant Jones out," interrupted Roderick firmly. "Remember, next to yourself, he's my dearest friend."

"Oh, well, there's Miss Barbara left. Now don't you think I would be quite irresistible as compared with either of those lawyer fellows?" He drew himself up admiringly.

"You might be liable to get your hide shot full of holes," replied Roderick.

"What do you mean?"

But Roderick did not explain his enigmatic utterance.

"I think I'll have a lay-down," he said, "and rest my stiff bones." He got up; he said nothing to Whitley, but the bruised leg pained him considerably.

"All right," replied Whitley gaily. "Then I'll do a little further reconnoitering up at the ranch house. So long."

Warfield was glad to be alone. Apart from the pain he was suffering, he wanted to think things over. He was not blind to the truth that Gail Holden had brought a new interest into his life. Yet he was half saddened by the thought that almost a month had gone by without a letter from Stella Rain. Then Whitley's coming had brought back memories of Uncle Allen, Aunt Lois, and the old days at Keokuk. He was feeling very homesick—utterly tired of the rough cow-punching existence he had been leading for over six months.

CHAPTER XVI.

THE MYSTERIOUS TOILERS

OF THE NIGHT

IN A day or two the excitement over the great evening party at the Shields ranch had passed and the humdrum duties of everyday life had been resumed. Whitley Adams had completed his business at Encampment and taken his departure with the solemnly renewed promise to Roderick that for the present the latter's whereabouts would not be disclosed to the good folks at Keokuk although their anxiety as to his safety and good health would be relieved. Grant Jones had torn himself away from his beloved to resume his eternal—and as he felt at the moment infernal—task of getting out the next issue of his weekly newspaper. Gail Holden had ridden off over the foothills, the Shields sisters had returned to their domestic duties, and all the other beauties of the ballroom had scattered far and wide like thistledown in a breeze. The cowboys had reverted to chaps and sombreros, dress clothes had been stowed away with moth balls to keep them company, and the language of superlative politeness had lapsed back into the terser vernacular of the stock corral. Roderick was pretty well alone all day in the bunk house, nursing the stiff leg that had resulted from the broncho-busting episode.

Between embrocations he was doing a little figuring and stock-taking of ways and means. During his six months on the ranch most of his salary had been saved. The accumulated amount would enable him to clear off one-half of his remaining indebtedness in New York and leave him a matter of a hundred dollars for some prospecting on his own account during the summer months among the hills. But he would stay by his job for yet another month or two, because, although the words had been spoken in the heat of the moment, he had pledged himself to meet the cowboy Scotty Meisch in the riding contest at the Frontier Day's celebration. Yes, he would stick to that promise, he mused as he rubbed in the liniment Gail Holden, when she had come to bid him good-by and express her condolence over his accident, had announced her own intention of entering for the lariat throwing competition, but he would never have admitted to himself that the chance of meeting her again in such circumstances, the chance of restoring his prestige as a broncho-buster before her very eyes, had the slightest thing to do with his resolve to delay his start in systematic quest of the lost mine.

Meanwhile Buell Hampton seemed to have withdrawn himself from the world. During the two weeks that had intervened between the invitation and the dance, he had not called at the ranch. Nor did he come now during the weeks that followed, and one evening when Grant Jones paid a visit to the Major's home he found the door locked. Grant surveyed with both surprise and curiosity the addition that had been made to the building. It was a solid structure of logs, showing neither door nor window to the outside, and evidently was only reached through the big living room.

He reported the matter to Roderick, but the latter, his stiff leg now all right again, was too busy among the cattle on the ranges to bother about other things.

But Buell Hampton all this time had been very active indeed. During the winter months he had thought out his plans. Somehow he had come to look upon the hidden valley with its storehouse of golden wealth as a sacred place not to be trespassed on by the common human drove. Just so soon as the melting snows rendered the journey practicable, he had returned all alone to the sequestered nook nested in the mountains. He had discovered that quite a little herd of deer had found shelter and subsistence there during the months of winter. As he came among them, they had shown, themselves quite tame and fearless; three or four does had nibbled the fresh spring grass almost at his very feet as he had sat on the porphyry dyke, enjoying the beautiful scene, alone in his little kingdom, with only these gentle creatures and the twittering birds for companions.

And there and then Buell Hampton had resolved that he would not desecrate this sanctuary of nature—that he would not bring in the brutal eager throng of gold seekers, changing the lovely little valley into a scene of sordid greed and ugliness, its wild flowers crushed underfoot, its pellucid stream turned to sludge, its rightful inhabitants, the gentle-eyed deer, butchered for riotous gluttony. No, never! He would take the rich God-given gift of gold that was his, gratefully and for the ulterior purpose of spreading human happiness. But all else he would leave undisturbed.

The gold-bearing porphyry dyke stretching across the narrow valley was decomposed; it required no drilling nor blasting; its bulk could easily be broken by aid of sledge hammer and crowbar. Two or three men working steadily for two or three months could remove the entire dyke as it lay visible between mountain rock wall and mountain rock wall, and taking the assay value of the ore as already ascertained, from this operation alone there was wealth for all interested beyond the dreams of avarice. Buell Hampton debated the issues all through that afternoon of solitude spent in the little canyon. And when he regained his home he had arrived at a fixed resolution. He would win the treasure but he would save the valley—he would keep it a hidden valley still.

Next evening he had Tom Sun, Boney Earnest and Jim Rankin all assembled in secret conclave. While the aid of Grant Jones and Roderick Warfield would be called in later on, for the present their services would not be required. So for the present likewise there would be nothing more said to them—the fewer in the "know" the safer for all concerned.

It was agreed that Tom Sun, Jim Rankin and the Major would bring out the ore. Jim was to hire a substitute to drive his stage, while Tom Sun would temporarily hand over the care of his flocks to his manager and herders. Boney Earnest could not leave his work at the smelter—his duties there were so responsible that any sudden withdrawal might have stopped operations entirely and so caused the publicity all were anxious to avoid. But as he did not go to the plant on Sundays, his active help would be available each Saturday night. Thus the plans were laid.

But although Buell Hampton had allied himself with these helpers in his work and participants in the spoil, he yet guarded from them the exact locality of his find. All this was strictly in accordance with goldmining usage among the mountains of Wyoming, so the Major offered no apology for his precautions, his associates asked for or expected none. Each man agreed that he would go blindfolded to the spot where the rich ore was to be broken and packed for removal.

Thus had it come about that, while Buell Hampton seemed to have disappeared from the world, all the while he was very busy indeed, and great things were in progress. Actual work had commenced some days before the dance at the Shields' home, and it continued steadily in the following routine.

The Major, Tom Sun and Jim Rankin passed most of the day sleeping. At night after dark, they would sally forth into the hills, mounted on three horses with three pack burros. A few miles away from Encampment the Major would blindfold his two assistants, and then they would proceed in silence. When they arrived near Spirit Falls the horses and burros would be tethered and Major Hampton would lead the way down the embankment to the river's bank, then turn to the left, while Tom Sun, blindfolded, extended one hand on Buell Hampton's shoulder and still behind was Jim Rankin with his hand extended on Tom Sun's shoulder.

Thus they would make their way to a point back of the waterfall, and then some considerable distance into the mountain cavern where the blindfolds were removed. With an electric torch the Major lighted the way through the grotto into the open valley.

A little farther on was the dyke of porphyry, quartz and gold. Here the sacks would be filled with the rich ore—their loads all that each man could carry. Footsteps were then retraced with the same precautions as before.

Placing the ore sacks on the backs of their burros, the night riders would climb into their saddles and slowly start out on the return journey, the Major driving the burros ahead along a mountain path, while Tom Sun and Jim Rankin's horses followed. After they had gone on for a few miles Major Hampton would shout back to his assistants to remove the blindfolds, and thus they would return to the town of Encampment in the gray dawn of morning, unloading their burros at the door of Major Hampton's house. Jim Rankin would take charge of the stock and put them in a stable and corral he had prepared down near the banks of the Platte River just over the hill. Tom Sun would show his early training by preparing a breakfast of ham and eggs and steaming coffee while the Major was placing the ore in one hundred pound sacks and carrying them back into the blockade addition he had built to his home. He would then lock the heavy door connecting the storehouse with the living room.

Usually the breakfast was ready by the time the Major had finished his part of the work and Jim Rankin had returned. After the morning meal and a smoke, these three mysterious workers of the night would lie down to sleep, only to repeat the trip the following evening. Each Saturday night, as has been explained, Boney Earnest was added to the party, as well as an extra horse and burro.

Buell Hampton estimated that each burro was bringing out one hundred pounds nightly, or about three hundred pounds every trip for the three burros, with an extra hundred pounds on Saturday night. If this ore yielded $114.00 per pound, the assay value already paid him, or call it $100.00, it meant that he was adding to his storehouse of treasure about $220,000.00 as the result of each week's labors. Thus in three months' time there would be not far short of $3,000,-000.00 worth of high grade gold ores accumulated. If reduced to tons this would make nearly a full carload when the time came for moving the vast wealth to the railroad.

One night in the midst of these operations, when Jim Rankin and Tom Sun supposed they were on the point of starting on the usual trip into the hidden valley, Buell Hampton filled his pipe for an extra smoke and invited his two faithful friends to do likewise. "We are not going tonight," said he. "We will have a rest and hold a conference."

"Good," said Jim Rankin. "Speakin' wide open like, by gunnies, my old bones are gettin' to be pretty dangnation sore."

"Too bad about you," said Tom Sun. "Too bad that you aren't as young as I am, Jim."

"Young, the devil," returned Jim. "I'm prognosticatin' I have pints about me that'd loco you any time good and plenty. 'Sides you know you are seven years older than me. Gosh 'lmighty, Tom, you an' me have been together ever since we struck this here country mor'n forty years ago."

Tom laughed and the Major laughed.

It was arranged that when the carload was ready Jim Rankin was to rig up three four-horse teams and Grant Jones and Roderick Warfield would be called on to accompany the whole outfit to Walcott, the nearest town on the Union Pacific, where a car would be engaged in advance for the shipment of the ore to one of the big smelters at Denver. The strictest secrecy would be kept even then, for reasons of safety as well as to preserve the privacy desired by Buell Hampton. So they would load up the wagons at night and start for the railroad about three o'clock in the morning.

Thus as they smoked and yawned during their night of rest the three men discussed and decided every detail of these future plans.

CHAPTER XVII.

A TROUT FISHING EPISODE

FOR a time Roderick had hung back from accepting the invitation to call at the Conchshell ranch, as the Holden place was called. In pursuing the acquaintanceship with Gail he knew that he was playing with fire—a delightful game but one that might work sad havoc with his future peace of mind. However, one day when he had an afternoon off and had ridden into Encampment again to be disappointed in finding no letter from Stella, he had felt just the necessary touch of irritation toward his fiancée that spurred him on to seek some diversion from his thoughts of being badly treated and neglected. Certainly, he would call on General Holden—he did not say to himself that he was bent on seeing Gail again, looking into her beautiful eyes, hearing her sing, perhaps joining in a song.

He was mounted on his favorite riding horse Badger, a fine bay pony, and had followed the road up the North Fork of the Encampment River a number of miles. Taking a turn to the left through the timbered country with rocky crags towering on either side in loftiest grandeur, he soon reached the beautiful plateau where Gail Holden's home was located. The little ranch contained some three hundred acres, and cupped inward like a saucer, with a mountain stream traversing from the southerly to the northerly edge, where the Conchshell canyon gashed through the rim of the plateau and permitted the waters to escape and flow onward and away into the North Fork.

As Roderick approached the house, which was on a knoll planted with splendid firs and pines, he heard Gail singing

"Robert Adair." He dismounted and hitched his horse under the shelter of a wide spreading oak. Just as he came up the steps to the broad porch Gail happened to see him through one of the windows. She ceased her singing and hastened to meet him with friendly greeting.

"Welcome, Mr. Warfield, thrice welcome, as Papa sometimes says," said Gail, smiling.

"Thank you," said Roderick, gallantly. "I was riding in this direction and concluded to stop in and accept your kind invitation to meet the General."

"He will be delighted to see you, Mr. Warfield, I have told him about your singing."

"Oh, that was making too much of my poor efforts."

"Not at all. You see my father is very fond of music—never played nor sang in his life, but has always taken keen delight in hearing good music. And I tell you he is quite a judge."

"Which makes me quite determined then not to sing in his presence," laughed Roderick.

"Well, you can't get out of it now you're here. He won't allow it. Nor will I. You won't refuse to sing for me, will you? Or with me?" she added with a winning smile.

"That would be hard indeed to refuse," he replied, happy yet half-reproaching himself for his very happiness.

"Daddie is walking around the grounds somewhere at present," continued Gail. "Won't you step inside and rest, Mr. Warfield? He'll turn up presently."

"Oh, this old rustic seat here on the porch looks exceedingly comfortable. And I fancy that is your accustomed rocker," he added, pointing to a piece of embroidery, with silk and needles, slung over the arm of a chair.

"You are a regular Sherlock Holmes," she laughed. "Well, I have been stitching all the afternoon, and just broke off my work for a song."

"I heard you. Can't you be persuaded to continue?"

"Not at present. We'll wait till Papa comes. And the weather is so delightfully warm that I will take my accustomed rocker—and the hint implied as well."

Again she laughed gaily as she dropped into the commodious chair and picked up the little square of linen with its half-completed embroidery.

Roderick took the rustic seat and gazed admiringly over the cup-shaped lands that spread out before him like a scroll, with their background of lofty mountains.

"You have a delightful view from here," he said.

"Yes," replied Gail, as she threaded one of her needles with a strand of crimson. "I know of no other half so beautiful. And it has come to be a very haven of peace and happiness. Perhaps you know that my father last year lost everything he possessed in the world through an unfortunate speculation. But that was nothing—we lost my dear mother then as well. This little ranch of Conchshell was the one thing left that we could call our own, and here we found our refuge and our consolation."

She was speaking very softly, her hands had dropped on her lap, there was the glisten of tears in her eyes. Roderick was seeing the daring rider of the hills, the acknowledged belle of the ballroom in yet another light, and was lost in admiration.

"Very sad," he murmured, in conventional commiseration.

"Oh, no, not sad," she replied brightly, looking up, sunshine showing through her tears. "Dear mother is at rest after her long illness, father has recovered his health in this glorious mountain air, and I have gained a serious occupation in life. Oh, I just love this miniature cattle range," she went on enthusiastically. "Look at it"—she swept the landscape with an upraised hand. "Don't all my sweet Jerseys and Hainaults dotted over those meadows look like the little animals in a Noah's ark we used to play with when children?"

"They do indeed," concurred Roderick, with heartily responsive enthusiasm.

"And I'm going to make this dairy stock business pay to beat the band," she added, her face fairly aglow. "Just give me another

141

year or two."

"You certainly deserve success," affirmed Roderick, emphatically.

"Oh, I don't know. But I do try so hard."

Her beautiful face had sweet wistfulness in it now. Roderick was admiring its swift expressive changes—he was saying to himself that he could read the soul of this splendidly frank young woman like a book. He felt thrilled and exalted.

"But here comes Papa," exclaimed Gail, springing delightedly to her feet

Roderick's spirits dropped like a plummet. At such an interesting psychological moment he could have wished the old General far enough.

But there was a pleasant smile on his face as Gail presented him, genuine admiration in the responsive pressure of his hand as he gazed into the veteran's handsome countenance and thanked him for his cordial welcome.

"Glad to meet you, Mr. Warfield," General Holden was saying. "My friend Shields has spoken mighty well of you, and Gail here says you have the finest baritone voice in all Wyoming."

"Oh, Daddie!" cried Gail, in blushing confusion.

"Well, I'm going to decide for myself. Come right in. We'll have a song while Gail makes us a cup of tea. An old soldier's song for a start—she won't be listening, so I can suit myself this time."

And Roderick to his bewilderment found himself clutched by the arm, and being led indoors to the piano like a lamb to the slaughter. Gail had disappeared, and he was actually warbling "Marching through Georgia," aided by a thunderous chorus from the General.

"As we go marching through Georgia," echoed Gail, when at the close of the song she advanced from the domestic quarters with sprightly military step, carrying high aloft a tea tray laden with dainty china and gleaming silverware.

All laughed heartily, and a delightful afternoon was initiated—tea and cake, solos and duets, intervals of pleasant conversation, a Schubert sonata by Gail, and a rendition by Roderick of the Soldiers' Chorus from Faust that fairly won the old General's heart.

The hours had sped like a dream, and it was in the sunset glow that Roderick, having declined a pressing invitation to stay for dinner, was bidding Gail good-by. She had stepped down from the veranda and was standing by his horse admiring it and patting its silky coat.

"By the way, you mentioned at the Shields' party that you expected to go trout fishing, Mr. Warfield. Did you have good luck?"

Roderick confessed that as yet he had not treated himself to a day's sport with the finny tribe. "I was thinking about it this very morning," he went on, "and was wondering if I had not better secure a companion—someone skilled with rod and reel and fly to go with me, as I am a novice."

"Oh, I'll go with you," she exclaimed quickly. "Would be glad to do so."

"That's mighty kind of you, Miss Holden," replied Roderick, half hesitatingly, while a smile played about his handsome face. "But since you put it that way I would be less than courteous if I did not eagerly and enthusiastically accept. When shall we go?"

"You name the day," said Gail.

Roderick leaned hastily forward and placing one hand on his heart said with finely assumed gallantry: "I name the day?"

"Oh, you know quite well I do not mean that."

She laughed gaily, but all the same a little blush had stolen into her cheeks.

"I thought it was the fair lady's privilege to name the day," said Roderick, mischievously.

"Very well," said Gail, soberly, "we will go trout fishing tomorrow."

"It is settled," said Roderick. "What hour is your pleasure?"

"Well, it is better," replied Gail, "to go early in the morning or late in the evening. Personally I prefer the morning."

"Very well, I will be here and saddle Fleetfoot for you, say, at seven tomorrow morning."

And so it was agreed.

It was only when he was cantering along the roadway toward home that Roderick remembered how Barbara Shields had on several occasions invited him to go trout fishing with her, but in some way circumstances had always intervened to postpone the expedition. In Gail's case, however, every obstacle seemed to have been swept aside—he had never even thought of asking Mr. Shields for the morning off. However, that would be easily arranged, so he rode on in blissful contentment and happy anticipation for the morrow.

The next morning at the appointed time found him at Conchshell ranch. Before he reached the house he discovered Fleetfoot saddled and bridled standing at the gate.

Gail came down the walk as he approached and a cheery good-morning was followed by their at once mounting their horses and following a roadway that led eastward to the South Fork of the Encampment River.

"You brought your flies, Mr. Warfield?"

"Oh, yes," replied Roderick. "I have plenty of flies—both hackle and coachman. These have been specially recommended to me, but as I warned you last night I am a novice and don't know much about them."

"I sometimes use the coachman," said Gail, "although, like yourself, I am not very well up on the entomology of fly fishing."

Soon the road led them away from the open valley into a heavy timber that crowned the westerly slope of the river. They soon arrived at their destination. Dismounting they quickly tethered their horses. Gail unfastened her hip boots from back of her saddle, and soon her bifurcated bloomer skirts were tucked away in the great rubber boots and duly strapped about her slender waist. Roderick was similarly equipped with wading boots, and after rods, lines and flies had been carefully adjusted they turned to the river. The mountains with their lofty rocky ledges—the swift running waters rippling and gurgling over the rocky bed of the river—the beautiful forests that rose up on either side, of pine and spruce and cottonwood, the occasional whistle and whirr of wild birds—the balmy morning air filled life to overflowing for these two disciples of Izaak Walton bent upon filling their baskets with brook and rainbow trout.

"The stream is sufficiently wide," observed Gail, "so we can go downstream together. You go well toward the west bank and I will hug the east bank." Roderick laughed.

"What are you laughing at?" asked Gail.

"Oh, I was just sorry I am not the east bank." The exhilarating mountain air had given him unwonted audacity.

"You are a foolish fellow," said Gail—"at least sometimes. Usually I think you are awfully nice."

"Do you think we had better fish," asked Roderick, whimsically, "or talk this matter over?"

Gail looked very demure and very determined.

"You go right on with your fishing and do as I do, Mr. Roderick Warfield. Remember, I'm the teacher." She stamped her little booted foot, and then waded into the water and cast her fly far down stream. "See how I cast my line."

"You know a whole lot about fishing, don't you?" asked Roderick.

"Oh, yes, I ought to. During occasional summer visits to the ranch I have fished in these waters ever so many times. You must not talk too much," she added in a lower voice. "Trout are very alert, you know."

"If fish could hear as well as see

Never a fish would there be in our baskets." And she laughed softly at this admonition for Roderick to fish and cease badinage.

"Which way is the wind?" asked Roderick.

"There is none," replied Gail.

"When the wind is from the North

The skilful fisherman goes not forth," quoted Roderick.

"Don't that prove I know something about fishing—I mean

145

fly fishing?"

"You have a much better way to prove your sport-manship," insisted Gail. "The fish are all around you and your basket is hanging empty from your shoulder."

"Rebuked and chided," exclaimed Roderick, softly.

They continued to cast and finally Gail said: "I have a Marlow Buzz on my hook."

"What is that?" inquired Roderick.

"Oh, it is a species of the Brown Palmer fly. I like them better than the hackle although the coachman may be equally as good. Look out!" she suddenly exclaimed.

Roderick turned round quickly and saw her line was taut, cutting the water sharply to the right and to the left while her rod was bent like a bow. She quickly loosened her reel which hummed like a song of happiness while her line sliced the waters like a knife.

"Guess you have a rainbow," cried Roderick excitedly, but Gail paid no attention to his remark.

Presently the trout leaped from the water and fell back again, then attempted to dart away; but the slack of line was not sufficient for the captive to break from the hook.

The trout finally ceased its fight, and a moment later was lifted safely from the water and landed in Gail's net. But even now it continued to prove itself a veritable circus performer, giving an exhibition of flopping, somersaulting, reversed handsprings—if a fish could do such things—with astonishing rapidity.

"Bravo," shouted Roderick, as Gail finally released the hook and deposited the fish in her basket.

Less than a minute later Roderick with all the enthusiasm and zeal imaginable was letting out his reel and holding his line taut, for he, too, had been rewarded. And soon he had proudly deposited his first catch of the day in his fish basket.

On they went down the river, over riffles and into deep pools where the water came well up above their knees; but, nothing daunted, these fishermen kept going until the sun was well up in the eastern sky. At last Gail halloed and said: "Say, Mr. Warfield, my basket is almost full and I am getting hungry."

"All right," said Roderick, "we will retrace our steps. There is a pretty good path along the east bank."

"How many have you?" asked Gail.

"Twenty-six," replied Roderick as he scrambled up the bank.

"I have thirty-one," said Gail, enthusiastically.

Roderick approached the bank, and reaching down helped her to a footing on the well-beaten path. Then they started upstream for their horses.

It was almost eleven o'clock when they arrived at their point of departure and had removed their wading boots. Gail went to her saddle and unlashed a little luncheon basket.

She utilized a large tree stump for a table, and after it had been covered with a napkin and the dainty luncheon of boned chicken, sardines and crackers had been set forth, she called to Roderick and asked him to fill a pair of silver collapsible drinking cups which she handed to him. He went to the brook and returned with the ice-cold mountain vintage.

"I am just hungry enough," said Gail, "to enjoy this luncheon although it is not a very sumptuous repast."

Roderick smiled as he took a seat upon the felled tree.

"Expect you think you will inveigle me into agreeing with you. But not on your life. I would enjoy such a luncheon as this any time, even if I were not hungry. But in the present circumstances—well, I will let you pass judgment upon my appetite after we have eaten."

"As they say on the long army marches in the books," said Gail, gaily, "I guess we had better fall to." And forthwith with much merriment and satisfaction over their morning's catch they proceeded to dispose of the comestibles.

It was only a little after noon when they reached the Conchshell ranch, and soon thereafter Roderick's pony was galloping along the road on his homeward way. He had never enjoyed such a morning in all his life.

CHAPTER XVIII.

A COUNTRY FAIR ON THE FRONTIER

THERE was great excitement among the bunch of cowboys on the Shields' ranch when the local newspapers came out with startling headlines and full announcements in regard to the annual frontier celebration. That night every line of the full page advertisements, also the columns of editorial elaborations on the contests and other events, were read aloud to an eager assemblage of all hands in front of the bunk house.

The *Dillon Doublejack* predicted that this year's celebration would undoubtedly afford the greatest Wild West show ever witnessed outside of a regular circus display organized as a money-making undertaking. Everything was going to be just the real thing—the miners' drilling contest, the roping competition, the bucking-broncho features, and so on. More than a score of outlaw horses that had thrown every cow-puncher who ever attempted to ride them had already been engaged. The *Doublejack* further declared that the tournament would be both for glory and for bags of yellow gold, with World's Championships to the best rider, to the best bucking broncho buster, to the best trick roper, to the fastest cowpony, and to the most daring and lucky participant in the bull-dogging of wild steers.

In the columns of the Encampment *Herald* special attention was drawn to the fact that in the rough riding and outlaw bucking contest for the world's championship there was a purse of $1,000 to be divided—$450 for first prize, $300 second prize, $150 third prize and $100 fourth prize, while in addition Buck Henry, the banker, offered a $200 championship saddle to the rider who took first place. It was also announced that the fair association would pay $50 in cash for every horse brought to the grounds that was sufficiently unmanageable to throw every rider; each participant to ride any horse and as often as the judges might deem necessary to determine the winner; chaps and spurs to be worn by the riders, and leather pulling would disqualify.

Both papers referred to the band concerts as a feature of great interest throughout the three days of the fair. Everything was to be decorated in colors—red and green, black and yellow, blue and white, pink and scarlet—from the grandstand down to the peanut boy. The race track was fast and in excellent condition, and everything would be in readiness at the appointed time.

After each item of news was read out there was a buzz of comment among the assembled cowboys, challenges were made, bets freely offered and accepted. As the gathering dispersed Roderick Warfield and Scotty Meisch exchanged significant glances but spoke no word—they had been as strangers to each other ever since their fierce quarrel on the morning of the broncho-busting exercises. Roderick was glad that the day was near at hand when the fellow would be made to eat his words. And with the thought also came thoughts of Gail Holden. Gee, but it would be fine to see her ride in such a contest of nerve and skill!

At last the eventful morning dawned and the people swarmed into Encampment from all the surrounding country. They came from far below Saratoga to the north. The entire Platte Valley from as far south as the Colorado state line and beyond were on hand. In fact, from all over the state and even beyond its confines the whole population moved in to participate in this great frontier day celebration. A crowd came over from Steamboat Springs and brought with them the famous outlaw horse Steamboat, who had never been ridden although he had thrown at least a dozen cowpunchers of highest renown.

When the programmes were distributed, Firefly was found upon the list of outlaw horses, and also to the surprise of many of his friends the name of Roderick Warfield appeared as one of the contestants in both the bull-dogging and bucking broncho events.

It was a veritable Mecca of delight for the miners in their drilling contests and for the cowboys in their dare-devil riding of outlaw horses—testing their prowess and skill in conquering the seemingly unconquerable. The lassoing of fleet-footed and angry cattle, the bull-dogging of wild steers gathered up from different parts of the country because of their reputation for long horns and viciousness, were spectacles to challenge the admiration of the immense throng seated in the grandstand and on the bleachers.

It was just ten o'clock on the morning of the first day when the judges sounded the gong and started the series of contests. The first event was a cow-pony race, with no restriction as to the sex of the riders. Ponies were to be fourteen hands two inches or under. There were seven starters. Up in one corner of the grandstand sat Grant Jones surrounded by a bevy of beautiful girls. Among them of course was Dorothy Shields. All were in a flutter of excitement over the race that was about to be run; for Gail Holden was among the contestants.

Gail Holden, quiet, unassuming, yet full of determination, looked a veritable queen as she sat her pony Fleetfoot clad in soft silk shirtwaist, gray divided skirt, and gray soft felt hat. With a tremor of delight Roderick noticed that she wore on her sleeve as her colors one of his college arm-bands, which he had given her when calling at the Conchshell ranch one evening after the trout fishing expedition.

At last the bell sounded and the word "Go" was given. A shout went up from the grandstand—"They're off—they're off." And away the seven horses dashed—-four men and three lady riders. At the moment of starting Gail had flung her hat to the winds. She used no quirt but held her pony free to the right and in the open. It was a half-mile track and the race was for one mile. When they swept down past the grandstand on the first lap Fleetfoot had gained third place. A pandemonium of shouts went up as the friends of each madly yelled to the riders to urge their mounts to greater speed. At the far turn it was noticed that Fleetfoot was running almost neck and neck with the two leaders, and then as they came up the stretch, running low, it seemed as if the race would finish in a dead heat between all three ponies.

Just then Gail reached down and was seen to pat her pony upon the neck and evidently was talking to him. Fleetfoot leaned forward as if fired with fierce determination to comply with her request for still greater effort His muscles seemed to be retensioned. He began creeping away inch by inch from his adversaries, and amid the plaudits and shouts of the people in the grandstand and bleachers, who rose to their feet waving handkerchiefs and hats in a frenzy of tumultuous approval, Gail's horse passed first under the wire—winner by a short head, was the judges' verdict.

The second feature was a great drilling contest of the miners from the surrounding hills. There were twelve pairs of contestants, and Grant Jones became wild with excitement when friends of his from Dillon were awarded the championship.

And thus event followed event until the day's program was completed.

Gail and Roderick were bidding each other goodnight at the gateway of the enclosure.

"I owe you my very special thanks," he said as he held her hand.

"What for?" she enquired.

"For wearing my old college arm-band in the pony race."

"Oh," said Gail, blushing slightly, "I had to have something to keep my sleeve from coming down too far on my wrist Besides they are pretty colors, aren't they?"

But Roderick was not going to be sidetracked by any such naive questioning.

"I refuse pointblank," he answered, smiling, "to accept any excuse for your wearing the badge. I insist it was a compliment to me and shall interpret it in no other way."

Her blush deepened, but she made no further protest. General

Holden had approached. She turned and took his arm.

"Until tomorrow then," exclaimed Roderick, raising his hat to both father and daughter.

"Until tomorrow," she quietly responded.

The morrow brought resumption of the tournament. Gail Holden was to display her prowess in throwing the lariat, while Roderick had entered his name in the bull-dogging event.

In the roping contest Gail was the only lady contestant. The steers were given a hundred feet of start, and then the ropers, swinging their lariats, started after them in a mad gallop.

Gail was again mounted on Fleet foot, and if anything ever looked like attempting an impossibility it was for this slender girl with her neatly gloved little hands, holding a lariat in the right and the reins of the pony in her left, to endeavor to conquer and hogtie a three-year-old steer on the run. And yet, undismayed she undertook to accomplish this very thing. When the word was given she dashed after the fleeing three-year-old, and then as if by magic the lariat sprang away from her in a graceful curve and fell cleverly over the horns of the steer. Immediately Fleetfoot set himself for the shock he well knew was coming.

The steer's momentum was so suddenly arrested that it was thrown to the ground. Gail sprang from the saddle, and the trained pony as he backed away kept the lariat taut. Thus was the steer hogtied by Gail's slender hands in 55 3/5 seconds from the time the word was given.

All of the lassoers had been more or less successful, but the crowd stood up and yelled in wildest enthusiasm, and waved their hats and handkerchiefs, as the time for this marvelous feat by Gail was announced from the judges' stand.

In the afternoon the bull-dogging contest was reached, and Grant Jones said to those about him: "Now get ready for some thrills and breathless moments."

When the word was given a wild long-horned steer came rushing down past the grandstand closely followed by a cowboy on his fleet and nimble pony. In the corral were perhaps a score of steers and there was a cowboy rider ready for each of them. Four or five steers were bull-dogged one after the other. Some had been quickly thrown to the ground by the athletic cowboys amid the plaudits of the onlookers. But one had proven too strong for the skill and quickness of his adversary, and after rather severely injuring the intrepid youthful gladiator rushed madly on down the race track.

Presently Roderick Warfield came into view astride his favorite pony, Badger, riding at full tilt down the race course, chasing a huge cream-colored steer with wide-spread horns, cruelly sharp and dangerous-looking. As horse and steer came abreast Roderick's athletic form swayed in his saddle for a moment, and then like a flash he was seen to leap on to the steer's back and reaching forward grab the animal's horns. An instant later he had swung his muscular body to the ground in front of his sharp horned adversary and brought him to an abrupt halt.

Gail Holden's face grew pale as she watched the scene from among a group of her girl friends on the grandstand.

The object of the bull-dogging contest is to twist the neck of the steer and throw him to the ground. But Roderick accomplished more. The steer lifted him once from the ground, and the great throng of people on the grandstand and bleachers, also the hundreds who had been unable to obtain seating accommodation and were standing along the rails, held their breath in bated silence. The powerful cream-colored steer threw his head up, and lifting Roderick's feet from their anchorage started on a mad run. But when he lowered his head a moment later Roderick's feet caught the earth again, and the steer was brought to a standstill. Then the milling back and forth began. Roderick's toes sank deep into the sand that covered the race track; the muscles of his neck stood out in knots. Finally, with one heroic twist on the long horns as a pry over a fulcrum, he accomplished the feat of combined strength and endurance, and the intense silence of the great throng was broken by a report like the shot of a pistol as the bull-dogged steer fell heavily to the earth—dead. The animal's neck was broken.

There are very few cases on record where a steer's neck has been broken in bull-dogging contests. Roderick therefore had gained a rare distinction. But technically he had done too much, for the judges were compelled to withhold from him the honors of the championship because in killing the animal he had violated the humane laws of the state, which they were pledged to observe throughout the series of contests. But this did not affect the tumult of applause that acclaimed his victory over the huge and vicious-looking steer. Afterwards when his friends gathered around him in wonderment at his having entered for such an event he confessed that for several weeks he had been practicing bull-dogging out on the range, preparing for this contest.

In the afternoon of the last day, the finals of the bucking-broncho competition were announced from the grandstand. There were only three contestants remaining out of the score or more of original entries, and Roderick Warfield was among the number. Scotty Meisch was there—the cowboy whom Roderick had challenged—also Bud Bledsoe, the bodyguard and sleuth of W. B. Grady. Three of the unconquered outlaws were brought out—each attended by two wranglers; the names of the horses were put in a hat and each cowboy drew for his mount. Roderick Warfield drew Gin Fizz, Bud Bledsoe drew Steamboat and Scotty Meisch drew Firefly. And in a few moments the wranglers were busy.

Three horses and six wranglers working on them at the same time! It was a sight that stirred the blood with expectation. These horses had been successful in throwing the riders who had previously attempted to subdue them. The outlaws were recognized by the throng even before their names were called from the grandstand.

The method of the game is this: One wrangler approaches the horse while the other holds taut the lariat that has been thrown over his neck; and if the freehanded wrangler is quick enough or lucky enough he seizes the horse by the ears and throws his whole weight on the animal's head, which is then promptly decorated with a hackamore knotted bridle. A hackamore is a sort of a halter, but it is made of the toughest kind of rawhide and so tied that a knot presses disastrously against the lower jaw of the horse. After being haltered the outlaw is blindfolded with a gunnysack. To accomplish all this is a dangerous struggle between horse and the wranglers. Then the word "Saddle" is shouted, and the saddles are quickly adjusted to the backs of these untamed denizens of the wild. It takes considerable time to accomplish all this and have the girths tightened to the satisfaction of the wranglers first and of the rider last. Invariably the rider is the court of final resort in determining that the outlaw is in readiness to be mounted.

At last the moments of tense expectancy were ended. It was seen that one of the outlaws was ready, and at a call from the judges' stand, Scotty Meisch the first rough-rider leaped on to the back of his untamed horse.

The "Ki-yi" yell was given—the blindfold slipped from Firefly's eyes, and the rowels of the rider sunk into the flanks of his horse. Bucking and plunging, wheeling and whirling, all the time the rider not daring to "pull leather" and so disqualify himself under the rules, the outlaw once again proved himself a veritable demon. In just two minutes after the struggle began Scotty Meisch measured his length on the ground and Firefly was dashing for the open. The scene had been a thrilling one. Roderick noticed that Scotty had to be helped off the track, but he felt no concern—the rough-rider parted from his mount in a hurry may be temporarily dazed but is seldom seriously hurt.

Steamboat was the next horse. Bud Bledsoe was wont to brag there was nothing wore hair that he could not ride. But Steamboat, when he felt the weight of a rider on his back, was as usual possessed of a devil. But Bledsoe was not the man to conquer the noted outlaw, and down he went in prompt and inglorious defeat.

Gin Fizz was a magnificent specimen of horseflesh—black as

midnight with a coat of hair that shone like velvet. His proud head was held high in air. He stood like a statue while blindfolded and Roderick Warfield was making ready to mount.

The vast assemblage in the grandstand held their breath in amazement and wondered what would become of the rider of the giant black.

Then Roderick quickly mounted, and men and women rose to their feet to see the terribleness of it all. Roderick sent his spurs deep into the flanks of the black and plied the quirt in a desperate effort quickly to master and subdue the outlaw.

The horse reared and plunged with lightning quickness, and at times was the center of a whirlwind of dust in his determined zig-zag efforts to dislodge his rider. He rose straight up on his hind legs and for a moment it looked as if he were going to fall over backwards. Then seemingly rising still higher in air from his back feet he leaped forward and downward, striking his front feet into the earth as if he would break the saddle girth and certainly pitch the rider over his head. He squatted, jumped, corkscrewed and sun-fished, leaped forward; then he stopped suddenly and in demoniacal anger, as if determined not to be conquered, he threw his head far around endeavoring to bite his assailant's legs. But at last the horse's exertions wore him down and he seemed to be reluctantly realizing that he had found his master. In the end, after a terrible fight lasting fully seven minutes, he quieted down in submission, and Gin Fizz thus acknowledged Roderick's supremacy. He was subdued. Roderick drew rein, patted him kindly, dismounted and turned him over to the wranglers. Gin Fizz was no longer an outlaw; he suffered himself to be led away, trembling in every limb but submissive as a well-trained cow-pony.

Approaching the judges' stand, Roderick received a tremendous ovation both from the onlookers and from his brother cowboys. The championship ribbon was pinned to his breast, and now he was shaking hands promiscuously with friends, acquaintances and strangers. But all the while his eyes were roaming around in

THE TREASURE OF HIDDEN VALLEY

search of Gail Holden.

At last he was out of the crowd, in a quiet corner, with Grant Jones, the Shields sisters, and a few intimates.

"Where is Miss Holden?" he enquired of Barbara.

"Oh, she took poor Scotty Meisch to the hospital in an automobile. She insisted on going."

"He's not badly hurt, is he?" he asked drily.

"Oh, no. Just shaken up a lot. He'll be all right in a week's time, Dr. Burke says."

"Then Gail—I mean Miss Holden—didn't see Gin Fizz broken?"

"No. But she'll hear about it all right," exclaimed Barbara enthusiastically. "My word, it was great!" And she shook his hand again.

But the day of triumph had ended in disappointment for Roderick Warfield. He slipped away, saddened and crestfallen.

"It was all for her I did it"—the thought kept hammering at his brain. "And she never even stopped to see. I suppose she's busy now bathing the forehead of that contemptible little runt in the hospital. Stella wouldn't have turned me down like that."

And he found himself thinking affectionately and longingly of the little "college widow." He hadn't been to the post office for three days. The belated letter might have arrived at last. He would go and see at all events; and to drown thought he whistled "The Merry Widow" waltz as he grimly stalked along.

CHAPTER XIX.

A LETTER FROM THE.

COLLEGE WIDOW

YES, there was a letter from Stella Rain. Roderick took it eagerly from the hands of the clerk at the general delivery window. A good number of people were already crowding into the post office from the fair grounds. But he was too hungry for news to wait for quieter surroundings. So he turned to a vacant corner in the waiting room and ripped open the envelope. The letter was as follows:

"Roderick:—

"I am sure that what I am about to tell you will be for your good as well as my own. It seems so long ago since we were betrothed. At that time you were only a boy and I freely confess I liked you very, very much. I had known you during your four years in college and you were always just splendid. But Roderick, a real love affair has come into my life—something different from all other experiences, and when you receive this letter I shall be Mrs. Vance Albertrum Carter.

"Mr. Carter, financially, is able to give me a splendid home. He is a fine fellow and I know you would like him. Let me be to you the same as to the other boys of old Knox—your

friend, the 'college widow.'

"*Very sincerely,*
"*Stella Rain.*"

Not a muscle of his face quivered as he read the letter, but at its close he dropped both hands to his side in an attitude of utter dejection. The blow had fallen so unexpectedly; he felt crushed and grieved, and at the same time humiliated. But in an instant he had recovered his outward composure. He thrust the letter into his pocket, and shouldered his way through the throng at the doorway. He had left Badger in a stall at the fair grounds. Thither he bent his steps, taking a side street to avoid the crowd streaming into the town. The grandstand and surrounding buildings were already deserted. He quickly adjusted saddle and bridle, and threw himself on the pony's back.

"'She knows I would like him,'"he muttered, as he gained the race track, the scene of his recent triumphs, its turf torn and dented with the hoofs of struggling steers and horses, thronged but an hour before with a wildly excited multitude but now silent and void. "'Like him'." he reiterated bitterly. "Yes—like hell."

And with the words he set his steed at the farther rail. Badger skimmed over it like a deer and Roderick galloped on across country, making for the hills.

That night he did not return to the bunk house.

It was high noon next day when he showed up at the ranch. He went straight to Mr. Shields' office, gave in his resignation, and took his pay check. No explanations were required—Mr. Shields had known for a considerable time that Roderick was leaving. He thanked him cordially for his past services, congratulated him on his championship honors at the frontier celebration, and bade him come to the ranch home at any time as a welcome guest. Roderick excused himself from saying good-by for the present to the ladies; he was going to stay for a while in Encampment with his friend Grant Jones, and would ride out for an evening visit before very long. Then he packed his belongings at the bunk house, left word with one of the helpers for trunk and valise to be carted into town, and rode away. Badger was Roderick's own personal property; he had purchased the pony some months before from Mr. Shields, and as he leaped on its back after closing the last boundary gate he patted the animal's neck fondly and proudly. Badger alone was well worth many months of hard and oftentimes distasteful work, a horse at all events could be faithful, he and his good little pony would never part—such was the burden of his thoughts as he left the Shields ranch and the cowboy life behind him.

Grant Jones was in Encampment, and jumped up from his writing table when Roderick threw open the door of the shack and walked in.

"Hello, old man, this is indeed a welcome visit. Where in the wide world have you been?"

He turned Roderick around so the light would fall upon his face as he extended his hand in warmest welcome, and noticed he was haggard and pale.

"Oh," said Roderick, "I have been up in the hills fighting it out alone, sleeping under the stars and thinking matters over."

"What does this all mean, anyway, old man? I don't understand you," said Grant with much solicitude.

"Well, guess you better forget it then," said Roderick half abruptly. "But I owe you an apology for going away so unceremoniously from the frontier gathering. I know we had arranged to dine together last night But I just cleared out—that's all. Please do not ask me any questions, Grant, as to why and wherefore. If in the future I should take you into my confidence that will be time enough."

"All right, old man," said Grant, "here is my hand. And know now and for all time it don't make a derned bit of difference what has happened, I am on your side to the finish, whether it is a desperate case of petty larceny or only plain murder."

Grant laughed and tried to rouse his friend into hilarity.

"It is neither," replied Roderick laconically. "All the same I've got some news for you. I have quit my job."

"At the Shields ranch?" cried Grant in astonishment. "Surely there's been no trouble there?"

"Oh, no, we are all the best of friends. I am just tired of cow-punching, and have other plans in view. Besides, remember the letter we got pushed under the door here on the occasion of my last visit. Perhaps I may be a bit skeered about having my hide shot full of holes, eh, old man?" Roderick was now laughing.

But Grant looked grave. He eyed his comrade tentatively.

"Stuff and nonsense. The lunatic who wrote that letter was barking up the wrong tree. He mistook you for the other fellow. You were never seriously smitten in that quarter, now were you, Rod, old man?"

"Certainly not. Barbara Shields is a fine girl, but I never even dreamed of making love to her. I didn't come to Wyoming to chase after a millionaire's daughter," he added bitterly.

"Oh, that's Barbara's misfortune not her fault," laughed Grant. "But I was afraid you had fallen in love with her, just as I fell head over heels in love with Dorothy—for her own sake, dear boy, and not for anything that may ever come to her from her father."

"You were afraid, do you say?" quizzed Roderick. "Have you Mormonistic tendencies then? Do you grudge a twin to the man you always call your best friend?"

"Oh, you know there's no thought like that in my mind," protested Grant. "But you came on to the field too late. You see Ben Bragdon was already almost half engaged."

"So that's the other fellow, is it?" laughed Roderick. "Oh, now I begin to understand. Then things have come to a crisis between Barbara and Bragdon."

"Well, this is in strict confidence, Rod. But it is true. That's why I was a bit nervous just now on your account—I kind of felt I had to break bad news."

"Oh, don't you worry on my account. Understand once and for all that I'm not a marrying man."

"Well, we'll see about that later on," replied Grant, smiling. "But I should have been real glad had you been the man to win Barbara Shields. How jolly happy we would have been, all four together."

"Things are best just as they are," said Roderick sternly. "I wouldn't exchange Badger, my horse out there, for any woman in the world. Which reminds me, Grant, that I've come here to stay with you for a while. Guess I can put Badger in the barn."

"Sure—you are always welcome; I don't have to say that. But remember that Barbara-Bragdon matter is a dead secret. Dorothy just whispered it to me in strictest confidence. Hard lines that, for the editor of such an enterprising newspaper as the *Dillon Doublejack*. But the engagement is not to be announced until the Republican nomination for state senator is put through. You know, of course, that Ben Bragdon has consented to run against Carlisle and the smelter interests."

"I'm glad to hear it And now we have an additional reason to put our shoulders to the wheel. We've got to send Ben Bragdon to Cheyenne for Barbara's sake. Count me in politics from this day on, old man. You see I am out of a job. This will be something worth while—to help down that blood-sucker Grady, and at the same time secure Bragdon's election."

"Ben Bragdon is the best man for Wyoming."

"I know it. Put me on his committee right away."

"You'll be a tower of strength," exclaimed Grant enthusiastically. "The champion broncho-buster of the world—just think of that."

Roderick laughed loud and long. This special qualification for political work mightily amused him.

"Oh, don't laugh," Grant remonstrated, in all seriousness. "You are a man of note now in the community, make no mistake. You can swing the vote of every cow-puncher in the land. You are their hero—their local Teddy Roosevelt."

Again Roderick was convulsed.

"And by the way," continued Grant, "I never had the chance to congratulate you on that magnificent piece of work on Gin Fizz. It was the greatest ever."

"Oh, we'll let all that slide."

"No, siree. Wait till you read my column description of the immortal combat in the *Doublejack*." He turned to his writing desk, and picked up a kodak print. "Here's your photograph—snapped by Gail Holden on the morning of the event, riding your favorite pony Badger. Oh, I've got all the details; the half-tone has already been made. The *Encampment Herald* boys have been chasing around all day for a picture, but I'm glad you were in hiding. The *Doublejack* will scoop them proper this time."

But Roderick was no longer listening. The name of Gail Holden had sent his thoughts far away.

"How's Scotty Meisch?" he asked—rather inconsequentially as the enthusiastic editor thought.

"Oh, Scotty Meisch? He's all right. Slight concussion of the brain—will be out of the hospital in about two weeks. But Miss Holden, as it turned out, did the lad a mighty good turn in rushing him to the hospital He was unconscious when they got there. She knew more than Doc Burke—or saw more; or else the Doc could not deny himself the excitement of seeing you tackle Gin Fizz. But there's no selfishness in Grail Holden's make-up—not one little streak."

In a flash Roderick Warfield saw everything under a new light, and a great glow of happiness stole into his heart. It was not indifference for him that had made Gail Holden miss the outlaw contest. What a fool he had been to get such a notion into his head.

"Guess I'll go and feed Badger," he said, as he turned away abruptly and left the room.

"When you come back I've a lot more to talk about," shouted Grant, resuming his seat and making a grab for his lead-pencil.

But it was several hours before Roderick returned. He had baited the pony, watched him feed, and just drowsed away the afternoon among the fragrant bales of hay—drowsing without sleeping, chewing a straw and thinking all the time.

At last he strolled in upon the still busy scribe. Grant threw down his pencil.

"Thought you had slipped away again to the hills and the starlight and all that sort of thing. I'm as hungry as a hunter. Let's go down town and eat."

"I'm with you," assented Roderick. "But after dinner I want to see Major Buell Hampton. Is he likely to be at home?"

"It was about Buell Hampton I was going to speak to you. Oh, you don't know the news." Grant was hopping around in great excitement, changing his jacket, whisking the new coat vigorously. "But there, I am pledged again to secrecy—Good God, what a life for a newspaper man to lead, bottled up all the time!"

"Then when am I to be enlightened?"

"He sent for me this morning and I spent an hour with him. He also wanted you, but you were not to be found. He wants to see you immediately. Tonight will be the very time, for he said he would be at home."

"That's all right, Grant. But, say, old fellow, I want half an hour first with the Major—all alone."

"Mystery after mystery," fairly shouted the distracted editor. "Can't you give me at least this last news item for publication? I'm losing scoops all the time."

"I'm afraid you must go scoopless once again," grinned Roderick. "But after dinner you can do a little news-hunting on your own account around the saloons, then join me later on at the Major's. That suit you?"

"Oh, I suppose I've got to submit," replied Grant, as he drew on his now well-brushed coat. "But all through dinner, I'll have you guessing, old man. You cannot imagine the story Buell Hampton's going to tell you. Oh, you needn't question me. I'm ironclad—bomb-proof—as silent as a clam."

Roderick laughed at the mixed metaphors, and arm in arm the friends started for their favorite restaurant.

CHAPTER XX.

THE STORE OF GOLD

ACOUPLE of hours later Roderick arrived at Buell Hampton's home. The Major was alone; there were no signs of Jim Rankin or Tom Sun; no traces of the recent midnight toil. The room looked just the same as on the occasion of Roderick's last visit, now more than two months ago, except for a curtain hanging across one wall.

Buell Hampton was seated before the great fireplace and notwithstanding the season of the year had a small bed of coals burning.

"It takes the chill away, for one thing," he explained after greeting his visitor, "and then it gives me the inspiration of real live embers into which to look and dream. There are so many poor people in the world, so much suffering and so many heartaches, that one hardly knows where to begin."

"Well, Major," said Roderick, "I am glad to find you in this mood. I'm one of the sufferers—or at least have been. I have come to you for some heartache balm. Oh, I'm not jesting. Really I came here tonight determined to give you my confidence—to ask your advice as to my future plans."

"I am extremely glad you feel toward me like that, my lad," exclaimed Buell Hampton, grasping Roderick's arm and looking kindly into his eyes. "I have always felt some subtle bond of sympathy between us. I have wanted to help you at the outset of a promising career in every way I can. I count it a privilege to be called in to comfort or to counsel, and you will know later that I have something more for you than mere words of advice."

"Well, it is your advice I want most badly now, Major. In the first place I have thrown up my job with Mr. Shields."

"Tired of cow-punching?" nodded Buell Hampton with a smile. "I knew that was coming."

"In the second place I want to be perfectly candid with you. I have a prospecting venture in view."

"That I have guessed from several hints you have dropped from time to time."

"Well, you spoke a while ago about your reserving some little interest for me in your great gold discovery. That was mighty kind, and rest assured I appreciate your goodness to one who only a few months ago was a stranger to you."

"You forget that I am a reader of character—that no kindred souls are strangers even at a first meeting, my son."

Buell Hampton spoke very softly but very clearly; his gaze rested fixedly on Roderick; the latter felt a thrill run through him—yes, assuredly, this great and good man had been his friend from the first moment they had clasped hands.

"You were very good then, Major," he replied, "in judging me so kindly. But I am afraid that I evoked your special sympathy and interest because of the confidences I gave you at one of our early meetings. You will not have forgotten how I spoke in a most sacred way about certain matters in Galesburg and what I intended to do when I had sufficient money to carry out my plans."

"I remember distinctly," said the Major. "Your frank confidence greatly pleased me. Well, has anything happened?"

"There is just one man on earth I will show this letter to, and you, Major, are the man."

Saying this Roderick handed over Stella Rain's letter.

After the Major had carefully perused it and put it back in the envelope, he reached across to Roderick.

"No," said Roderick, "don't give that letter back to me. Kindly lay it on the red coals and let me see it burn to gray ashes. I have fought this thing out all alone up in the hills, and I am now almost glad that letter came, since it had to be. But let it vanish now in the flames, just as I am going to put Stella Rain forever out of my thoughts. Yesterday the receipt of this letter was an event; but from now on I shall endeavor to regard it as only an incident."

Silently and musingly the Major complied with Roderick's request and consigned the letter to the glowing embers. When the last trace had disappeared, he looked up at Roderick.

"I will take one exception to your remarks," he said. "Do not think unkindly of Stella Rain, nor even attempt to put her out of your thoughts. Her influence over you has been all for good during the past months, and she has shown herself a very fine and noble woman in the gentle manner in which she has broken the bonds that had tied you—bonds impulsively and all too lightly assumed on your part, as she knew quite well from the beginning. I have a profound admiration for your little 'college widow,' Roderick, and hold her in high esteem."

There was just the suspicion of tears in Roderick's eyes—a lump in his throat which rendered it impossible for him to reply. Yes; all bitterness, all sense of humiliation, were now gone. He too was thinking mighty kindly of sweet and gentle Stella Rain.

"Remember," continued the Major quietly, "you told me how she warned you that some other day another girl, the real girl, would come along. I guess that has happened now."

Roderick started; there was a protesting flush upon his cheek.

"Even though you may not yet fully realize it," quietly added the Major.

"What do you mean?" faltered Roderick; the flush of offended dignity had now turned into the blush of confusion.

The Major smiled benignantly.

"Oh, my young friend, remember again that I read men's minds and hearts just a little. There must be some new influence in your life."

"How do you know that—how can you say that?"

Buell Hampton laid a hand on the young man's shoulder and smiled.

"Because otherwise you would be still up among the hills

alone, young man. Your fight in the wilderness would have lasted for forty days—not for a single night. The fever of love does not die down so suddenly without an antidote. The resignation you have shown while we burned that letter is not merely a negative condition of mind. There is something positive as well."

"Oh, I can't admit that," protested Roderick. "Or at least I dare not allow myself to think like that," he corrected himself hurriedly.

"Well, we shall see what we shall see. Meanwhile all is well. The rich harvest of experience has been reaped; the fertile soil awaits the next tillage. The important moment of every life is 'The Now.' And this is what we have to think about tonight, Roderick."

"Precisely, Major. And that is just why I opened the conversation. As I said at the outset, you assigned me an interest in your gold mine for a specific object that no longer exists."

"On the contrary," replied Buell Hampton, "I assigned it on general principles—on the general principle of helping a worthy young man at the critical period of starting into useful life-work. But I may tell you also," he laughed lightly, "that I had in my mind's eye valuable and important future services whereby the interest would be paid for most adequately."

"And these services are what?" asked Roderick, with a delighted gleam in his eyes.

"We'll come to that presently. Where is Grant Jones?"

"He was to follow me here in half an hour. Time's almost up, unless he's on the trail of a newspaper scoop." Roderick was smiling happily now.

"Well, we shall await his coming. What do you say to a little music to beguile the time?"

The Major glanced at his violin resting on a side table.

"Nothing would give me greater pleasure," responded Roderick, jumping up with alacrity and handing to the master his old Cremona.

"I am glad you like music," said Buell Hampton, as he began to tighten his bow. "Its rhythmic cadences of tone are a language universal. Its power is unseen but felt, captivating and enthralling alike the cultured and the untutored. The harmony of tone enwraps the soul like a mantle. It influences heart and intellect It may depress in saddest tears or elevate to highest ecstasy. Music is the melody of the Gods. It is like an ethereal mist—a soft and dainty distillation of a thousand aromatic perfumes, inspiring and wholesome to the soul as the morning dew is to buds and blossoms."

As he spoke he had been gently thrumming the strings, and now he placed the violin to his chin. Soft and plaintive melodies alternating with wild and warring airs followed one after the other until the entire room seemed to be quivering with melody. For fully an hour, unconscious of the passing time, the Major entertained his guest, and concluded with a rapid surging theme as if it were a call to battle and for greater achievements.

Grant Jones had not yet arrived. Roderick recovered from the trance into which the music had thrown him. He thanked the Major for the pleasure he had given, then threw a glance at the doorway.

"Where the deuce can he be?" he murmured.

But at the very moment the door opened, and in walked the belated editor.

"Where have you been all this time?" asked Roderick, half petulantly.

"On the porch of course," replied Grant. "Do you think I was going to interrupt such divine melody?"

Buell Hampton smiled pleasedly while he laid down the violin on the table.

"Well," he said, "be seated, Grant, my boy. I am going to lose no further time. I have some figures to work on tonight. This is my first night at home, Roderick, for many weeks. Grant already knows the story. Now I shall tell it to you."

And straightway the Major related how Jim Rankin, Tom Sun, and Boney Earnest had garnered the midnight harvests of gold. Then he drew aside the curtain hanging on the wall, unlocked the stout door which it concealed, and, to Roderick's amazement,

170

displayed the piled up sacks of golden ore.

"All quite equal to the rich samples you handled here several months ago," said Buell Hampton, as he waved his hand toward the accumulated treasure.

"Great Cæsar!" gasped Roderick. "There must be hundreds of thousands of dollars there."

"The total will run into millions, young man," smiled the Major. Then he closed the door, relocked it, and dropped the curtain. But he did not resume his seat.

"Now this is where your services, and those of Grant Jones will come in. This great wealth must be safely transported to Denver. And as I have already explained to you tonight, I still want to guard jealously my secret of the Hidden Valley on whose resources I may or may not draw again—this the future must decide. All of us who are interested have abundance for the present; we are equipped for many good works. The removal of this large quantity of ore, without attracting public attention here, requires good judgment on the part of men who can be absolutely trusted. You are the men selected for the responsible duty. And remember it will be dangerous duty should our secret leak out. The days of hold-ups are passing in the West, but have not yet passed; for as you both know there are still a good few desperadoes among the wilds of our Wyoming mountains."

"My God—what loot!" murmured Roderick, glancing toward the curtain.

"Yes—a rich loot," acquiesced the Major. "Now you young men will understand that your interests are my own—that while I am delighted to share this treasure with my chosen friends, these friends have been and continue to be quite indispensable to me. Roderick, your question earlier in the evening is answered— you will have a rightful share in this gold. Get ready in about a week's time to earn it Now go tonight. I will see you later on to unfold my plans for the journey in closer detail."

"Great guns," groaned Grant Jones, as the two young men gained the roadway. "What a newspaper story—what a scoop!

And not one damned word can be put in type."

CHAPTER XXI.

A WARNING

BY SUBTLE alchemy of thought Roderick's feelings toward Scotty Meisch had become entirely changed. On the ranch he had treated the rough, uncultivated and at times insolent youth with contempt that was scarcely concealed. He was not of his class; and Roderick by his manner had shown that he counted Scotty as outside the pale of good breeding—a fellow not to be associated with except in the necessary work of roping a steer or handling a mob of cattle. It had been almost an act of condescension on his part to accept Scotty's challenge to try out their respective riding abilities at the frontier fair. Any hurt the lad might have received in the contest was part of the day's game, and at the moment Roderick had treated the incident with indifference. But now he found himself feeling quite solicitous as to the poor fellow's condition. Of course Gail Holden, who had interested herself in the injured cowboy, had nothing to do with this change of sentiment—at least Roderick's consciousness took no cognizance of her influence in the matter. All the same, as he walked over to the hospital on the following afternoon to inquire about the invalid, he was conning in his mind the chances of perhaps meeting Gail there.

However Scotty Meisch was alone when Roderick was admitted to the ward. There was only another occupant of the long room, occupying a cot at the farther end. The nurse as she brought Roderick to Scotty's bedside declared that her patient was getting along fine, and that a visit from a friend would cheer him up and do him good. Roderick smiled as he sat down at the foot of the bed and the nurse moved away to attend to other duties. Except for a bandaged head the cowboy looked fairly fit.

"How are you, old man?" Roderick asked in a kindly tone.

Scotty seemed quite disconcerted by this friendly greeting. He looked sheepish and shame-faced.

"Oh, I'll be all right in no time," he mumbled. "Expect you think I'm a mean cuss," he added, after a moment's pause, glancing at Roderick then hastily looking away again.

"I haven't said so," replied Roderick in a pleasant and assuring way.

"No, I know you hain't said it. But I've never, liked you from the first time we met over at the Shield's ranch. I don't know why—damned if I do. But I didn't like you and don't like you now, and I'm gosh'lmighty ashamed of myself fer bein' so ornery."

"You shouldn't speak of yourself so harshly," said Roderick, somewhat interested in the turn the conversation was taking.

"I don't deserve any kindness at your hands," Meisch went on. "I sure planned to kill you onct 'til I found out you weren't sweet on Barbara Shields. Oh, I'm a low-down cuss, but I'm ambitious. You hain't the feller I'm after any more. It's that lawyer Carlisle and I'll git him, you jist see. He's got to keep out of my way," and as Scotty, with a black scowl on his face, said this he looked the part of an avenging demon right enough.

"I know," he continued, "Barbara is older than I am, but I'm dead gone on her, even if she don't know it, an' I'll do things yet to that feller Carlisle." Roderick was fairly perplexed by these references to Barbara Shields and the disclosure of the rough cowboy's feelings toward his employer's daughter. For a moment he could not find the proper word to say. He just ventured a platitude, kindly spoken as it was kindly intended: "Oh, you must get over these broodings, Scotty."

"It's not broodings—it's business, and I mean it," he muttered. "Oh, you needn't look so darned solemn. I've no more bad feelin's agin you. But when you first came to the ranch, you know you couldn't ride any better than a kid. But you began givin' yourself airs, an' then when I thought you were goin' to cut me out with Barbara I jist got plum crazy. That's why I sent you fair warnin'."

A light broke in on Roderick.

"So it was you who slipped that note under Grant Jones' door, was it?" he asked in great surprise.

"Yas. You can know it now; who cares? But it was only later I saw I was on a blind trail—that it was the other one you're after—goin' fishin' an' all that sort o' thing."

Roderick reddened.

"Oh, that's all fudge too," he exclaimed uneasily.

"I'm not so sure 'bout that," replied Scotty, with a cunning look in his eyes. "'Sides, she's dead gone on you, that's a cert. She was here all yesterday afternoon, and could speak about nothin' else—praised yer ridin' and allowed she was tarnation sorry to have missed seein' you on Gin Fizz. Which reminds me that I've got to comgratulate you on the championship." He slipped a hand timidly and tentatively from under the bed-spread. "Oh, I can admit myself beat when I'm beat. You've grown to be a better'n rider than me. I'm only a little skinny chap at the best, but you showed yourself strong enough to kill that great big steer in the bull-doggin'. You've got me skinned, and you hold the championship right enough. Shake."

And Scotty at last mustered up the moral courage to extend his hand. Roderick took it and shook it warmly. So Gail had been talking about him!—his heart had leaped with joy.

"I'm glad to hear you speak like that, Scotty," he said with great cordiality. "You and I can come to be mighty good friends."

"Gee, but I wish I looked like you," remarked Scotty, lapsing into a half smile. "Shake hands again with me, won't you?"

Roderick reached over and once more bestowed a good honest squeeze; and he improved the occasion by begging Scotty not to indulge in evil thoughts about killing people or anything of that sort.

"What makes you kind t' me?" asked the lad as he looked inquiringly at Roderick.

"I don't know that I have been particularly kind to you," replied Roderick. "I begin to realize that I should have been here before now to help cheer you up a bit while convalescing."

Scotty turned from Roderick and looking at the ceiling was silent for a few moments. At last he said: "Expect if I'd stay here a long, long time you'd keep on bein' kind t' me. Possibly you would bring Barbara with you on some of your visits. But I know I'm goin' t' get well, that's the pity of it all. I wouldn't be in bed now if the doctor hadn't said I got ter stay here for a few days. When I'm well, why, then it's all off with you an' Scotty. You won't pay any more attention to me when I'm once more sound as a nut an' ridin' range than you would a low down coyote."

"Why should I become indifferent to you?" inquired Roderick.

"Oh, no reason why you should, only you will," replied Scotty. "You are of the high-falutin' an' educated kind an'—well, I never went to school more'n two weeks in my life. I got tired of the educatin' business—stole a horse and never did go back. An' they never caught me, nuther."

He brightened up when he said this and laughed at his cleverness as if it were a most pleasant remembrance.

"Where was your childhood home?" inquired Roderick.

"Now, right there," replied Scotty, "is where yer presumin'. You're not talkin' to me. D'ye suppose I'm goin' ter tell yer and have this whole business piped off and those fellers come out here an' pinch me for hoss-stealin'. Not on yer life, so long as Scotty Meisch knows himself."

Roderick smiled as he said: "Surely, Scotty, you are a very suspicious person. I had no thought of doing what you suggest."

"Waal," drawled Scotty, "if you'd have been as near goin' to the penitentiary as often as I have, you'd learn to keep yer mouth shut when people begin to inquire into your past hist'ry an' not unbosom yerself. Fact is, my hist'ry won't stand investigatin'. It's fuller of thin places an' holes than an old-fashioned tin corn grater. You know what a grater is, don't you? It's a tin bent over into a half moon an' nailed to a board with holes punched from inside out to make it rough. Where I come from we used to husk new corn just as soon as it was out of the milk an' grate it into meal. About the only thing we had to live on was cornmeal mush an' milk. Wish I had some now. I'm hungrier than hell for it."

The primitiveness of it all rather appealed to Roderick, and he called the nurse and asked if she wouldn't serve the patient with some cornmeal mush with milk for dinner that evening.

"Certainly," she replied, "if Dr. Burke does not object," and went away to make inquiries. In a little while she returned and said: "The doctor says a nice bowl of cornmeal mush and milk would be just the thing for Mr. Meisch." And it was so arranged.

When the nurse had gone Roderick noticed a tear trickling down the cheek of Scotty and in order not to embarrass the boy he turned away and stood looking out of the window. Presently Scotty said: "I wish ter hell I was decent, that's what I wish."

Without turning from the window Roderick inquired: "How old are you, Scotty?"

"Guess I'm about nineteen. I don't know fer sure. They never did tell me when my birthday was."

"How would you like to go to school, Scotty? Brace up and be an educated chap like other fellows."

"Me learn to read an' write?" exclaimed Scotty. "Look here, Mr. Warfield, are you chaffin' me? That's what some Englishmen called it when they meant teasin' and so I say chaffin'. Might as well use all the big words a feller picks up on the way." Roderick laughed aloud at Scotty's odd expressions and turned to him and said: "Scotty, you aren't a bad fellow. You have a good heart in you."

"I don't know about that," said Scotty, shaking his head. "One time there was a feller told me that tough cusses like me don't have hearts—just gizzards."

"Well," said Roderick, laughing, "my time has come to go now but I want to tell you I like you, Scotty. You seem to me to be the making of a very decent sort of chap, and if you will be a real good fellow and are sincere about wanting to go to school and make something of yourself, I believe I can arrange for you to do so."

"Honest, Mr. Warfield, honest? Are you tellin' me the truth or is this a sick bed jolly?"

"Certainly I am telling you the truth," replied Roderick. "You think it all over until I come and see you again."

"When'll you come? Tomorrow?"

"Yes," replied Roderick, "I'll come tomorrow."

"All right," said Scotty, "I'll sure look for yer." The next day when Roderick called, Major Buell Hampton and Grant Jones accompanied him. They had a long talk with Scotty whose rapid recovery showed improvement even from the previous day. After the subject had been introduced by Roderick, who told Scotty that he had informed his friends of the lad's desire to go to school, Major Buell Hampton observed: "A printing office, Mr. Meisch, is a liberal education within itself. I have been talking this matter over with Mr. Jones, the Editor of the *Dillon Doublejack,* and with Mr. Warfield, and we have mutually agreed that if you are in earnest about leaving the range for a while and will learn to read books and generally improve your mind, we shall give you the opportunity. As soon as you are able to leave the hospital, how would you like to go over to the little town of Dillon with Mr. Grant Jones, this gentleman at my right, and go into his printing office?"

"You would be my devil to start in with," said Grant, good-naturedly.

"Guess that'd about fit me," responded Scotty with a grin. "I'm a sort of a devil anyway, ain't I?" and he looked toward Roderick.

"Mr. Jones means a different kind of a devil, Scotty," laughed Roderick. "What Major Buell Hampton suggests to you is most excellent advice, and I think you had better accept the offer. This job will give you a home, and you will work in the printing office. You will soon learn to read books, and also you will become a typesetter which, as Major Hampton told you, is a practical education within itself and will lead to better things and greater things along educational lines. Of course, it may be some time

178

before that knock on your head gets all right."

"Oh, don't worry about my old bean," said Scotty with a smile, as he touched the bandage that encircled his cranium.

Finally Scotty said he believed he would like to try the new job. "You know, I've been knocked 'round over the world an' kicked an' thumped an' had my ears cuffed an' my shins barked so much that I don't hardly know what to make uv you fellers. If I was sure you wasn't stringin' me an' really meant it all as a kindness, why, I'll be goshdamed if I wouldn't git up out o' bed this minute an' start for Dillon. That's what I'd do. I ain't no piker."

This speech was very amusing to Grant Jones; and he assured the injured boy that he himself was not going over to Dillon for perhaps a week, by which time if he were attentive to the instructions of the doctor he probably would be able to accompany him.

"I'll take you over," said Grant, "and we'll batch it together so far as a place to sleep is concerned in the printing office. There is a good boarding house just across the street where you can get your meals."

"Who's goin' ter pay for them?" asked Scotty. "I ain't got any money."

"That," said Roderick, "is what Major Buell Hampton is going to do for you. Not only will he pay your board for one year until your work is worth wages in the printing office, but he will also get you some new clothes and a new pair of shoes and rig you out in good shape, old man."

"Gee, but you're good to me, Major Hampton, and Warfield too. Yer ought ter cuff my ears instead uv bein' so all-fired kind."

With this the loveless boy turned towards the wall and covered his face. Both Major Hampton and Grant, as well as Roderick, were noticeably affected, and the three walked over toward the window while Scotty was collecting himself.

"I say," said Grant, sotto voce, "in the language of Jim Rankin, the worst that poor little devil will get—if he goes with me—will be the best of it."

Then the visitors turned round to say good-by. The invalid had had about enough excitement for one day.

Just as they were departing, Scotty beckoned Roderick to his side.

"Stop a minute or two with me—alone," he whispered. "I wants ter tell you somethin'."

Roderick excused himself to the others; he would join them on the porch presently.

Scotty's face wore a keen eager look.

"Say, if I helps you," he began, "I'll be doin' a good turn, won't I, to the girl that saved my life by hurryin' me along to this 'orspital here?"

"I believe she will count it as a favor," replied Roderick. "How can you help me, Scotty?"

"An' I'll be doin' you a favor," continued the lad, without answering the direct question, "if I do a good turn to your friend with the name that reminds me of Bull Durham terbaccer?"

"Buell Hampton," laughed Roderick.

"The Major you also call him. Wal, I can drop him a word o' warnin' too."

"Oh, he has never a thought about love affairs," replied Roderick, smiling.

"But this is a warnin' of another kind. Listen." And Scotty drew himself up to a sitting posture on the bed. "Come nearer."

Roderick complied; his ear was close to Scotty's lips. The cowboy spoke in a whisper.

"The Major's got a pile o' rich ore stored in his house. There's a bunch o' fellers agoin' to get it, an' they'll shoot to kill as sure as God made hell."

Roderick mastered his emotion of surprise.

"When is this to take place, Scotty?" he asked quietly.

"Any night after tonight. Tonight they've fixed to square accounts with some sheep herders over Jack Creek way. Then they're goin' for the Major."

Roderick gripped the other's hand.

180

"Scotty, you have done me the biggest service in the world," he said earnestly. "But one thing more—who are these men?"

"I dassn't tell. They'd plug me full o' holes the moment I got out o' here."

Roderick felt perplexed. He did not like to press for information that might seem to threaten danger for Scotty himself.

The latter was watching his face furtively.

"I know you're straight—you'll never give a feller like me away if I tell you one name."

"Never. You may stake your life on that."

"Wal, I don't care what happens to him anyway. He's a bad egg—a rotten bad egg clean through. And I'm done with him from now right on. I'm goin' to take that printin' devil's job and act on the square."

"That's right, Scotty. And we'll all help you to get clear of bad companions and bad influences. So it's all right for you to give me that name."

"An' she'll be pleased too, won't she, that Holden young lady?"

"She'll be always grateful to you for saving Buell Hampton."

"That's 'nuff for me. The leader o' that gang is—"

Scotty paused a moment; Roderick waited, silent and still.

"Bud Bledsoe," whispered the lad. "Now I've stopped hatin' you, I've sort o' turned to hatin' him and all his kind. But you'll not give me away, Warfield? I wants ter hold down that printin' job—that editor feller will make a man of me, that's just how I feel."

"And just as we all feel," said Roderick. "Now, Scotty, you must lie down. Let me fix your pillow for you. You've got some fever yet, I can see. You must rest, old fellow. You look tired."

"Yes; I'm doggoned tired," murmured the lad wearily, as he sank back on the pillow and closed his eyes.

"He is sleeping now, I think," said Roderick to the nurse as he passed quietly out of the ward.

CHAPTER XXII.

THE TRAGEDY AT JACK CREEK

AFTER a brief consultation on the hospital veranda, Buell Hampton, Roderick and Grant decided on an immediate consultation with Jim Rankin. They found the ex-sheriff busy among the horses down at the brush stable over the hill from the Major's home.

Jim received the startling news with great complacency.

"I've been expectin' tumultuous news o' this kind for quite a while," he said. "Oh, I'm up to all the didoes o' both the cowpunchers and the sheep herders. Never mind how I got to know them things. I just know 'em, and that's 'nuff said, good and plenty, for all present. If the cowpunchers are going to Jack Creek tonight, there will be hell a-poppin'."

"Not murder, surely?" exclaimed Roderick.

"Wal, there's no sayin' how them things end," replied Jim. "You see it's this way. The cowpunchers claim they're afeard the sheep'll cross over Jack Creek, an' they'll go armed with great big clubs as well as shootin' irons. They'll undertake, I'm 'lowin', ter kill with their dubs a whole lot o' sheep, maybe the hull kit an' bilin' uv 'em, shoot up the mess wagons where the sheep herders are sleepin', an' the chances are nine outer ten that they'll kill the herders an' then jist nachur'ly burn the wagons an' the corpses, kill the shepherd dogs too an' throw them on ter the fire and generally do a hellish piece uv intimidatin' work. They'll burn the wagons ter hide evidence uv their guilt. You bet they'll git keerless with their artillery."

"Good God!" murmured Roderick in horror and surprise.

"We must stop this murderous business," remarked Buell Hampton.

"And get hold of Bud Bledsoe before he can do further harm," suggested Grant Jones. "Let's hunt up the sheriff."

"Now, just go slow, g'nlemen, please," replied Jim, expectorating an inconvenient mouthful of tobacco juice and wiping his lips with the back of his hand. "Jist you leave this business to me. I've been prognosticatin' trouble for months back, an' know jist how to act. No sheriff is wanted—at least not the bum sheriff we've got at the present time. He needs no warnin' from us—mark my words. And even if he didn't chance to know what we might be tellin' him, when he did know, it would be his pertic'lar business to arrive after the killin'—that's politics. Do you git me, Major?"

"I'm afraid I get you all right, Jim," replied Buell Hampton gravely.

"Well, let us go and see Ben Bragdon," proposed Roderick.

"Not on your life," replied Jim excitedly. "Hell, man, he's the attorney fur the cattle fellers."

"He is a gentleman," exclaimed Roderick, "and if he is the attorney for the cow men, so much the better. He would advise the bosses of this contemplated lawbreaking raid and murder, and of course they would immediately take steps to keep the cowboys from committing such wickedness."

Jim Rankin's black eyes fairly snapped as he looked Roderick straight in the face and exclaimed: "Roderick, are yer as big a tenderfoot as that? Don't yer know the cowboys don't go out murderin' uv their own accord on these here cut-throat raids? They go, by gunnies, 'cause they're paid by the higher ups ter do these dastardly killin' acts. Why, gosh 'lmighty, Ben Bragdon draws a monthly retainer fee uv several figures ter protect the higher ups an' there yer are, plain as a handle on a gourd. No, by gunnies, while the Major and Mr. Jones keep guard here, you an' me, Roderick, will have ter go alone an' jist nachurally take the law into our own hands. We'll have plenty uv shootin' irons an' loco the cowboys by shootin' an' wingin' two or three uv 'em,

183

Bud Bledsoe in pertic'lar. Oh, you bet I know how to do this job," and he chuckled reassuringly.

"Well, I don't," replied Roderick. "I don't pretend to know these cold-blooded murdering ways of the West or anything of this lawless feud that is going on between the cattlemen and the sheep men. However, I will go with you, Jim. When shall we start?"

"Immediately after supper. There's no moon and it looks a little squally. It will be darker than a stack of black cats, but by gunnies, I know the way. All you've got to do is to have yer shootin' irons ready, follow me and shoot when I shoot Now I guess there's no need my onbosomin' myself any more," he added with a comprehensive glance around.

Roderick was unable to repress a smile.

"All right, Jim, I'm game, and ready for the lark."

"By gunnies, it ain't no lark howsumever; I know yer game," replied Rankin. "You bet you I kin tell a scrapper when I see him. Now not a word to anyone else besides us four—exceptin' of course, Boney Earnest I'm goin' over to the smelter right now, and will arrange for him to be here tonight to help the Major."

"And Tom Sun?" asked Roderick, anxiously.

"Oh, he's in no danger. Them fellers are after his herders but not after the big man. They know better—the law would be poppin' like hell if they ever made the mistake o' hurtin' one o' the higher-ups."

"Besides, Mr. Sun is at Rawlins today on business," observed Buell Hampton. "He is riding, and is to come straight here. But he told me not to expect him until midnight."

"Which the cowpunching gang know quite well," said Jim emphatically. "You bet they are playin' up tonight jist because they cal'clate on his absence. Now we'll be a-movin'. Major, get your rifles well oiled—you may need 'em. My ridin' hoss is over at the livery barn, and you an' me, Roderick, will start from there at eight o'clock sharp. Oh, you bet we'll have tumultuous doin's. Jist you an' me 'll show these killin' cusses they're holdin' bob-tailed flushes fur oncet. They won't show up here for the gold ore after we're through with 'em. Reminds me uv the old sheriff days, boys. An' its 'lmighty good to be back to them," he added, pushing his hat back on his head determinedly.

"I think we must put you up for sheriff again next election," laughed Grant Jones.

"That's just what I'm prognosticatin'," replied the rugged old frontiersman, with a grim smile. "Folks will see who's the real sheriff tonight—me or that white-livered double-dealin' cur. Mills." And he strode away in the direction of the smelting plant, chewing his tobacco cud vigorously.

At the appointed hour that night Roderick was at the livery barn, and got ready his faithful horse, Badger. He had only waited a few minutes when Jim Rankin made his appearance. They were soon in their saddles and headed for Jack Creek.

The night was very dark, and despite the would-be sheriff's vaunted knowledge of the country they lost themselves several times, and on one occasion had to retrace their steps four or five miles. Wherever it was possible they urged their horses on as rapidly as was prudent, but often for long distances it was a case of picking their way at a walking pace through the inky blackness. It was within an hour of midnight when at last they turned from the main road to the westward along the north bank of Jack Creek, which was the dividing line between the flockmasters' and the cattle men's range. Rankin explained that the bands of sheep were being held about two miles on to the westward.

They had not gone very far up the creek when they were startled by the sight of two great fires burning like haystacks. They spurred their horses and hurried as fast as possible over the uncertain and little used road, and soon came upon a weird and terrible scene. Some three or four hundred sheep had been clubbed to death and lay like scattered boulders over the ground, while the two covered wagons where the herders cooked their meals and likewise slept were fast burning to ashes.

"By gunnies," said Jim Rankin, "we didn't get here quick enough. They've sure done their hellish work. I'll bet there's two sheep herders an' two shepherd dogs bumin' to cinders in them there fires. It's hell, ain't it? They beat us to it for sure. But usually them doin's don't come off 'til one or two o'clock in the mornin'."

"Where are the balance of the sheep?" inquired Roderick. "I thought you said there were several thousand."

"Why, boy," said Jim, "they're chasin' down toward Saratoga as if the wolves were after them. There's 'bout three thousand sheep in each band an' there were two bands uv 'em."

Just then four masked men rode up out of the darkness toward the burning outfits, but quickly checked their horses when they saw the two mounted strangers.

"Don't shoot, Roderick, don't shoot," whispered Jim. "By gunnies, they've got us covered. Don't lift your artillery. They'll kill us sure if yer do." Then he raised his trembling voice in a shout: "Hey, you fellers, we seed somethin' burnin' here. Wonder what 'tis?"

A deep guttural voice came back: "You two 'll find it a dam sight more healthy to git back on the main road an' tend to your own business. You have got jist one minute to start."

"Come on," said Jim, agitatedly, whirling his horse, putting spurs to him and leaving Roderick trailing far behind.

Roderick rode along toward the main road which they had just left after crossing over Jack Creek. He was disgusted with it all and with Jim Rankin's poltroonery in particular. The sight he had seen by the gleaming light of the burning wagons was ghastly. The innocent, helpless sheep that had been clubbed to death through the selfishness of men. He was in no mood for hilarity. It was a sight that would remain with him and haunt him. Then too, he had received a new measure of Jim Rankin.

But Roderick Warfield had all the blind audacity of youth and did not give the old westerner Jim Rankin the credit he deserved. Jim Rankin was versed in the ways of these western transgressors, and knew the price he and Roderick would have to pay for "butting in" on a quarrel between the cattle and the sheep men that was no direct concern of outsiders. This price was death, swift and merciless.

When Roderick reached the highway he pulled his horse to the right toward the bridge that spanned Jack Creek. As he approached the bridge he heard someone say: "Here he comes now." The voice was not Jim Rankin's.

"Hello," came a call in yet another voice, just as his horse reached the bridge.

"Come on, Roderick," cried Jim Rankin, "I'm here."

"Who's with you?" inquired Roderick.

"They'll tell you," replied Jim.

Roderick rode up and found three men with drawn revolvers, and one of them proved to be the sheriff of the county and the others his deputies.

"Gentlemen," said the sheriff, "you are accused of killing a lot of sheep up here on Jack Creek and burning a couple of wagons, and I arrest you in the name of the law."

"What does this mean?" inquired Roderick, hotly.

"It means," said the sheriff, "you fellers will fork over your shootin' irons quietly and submit to being handcuffed."

"Look here, Mills," said Rankin, resentfully, "you're goin' too dangnation far, by gunnies. I'll be responsible for young Warfield, here. I'll go his bail. Dangnation, don't press me any furder or I'll git peevish."

"Well," replied Sheriff Mills, hesitatingly, "who will be responsible for you?"

"Why, Gosh'lmighty, Mills, we've know'd each other fur twenty-five years. You go my security yourself or by the great horn spoon you'll not kerry Rawlins precinct next election."

"Watch that young feller," instructed the sheriff to his deputies. "Ride over this way, Jim, where we can speak privately."

A few moments later Rankin called out: "Come on, Roderick, let's be goin'. It's gettin' late. Everything's all right." And together they headed their horses for Encampment and rode on in the darkness.

Jim Rankin presently said: "Well, by gunnies, Tom Sun has

leastways got to hand it to us fur tryin'."

Roderick made no immediate reply and they continued their way in silence.

At last Roderick spoke.

"You were mighty friendly with that white-livered, double-dealing cur, the sheriff—that's what you called him a few hours ago."

"Yes, but he wasn't present with a gun in his hand," replied Jim. "He sure 'nuff had the drop on us."

"How did you square him then?"

"Politics," came the sententious answer. "And I guess I put one over him at that. Somebody's goin' to git a dangnation throw-down, an' don't you forgit it."

An hour later they descended at the livery barn. The sky had cleared, and they had ridden fast under the starlight. Roderick looked the ex-sheriff squarely in the face.

"Now, Jim Rankin, the next move in the game is going to be mine. Get your three fours hitched up at once, and bring them down one by one as fast as they are ready, to the Major's. We load that ore tonight, and start for the railroad before daylight. Do you get me, my friend?"

Jim Rankin for a moment looked into Roderick's eyes.

"I guess I git you, Mr. Warfield," he replied, as he meekly turned away toward the stables where the twelve powerful draught horses had been held in preparedness for a week past.

CHAPTER XXIII.

THE FIGHT ON THE ROAD

DAYLIGHT had not yet broken when the three four-horse wagons were loaded and ready for the road. Not a moment had been lost after Roderick's arrival at the Major's. That night he had had a grim glimpse of what western lawlessness among the mountains might mean, and had speedily convinced the Major that his policy of instant departure was the wise one. Bud Bledsoe and his gang would rest at least one day, perhaps two or three days, after their devilish exploit with the sheep-herders, and when they came reconnoitering around the blockhouse in which the ore was stored it would be to find the rich treasure gone. The teams by that time would be at Walcott, or at least well on the way to their destination.

The little bunch of friends had set to work with a will. Jim Rankin got the first team down within half an hour, and by that time the Major, Tom Sun, who had duly turned up from Rawlins, Boney Earnest, Grant Jones and Roderick had a goodly pile of the one-hundred-pound ore sacks stacked in front of the house, ready to be lifted into the wagon. Without a hitch or delay the work proceeded, and now that the loading was completed, and the rifles and ammunition had been stowed under the drivers' seats, the tension of suppressed excitement was relaxed. Pipes were alight during a final consultation.

The three tough old westerners, it was settled, were to drive. Boney had announced his absolute determination to come along—the smelter could go to blazes, he had applied some days before for a week's leave anyways and if W. B. Grady chose

189

to buck because he took it now, well he could "buck good and plenty, and be damned to him." Tom Sun was keeping in stern repression his wrath against the miscreants who had massacred his sheep and probably killed his herders as well; it would be stern satisfaction for him to have a fight on the road, to settle accounts with Bud Bledsoe by the agency of a rifle bullet. Jim Rankin, after his quiet taking-down by Roderick at the livery stable, had recovered his accustomed self-assurance and bellicosity, and was "prognosticating" all manner of valorous deeds once it came to guns out on both sides and fair shooting.

While these three would manage the teams, Buell Hampton, Grant and Roderick would scout ahead on their riding horses, and provide a rear guard as well so that the alarm of any attempted pursuit could be given. Badger had been fed and rested, and looked fit for anything despite the night's ride to Jack Creek.

Jumping into the saddle Roderick, accompanied by Grant Jones, who knew the road well, led the way. The wagons followed, while the Major delayed just long enough to lock up the house, including the now empty inner chamber, and clear away the traces of the night's work. The whole cavalcade was three or four miles out of Encampment before the sun had risen and the townsfolk were astir.

The distance to be traversed was just fifty miles, and that night the first camp was made beyond Saratoga. No public attention had been drawn to the wagons; none of the people encountered on the road or at stopping places had any reason to think that these ordinary looking ore-sacks held gold that was worth a king's ransom. There had been no signs of ambushed robbers ahead nor of pursuit in the rear. But that night, while a few hours of sleep were snatched, watch was kept in turn, while each sleeper had his rifle close at hand. With the first glimmer of dawn the journey was resumed.

It was well on in the afternoon when the Major spied, some distance out on the open country to the left, the dust raised by a small party of horsemen. He rode up to the wagons to consult his friends. He had just pointed out the sign to Jim Rankin, when the riders disappeared behind a rocky ridge.

Jim had been shading his eyes while gazing fixedly. He now dropped his hand.

"By gunnies, they are after us right enough," he exclaimed. "That was Bud Bledsoe in the lead—I know his ginger-colored pony. They're going to cross Pass Creek lower down, then they will swing around into White Horse Canyon, coming back to meet us after we've crossed the bridge and are on the long steep hill just beyond. Dang me if that ain't their game."

The Major rode ahead to warn Grant and Roderick. The bridge over Pass Creek was only three miles from Walcott. If the three scouts could gain the crest of the steep slope, before the robbers, the advantage of position would be theirs.

Roderick grasped the plan of campaign in an instant, and, digging his spurs into Badger's flank, galloped off full pelt. Grant and the Major followed at the best pace of their less mettled ponies.

It was less than a mile to the bridge, and Badger was soon breasting the hill at a swinging canter. Just before reaching the summit Roderick descended, and throwing the bridle over the pony's head tethered it in cowboy fashion. "I'll be back in a minute, old fellow," he said, as he gave Badger an affectionate pat on the neck. Then, rifle in hand, he walked up the remaining few yards of the slope, and cautiously peered over the crest into White Horse Canyon.

Great Scott! seven or eight horsemen away down at the foot of the descending incline were just scrambling out of the waste of cacti and joshuas on to the roadway! The first comers were waiting for the stragglers, and a pow-wow was evidently being held. Roderick gripped the butt of his rifle. But he heard the clatter of hoofs behind him, and drew back for the time being. Waving a cautioning hand to Buell Hampton and Grant as they approached, he gave the news in a few words. It took only a minute to tie all three horses securely to the low-growing grease-wood that here skirted the road—the animals, although well-trained, might be stampeded by the shooting. Then, rifles in hand, Roderick, Grant and the Major crept up to the crest of the ridge. Before reaching it the sharp tattoo of horse hoofs smote their ears.

"That's Bud Bledsoe in the lead on the ginger pony," exclaimed Buell Hampton.

Nothing more was needed by Roderick; if Bud Bledsoe was there, the gang were lawbreakers and bent on further villainy.

"Bang!" went Roderick's rifle; and the ginger-colored horse plunged forward on his knees, and then rolled over, kicking wildly in the air. Two horses behind stumbled over the obstruction, and instantly there was a confused heap of struggling beasts and men. Four other riders had reined in their steeds just in time, and were standing stock-still on the highway.

"Keep it up, but don't kill," muttered the Major, just before he fired his own rifle. Almost at the same instant came "bang" from Grant's shoulder, and a second shot by Roderick.

At this fusillade the four cowboys still mounted jumped their horses into the sage brush and cacti and were gone like a streak across country. One of the fallen horses had struggled to its feet, and a figure leaped into the saddle. It was Bud Bledsoe— Roderick knew him by his gorilla-like figure. Leaving his two fallen comrades to their fate, the leader raced after the fleeing quartette. Three rifle bullets whizzed past him to quicken his pace. Then the marksmen on the ridge stood erect.

Two motionless human figures lay on the road at the bottom of the hill; the ginger horse had rolled in among the bushes in his death throes, the other was limping along with a broken leg. Roderick ran down the slope on foot, leaving the others to follow with the horses.

The first man he reached was dead, his neck broken by the fall. Roderick recognized him at a glance—for when once riding the range with a bunch of cowboys they had passed a lone rider on a mountain trail and the name had been passed around—

Butch Cassidy, a horse rustler, and an outlaw of the hills. The other fellow was bleeding from a wound in his breast; there was a gulping gurgle in his throat. He had evidently been hit by Grant's first bullet, which had been fired too quick for any heed to be paid to Buell Hampton's merciful injunction. Just as Roderick raised the limp hand the wounded man opened his eyes; then he uttered one great sob and died.

A few minutes later bullets from Grant's revolver put the injured horses out of pain.

In the dusk of the falling night the dead men were borne on the ore wagons into Walcott. The station agent recognized the second corpse as that of a notorious gambler and hold-up artist, an old associate of Big-Nosed George in early days. The railroad man treated the bodies as trash, but condescended to wire down the line for the coroner and the sheriff. The car, which had been ordered several days before, was on the side track awaiting the ore shippers, and he counselled that there should be no delay in loading, as a through freight for Denver was due shortly after midnight. So the fight was forgotten, and the work of transferring the ore sacks from the wagons was soon in progress, all present, even the Major, lending a hand.

After the task had been completed, the bill of lading prepared and all charges prepaid, Jim Rankin, Boney Earnest, Tom Sun and Grant Jones boarded the car. They were well provided with blankets for bedding and still carried their rifles. Buell Hampton and Roderick remained to arrange for the sending back of the teams and saddle horses; they would follow on the morning passenger train, and the whole party would reach Denver practically at the same hour next night.

No further incident occurred. But not until the carload of ore had been duly delivered, sampled, and weighed did the four faithful and well-armed guards relax their vigilance. The purchasers were the Globe Smelter Company, with whose manager Boney Earnest had personal acquaintance.

While secrecy was exercised concerning this remarkable ore

shipment, yet the news gradually crept out and it became known that something phenomenal had occurred. The newspaper reporters hovered around the Globe Smelter endeavoring to pick up a few crumbs of information.

Buell Hampton and his friends were registered at the Brown Palace Hotel where they had arranged for connecting rooms. Two days afterwards Buell Hampton announced to his friends, in the privacy of his room, that the returns were all he had anticipated. The money had been duly deposited to his credit, and now he wrote checks running into five figures for each of his friends, and admonished them separately and collectively to deposit the money in some Denver bank to their individual credit, then return to their Encampment homes and each continue his avocation as if nothing had happened to improve their financial affairs.

"As for myself," said the Major, "I have a mission to perform, and I probably will not return to Encampment for a matter of fifteen or twenty days."

That night Major Hampton left for New York carrying with him certified checks for a large sum of money, and on the following morning the others took train for Wyoming. Within a few days all had resumed their accustomed routine. Jim Rankin was back on his stage coach making his usual trips; Boney Earnest, after an acrimonious scrap with Grady over the question of absence without leave, was in his old place before the blast furnace; Tom Sun regained his home at Split Rock, north of Rawlins, Grant Jones returned to his editorial duties, Roderick to his preparations for a prospecting expedition.

Both Grant and Roderick had brought with them checks for a few thousand dollars, which they deposited in the local bank to the great surprise of the cashier. And even before leaving the bank they began to realize that their importance in the community had already gone up a hundred per cent. Such is the prompt efficacy of a substantial bank balance!

CHAPTER XXIV.

SUMMER DAYS

WITHIN less than a year of his leaving Keokuk to play football with the world, as Uncle Allen Miller had phrased it, Roderick Warfield had established himself in a sound financial position. So far he had not been made the "pig-skin" in life's game. While he was filled with grateful feeling toward Buell Hampton, and recognized the noble generosity of his friend, he had at the same time the satisfaction of feeling that he had done at least a little toward earning a share in the proceeds derived from the carload of rich ore. And once he found his own mine, his father's mine, it would be his turn to follow the golden rule and share liberally with those around him.

When he had handed in the Denver check at the local bank, he had already found a new deposit to his credit there—a sum of money to which he had never given a thought from the moment it was won. This was the $450 coming to him as the World's Championship prize in the rough-riding and outlaw-busting competition at the frontier celebration. It was with intense delight that Roderick decided to apply this windfall to finally clearing off his New York liabilities. He felt like walking even a bit more erect than ever now that he would owe not a dollar in the world. After luncheon he returned to the bank and secured eastern drafts.

But there was a balance remaining, and Roderick at once thought of the lad who had not only suffered defeat in the contest but injury as well. Major Hampton had already undertaken the provision of clothes and other outfit for Scotty Meisch. Roderick thought for a moment; then he walked across to the Savings Bank and started an account in the cowboy's name with a credit of $100. He carried the little pass-book with him to the hospital.

He found Scotty reclining in a long chair on the veranda. The invalid was convalescent, although looking pale from the unwonted confinement. His face brightened with joy when Roderick, looking down with a pleasant smile, patted him on the shoulder and gripped his hand.

"Gee, but it's good to see you again," murmured the boy. "It seems like a hell of a time since you were here. But I got the postcard you sent me from Denver."

"Yes, Scotty, as I wrote you, Grant Jones and I, also the Major, have all been to Denver. We were called away unexpectedly or would have paid you a parting visit. But I've come around at once, you see. Grant Jones and I got back only this afternoon. Mr. Jones is going to take you over to Dillon next week. Meanwhile I have brought you this little book, old fellow."

Scotty glanced at the pass-book, wonderingly and uncomprehendingly. He turned it over and over.

"An' what's this piece o' leather goods for?" he asked.

"That means you've got $100 to your credit in the Savings Bank, Scotty—the consolation prize, you remember, in the broncho-busting contest."

"Consolation prize be damned. There was no consolation prize."

"Oh, yes, there was."

"Not by a danged sight You've gone an' done this, Warfield."

"Well, I got the big money, and hasn't the winner the right to give off a bit of it as a consolation prize? Just stuff that book in your pocket, Scotty, and may the hundred dollars soon roll up to a thousand, old fellow."

"Great guns, but you're powerful kind to me—all of you," murmured the cowboy. There were tears in his eyes.

"And by the way, Scotty," continued Roderick, talking gaily, "that reminds me, I've got to go across to Englehart's store and take over that grand championship saddle he was showing in his window—Banker Buck Henry's special prize, you remember. I had almost forgotten about it. Why, it's mine—stamped leather, solid silver mounts, and all the gewgaw trimmings. How will I look riding the ranges with that sort of outfit?"

"You'll look just grand," exclaimed Scotty admiringly. "But you won't use that on the range. It will be your courtin' outfit."

Scotty smiled wanly, while Roderick laughed in spite of himself. The invalid felt emboldened.

"Oh, she's been over here every day during your absence," he continued. "Gee, but she's pretty, and she's kind! And let me tell you somethin' else. Barbara's been a-visitin' me too. Just think o' that."

"Ah, all the girls are good, Scotty—and Wyoming girls the best of all," he added enthusiastically. There was safety in the general proposition.

"Barbara an' I has made it all up," continued the lad, still smiling, wistfully yet happily. "She's dead stuck on that lawyer chap, Bragdon, and we shook hands over it. I wished her luck, and promised to vote for Bragdon at the election for state senator. An' what do you think she did when I told her that?" he asked, raising himself in his chair.

"She said 'Bully for you,' I bet," replied Roderick. "She did more. She kissed me—fair and square, she kissed me," Scotty put his finger-tips to his forehead. "Oh, only there," he added, half regretfully. "But I'll never forget the touch of her lips, her sweet breath in my face." And he patted the spot on his brow in appreciative reminiscence.

"That's politics, as Jim Rankin would say," laughed Roderick, more to himself than to the cowboy.

"Wal, it's the sort o' politics I like," replied Scotty. "If she'd even only cuff my ears every time I voted, I'd be a repeater for Bragdon at the polls."

"Well, we'll both vote the Bragdon ticket, Scotty. A girl like Barbara Shields is worth making happy, all the time. And later on, old fellow, the proper girl will be coming along for you."

"Looks as if she was comin' along for you right now," grinned Scotty, glancing toward the steps of the veranda.

And a moment later Roderick was shaking hands with another hospital visitor, gazing into Gail Holden's blue eyes, and receiving her warm words of greeting over his safe return.

"We heard something about a fight near Walcott, you know, Mr. Warfield—about a mysterious carload of ore. Two hold-up men were killed, and your name was mentioned in connection with the affair. I felt quite anxious until Mr. Meisch received his postcard from Denver. But you never thought of writing to me," she added, reproachfully.

"I did not dare," murmured Roderick in a low tone intended only for her ears.

But Scotty heard and Scotty saw.

"This is the very hour the nurse says I've got to sleep," he said. "You'd better be clearin' out, War-field."

"And me too?" asked Gail, laughingly.

"The pair o' you," replied the invalid, as he lay back languorously and closed his eyes.

"I guess we'd better be going," laughed Roderick.

"Perhaps Mr. Meisch is awake enough yet," said Gail, "to hear that I brought over a chicken for his supper."

"Tell the nurse I'll have it fried, please," yawned Scotty, as, without opening his eyes, he turned over his head in slumberous fashion.

"Come away then, Miss Holden," said Roderick. "I suppose you rode over on Fleetfoot. I'll saddle Badger, and we'll have a gallop across country."

"No doggoned politics there," exclaimed the cowboy, awaking suddenly, as he watched the handsome couple disappear. "That's the real thing, sure."

The summer days glided past. The Major had returned from New York and had quietly resumed his old life of benevolence among the poor. But soon there seemed to be no more poverty in or around Encampment. Roderick, keeping the mining town as his headquarters, made a series of expeditions into the mountains, systematically searching every range and every known canyon. He would be absent for several days at a time, sometimes with Jim Rankin for a companion, Grant Jones once or twice accompanying him, but latterly with Boney Earnest as his *fidus Achates*. For Boney had severed his connection finally with the Smelter Company, after a quarrel with Grady that had ended in the blast furnace foreman knocking his employer down. Such is the wonderful independence that comes from a bank balance—even a secret bank balance that may not command the deference accorded to known financial prosperity.

Between his prospecting expeditions Roderick spent an occasional evening either at the Conchshell Ranch or at the Major's, with a flying call now and then at the Shields home, especially when Grant was on one of his periodical visits to Encampment.

The month was now September. The rugged mountains still guarded their secret, and Roderick was beginning to fear that the quest for his father's mine was indeed going to be a vain one. But there came an interlude to his range-riding and gold-dreaming. The state conventions were approaching. Even love became a minor matter to politics. The air was surcharged with electricity

CHAPTER XXV.

RUNNING FOR STATE SENATOR

AT BREAKFAST table one morning Roderick noticed in the *Encampment Herald* a featured article about the forthcoming Republican convention.

"Oh, yes," replied Grant, when Roderick called his attention to it, "this convention trouble has been brewing for some time. Personally, as you know, I am a Republican, even though my paper, the *Dillon Doublejack*, is a dyed-in-the-wool Democratic organ."

"What trouble," asked Roderick, "can there possibly be about a county convention?"

"It's a senatorial convention," explained Grant. "There is an old saying," he went on, "that every dog has his day. But unfortunately politically speaking there are more dogs than days, and when two or three contestants try to get in on the same day, why, somebody is going to get bitten. There is only one state senatorial job from this district but there may be half-a-dozen fellows who feel called upon to offer themselves upon the political altar of their country."

"Have noticed a good many fellows down from the hills recently," replied Roderick.

"Well, that's politics," said Grant. "They take a lay off from their work in the hills—come down here to fill up on free political whiskey furnished by the various candidates. Oh, take it from me," said Grant, looking wise and shaking his head, "these delegates are a booze-fighting bunch for fair."

For a moment or two the journalistic oracle busied himself with his toast and butter.

"You watch the columns of my paper," he resumed. "I'm going to show up these whiskey drinking, habits of the delegates good and plenty in this week's issue of the *Doublejack*. In the language of Jim Rankin I get a heap peevish with all this political foolishness. Still," Grant went on, "I presume it is a part of the political machinery of the frontier. One thing," he concluded, "we all become unduly excited in these ante-convention days."

Political excitement had indeed waxed warm, and the little mining town had seemingly ceased to think about its mines, its great smelting plant, rich strikes in the hills and everything else—even the cattle men and the sheep men appeared to have forgotten their feuds together with their flocks and herds in the general excitement over the nomination for state senator from southern Carbon County.

Grant Jones in his Doublejack editorials made emphatic and urgent appeal to the people to remember the doctrines of the old Simon-pure Jacksonian democracy and agree upon a good Democratic nominee. With a split in the Republican ranks the chances were never better for the election of a Democratic senator. He pointed out that if Bragdon won the nomination the Carlisle clique would secretly knife the Bragdon forces at the polls by voting the Democratic ticket, and on the other hand if Carlisle should best Bragdon in the nominating contest then the Bragdon following would retaliate by supporting the Democratic nominee so as to defeat Carlisle in the end.

On the Republican side W. Henry Carlisle, the astute lawyer, was backed by the smelter interests, while Ben Bragdon, the eloquent, was supported by the antismelter forces generally and also by Earle Clemens, editor of the *Encampment Herald,* one of the best known and most highly respected party leaders in the state.

The so-called smelter interests were certainly discredited because of the domineering insolence of W. B. Grady and his unfair treatment of the men. Not only did Grady practice every sort of injustice upon the employees of the great smelting plant in all its various departments, but he also quarreled with the ranchmen in the valley whenever he had dealings with them even to the extent of buying a load of hay.

As convention day approached there was a noticeable feeling of unrest and nervousness. Factional strife was running at high tension.

The wise men of the party said they could plainly see that unless harmony in the Republican ranks obtained at the convention the nominee would be defeated at the polls, and that if Ben Bragdon's nomination were insisted upon by his friends without in some way conciliating the Carlisle faction the Democrats would be almost certain to win at the following November's elections.

It was pretty generally conceded that Ben Bragdon, controlled the numerical strength of the delegates, but the wiseacres would ask in their solicitude: "Is it wisdom to take such a chance? Does it not invite a split in the ranks of our party? In other words, does it not mean defeat for the Republican candidate on election day?"

Carlisle was a power to be reckoned with, and had a clannish, determined following in political affairs, and although he and his friends might be outnumbered and beaten in the nominating convention, yet what would follow if Bragdon's nomination were forced upon them? What would be the result? Would not Carlisle's following secretly slash the rival they had been unable to defeat at the nominating convention?

A "dark horse" seemingly was the only way out of the dilemma, and the more conservative delegates insisted that Bragdon and his friends must be brought to understand and recognize the possibilities of almost certain defeat unless harmony could be insured; otherwise Bragdon must be compelled to withdraw.

Early in the morning before the day named for the senatorial convention to assemble at Rawlins the delegates at Encampment and several hundred friends of the respective candidates started overland for the convention city.

There were two roads from Encampment to Rawlins—one that branched off from the so-called main road and went along the

Platte River bottom. The distance by either route was about sixty miles. Carlisle and his following went one road, while Bragdon and his following traveled by the other road, both arriving at the hotel in Rawlins at the same time with panting horses. It was a mad race, each faction trying to show supremacy over the other even at the cost of horseflesh.

The delegates gathered in knots of three and four in the lobby of the hotel, in the barroom and in the private rooms during the afternoon and evening before convention day.

The trains had arrived from the East and the West, and the delegates from all over the senatorial district were present and ready for the fray that was certain to come off the following day— indeed, Rawlins, the county seat, was alive with politicians and the Ferris House, the leading hotel of the place, was a beehive of activity. The Democratic spectators were jubilant and made their headquarters at Wren's saloon.

It was at the Ferris House that W. Henry Carlisle had opened his headquarters in opposition to Ben Bragdon. The Carlisle people said they had no alternative candidate. Any one of a score of men might be named in the district, each of whom would be satisfactory; in fact, anyone excepting Ben Bragdon, provided, of course, it was found that Carlisle could not be nominated, which they were far from conceding.

Bragdon and Carlisle had often before locked horns in hotly contested lawsuits up in the-hills, but in addition to their legal fights for supremacy there had been one special controversy that had resulted in a big financial loss for which each held the other responsible. It involved a bitter fight over a mining claim wherein both Bragdon and Carlisle had financial interests, and both had finally lost. It was a rich property and had by decree of the courts been awarded to a third party. But the decision did not lessen the feud. The impelling motive in their political contest was not half so much, perhaps, for the honor of being state senator as it was a consuming desire in the heart of each to best and lick the other.

Some of the delegates, even those who were inclined to be

friendly to Bragdon's candidacy, acknowledged that seemingly he had made no effort to pacify either Carlisle or his friends, and thus, in a way, had proven himself deficient as a political leader and standard-bearer for the party.

Others claimed that a reconciliation was impossible, that the breach was entirely too wide to be patched up at the eleventh hour. Still others were of the opinion that if the Bragdon forces would concede the chairmanship of the convention to Carlisle and his friends and thus give substantial evidence of a desire to harmonize and be friendly, past differences could be adjusted, with the result not only of Bragdon's nomination but his election as well.

Those high in the leadership of the Bragdon forces laughed incredulously and scorned to consider such a compromising surrender, and further expressed their disbelief in the sincerity of Carlisle and his crowd even if the Bragdon following were willing to make such a concession.

"No," said Big Phil Lee, Bragdon's chief lieutenant, "I'm a Kentucky Democrat, boys, as you all know, but in this fight I'm for Bragdon—a Bragdon Republican—and we've got the whip-hand and by the Eternal we will hold it. We Bragdon fellows have already agreed upon a chairman and a secretary for both the temporary and permanent organizations of tomorrow's convention, and we have selected Charlie Winter to name Bragdon in a nominating speech that will be so dangnation eloquent—well, it will simply carry everybody off their feet. He is the boy that can talk, you bet he is. Oh, you bet we've got 'em licked, Carlisle and all his cohorts. And let me tell you something else," continued Big Phil Lee, gesticulating, "we'll hold them responsible for the final result. If Bragdon's not elected, it will be because Carlisle and his gang knife him at the polls. Just let them do such a dirty contemptible piece of political chicanery and they'll be marked men ever afterwards in this senatorial district, and not one of them could be elected even to the office of dog pelter."

CHAPTER XXVI.

UNEXPECTED POLITICAL HARMONY

IT WAS just such talk as Big Phil Lee's that kept the Bragdon forces lined up and defiant to the point of an open rupture and a total disregard for the minority, while the Democrats cheered Big Phil Lee's remarks with enthusiastic hoorays.

The individual who really held the destiny of the party that year in the hollow of his hand and within the next few hours proved himself the Moses to lead all factions from the paths of bickering into the highway of absolute harmony, was the newspaper man, Earle Clemens. All through the evening hours the editor of the *Herald* had been a most eloquent listener. He was on good terms with everybody, jovial and mixed with all factions, and yet was scrupulously careful to avoid giving any expression of advice or stating an opinion. He had, however, been very outspoken in his editorial advocacy for harmony.

Earle Clemens was not only known and respected all over the state as an able newspaper man, but he was the possessor of a rich tenor voice that had delighted many an audience up in the hills, and then, too, he had composed the melody of the state song, entitled "Wyoming"—all of which tended to his great popularity and powerful influence.

While it was quite generally known that Clemens was perhaps closer in his friendship for Bragdon than any other man in the district, dating from way back when the generous-hearted young lawyer had helped Clemens at a time and in a way that money could not buy or repay, yet the editor of the *Herald* had all along insisted that unless the Bragdon sympathizers effected a reconciliation with the Carlisle crowd, it virtually meant, if Bragdon's nomination were forced upon the convention, a Democratic victory at the coming November election.

In his last editorial, before the convention was to assemble, he had, in reply to Democratic newspaper gibes about a high old row which was likely to obtain at the oncoming Republican convention, branded the writers one and all as political falsifiers. He boldly announced that not a single discordant note would be heard when the Republican host came to nominate its standard bearer, and furthermore that the choice would be emphasized by a unanimous vote of the delegates. And in the final event the Republican candidate, he declared, would be elected by such an overwhelming popular vote that it would make the false Democratic prophets and bolting Republican malcontents, if there were any, "hunt the tall timber."

The Democratic press in reply had said that the editor of the *Herald* was whistling to keep up his courage, and of course much amusement had been caused by the spirited controversy. So when the eventful day arrived fully as many Democrats journeyed to Rawlins to see the fun as there were Republican delegates. Of course, as good Democrats, they lost no opportunity to help embitter the two factions and widen the breach between the Bragdon and the Carlisle forces.

Editor Earle Clemens, however, had ideas of his own that he told to no one. The electric light was shining in his room long after midnight and his small hand typewriter, which he always carried in his grip, was busy clicking away—presumably writing copy for the columns of his paper. What really occurred however, was this: He wrote two letters on the hotel stationery—one addressed to Hon. Ben Bragdon, and the other addressed to Hon. W. Henry Carlisle, and the envelopes were marked private.

After the letters were duly typewritten, he placed an electric light under a pane of glass with which he had provided himself, elevating the glass by supporting the ends with a couple of books, and then from letters that he had at some former time received from both aspirants cleverly traced and signed the signature of W. Henry Carlisle to one letter and in like manner signed the signature of Ben Bragdon to the other letter—yes, brazen forgeries.

After inclosing them in their respective envelopes, he stole softly out into the hallway and slipped one under the door of Carlisle's room and the other under the door of Bragdon's room. Then he went downstairs and bribed the night clerk to call both Bragdon and Carlisle at sharp fifteen minutes before six o'clock. This done, Clemens hastened back to his own apartment for a few hours' sleep, wondering as he disrobed if the "end would justify the means."

"There is no question," he said to himself as he climbed into the bed, "but that the Republican ox is in the ditch and heroic measures are necessary."

The following morning, when W. Henry Carlisle was awakened by the night clerk calling out softly the hour of seven o'clock, he hastily arose and began dressing, but before he had half finished he spied the letter that had been pushed under his door. Picking it up, he broke the seal and this is what he read:

"My dear Carlisle:—

"It probably requires more bravery to make an apology and to ask to be forgiven than it does to settle differences between gentlemen by the now antiquated 'code.'

"I here and now tender my apologies for any unkind words I may in the past have spoken derogatory to you, and as an evidence of my candor will pledge you the support of myself and friends for both temporary and permanent chairman at tomorrow's convention, if you reciprocate this offer of a reconciliation.

"If you are big enough and broad enough and generous

enough to accept this overture and desire to bury all past differences and from now on work in harmony together, each helping the other, as did Jonathan and David of old, why, the opportunity is offered, and we will let bygones be bygones.

"If you accept this apology, meet me at the hotel bar early tomorrow morning and merely extend your hand of friendship in greeting. I will understand; but please do not humiliate me by mentioning the fact, even to your best friends, that I have written this letter, and above all do not refer to it at our meeting tomorrow morning or at any future time. It is quite enough if these old differences are wiped off the slate between you and myself without commenting, or permitting comments to be made. I am not unmindful, Carlisle, that you are a great big able man and I want you to be my friend, and I wish to be yours. You have the power to make my nomination for state senator unanimous.

"I have the honor of subscribing myself

"Very sincerely yours,

"Ben Bragdon."

Across the hall Ben Bragdon was also reading a letter, which was almost a duplicate of the one that Carlisle was perusing, except that the conditions were reversed. Carlisle, in his letter of apology, offered to support Bragdon for the nomination, provided the hatchet was buried and the Bragdon forces would support him for temporary and permanent chairman.

At the conclusion of the reading of these respective letters, each wore an exultant look of mastery on his face. For the time being at least all other differences were forgotten. In the hearts of both was the thought: "It's mighty decent of him; he really is a bigger man than I thought."

Carlisle was the first man to leave his room and going quickly downstairs passed hurriedly into the hotel bar, which at that early hour was deserted except for the immaculate, white-aproned bartender.

"What will it be this morning, Mr. Carlisle?" was the respectful inquiry of the attendant.

"Nothing just yet," replied Carlisle, "I am waiting for a friend."

A moment later Ben Bragdon came in, whereupon both of these skillful politicians vied in meeting each other more than half-way and extending the right hand of good fellowship in kindliest greetings.

"Guess we're a little early," stammered Bragdon in a futile attempt to appear at ease and free from embarrassment. They both laughed a little, and Carlisle remarked that fortunately the bartender was at his post even if the delegates were slow about getting started on the day's work.

Just then the night clerk appeared and apologized for calling them so early. "Don't know how it happened," he stammered, "but I made a mistake of an hour. I called you gentlemen at six instead of seven. I hope you'll not—"

"Oh, that's all right," exclaimed Bragdon and Carlisle in unison, as they good-naturedly waved him aside with their assurance that they were glad to be up and about.

"A couple of Martini cocktails," said Bragdon to the attendant. The cocktails were soon before them and tossed off in a jiffy, with the mutual salutation of "Here's how."

"Come again, my man; make it half a dozen this time—three apiece," said Carlisle, laughing and throwing down a twenty dollar gold piece. "Might as well have a good appetizer while we're about it, and then we'll relish our breakfast, good or bad."

They chatted about the weather while the cocktails were being prepared. Finally the cocktails were pushed along the bar counter, three in front of each.

"All right," said Bragdon, as they each lifted a glass. "Here's to your good health!"

"Thanks," said Carlisle, "but since we have three cocktails apiece before us, suppose we drink to the past, the present, and the future!"

"Good!" replied Bragdon, beaming with approval. "Splendid idea and happily put" He then ordered some of the highest priced cigars the house afforded and insisted on Carlisle filling his pockets, while he stowed away a goodly number himself.

Soon after the fourth cocktail disappeared, they started for the dining-room arm in arm, chatting away to one another like two old cronies who had just met after a long separation. They found seats at a table in a far corner and in their eagerness to say the right thing to one another took no notice that a few of the delegates were already at tables in different parts of the room. The delegates laid down their knives and forks and looked toward Bragdon and Carlisle in astonishment. Then they whispered among themselves, whereupon four or five left the room quietly and hastened with all speed to carry word to the other delegates, most of whom were still in their apartments.

The news spread like wildfire, and a general scramble followed in hurriedly dressing and rushing downstairs to witness with their own eyes such an unexpected turn in political affairs between two men who had been at daggers drawn.

Within a very short time the dining-room was well filled with delegates, but neither Bragdon nor Carlisle paid any attention; nor were they seemingly conscious that all eyes were turned upon them. Each was felicitating himself on the turn of events. Then, too, their amiability, as well as their appetites, had no doubt been whetted into keenest activity by the cocktails.

Ben Bragdon, after breakfast, gave orders that the Hon. W. Henry Carlisle was to be made both temporary and permanent chairman, and Carlisle likewise announced that the Hon. Ben Bragdon was to be nominated as senatorial candidate by acclamation; and each issued his instructions in such a matter-of-fact, yet stubbornly blunt fashion, that no one offered any objection or asked any questions.

The delegates looked at each other, nudged one another in the ribs and indulged in many a sly wink of suppressed amusement. But they all quickly recognized the political advantage insured by a coalition of the Bragdon and Carlisle forces, and the utter dismay this would cause in the camp of the Democrats. Therefore they all became "programme" men and took their orders meekly. So when the convention finally met and got down to business with Carlisle presiding, it at once proceeded to nominate Ben Bragdon by a unanimous vote.

Seemingly everybody cheered on the slightest provocation and everybody was in excellent good nature, and after the convention had completed its labors and adjourned, it was conceded to have been one of the most harmonious political gatherings ever held in the state. Thus was the prediction of Earle Clemens, the newspaper scribe, fulfilled to the very letter.

The convention over, the delegates drifted back to the Ferris House and not long after Big Phil Lee called at Clemens' room. The editor was picking away at his typewriter, preparing a report for the columns of his paper. Grant Jones, Roderick Warfield, and two or three others were in the room, smoking and talking. But Clemens paid no attention, so intent was he on his work. Big Phil Lee, who without doubt had been Bragdon's loudest shouter, said: "Say, Clemens, I compliment you on your prophetic editorials. I reckon you are writing another one. You said the convention would be harmonious, and how in the demnition bow-wows your prophecy happened to come true nobody knows. But it did."

"Thanks," replied Clemens, in his light-hearted jovial way, and then looking out of the window for a moment, added: "I say, Lee, don't it beat hell what a little clever horse sense will accomplish at times in a political convention?"

"What do you mean by that?" asked Big Phil, quickly. "You seem to be posted. By gad! I think it's high time I was taken into the inner councils myself and had the seemingly inexplainable made clear to me."

"Search me," replied Clemens in a subdued voice, as he bit the tip of another cigar and struck a match. "Neither Bragdon nor Carlisle has invited me into any of their secret conferences."

Big Phil Lee looked a bit incredulous, shook his head in a nonplussed sort of way and said: "Well, so long, boys. I'm goin' down to the hotel parlor where Bragdon is holding his reception. They are falling over one another congratulating Carlisle about as much as they are Bragdon."

As the door closed behind him, Clemens looked up from his typewriter and said to Grant Jones, laughingly: "Say, Grant, remember what the Good Book says?"

"Says lots of things—what do you refer to?" asked Grant

Clemens replied: "Blessed are the peacemakers."

Grant Jones came over close to him and said: "Look here, Clemens." And he fixed him with his eyes as if searching for an answer to that which was veiled in mystery. But Clemens stood the ordeal and presently Jones burst out laughing: "It's all right, Clemens, the *Herald* has sure put one over on the *Doublejack* this time. I don't know how it was done, and maybe I never will know. But take it from me, it was clever—damned clever!"

Clemens made no reply, but removing his cigar winked at Roderick Warfield who was sitting near, puffed rings of smoke toward the ceiling and afterwards whistled softly the air of "Wyoming," the state song, even while he smiled the smile of a knowledge that surpasses understanding.

Delegates and sightseers, Republicans and Democrats, who had journeyed to see a hotly contested nomination, ostensibly for the state senate but really for political supremacy, were good-natured and jovial when they started on the return trip. Big Phil Lee shouted to Earle Gemens who was on the other stage and said: "We are such a happy family, I presume we will return on the same road instead of dividing and horse racing."

Clemens and the other returning passengers on the hurricane deck laughed good-naturedly and said: "Sure, we will stick together from now on and fight the Democrats." Presently the crowd commenced singing vigorously—if a bunch of discordant voices could be so described—various popular airs of the day.

That evening a reception was given Ben Bragdon at the hotel Bonhomme in Encampment, and the affair was presided over by W. Henry Carlisle. It was interpreted that the breach between these two attorneys had been effectually healed to the discomfiture of the Democrats. But no one save and except Earle Clemens knew how it had been brought about.

Roderick Warfield slipped away early from the scene of jubilation, and carried the glorious news to the Shields' ranch that Ben Bragdon had been unanimously nominated. Barbara, with the flush of radiant joy on her face, could no longer deny the soft impeachment, and he boldly congratulated her on her coming wedding to the senator-elect for southern Wyoming.

CHAPTER XXVII.

THE UPLIFTING OF HUMANITY

THE following evening Roderick called at the Major's home, and found a visitor there, a stranger yet very well known to him by reputation. This was no other than the Reverend Stephen Grannon, the travelling parson, of whose fame as a doer of good deeds at the cost of complete self-sacrifice and self-denial, Roderick had often heard.

"Delighted to see you, Roderick," said the Major. "Come right in. You know, of course, the most noted man in the camp—the man with the saddle bags. What? Never met yet? Well, it is a great pleasure to me to make you two acquainted."

After cordial greetings had been exchanged Major Hampton continued: "We have just been discussing some of the great problems of humanity. Pardon me, my dear friend, but I wish to say to Mr. Warfield that if I were called upon today to name the greatest humanitarian with whom I am acquainted I certainly should say—the Reverend Stephen Grannon."

"You do me too much honor," interposed the parson hastily. "You compliment me far too highly." Major Hampton went on as if the Reverend Stephen Grannon had made no interruption: "The school of humanitarianism is small in number, but the combined results of their labors directed through the channels of service in the behalf of humanity bear the stamp of greatness. The sincere lover of his fellows recognizes that the poor of this world have borne and are still bearing the burdens of the race. The poor have built all the monuments along the world's highway of civilization. They have produced all the wealth from the hills and from the soil The poor of the world have endured the hardships of conquering the wilds and erecting outposts on the border of civilization. Indeed they conquer everything except the fetters that bind them and hold them as an asset of great corporate power that is heartless and soulless and indifferent to the privations and sufferings of the individual."

The Reverend Stephen Grannon gave it as his view that the mission of a humanitarian was not to hinder the world's progress, nor even to prejudice anyone against the fortune gathering of the rich, but rather to dispel the darkness of injustice and assist the great army of the impoverished to a better understanding of their rights as well as their powers to conquer the evils that have throughout the ages crept into and clung to our civilization.

"Poverty," he remarked, "is the cause of much misery and often the impelling motive to immorality and crime in many forms. Men often sell and barter their votes and birthrights in this free country to bribe givers—wily politicians—while our girls are not infrequently lured into selling their very souls for ribbons and the gaudiness and shams of the world."

"What is the cure?" asked Roderick, greatly interested.

"The cure," responded the preacher, "is the regeneration of mankind through the leavening and uplifting power of the principles taught by the humble humanitarian of Galilee, the great prince of righteousness."

"Yes," chimed in Major Hampton, "the Reverend Stephen Grannon has given you the solution for the problem. Add to this a higher education. The more highly educated the individual," continued the Major, "the greater the crime if they break the law."

"But," said Roderick, "this is a free country and we have free schools. Why do not the poor have a better education?"

Reverend Grannon turned quickly to Roderick and replied: "You come with me to the twenty-odd mining camps, Mr. Warfield, surrounding this town of Encampment—come with me up in the hills where there are no schools—see the little children growing up in carelessness because of the impossibility on the part of their fathers and mothers to provide them with school privileges. In the school room the teacher becomes the overseer not alone of their studies but of their morals as well. Let me take you down in the mines," he continued, speaking with great earnestness, "and see the boys from twelve years to twenty-one years working day after day, many of them never having had school privileges and therefore unable to read or write."

He paused for just a moment, then resumed: "It brings to my mind what a very wise man once wrote. It was King Solomon, and among many other splendid truths he said: 'The rich man's wealth is his strong city; the destruction of the poor is their poverty.'.rdquo;

"Roderick," said the Major as he lit his meerschaum and blew the smoke towards the ceiling, "my heart is very light tonight, for I have arranged with the assistance of the Reverend Stephen Grannon to help relieve this lamentable situation in those mining camps up in the mountains away from school privileges. I have recently taken the matter up with the county commissioners and have agreed to build twenty schoolhouses. Each schoolhouse will consist of two rooms. One will be for the smaller children during the day and also to serve as a night school for the young men and young women who are employed in manual labor during working hours. The other room is a library sufficiently large and spacious to accommodate the young men of each mining community and thus keep them away from saloons, brothels, and prize ring attractions. One hour each evening will be taken up by a reader and a regular course of entertaining books will be read aloud in a serial way. The books in the library will be loaned out on tickets and the usual library rules observed."

"Splendid," said Roderick, "that sounds practical to me."

"It is practical," said the Reverend Stephen Grannon, "and thanks to Major Buell Hampton this plan which I have cherished for so many years will soon be put into effect."

Looking at his watch he turned to the Major and said: "By the way, Major, I have a couple of poor families to visit tonight.

I have promised them, and they will be disappointed if I do not come." He arose as he said this.

"My good friend," replied Buell Hampton, "I am sorry you cannot remain longer with us, but I would not keep you from your duties."

The Reverend Stephen Grannon put on his top coat, as the evenings were growing chilly, and after shaking hands took his departure.

When he was gone and the door closed, Major Hampton turned to Roderick and holding up one hand said reverently: "Of such is the kingdom of heaven. In all my lifetime, Roderick, I have never known another such splendid character. I have closely observed his work ever since I came to this camp. Perhaps in his entire lifetime he has not collected fifty dollars in money. He says he does not want money."

"But he must have money to live on."

"Above all money considerations," said the Major, looking into the darkened corner of his living room, "he wants to save souls here on this earth so that he will have more jewels in his crown over yonder—these are his own words. There is not a family in the surrounding country that he is not acquainted with. If there is sickness he is the first one there. Where the greatest poverty abounds you will find him. He goes out and solicits alms for those in distress, but keeps nothing for himself excepting the frailest living. Go through the valley or up in the mountain gorges or still farther up in the mining camps where the snow never melts from the shady side of the log cabins, and you will find this noble character, Reverend Stephen Grannon, doing his good work for the poor—ministering to their wants and endeavoring to lift humanity into higher walks, physically, morally, and spiritually."

"I am glad you have told me all this," replied Roderick. "It increases my already high opinion of the parson."

"He is a veritable shepherd among the people," continued Major Hampton. "Reverend Grannon is the true flockmaster of Wyoming. The people are frequently unruly, boisterous, intemperate and immoral, yet he treats them with greatest consideration and seeks to persuade and lead them away from their sins and transgressions. Yes, he is a great flockmaster—he is well named The Flockmaster."

Both were silent for a few moments. Then the Major, as if suddenly remembering something, looked up and said: "He tells me Scotty Meisch is getting along fine over in the *Dillon Doublejack* printing office."

"I am glad to hear that," exclaimed Roderick. "It is good to have saved at least one lad from going the way of those outlaws of Jack Creek. I have never forgotten that ghastly midnight scene— the massacred sheep and the burning herders' wagons."

"Well, what can you expect?" asked the Major. "When the social waters are poisoned at the fountain head, the whole course of the stream becomes pernicious. In this state of Wyoming the standard of political decency is not high. The people have no real leaders to look up to. The United States Senator, F. E. Greed, sets a pernicious example to the rising generation. He violates laws in scores of instances because of his greed and grafting proclivities, and his bribed supporters go on year after year supporting him. What the state needs is a leader. High-minded leaders are priceless. Their thoughts and their deeds are the richest legacy to a state or a community. Great leaders are beacon lights kindled upon the mountain peaks of the centuries, illuminating the mental and moral atmosphere of civilization. The history of the world—of a nation, of a state and of a community—is the story of their epochal deeds, while man's advancement is only the lengthened shadow of their moral, spiritual and temporal examples. Leaders come up from the crowd, from among the poor and the lowly. They are immediately recognized by the great mass of the people and invariably crowned, although sometimes it is a crown of thorns that they are compelled to wear and endure for upholding priceless principles in their endeavor to lead humanity to a higher plane. However," concluded the Major, "the world is growing better. The nimble-fingered, tilltapping, porch-climbing derelicts in politics and commercialism are becoming unpopular. The reprehensible methods in all avenues of life are being condemned instead of condoned—the goats are being cast out from among the sheep."

"You interest me very much, Major," said Roderick. "Your ideals are so high, your aims so decent and right, that it is a pleasure to hear you talk. I am a firm believer," Roderick went on, "in the justice of the doctrine that all men are created free and equal."

"It is a sad commentary," replied Major Hampton, "in this land where liberty is cherished and our Government corner-stoned upon the theory that all men are free and equal, that even the soberest of us are compelled, my dear Roderick, to regard such affirmations as blasphemous. To illustrate: An employee in one of the big manufacturing combinations committed a burglary—almost petty larceny in its smallness—another case of Jean Valjean stealing bread for his children—and yet he was tried before an alleged court of justice and sent to the penitentiary for ten years. The head of the same institution pillaged multiplied millions from the poor in unjust and lawless extortions. When he was caught red-handed in his lawbreaking, instead of sharing a prison cell with the poor man our courts indulgently permitted this great highwayman six months' time in which to reorganize and have legalized his methods of stealing."

"Such rank injustice," exclaimed Roderick, "makes my blood tingle with indignation. It is surely high time a determined crusade was led against the privileged classes."

The Major made no reply but after a little, looking up from the open grate and turning to Roderick, he asked him if he was aware that the next day was the annual meeting of the stockholders of the Encampment Mine and Smelting Company.

"Oh, is it?" said Roderick. "Some time ago I noticed something in the newspapers about the meeting, but as it was of no particular moment to me I had forgotten it."

"Yes," said Major Hampton, "and I guess I will now tell you

that I have been holding a secret from you."

"That so?" exclaimed Roderick questioningly.

"You will remember," the Major went on, "that I left you in Denver after we made the big ore shipment and that I was away for three or four weeks. Well, I went to New York, employed two or three big brokers down on Wall Street, and commenced buying Encampment Mine and Smelter Company stock on the exchange. Working jointly with a new friend I have discovered, a professional man of finance yet a true friend of humanity, I have absolute control of the stock today."

"You have?" exclaimed Roderick. "You own a control of the stock in this great smelter and the Ferris-Haggerty mine?"

"Yes, the whole enterprise is virtually in our ownership. Well, something is going to happen tomorrow at the stockholders' meeting which I fear will not be pleasant to certain individuals. But duty compels me to pursue a course I have mapped out. My chosen work in life is to serve the poor, yet in trying to fulfill this mission I harbor no resentful thoughts against the rich as a class nor do I intend for them any unfair treatment."

"If the people only knew," remarked Roderick, softly, "you are without doubt one of the richest men in this part of the country and yet you so honestly prefer the simple life."

"There are two kinds of rich people," continued the Major. "One class is arrogant and unfeeling; they hoard money by fair means or foul for money's sake and for the power it brings. The other class use their wealth not to oppress but to relieve the worthy poor. Personally, Warfield, I do not regard the money which accident has made mine as being in any sense a personal possession. Rather do I hold it as a trust fund. Of course I am grateful. The money enlarges my opportunity to do things for my fellows that I wish to do."

The Major paused a moment, then resumed: "Do you remember, Roderick, when I first told you, Jim Rankin and the others about my hidden mine that I said there were six men in the world whom I held in highest esteem?"

221

"I remember well," assented Roderick.

"Well, five of you were present then—Tom Sun, Boney Earnest, and Grant Jones, with yourself and Jim. For the absent sixth one I specifically reserved a share in my prosperity, although at the time I withheld his name. Now you know it He is the one entitled to most consideration among us all—the Reverend Stephen Grannon."

"Of course he is," concurred Roderick, with hearty conviction. "He can do more good in the world than all the rest of us together, yourself excepted, Major."

"At present, perhaps," said Buell Hampton. "But let his shining example be an incentive to you all—to us all. Well, in a confidential way, I will tell you, Roderick, that when in New York I also purchased a large block of bonds that yields an income of something like $20,000 per year. This income I have legally turned over with proper writings to the Reverend Stephen Grannon, and already I think you will discover a vast improvement in the mining camps and throughout the valleys among the poor. For Stephen Grannon is a godly man and a true humanitarian."

"My word, but that's great—that's grand!" murmured Roderick with deep enthusiasm. And he gazed at Buell Hampton's noble soul-lit face admiringly.

The Major rose to his feet—his usual method of intimating that he wished to be alone. Roderick grasped his hand, and would have spoken further, but Buell Hampton interrupted him.

"Say no more, my dear boy. I am glad that you have been interested in what I had to say tonight. The veil was lifted and you saw me as I am—anxious to be of benefit to my fellows. I shall indeed be proud if you find these doctrines not merely acceptable to yourself, but in some degree at least stimulative in your acts toward the worthy poor and lowly as the years come and go."

As Roderick walked slowly along the street deep in thought over Buell Hampton's words, he came suddenly upon W. B. Grady and several well dressed strangers at a street corner. The visitors, he surmised, were eastern directors of the big smelting company who had come to Encampment for the stockholders' meeting on the morrow.

CHAPTER XXVIII.

JUSTICE FOR THE WORKERS

THE next morning at ten o'clock, Major Buell Hampton walked down to the smelter office. He was met at the door of the directors' room by the general manager, Mr. W. B. Grady. Despite a bold front Grady looked careworn and anxious.

"Hold on there," he said as the Major started to enter. "What do you want?" He spoke roughly. "This is a meeting of some gentlemen who are interested in the Smelter."

"Very well," said the Major. "I came down to attend the stockholders' meeting."

"Well, you can't go in," said Grady. "Stockholders' meetings of this company are private. We do not furnish entertainment and gossip for onlookers like a justice of the peace court."

"That may all be true—I hope it is true, Mr. Grady," said the Major, and he looked him in the eyes with more of pity than of anger depicted on his face. The crafty manager cringed before the critical inspection.

"I am here strictly on business," continued Buell Hampton. "I am a stockholder."

"You a stockholder in our Smelter Company?"

"I have that honor," replied the Major, tersely. "Or at least I hold powers of attorney from the largest group of stockholders in your company."

An ashen grey crept into Grady's face.

"What do you mean?" he faltered. "You are not a shareholder of record on our books."

"No, but you will find as shareholders of record the names of

Charles T. Brown, George Edward Reed, Herbert Levy, Daniel W. Higbee, and a few others about whom I need not bother."

A new light broke over Grady. He looked more sickly than ever.

"These are recent purchasers of stock," he said, "in New York and also, if I remember rightly, in Iowa."

"Precisely, and together these buyers now hold the controlling interest in your company. Here are the legal documents constituting me the attorney for all these men." He drew a neat little packet of papers from the breast pocket of his coat. "In other words I am these men—I hold the controlling power, although I did not choose to disclose the fact until this morning. Now, will you please let me pass? Thank you."

If a pistol had been thrust against the ribs of W. B. Grady, he could not have looked more utterly scared. He had stepped aside to let the Major pass and now bluff and bluster changed swiftly to sycophancy.

"All right, Major Hampton," he said, in his most ingratiating manner. "Walk right in and let me introduce you to some of the other stockholders. Of course, only a few of them are here."

The Major followed him into the directors' room and was duly presented.

"This," said Grady with patronizing suavity, "is an old fellow townsman of ours here in Encampment and a friend of mine. Here, Major, take this chair," insisted Grady. "You see we are all a happy family together."

Major Hampton could not but contrast the fawning manner of the general manager before his superiors, the directors of the Company, with his notoriously overbearing and insolent treatment of the workingmen.

"Well," said the chairman, "fortunately we have a very good manager."

"Thank you," said Grady with increased affability.

"For myself, I am pleased and delighted at the general manager's report which I presume it will be in order now to have read. I think we have all seen it in advance."

The Major shook his head in dissent but made no comment.

Thereupon the meeting was called to order, and after the preliminaries were concluded Mr. W. B. Grady proceeded to read a rather brief but very interesting annual report.

His report was not only a business summary of a most successful fiscal year, but also abounded with more or less veiled laudations of himself in his capacity of manager.

Attorney Wm. Henry Carlisle, who combined with his legal position a seat on the board of directors, advised that the election of a directorate for the ensuing year was in order. By this time it was known to the other shareholders present that Major Buell Hampton owned or represented a control of the stock. This rather upset the cut-and-dried program.

W. B. Grady, addressing the chairman, said that he presumed Major Buell Hampton would appreciate being elected a member of the board of directors, and if the Company's attorney, Mr. Carlisle, did not object perhaps it would be well for him to vacate his seat so as to make room for the new incumbent.

Carlisle's face grew very red at this attempted slight but he said nothing.

Major Buell Hampton arose, and addressing the chairman said: "Since I have acquired control of the stock of this Company, I have decided that Mr. Grady shall not be re-elected as a director. But in the first place I wish to ask of all stockholders present what their intentions are regarding the declaring of a dividend?"

With this he resumed his seat.

By every lineament on Grady's face one could see that he was furious.

"I presume," said the chairman, "that it would be proper to follow the suggestion of Mr. Grady, our general manager, and declare a dividend of seventy-two per cent on the capital stock."

Major Buell Hampton, again addressing the chair, remarked that seventy-two per cent, was certainly a fat dividend. But for himself he had purchased a control of the Company's stock for the purpose of introducing some innovations in its management, and in order that there might be no misunderstanding he felt it was now proper to present his views. If any of the directors were not in harmony, why, of course, it would be inadvisable for them to stand for re-election to a directorate over which he intended henceforth to exercise a close supervision.

"I now wish to ask the directors of the Company this question," added the Major. "What about Boney Earnest's dividend?"

He paused for a reply.

For a moment the stockholders and representatives of stockholders present seemed almost dumfounded. They turned to the manager, Mr. Grady, who answered the Major by saying he did not know that Boney Earnest, the dismissed blast furnace foreman, was a stockholder or had any investment in the concern—"it was all news to him," he added with a weak attempt at levity.

Major Hampton had remained standing, and by silent consent all waited for him to reply to this statement.

"Yes, gentlemen," he said quietly, "Boney Earnest may not be a stockholder of record. But all the same he had his all invested in this smelting plant. Day after day, during year after year, he stood before the blast furnace, doing work of a class which few men could endure. It is true he received a daily wage until the date of his dismissal, but he had invested in addition to his daily duties almost a life-time of ripe experience in the particular work he was doing for this concern. In short, he had his all—his strength, his brain and his experience—invested. In these circumstances I object," continued Major Hampton, "to a dividend of seventy-two per cent. I notice from the manager's report that he has made ample allowances for betterments, replacements, and surplus, and even with all these very proper provisions, the enormous possible dividend of seventy-two per cent, still remains. An original capital stock of $500,000 and an annual dividend of $360,000, certainly is a magnificent showing."

Buell Hampton paused and all present clapped their hands gleefully, as if the Major was coming around to their way

227

of thinking.

After silence was restored he proceeded: "Money is worth probably from five per cent, to six per cent, per annum on solid, non-hazardous investments and at least double these figures or more on mining investments which must be regarded as extremely hazardous. It is not, however, worth seventy-two per cent. per annum. Therefore, gentlemen, we will declare a dividend of six per cent, on the capital stock, which will require $30,000. We will then add the capital stock to the pay roll. The pay roll for the last year in round numbers is $1,100,000. The capital stock is $500,000 or a total of both of $1,600,000. We will then declare the remaining $330,000 of earnings into a dividend on the entire $1,600,000 of capital stock and annual pay roll combined, which amounts to a little over twenty per cent. This will give to the shareholders of our company's stock a little more than a twenty-six per cent, dividend."

The Major sat down. Consternation was apparent on every countenance.

"Major," said one of the eastern directors, "may I ask you what would happen and what you would do in carrying out your altruistic dream if the earnings did not amount to even six per cent, on the money actually invested?"

The Major arose again and with great politeness replied: "Probably we would not declare a dividend. If we had but $30,000 that could be legitimately applied to dividend purposes, the amount would belong to the stockholders. But anything above this preferred dividend to the shareholders should be declared on the annual pay roll combined with and added to the capital stock of the company, both classes of investors participating in the surplus over and above six per cent, preferred dividend. The question with me," added the Major, "is this? How many of you directors are in sympathy with the suggestion I have made?"

There came no answer, and he continued: "A while ago I expressed myself against your manager for a position on the directorate. I always have a reason for my decisions. It has come to me," continued the Major, "that while the original cost of this plant may have been $500,000 yet by the wicked manipulation of the 'system' the original shareholders were completely frozen out—legally robbed if you please, of their investment and it is quite probable the Pennsylvania crowd, the present owners or at least those who were the owners before I purchased a control, paid very little in real money but much in duplicity and ripened experience in the ways of the fox and the jackal. I have learned on excellent authority that Mr. W. B. Grady, by stealth and cunning, secured the underlying bonds from one of the former builders of this great plant, and robbed him and left him penniless in his old age. Unless other means of restitution be devised, the reimbursing of those stolen sums out of my private purse will be one of my first duties and one of my greatest pleasures."

Grady rose, his face flushed with passion. But Buell Hampton waved him down with his hand and calmly proceeded: "I will state another innovation. There are seven directors who control the destinies of this company. I now insist that the company's attorney shall be instructed to have the by-laws so amended that the head of each department, beginning at the mine where we extract the ore, then the tramway which carries the ore to the smelter and all the various departments in the smelter including the converter—shall be elected annually by the workers themselves in each of the seven departments. In this way there will be seven foremen; and these seven foremen shall be officially recognized by the amended by-laws of this company as an advisory board of directors, entitled to sit and vote with the regular directors at each monthly meeting and likewise with the stockholders in their annual meeting."

Had a bomb-shell been thrown into the stockholders' meeting greater consternation could not have been evinced'. Finally Attorney Carlisle moved that an adjournment be taken until ten o'clock the next day, at which time the stockholders would re assemble and further consider the unexpected and doubtless vital questions now under consideration. The motion prevailed.

Of course the entire matter hinged first of all upon the election of a directorate. During the adjournment Attorney Carlisle, peeved at Grady's readiness to drop him from the directorate, called on Major Hampton and assured him he was in accord with the views he had expressed and that his every suggestion could be legally complied with by amending the by-laws.

Buell Hampton, however, did not take the hint implied. He was courteous but firm. The old régime had to go—the management must be changed, lock, stock and barrel. Therefore there could be no further utilization of Mr. Carlisle's services as attorney for the company. Baffled and discomfited the lawyer withdrew. He was full of indignation, not against Major Hampton, but against Grady, for he had warned the latter against selling a certain block of stock to part with which had jeopardized control of the corporation. But Grady, in need of money, had replied that there was no risk, the buying being sporadic and the existing directorate in high favor with the stockholders because of its ability and readiness to vote big dividends.

Grady had little dreamed that already considerable blocks of the stock had passed, under various names, into the control of the Keokuk banker, Allen Miller, to whom he had some time before mortgaged his Mine and Smelter Company bonds, and who had reasons of his own for displacing Grady and crippling him still more badly in his finances. Nor had he sensed the danger that the scattered sales of stock in the East had been in reality for a single buyer, Major Buell Hampton. Therefore he had been caught quite unprepared for the combination of forces that was able now to throw him down and out at the first meeting of stockholders. For once the fox had slept and had been caught napping in the short grass, away from the tall timber.

Carlisle had of late been too busy "doing politics," and had allowed matters to drift even though he had seen possible rocks ahead. Now the two old-time confederates were blaming each other—Carlisle denouncing Grady for parting with the stock control, Grady upbraiding Carlisle for neglect in not having taken steps to discover who were the real buyers of the shares being gradually transferred on the company's stock books. The blow, however, had fallen, and there was no means of blocking the transfer of power into new hands.

When the stockholders' meeting reconvened the following morning, Major Buell Hampton submitted the names of five men whom he desired on the directorate. They were—Roderick Warfield, Grant Jones, Boney Earnest and himself, together with Ben Bragdon, who would also take up the duties of attorney for the company. This left only a couple of places to be filled by the eastern stockholders. Two names from among the old directors were offered and accepted. Indeed the selection of directors became a unanimous affair, for seeing themselves utterly defeated both Grady and Carlisle, glaring at each other, had left the room.

Major Hampton's views on corporations and dividends, and his new plan of management for the Smelter Company spread all over the camp with astonishing rapidity, and there was general rejoicing among the miners and laborers.

One employee in the smelter who had been with the company for some three years made the discovery that, while he was receiving three dollars per day, which meant an annual income to himself and family of $1095, his dividend would bring him an extra lump sum of $219 annually.

When figuring this out to his wife he said: "Think of the pairs of shoes it will buy for our kiddies, Bess."

And the woman, an Irishwoman, had replied: "Bless the little darlin's. And hats and coats as well, not to speak of ribbons for the girls. God bless the Major. Sure but he's a wonderful man."

Several workers sitting in a corner of the Red Dog saloon were calculating with pencil and paper their annual dividends on the already famous Buell Hampton plan.

"Boys," said one of them after they had their several accounts figured to the penny, "maybe we won't make the dividend bigger next year—what?"

"I should say," responded another. "I'll do at least twice the work every day of the coming year, because there's now an object for us poor devils to keep busy all the time. We're sharing in the profits, that's just what it means."

"There'll be a great reduction in breakage and waste," remarked another employee.

"The directors can leave it to us to make the next year's dividend a dandy one."

These were just a few of the grateful encomiums flying around.

On the day following the stockholders' meeting the newly elected directors convened, all except Grant Jones, who was over at Dillon and had not yet been advised of his election. After Major Buell Hampton had been voted into the chair a communication from W. B. Grady was read, stating that he wished to know at once if the directors desired his services for the ensuing year; if so he required a written contract, and should the directors not be ready to comply with this ultimatum they could interpret this letter as a formal resignation. There was a general smile around the directors' table at this bluffing acceptance of the inevitable. It was promptly moved, seconded, and carried unanimously that Mr. W. B. Grady be at once relieved from all further connection with the Smelter Company's plant and business.

Major Hampton then explained that in accordance with his scheme the men in the various departments would be invited at an early date to elect their foremen, and these foremen in turn would have the power, not to elect a general manager, but to recommend one for the final consideration of the directors. Until a permanent appointment was made he suggested that Boney Earnest, the blast furnace foreman dismissed by the late manager because of a personal quarrel, should take charge of the plant, he being a man of tried experience and worthy of absolute trust. This suggestion was promptly turned into a substantive motion and adopted by formal resolution. The meeting adjourned after Director Bragdon in his capacity as company attorney had been instructed to proceed immediately to the work of preparing the proper amendments to the by-laws and taking all legal steps necessary to put into operation the new plan.

Thus neither mine nor smelting plant was shut down, but everything went on without interruption and with greater vigor than before the momentous meetings of stockholders and directors. The only immediate visible effect of the company's radical change in policy was Grady's deposition from the post which had enabled him to exercise a cruel tyranny over the workingmen.

And in the solitude of his home the dismissed manager, broken financially although those around him did not yet know it, was nursing schemes of revenge against Buell Hampton, the man of mystery who had humiliated him and ousted him from power.

Where was his henchman, Bud Bledsoe?—that was the question throbbing in Grady's brain. But Bud Bledsoe was now an outlaw among the hills, with a price on his head and a sheriff's posse ready at a moment's notice to get on his heels.

"By God, I've got to find him," muttered Grady. And that night, in the falling dusk, he rode out alone into the mountain fastnesses.

CHAPTER XXIX.

SLEIGH BELLS

THE morning after the directors' meeting, when Roderick awakened and looked out of the window, he found the air filled with flakes of falling snow. He wasted no time over his toilet. Immediately after breakfast he bundled up snugly and warmly, went over to the livery stable and engaged a team and a sleigh. Soon after, the horses decorated with the best string of sleigh bells the livery could provide, he was holding the reins taut and sailing down through the main street of the little mining town headed for the country. He was going to the Shields ranch. Half a dozen invitations had been extended him during the past weeks, and he told himself he had been neglectful of his old employer.

When he reached the ranch and his team was duly stabled, the sleigh run in out of the storm, he was cordially welcomed by the family before a roaring fire of cheerfulness, and a multitude of questions were poured upon him.

"Why did you not come sooner and what about Major Hampton and the smelter? We have heard all sorts of wonderful things?"

"Why, what have you heard about the Major?" inquired Roderick, endeavoring to get a lead to the things that had evoked such surprise.

"I will tell you," said Barbara. "Papa heard of it the day before yesterday when he was in town. The stockholders were having a meeting, and people said it had turned out to the surprise of everyone that Major Hampton was the owner of a control of the company's stock."

"Yes," replied Roderick, "the rumor is correct. Great things have indeed happened. But haven't you heard from Ben Bragdon?"

"Not a word."

"Well, I suppose he has been too busy reconstructing the by-laws and the company's affairs generally. Major Hampton has put him in as attorney. There's a financial plum for you, Miss Barbara."

"And Mr. Carlisle?" she asked in great astonishment.

"Like W. B. Grady, he is down and out," replied Roderick. "There's been a clean sweep. And behold in me a full-blossomed member of the board of directors. Our chairman, the Major, has handed me over a small library of books about smelting of ores, company management, and so on. He tells me I've got to get busy and learn the business—that I'm slated as vice-president and assistant manager, or something of that kind. What do you think of all that, Mr. Shields? There's a rise in the world for your cowboy and broncho-buster of a few months ago."

The cattle king and all the others warmly congratulated Roderick on his rising fortunes. Dorothy now took the lead in the conversation.

"You folks, keep still a moment until I ask Mr. Warfield just one question," she said eagerly.

"Oh," exclaimed Roderick, quickly, "I can answer the question. No, Grant Jones has not been over to Encampment for quite a while."

A general laugh followed.

"He has a devil over at his office," added Roderick gravely.

"A what?" they exclaimed.

"A devil. You surely know what a devil in a printing office is? It is a young fellow who washes the ink from the rolls and cleans the type or something of that sort—sweeps out, makes fires and does a wholesale janitor business. If he is faithful for fifteen or twenty years, then he learns to set type and becomes a printer. Grant is breaking his new devil in. Scotty Meisch, formerly one of your father's cowboys, is his name."

"Oh, little Scotty," exclaimed Barbara. "I remember him."

"Well, does that necessarily keep Grant away?" asked Dorothy.

"Oh, no, he is not necessarily kept away. He is probably a believer, Miss Dorothy, that absence makes the heart grow fonder.' I was very disappointed," Roderick went hurriedly on, smiling, "that Grant was not in town to share the sleigh with me in coming over this morning. Of course he doesn't know it yet, but he also has been elected as one of the directors of the Encampment Mine and Smelter Company."

"He has?" exclaimed Dorothy, her face lighting: "My word, but he'll be all puffed up, won't he?"

"Oh, no," replied Roderick, "Grant is a very sensible fellow and he selects his friends and associates with marked discrimination."

"Well, that's what I think," concurred Dorothy emphatically.

She was not a little embarrassed by a second ebullition of general laughter. There was a flush of rising color on her pretty cheeks.

"Well, I don't care," she added bravely. "If I like anybody I let them know about it, and that's all there is to be said."

While luncheon was in progress, Roderick suggested that as the sleighing was very good and his sleigh a very large one—the seat exceedingly wide—the young ladies should come sleigh-riding with him in the afternoon.

"Splendid," shouted the sisters in unison. "Certainly, we will be delighted provided mother has no objections."

"Oh, no," said Mrs. Shields, good-naturedly. "This first snow of the season makes me feel like having a sleigh-ride myself. But, there, your seat certainly won't take four of us, and I know that Mr. Shields is too busy to think of getting out his sleigh this afternoon."

"Well, I'LL tell you what I'll do, Mrs. Shields," said Roderick, stirring his coffee. "I'll take you for a ride first. We will go as far as the river and back again, and then if the young ladies are real good why of course I'll give them the next spin."

"Oh, no," said Mrs. Shields, "you young people go on and have your sleigh ride and a good time."

"No," objected Barbara. "You shall have the first sleigh ride, Mama, and if you don't go then Dorothy and I stay at home."

"Come now, Mrs. Shields," urged Roderick, "accept my invitation, for I see if you don't I shall not be able to persuade the young ladies to come."

"Yes, Mother," said Dorothy, "it is just lovely of him to invite you, and certainly the sleigh ride will be invigorating. The truth is, we girls will enjoy the ride afterwards doubly if we know you have had the first ride of the season before we have ours."

"Very well," said Mrs. Shields, "since you all insist, so let it be."

Soon after Roderick's team was hitched to the sleigh and came jingling down to the front gate. Mrs. Shields was tucked snugly in under the robes and away they dashed with sleigh bells jingling, down the road towards the Platte River several miles away.

When they got back Barbara and Dorothy were in readiness, and Roderick started away with them amid much merry laughter and promises from the girls to be home when they got home but not before. The snow was still falling in great big flakes and the cushion beneath the runners was soft and thick. Mile followed mile, and it was late in the afternoon when the sleighing party found themselves in Encampment. Roderick insisted that the young ladies should have supper at the Hotel Bonhomme; they would start on the return trip home immediately afterwards.

When the sleigh drove up to the hotel, who should be looking out of the front door but Grant Jones? He rushed outside and assisted the sisters to alight.

"I will be back in a few minutes," shouted Roderick, as he dashed away to the livery stable.

"Say, Joe," said Roderick while the horses were being unhitched, "I will want the rig again after dinner, and Grant Jones will also want a sleigh."

"All right," replied the stableman. "I can fix him out all right and everything will be in readiness. Just telephone and I'll send the rig over to the hotel."

At the dinner table Grant Jones was at his best. He had already heard about the Smelter Company affairs and his own election as a director, and waved the topic aside. It was the surprise of seeing Dorothy that filled him with good-humor and joviality. As the meal progressed he turned to Roderick and said: "Oh, yes, Roderick, I've just been hearing from Scotty Meisch that during the summer months you learned to be a great trout fisherman."

"Yes," replied Roderick with a smile, "I certainly had a great trout-fishing experience."

"Where?" asked Barbara quickly.

"On the South Fork of the Encampment River."

"Now, Mr. Roderick Warfield," said Barbara quite emphatically, "I invited you to go trout fishing with me a good many times, and you told me I should be the one to teach you the gentle art. Instead of this you go away and learn to catch trout all alone. How many did you catch?"

Roderick reddened with embarrassment.

"Twenty-six," he said.

"Well, that was a pretty good catch for a novice. How big were they?"

"About two pounds," Roderick answered, absent-mindedly.

Grant Jones was fairly choking with laughter. "I say, Barbara," he began.

"I didn't go trout fishing alone," interrupted Roderick quickly.

"Look here, Barbara," persisted Grant, calling to her across the table. But Barbara was all attention to Roderick.

"Who went with you?" she inquired.

"Miss Gail Holden," he replied and his face was actually crimson.

Barbara laid down her knife and fork and leaned back in her chair, placed her arms akimbo with her pretty hands on her slender waist line, and looked at Roderick as if she were an injured child. Finally she said: "Trifler!" Then everybody laughed at Roderick's confusion.

But he quickly recovered himself.

"Trifler yourself!" he laughed back in rejoinder. "What about

Ben Bragdon? What would he have said had we gone trout-fishing together?"

"You were not out of the running then," said Barbara archly.

"Oh, yes, I was, although the secret was to be kept until after the nomination for senator."

It was Barbara's turn now to blush. She looked around in some bewilderment. Grant had bestowed a vigorous kick on Roderick's shins beneath the table. Only then did Roderick realize that he had broken a confidence. Dorothy was eyeing Grant reproachfully. It was a case of broken faith all round.

"Well, you sisters have no secrets from each other," exclaimed Roderick, meeting the situation with a bright smile. "In just the same way Grant and I are chums and brothers. Besides it was a friendly warning. I was saved in time from the danger of shattered hopes and a broken heart, Miss Barbara."

"So went fishing for consolation," she replied with a smile.

"And found it," laughed Grant.

"Who says that?" demanded Roderick, sternly. "Miss Holden would have every reason seriously to object."

"The devil says it," replied Grant, assuming a grave countenance.

"That's a poor joke," said Roderick, offended.

"Oh, Scotty Meisch is an observant lad," remarked the editor drily.

"The printer's devil!" cried Dorothy, clapping her hands. And all four laughed heartily—Roderick most heartily of all despite his momentary dudgeon.

"Then since all these whispers are going about," remarked Barbara when quiet was restored, "I think it will be advisable for me to have a heart-to-heart talk with Gail."

"Oh, please don't," faltered Roderick. "Really, you know, there's no foundation for all this talk—all this nonsense."

"Indeed? Then all the more need for me to drop her a friendly warning—guard her against shattered hopes and a broken heart and all that sort of thing."

The tables were fairly turned, but Barbara, with quick woman's wit, saw that Roderick was really pained at the thought lest Gail Holden might learn of this jesting with her name.

"Oh, don't be afraid," she said, reassuringly. "We three will keep your secret, young man. We are all chums and brothers, aren't we now?" And with one accord, laughing yet serious too, they all shook hands to seal the bond, and any breaches of confidence in the past were forgiven and forgotten.

It had been a merry supper party, but it was now time to be starting for the ranch. As they rose from the table Roderick turned to Grant and said: "You will have to excuse me, old boy, as I am taking the ladies home."

"Taking the ladies home? Well, ain't I goin' along?" asked Grant, with a doleful look at Dorothy.

"No room in our sleigh," said Roderick coldly.

"Roderick," said Grant, half sotto voce, "you are cruel." But Roderick was unsympathetic and did not even smile. He turned away indifferently. Drawing Barbara aside, he told her in an undertone of the arrangements he had made with the livery stable for an extra sleigh.

"Then you'll be alone with me," she said, with an amused smile. "Won't you be afraid? Broken heart, etc?"

"Not now," he replied sturdily.

"Or of Mr. Bragdon? He mightn't like it, you know."

"Oh, I'm not afraid of him," laughed Roderick. "And I guess he will trust me—and you," he added gently and with a chivalrous little bow.

Shortly the sleighs were brought round to the hotel. Grant was beside himself with delight when he discovered the extra rig for himself and Dorothy, and he laughingly shouted to Roderick: "I say, old man, you're the best ever." Soon the merrymakers were tucked snugly beneath the lap robes, and were speeding over the glistening expanse of snow to the joyous tinkle of the silver bells.

CHAPTER XXX.

WHITLEY ADAMS BLOWS IN

RODERICK WARFIELD'S election to a seat on the board of directors of the Encampment Mine and Smelter Company had for him a series of most unexpected consequences. He had had no knowledge that Uncle Allen Miller and a number of his financial followers in Iowa were now large stockholders in the corporation. Nor had he been aware that Major Buell Hampton, after his journey to New York, had visited the Keokuk banker. The Major had learned from his brokers in Wall Street that Allen Miller was on the market for this particular stock and had already acquired a considerable holding. Hence his flying business visit to Keokuk, which had resulted in the combination of forces that had gained the control and ousted Grady, Carlisle, and their pawns on the old directorate.

Major Hampton had since been in continuous correspondence with the banker, but had never for a moment associated the names of Allen Miller and Roderick Warfield as having any possible connection by relationship or otherwise. The selection of the new board had been left entirely in Buell Hampton's hands after the banker had given his assent to the profit-sharing scheme. That assent had not been won without considerable argument. The plan upset all the banker's old theories about industrial enterprises. At the same time the shrewd old man of finance was reading the signs of the times, and had long since come to realize that a readjustment of the relations between capital and labor was inevitable. He was all the more inclined to make this experiment, in the first place because he was not going to be bothered with the working out of the practical details, and in the second place because the magnetic personality of Buell Hampton had at once inspired him with confidence both in his ability to do things and in his integrity. Therefore the shrewd old banker had fallen in with the Major's plans, and given him a free hand when entrusting him with the powers of attorney for himself and the other Iowan stockholders.

In point of fact there was another secret motive animating Allen Miller to this line of action. Unless he cooperated with Buell Hampton, the control would remain with W. B. Grady and his associates. And it was Grady whom the banker was after—Grady, the financial shark who had robbed his lifelong friend, General John Holden, of his underlying bonds in the original and now defunct smelter company, at the time when the amalgamation scheme had been devised to freeze out the first founders of the enterprise. General Holden had been the chief victim of this rapacious trick of financial jugglery, and Allen Miller was working secretly to undo the wrong. But the banker was animated not only by reasons of friendship. He had another incentive almost as strong. He wanted to satisfy his keen sense of personal pride toward Roderick Warfield. For the vital cause of quarrel between the old banker and the youth he loved yet had disowned was the unnamed girl he had thrust upon Roderick as a suitable bride because of her fortune. And this fortune had been proved to be illusory on the very day succeeding the rupture that had culminated in Roderick's fine display of scorn and anger, when he had flung himself out of the banker's room and started off for parts unknown to fight his own way in the world.

It was the financial disaster which had overtaken General Holden that had opened Allen Miller's eyes to the truth that he had been utterly wrong in his attempted methods of managing a headstrong, and as the old guardian had thought at the time a wayward, youth like Roderick Warfield. He had bitterly regretted the harsh words that had dared the offender to play football with the world and, as he now realized, had by their sarcastic bitterness driven the high-mettled young man from his boyhood home. He had never doubted Roderick's prowess to make a way for himself by his own unaided efforts, and, despite the quarrel, had always felt sure of the lad's affection. So Roderick one day would come back, to find the latchstring hanging outside the door of his home, the promised place in the bank still awaiting him, and—the pride and dogged determination of the old man would not yield the point—the rich, attractive, and in every way highly eligible bride still available. The only flaw in the program was Gail Holden's fall from fortune, and to repair this had been the object of the banker's continuous and strenuous endeavor.

He had grabbed at the chance of lending money on the Mine and Smelter Company bonds standing in the name of W. B. Grady, which bonds he considered were by moral right really the property of General Holden. But he had lent discreetly, postponing any big advance while he held the documents and nosed around for information that might give some valid reason to dispute their ownership. And in course of time he had made one surprising discovery. Obtaining from General Holden all correspondence with Grady, he had found one sentence in which the sponsor for the new amalgamation scheme had guaranteed the withdrawal of all underlying bonds in the old smelter company before the scheme would be put through. Yet this condition had not been complied with, for Allen Miller had, in the course of tracing every old bond, discovered that five were still in existence and had never been surrendered. They belonged to a widow away back in Pennsylvania who had gone to Europe and whose whereabouts at the time Grady apparently had not been able to ascertain. But the persistent old banker had followed the trail and through his agents in France had purchased this particular parcel of bonds at a high figure. They were few in number and insignificant in face value, but to Allen Miller they were priceless, for these underlying bonds put W. B. Grady in his power and could be made the means eventually of compelling restitution to General Holden of the fortune that had been filched from him. Grady would have to make good or face the criminal charge of a fraudulent transaction.

Buell Hampton had been told nothing about this—it was sufficient for Allen Miller's immediate purpose to have the company control wrested without delay out of Grady's hands. This would render litigation easier, perhaps avoid it altogether— the better alternative, for the law's harassing delays and heart-sickening uncertainties are proverbial. So when Buell Hampton had come to Keokuk in the cause of humanity, to fight for the toilers at the smelter and in the big mine, he had been agreeably surprised to find in the old banker such a ready listener to his philanthropic arguments. The alliance had been struck, with the result that Buell Hampton had been able to swing the stockholders' meeting exactly as he desired.

Up to the very eve of that meeting the Major had kept his counsel and held his hand. The merest hint of the power he possessed might have given time for so astute a knave as Grady to devise some means more or less unscrupulous of repelling the attack. Therefore Buell Hampton had not dropped one word of what he intended to do until he had spoken to Roderick in his home on the night before the stockholders' meeting. Little did either of them know at that time how vitally and directly Roderick was interested in the outcome of the Major's fight for the downtrodden poor.

After the eventful meetings of stockholders and directors it had been Buell Hampton's first duty to send a full report of the proceedings to Allen Miller of Keokuk, whose power of attorney had enabled him to effect the coup deposing Grady and giving a share of the profits to the actual toilers at the furnaces and in the mine. In the course of this report the names of the new directors were set forth. Judge of the old banker's utter amazement when his eyes fell upon the name of—Roderick Warfield. Surprise quickly yielded to joy and delight. The news was telephoned to Aunt Lois. The old banker could not leave town at the moment— an issue of city bonds required his close attention. But that very night an envoy was dispatched to Wyoming in the person of his bright and trusted young clerk, Whitley Adams.

And the first of the series of surprises for Roderick Warfield, one afternoon a few days after the sleigh ride, was the sight of his old college chum tumbling out of a bob-sled which, in default of coaching facilities, had brought him over from the railroad at Rawlins. Whitley had stopped the sled in the main street along which, in the crisp sunshine that had followed the heavy snowfall, Roderick happened to be strolling.

"Hello, old scout," cried the new arrival with all the ease of a veteran globe-trotter.

"Where in thunder did you drop from!" exclaimed Roderick, clutching at his hand.

"From Iowa's sun-kissed cornfields to Wyoming's snow-capped hills," laughed Whitley, humming the tune of the hymn he was parodying.

"What has brought you here?"

"Lots of things. A letter for you, to begin with."

"From whom?"

"Your Uncle Allen Miller."

"But he doesn't know I'm here, does he?"

"The whole world knows you're here, dear boy," replied Whitley, pulling the latest issue of the *Encampment Herald* out of his pocket. "Why, you've become famous—a director of the great smelting corporation." And he flourished the journal aloft.

"Who sent you that paper?"

"Major Buell Hampton, of course. At least he sent it to your uncle."

"Get out. You're kidding, Whitley."

"No kidding about me, old man. Those irresponsible days are now over." Whitley drew himself up with great dignity. "If Buell Hampton hasn't told you that he came to Keokuk and made the acquaintance of Banker Allen Miller, well, that's his affair, not mine. Where shall we have dinner? I'm as hungry as a grizzly."

"Wait a moment, Whitley. Do you mean to tell me Uncle Allen

knows the Major?"

"Sure. They've been as thick as thieves—or rather I should say as close as twins—Oh, that reminds me. How are dear Barbara and Dorothy?"

"Shut up—stop your nonsense. What were you going to say?"

"Oh, just this, that ever since the Major paid us a visit at Keokuk, letters have been passing nearly every week between him and the banker. I've seen all the correspondence."

"I have known nothing about this," said Roderick, in great perplexity.

"Well, doubtless you are not in the same confidential position as I occupy," replied Whitley airily. "But of course now that you are a director of the company you'll come to know—or at least should know; that's part of your duties—that Allen Miller is a big stockholder."

There flashed to Roderick's mind Buell Hampton's vague reference, on the night preceding the stockholders' meeting, to some new friend, a professional man of finance, with whom he held joint control of the company's stock.

"A true friend of humanity," he murmured, recalling the Major's words. "Great Scott, that's about the last identification tag I would have expected for Uncle Allen."

"Well, old chap," interposed Whitley, "don't mumble in conundrums. You take it from me that Buell Hampton and your uncle are financial pals—associates might be the more dignified word. That's no doubt why the Major nominated you for the board of directors."

Roderick paled.

"By God, if that's the case, I'll resign tomorrow. I've been standing on my own feet here. I owe nothing to Uncle Allen."

"There now, put all that touchy pride in your pocket, Roderick. By jingo, you're worse than Banker Miller himself. But I took the old gentleman down a few pegs the afternoon he learned that you were in Wyoming," Whitley rambled on, laughing. "He declared that I must have known your hiding place all the time."

"And you answered?"

"Owned up at once, of course. Told him that others besides himself could be trusted with a confidence—that neither he nor anybody else could have bulldosed me into betraying a client. A client—that's what I called you, old man. Oh, you can't give me business points nowadays. What do you think he said in reply?"

"Ordered you out of the room, I suppose."

"Not on your life! Commended my sagacity, my trustworthiness; told me again that I was a born banker, one after his own heart. And to show that he meant what he said, he raised my salary five dollars a week, and handed me over fifty dollars extra spending money for this trip. What do you think of that?"

"I can't express a thought—I'm too much surprised over the whole train of events."

"Oh, I suppose he knew I'd have to buy a few boxes of candy for the beautiful Wyoming girls," Whitley went on. "I had told him after my first trip here that they were regular stunners—that they had been buzzing about me like flies around a pot of honey. Oh, he laughed all right. I know how to manage the old fellow— was half afraid he'd be coming along himself instead of sending me this time. But he bade me tell you he couldn't possibly get away from Keokuk just now. Which reminds me—here's your letter, old man; and one, too, from Aunt Lois. She saw me off at the train, and gave me a kiss to pass on to you." Whitley, a bunch of letters in his hand, made a movement as if to bestow upon Roderick the osculatory salute with which he had been entrusted. But Roderick, smiling in spite of himself, pushed him back.

"You irrepressible donkey: Hand over my letters."

"Oh, yes, the letters." Whitley began to sort the bunch of correspondence. "This is for Buell Hampton. And this is for Ben Bragdon. I suppose he's in town?"

"Yes. But he's pretty busy."

"Won't be too busy to attend to me, I reckon. Then W. B. Grady"—he was fingering a neatly folded, legal looking document "I hope that Grady hasn't cleared out from Encampment yet."

"Not that I've heard. In fact I saw him on the street this morning. You seem to have business with everyone in town."

"Just about hits it, old man. And General John Holden. Ah, yes, that reminds me," Whitley suspended his sorting of the letters, and looked up. "How's the college widow, old man?"

Roderick reddened.

"That's all off," he answered stiffly.

"I guessed that's just what would happen. Best so, by a long chalk, So Stella Rain is free again. Guess I'll stop off on my way home, and take a run to Galesburg. Nice girl, you know, Stella. No saying but I might make an impression now she is"—

"Stella Rain is married," interrupted Roderick, speaking sharply and shortly.

"You don't say? Too bad."

"Happily married, I tell you—to some rich fellow."

"Oh, then, she threw you over, did she? Ho, ho, ho! But that's all right, old fellow. Saves all complications. And Gail, how's Gail? Oh, she's a pipit pin.

"By gad, Whitley, you shut up. Come and have your dinner. But you haven't given me my letters yet."

"Ah, I forgot Well this one is for General Holden. I've got to see him at once."

"What about?"

"Confidential business, my friend. Ask no questions for I want to be spared the pain of refusing you the slightest information. Great guns, Rod, we financial men, you know, hold more secrets than a father confessor. We've got to keep our mouths shut all the time, even to our best friends. This is my letter of credit to your local bank—no limit, mind you, on my sight drafts on Keokuk. Ah, yes, here are your letters—one from Aunt Lois, the other from your old guardian. Hope he has put a fat check inside."

"I don't need his checks—if there's any check here, you can take it back." And Roderick ripped open the envelope.

But there was no offending slip of colored paper enclosed, and he thrust both the letters unread into his pocket.

"Now we'll dine," he said.

"A moment, please." And Whitley turned to the driver of the bob-sled waiting in the middle of the road.

"Go and get your dinner, my man," he called out. "Then hitch fresh horses in that sled, and come to my hotel, the Bonhomme; that's the best place in town, if I remember right, Roderick," he said with a glance at his friend. Then he continued to the driver: "Charge everything to me, and don't be longer than a couple of hours. Now come along, Roderick. You dine with me—oh, I have an ample expense fund. But I'm sorry I'll have to leave you immediately after dinner."

Roderick was overwhelmed by all this grandiloquence. He hardly dared to take his old chum's arm as they walked along the street. But at last he stopped, burst out laughing, and slapped the man of affairs squarely between the shoulders.

"Whitley, old chap, you're a wonder. You play the part to perfection."

"Play the part?" protested Whitley, with a fine assumption of dignity. "I *am* the part—the real thing. I'm your rich old uncle's right hand man, and don't you forget it. Would a little ready cash now be a convenience?"

Then Whitley's arm went round his comrade's neck, and with a simultaneous whoop of laughter they passed into the hotel.

But during the next twenty-four hours Roderick saw very little of his college chum. And during the same period the said college chum accomplished some very remarkable things. Immediately after dinner the bob-sled sped out to Conchshell ranch, and General Holden signed the legal papers that attached, as a measure of precaution, the bonds standing in the name of W. B. Grady and now in the custody of the bank at Keokuk as security for a loan. And for half the night Attorney Ben Bragdon and Whitley Adams were closeted with W. B. Grady in a private parlor of the hotel, and the fight was fought out for legal possession of the fraudulently acquired bonds—a fight that put the issue squarely up to Grady whether he would accept Banker

Allen Miller's terms of surrender or face a criminal charge. It was in the grey of the breaking dawn that the vanquished Grady crept out of the hotel, wiping the beads of cold sweat from his brow, while Whitley was quietly folding up the properly signed transfers that gave back to General Holden bonds of equal value to those of which he had been robbed by false pretences and promises never fulfilled.

In the morning Whitley was again at the Conchshell ranch, and breakfasted with the General and his daughter. It was the latter who bound him to secrecy—to the solemn promise that neither he nor Mr. Bragdon should divulge to anyone the story of this restored family fortune. Gail declared that she was going to make good with her dairy cattle venture, that neither she nor her father wanted to return to the old life of fashion and society at Quincy, that they had no wish to appear as rich folks. Whitley listened to all the arguments, understood, and promised. And that the transfer of the bonds should not be connected with General Holden's name it was agreed that for the present they should pass to Banker Allen Miller as family trustee.

Whitley's chest had expanded fully two inches when he drove away, the trusted emissary for the carrying into effect of these decrees. He had had a few minutes alone with Gail and, introducing the name of Roderick Warfield in a casual way, had assured her that he, like everyone else, would know nothing about these strictly family affairs. She had blushed a little, reiterated her thanks, and at parting had, he could have sworn, given him an extra friendly pressure of her dainty little fingers.

Whitley drove straight to Ben Bragdon's office, and took the precaution of adding to the professional seal of secrecy a direct expression from the General of his wishes in the matter.

During the afternoon the young banker from Keokuk personally delivered the letter from Allen Miller addressed to Major Buell Hampton. Whitley had insisted upon Roderick accompanying him. The relationship between Roderick and Banker Miller was now revealed. The Major received the news without much surprise.

"In the loom of life," he said, with great solemnity, "the shuttle of destiny weaves the threads of individual lives into a pattern which is only disclosed as time goes on. Thus are the destinies of men interwoven without their knowing either the how or the why. Roderick, my dear fellow, from this day on we are simply more closely bound to each other than ever."

The evening was spent at the Shields ranch. Whitley congratulated Barbara on her engagement to Ben Bragdon, and then took Dorothy's breath away by congratulating her and the absent Grant Jones as well.

Dorothy blushed furiously, and disowned the soft impeachment; to which Whitley replied that unless her sweetheart got busy promptly and toed the line, he himself was coming back to Encampment to cut out so tardy a wooer. "Tell Grant Jones from me," he said, "that it's taking chances to leave the tempting peach upon the tree." She slapped his hand playfully for his audacity, and Roderick hurried the flippant financier out of the room.

At midnight, in the bright moonlight, Whitley departed for Rawlins to catch his train. Nothing could persuade him to prolong his visit—Banker Miller would be hopping around like a cat on hot bricks, the bank going to wreck and ruin if he did not hurry back, the girls of Keokuk growing quite jealous of the beauties of Wyoming.

Like a whiff of sweet perfume the joyous youth was gone.

CHAPTER XXXI.

RODERICK'S DISCOVERY

NOTWITHSTANDING their change in fortunes, Roderick and Grant still made the editor's shack their home—the old place endeared to them by many fond associations. A few days after Whitley Adams' visit they were seated at the breakfast table, and Grant had proposed that they should go deer hunting.

"Excellent weather," he explained, "as the snow is just deep enough up in the mountains to drive the deer down. Finest sport in the world. Nothing like going after big game."

"You almost persuade me," said Roderick, setting down his coffee and looking at Grant with increased interest. "All the same I hate to leave the smelter plant even for a day or two. You see I'm just beginning to get a hang of the business, and I've quite made up my mind to master it."

"Oh, let it rip. You're not tied down to the works, are you?"

"Certainly not—you don't imagine I think myself qualified as yet to be tied down. 'But what about guns?"

"Oh, well," said Grant, "I have a.32 Winchester, one that has got a record too, by gunnies, as Jim Rankin would say. Its record is great."

"How big a record?" inquired Roderick.

"Seven deer," answered Grant.

"All your own killing?"

"Well, no. To be downright truthful since you force me to particularize, I'll admit I never killed but one deer with it. But that does not interfere with the gun's record." And then he continued: "I have no doubt Major Hampton will be delighted to loan you his gun. He has a .30 calibre Government Springfield and in his hands it has accounted for many a buck."

After breakfast they called on Major Hampton.

"Good morning, gentlemen," said the Major as he opened the door and bade them welcome.

"We are going deer hunting," said Grant, quite enthusiastically. "I have a gun, but this-would-be-slayer-of-big-game, Roderick, is gunless and when we return he may be deerless. Was just wondering, Major, if you would care to loan your famous deer killer to him. Guess its long record," he added, "would fill a book."

"Why, certainly," replied the Major in an absent-minded way; and then presently he went on: "Do not interpret my hesitation as unwillingness to accommodate you. It is well you came just when you did, for within half an hour I myself will be starting for the mountains and my mind was pre-occupied with my own little preparations."

"Can't you come with us, Major?" asked Grant.

"But I won't be depriving you of your gun?" enquired Roderick simultaneously.

"I answer 'no' to both questions," was the smiling response. "I am going out on one of my lonesome excursions—to commune with Nature face to face for a brief spell. And when I go I need no rifle—even the very deer there are my trustful friends."

Then turning he took down his rifle from its accustomed place and brought it over to Roderick.

"This old Springfield has served me well," he said, smiling in his own magnificent way. "It was my friend in dark days of need. In my lifetime, gentlemen, I have never spilled the blood of any living thing wantonly, and I do not believe man is justified in taking the life of even a worm on the pathway, a rabbit in the hills, cattle or sheep in the fields, or a deer in the wilds unless it is for food and to sustain life."

Then suddenly looking at Grant the Major said: "I understand W. R. Grady is up in the hills?"

"Yes, so I have heard."

253

"What is he doing? Looking for a mine?"

"Possibly. They say he is at the Thomas Boarding House most of the time up at Battle."

"Guess," interrupted Roderick, "that he is not very happy since the new order of things—your new plan, Major—put him out of business."

"Perhaps he is getting in touch again with his old heeler, Bud Bledsoe," suggested Grant. "That outlaw gang has been lying low for quite a while, but I'm expecting to hear about some new bit of deviltry any day. Am in need of a corking good newspaper story."

"Well, since you are bent on hunting big game," laughed the Major, "these miscreants might provide you with all the exciting sport you are wanting."

"Oh, a brace of good fat bucks will be good enough for us. Where's the likeliest place to start from, Major? You're the local authority on these matters."

"You know where Spirit River Falls are?" asked Buell Hampton.

"I've heard of them but have never been there," replied Grant.

"I think that I've seen them from above," observed Roderick, "but I don't know the way to them."

"Well, you know where Gid Sutton's half-way house is located?"

"Certainly," replied Roderick. "I was there less than a month ago."

"Well, Spirit River Falls are located about six or seven miles south and east of the half-way house. I advise that one of you go up the South Fork of the Encampment River and the other keep to the right and go over the hills past Conchshell ranch into a park plateau to the south; then have your meeting place this evening in an old log structure that you will find about three-fourths of a mile directly through the timber southeast from the falls. If you are wise, you will load up two or three burros, send them with a trusty, and have him make camp for you in this old deserted hut. You will find a cup of coffee, a rasher of bacon and a few sandwiches very appetizing by the time you have tramped all day in your deer-hunting quest And the country all around is full of deer."

The young men thanked him warmly for his advice.

"In point of fact," continued Buell Hampton, "I'll be up in the same region myself. But I'm travelling light and will have the start of you. Moreover, we can very easily lose each other in that rugged country of rocks and timber. But don't mistake me for a buck, Roderick, if you catch sight of my old sombrero among the brushwood;" saying which he reached for the broad-brimmed slouch hat hanging against the wall.

"I'll take mighty good care," replied Roderick. "But I hope we'll run up against you, Major, all the same."

"No, you won't find me," answered Buell Hampton, with a quiet smile. "I'll be hidden from all the world. Follow the deer, young men, and the best of luck to you."

The two comrades started away in high feather, anticipating great results from the tip given them by the veteran hunter. Going straight to the livery barn, they rigged out three burros, and sent with them one of the stablemen who, besides being a fairly good cook, happened to be familiar with the trail to Spirit River Falls, and also knew the location of the "hunter's hut" as they found the old log structure indicated by Buell Hampton was locally named.

These arrangements concluded, Roderick and Grant started for the hills. Some half a mile from Encampment they separated—Jones going along the east bank of the South Fork of the Encampment River and Roderick following the North Fork until he came to Conchshell canyon. The day was an ideal one for a deer hunt. There was not a breath of wind. The sky was overcast in a threatening manner as if it were full of snow that was liable to flutter down at the slightest provocation.

As Roderick reached the plateau that constituted the Conchshell ranch he concluded to bear to the left and as he said to himself "Keep away from temptation." He was out hunting wild deer that day and he must not permit himself to make calls on a sweet-throated songster like Gail. On through the open fields and over the fences and into a thick growth of pines and firs, where he plodded his way through snow that crunched and cried loudly under his feet Indeed the stillness of everything excepting his own walking began to grate on his nerves and he said to himself that surely a whitetailed deer with ordinary alertness could hear him walking even if it were half a mile away.

As he trudged along mile after mile he was very watchful for game or tracks, but nothing stirred, no trace of deer was discernible in any direction. He was following the rim of a hill surmounting some boxlike canyons that led away abruptly to the left, while a smooth field or park reached far to the right where the hills were well covered with timber. Here and there an opening of several acres in extent occurred without bush or shrub.

It was perhaps one o'clock in the afternoon and he was becoming a bit leg-weary. Brushing the snow away from a huge boulder he seated himself for a short rest. Scarcely had he done so than he noticed that occasional flakes of snow were falling. "More snow," he muttered to himself, "and I am a good ways from a cup of coffee if I am any judge."

After he was rested he got up and again moved on. Just then, as he looked down into a box canyon, he saw three deer—a doe and two half-grown fawns. Quickly bringing his gun to his shoulder his first impulse was to fire. But he realized that it would be foolish for the animals were at least five hundred yards away and far below the elevation where he was standing.

"No," he said to himself, "I will leave the rim of this mountain and get down into the canyon."

He hastily retreated, and took a circuitous route intending to head off the deer. In due time he approached the brow of the precipitous bluff and after walking back and forth finally found a place where he believed he could work his way down into the canyon. It was a dangerous undertaking—far more so than Roderick knew—and might have proved his undoing.

He was perhaps half way down the side of the cliff, working his way back and forth, when suddenly some loose stones slipped from under his feet and away he went, sliding in a sitting position down the side of the mountain. He had sufficient presence of mind to hold his gun well away from him to prevent any possible accident from an accidental discharge. The cushioning of the snow under him somewhat slowed his descent, yet he could not stop. Down and down he went, meeting with no obstruction that might have given him a momentary foothold. Presently he saw, to his great relief of mind, that he was headed for a small fir tree that had rooted itself on a ledge near the bottom of the canyon. A moment later his feet came thump against its branches, and while the jar and shock of suddenly arrested motion were very considerable yet they were not enough to be attended with any serious consequences.

Somewhat dazed, he remained seated for a few moments. But soon he found his footing, and pulling himself together, brushed away the snow from his apparel and made sure that his gun was all right. After a glance around he picked his way down some distance farther into the canyon, and then turning to the right along a little ledge started in the direction where he expected to sight the deer higher up the hill.

Suddenly he stopped. There were the deer tracks right before him going down the gorge.

"By George," he muttered aloud, "I did not get far enough down. However, I will follow the tracks." And forthwith he started on the trail, cautiously but highly expectant.

The direction was westerly, but he had not gone far until the canyon made an elbow turn to the south and then a little farther on to the east. "I wonder," said Roderick to himself, "what sort of a maze I am getting into. This canyon is more crooked than an old-fashioned worm fence or a Wyoming political boss."

The box canyon continued to grow deeper and the rocky cliffs higher, zig-zagging first one way and then another until Roderick gave up all pretense of even guessing at the direction he was travelling.

"Strange I have never heard of this narrow box-canyon

before," he thought.

After walking briskly along for about an hour, keeping the tracks of the retreating deer in view, he suddenly came to an opening. A little valley was spread out before him, and to his amazement there were at least a hundred deer herded together in the park-like enclosure.

Roderick rubbed his eyes and looked up at the high and abrupt precipices that surrounded this open valley on every side. It seemed to him that the walls rose sheer and almost perpendicular several hundred feet to the rocky rim above. He followed on down, filled with wonderment, and presently was further astonished by finding several great bubbling springs. Each basin was fully a hundred feet across, and the agitated waters evidently defied freezing, for they fairly boiled in their activity, overflowing and coming together to form quite a big tumbling mountain stream.

Stealthily following on and keeping the great herd in view he mentally speculated on the surprise he would give Grant Jones when he came to display the proofs of his prowess as a hunter of the hills. Surely with his belt full of cartridges and the large number of deer in sight, although as yet too far away to risk a shot, he could add several antlered heads to Grant's collection. The stream grew larger. There were a number of other springs feeding their surplus waters into brooks which eventually all joined the main stream, and he mentally resolved that the next time Gail and he went trout-fishing they would visit this identical spot. He laughed aloud and asked the question: "Will she be mine so that we may come together for a whole week into this beautiful dell?"

The farther he advanced the less snow he found in the strange, rock-fenced valley. The grasses had grown luxuriantly in the summer season, and the deer were browsing in seeming indifference to his presence yet moving on away from him all the time. He began wondering if all this were a mirage or a reality. He looked a second time at the slowly receding herd and again he laughed aloud. "Such foolishness," he exclaimed. "It is an absolute reality, and right here I will make my name and fame as a hunter."

He stopped suddenly, for just across the stream, standing among the boulders and pebbles of an old channel, were four deer, not two hundred feet away. They were looking at him in mild-eyed wonder, one of them a noble, splendidly antlered buck. Lifting the Major's Springfield to his shoulder Roderick sighted along the barrel and fired. Three of the deer ran away. But the buck jumped high into the air, attempted to climb the opposite bank, failed and fell backward.

Hurriedly crossing over the stream and slipping in his excitement off the stones into knee-deep water, he came quickly up to the wounded deer. Instantly the animal bounded to his feet, but fell again. Roderick fired a second shot which reached a vital spot. The magnificent denizen of the hills had been vanquished in the uneven contest with man's superior knowledge and deadly skill.

The novice in huntsman's craft had received all sorts of book instructions and verbal explanations from Grant Jones. So he at once drew his hunting knife, thrust it into the jugular vein of the dying deer, and bled him copiously. Only the hunter knows the exultant feelings of mingled joy and excitement that possessed Roderick at that moment. His first deer! Resting the gun against a small cottonwood tree that grew on a raised bank between the old channel and the flowing waters, he walked to the stream, washed the crimson from his knife, and returned the weapon to its sheath.

Then he looked around to get his bearings. He knew he had come with the waters from what seemed to be a westerly direction. The stream was evidently flowing toward the east. As he walked along in the old channel over the sandbar he kicked the rocks and pebbles indifferently, and then stopped suddenly, gasped and looked about him.

On every side the mountains rose precipitately fully six or

seven hundred feet. There was no visible outlet for the stream.

"Is it possible," he exclaimed with bated breath, "that I am in the lost canyon? And this," he said, stooping down and picking up a nugget of almost pure gold—"is this the sandbar on which my father and Uncle Allen Miller found their treasure yeans and years ago? Marvelous! Marvelous! Marvelous!"

For the moment the slain deer was forgotten. His achievement as a hunter of big game no longer thrilled him. He was overwhelmed by a mightier surge of emotion.

"Yes," he said finally in a low voice of conviction, "this at last is the lost find!"

And he sank down on the gold-strewn pebbly sandbar, limp and helpless, completely overcome.

A minute later he had recovered his composure. He stood erect He gazed down the valley. The startled herd of deer had vanished into the brushwood and low timber.

But there, slowly ascending along the river bed, was the figure of Buell Hampton. Roderick stood stockstill, lost in amazement, waiting.

CHAPTER XXXII.

STAKING THE CLAIMS

SO IT is you who have found my Hidden Valley," said Buell Hampton as he drew near. His voice had a regretful ring, but as he grasped Roderick's hand he added cordially: "I thank God it is you, Roderick. When I heard the rifle shots I was afraid it might be Bud Bledsoe or some of his gang."

"Your hidden valley, Major?" murmured Roderick, interrogatively and with emphasis on the first word.

"Yes, my son—the valley from which I took the carload of rich ore we sold in Denver."

"Great guns, Major. I too have discovered gold—placer gold."

"Where?"

"At your feet. Look." And Roderick stooped and picked up a fine smooth-worn nugget as big as a pigeon's egg. "Look, look, look," continued Roderick. "It is all around us on this sandbar."

"I did not happen on this spot," said Buell Hampton. "The fact is I hardly explored the valley at all. I had all the gold I wanted or could ever want in my own find."

"Then where is that find?"

"Lower down the stream—a dyke of porphyry and white quartz. But you already know the kind of ore Jim Rankin, Tom Sun, and Boney Earnest helped me to get out of the valley. It is quite different from your gold."

The Major stooped, and collected a handful of good-sized nuggets.

"How did you come to find this place, Roderick?" he asked, gazing up at the sheer cliffs around them.

"I have been searching for it," he replied, "since ever I came to Wyoming. Oh, Major, it is a strange story. I hardly know where to begin. But wait. Sit down on that boulder. I have my father's letter with me. You can read it and will then understand."

From an inner pocket Roderick produced the map and letter which had never left his possession, night or day, since his Uncle Allen had handed him the sealed packet in the bank manager's room at Keokuk. Without a word Buell Hampton took the seat indicated, and after a preliminary glance at the map proceeded to read the long epistle left by the old miner, John Warfield, as a dying legacy to his son. Roderick sitting on his heels watched in silence while the other read.

"Your father was a sensible man," remarked Buell Hampton, as at last he refolded the paper. "I like the spirit in which he wrote—the fervent expression of his hope that this wealth will prove a blessing to you instead of a disquieting evil. Yes, you have undoubtedly found your father's lost mine. But, Roderick, why did you not tell me of this before? I would have gladly helped you to a quicker discovery. This map here I would have recognized at a glance as the map of my happy retreat, my Hidden Valley."

"Well, Major, I may seem to have been a bit reticent—or independent, may I call it? But you will remember that it was early in our intimacy when you showed me and the others those rich ore specimens in your home. And you yourself were reticent—bound us to secrecy, yet gave us no-single clue as to the whereabouts of your wonderful discovery."

"Because I wanted to protect this place from intrusion—I indulged in the dream that the treasure of the valley might be made to fall only into worthy hands, which dream could never be realized unless I guarded my secret from one and all."

"Your sentiment I quite understand. But don't you see, Major, it was this very reticence on your part that made me reticent—that virtually sealed my lips? I have often thought of showing you my father's letter, of telling the full reasons that brought me to Wyoming. But to have done so after you had shown us that ore

262

would have been simply to press you for further information—to have asked you to divulge the location of your mine which you had resolved to keep secret so that I might possibly be assisted in the quest for my father's lost claim. I couldn't do that I am sure you will now understand my feelings."

"Fine feelings, Roderick," exclaimed the Major, extending his hand. "Feelings after my own heart I understand them, and can only compliment you on your sturdy independence. But how did you get here?" And again he glanced up the precipitous mountains.

"Well, I think I might almost say I tumbled down into the canyon," laughed Roderick. "I slipped and tobogganed down a steep slope. Then I followed the tracks of four deer I was after, and found myself here. By the way, have you looked at my splendid buck?"

Buell Hampton rose, and as if by force of habit drew his hunting knife and proceeded to dress and gambrel the deer. Roderick watched the skilled hands at work. Before many minutes the carcass was hanging on the peg of a broken limb.

"Certainly, a fine buck," remarked the Major, stepping back admiringly. "Your first, I believe?"

"My very first."

"Not often that a man kills his first deer and discovers a gold mine on the same day, eh?" laughed Buell Hampton. "But where is Grant Jones?"

"I haven't seen him since morning. We followed your directions, and took opposite sides of the river."

"Then he will meet you tonight at the old log hut?"

"That's our arrangement. But how are we to get out of this box-canyon?"

"I can show you an easier way out than the toboggan slide by which you came in," replied the Major, smiling. "At the same time I think I should prefer to follow your tracks, so that in the future I may know this second means of access. I am afraid the secret of this little sequestered valley can be no longer kept from the world. I presume you are going to stake out a claim

263

and record it."

"You bet," laughed Roderick. "There's no sentiment about sequestered valleys or happy retreats in my make-up. Great Scott, there's a cool million dollars of gold lying around right here. I'm going to take no chances of the next man finding the spot. Isn't that common sense, Major?"

"No doubt," replied Buell Hampton, "it is common sense in your case. And you are obviously following your father's bidding in making the fullest and the best use of the wealth he tried so long in vain to rediscover. Are you familiar with the regulations as to staking out a claim?"

"Oh, yes, I've posted myself on all that."

"Well, choose your ground, and I'll whittle your stakes." He rose and again unsheathed his hunting knife.

"Major," cried Roderick, "along this old channel there's at least three men's ground. We'll stake for you and for me and for Grant Jones."

"But Grant Jones must have been on his claim before he can file on it. That's the law."

"We'll bring him down tomorrow morning."

"Then, go ahead," said the Major. "I think it is right and proper to secure all the ground we can. I believe it will be all for the best that it should be in our hands."

Within an hour stakes had been placed at the corners of the three placer claims, and the proper location notices, written on leaves torn from Buell Hampton's note book, affixed to a stake in the centre of each claim.

"I think that this complies with all legal requirements," remarked the Major, as they surveyed their workmanship. "Now, Roderick, tit for tat. You will come down the valley with me, and we shall secure, as lode claims, the porphyry dyke from which I have cut out merely the rich outcrop."

Another hour's labor saw the second task completed.

They were back at Roderick's sandbar, and had filled their pockets with nuggets.

"Now for the ascent," said Buell Hampton. "Tomorrow morning we shall return, and breakfast here on your venison. Hurry up now; the evening shadows are already falling."

The trail left by Roderick and the four deer through the canyon and along the *zigzag* gash in the mountains above the bubbling springs was clearly traceable in the snow. When the narrow ledge by which Roderick had descended into the gorge was reached the Major took the precaution of blazing an occasional tree trunk for future direction. Progress was easy until they reached the abrupt declivity down which the hunter had slipped. A little farther along the deer appeared to have descended the steep incline by a series of leaps. In the gathering dusk it was impossible to proceed farther; steps would have to be cut or a careful search made for some way around.

"We must go back," said Buell Hampton. "Now I will show you my means of access to the canyon—one of the most wonderful rock galleries in the world."

Retracing their footsteps they hastened along at the best speed possible, and soon reached the tunnel into which the river disappeared. Producing his electric torch, the Major prepared to lead the way. He lingered for just a moment to gaze back into the canyon which was now enveloped in the violet haze of eventide.

"Is it not lovely?" he murmured. "Alas, that such a place of perfect peace and beauty should come to be deserted and despoiled!"

Roderick was fingering the slugs of gold in his pocket. He followed the direction of the Major's eyes.

"Yes, it is all very beautiful," he replied. "But scenery is scenery, Major, and gold is gold."

The little torch flashed like an evening star as they disappeared into the grotto.

Buell Hampton and Roderick had gazed up the canyon.

But they had failed to observe two human forms crouched among the brushwood not fifty yards away—the forms of Bud Bledsoe and Grady, who had that morning tracked the Major

265

from his home to the falls, under the cataract, through the rock gallery, right into the hidden canyon, intent on discovering the secret whence the carload of rich ore had come, bent on revenge for Grady's undoing with the smelting company when the proper moment should arrive.

That night Buell Hampton, Roderick Warfield, and Grant Jones supped frugally at the hunter's hut on ham sandwiches and coffee. Down in Hidden Valley on the gold-strewn sandbar W. B. Grady and his henchman feasted royally on venison steaks cut from the fat buck Roderick's gun had provided. They had already torn down the location notices and substituted their own. And far into the night by the light of their camp fire the claim-jumpers searched for the nuggets among the pebbles and gathered them into a little heap, stopping only from their frenzied quest to take an occasional gulp of whiskey from the big flask without which Bud Bledsoe never stirred. When daylight broke, exhausted, half-drunk, both were fast asleep beside the pile of stolen gold.

CHAPTER XXXIII.

THE SNOW SLIDE

DURING the night a few flakes of snow had fallen—just the flurry of a storm that had come and tired and paused to rest awhile. The morning broke grey and sombre and intensely still; the mantle of white that covered the ground and clung to bushes and tree branches seemed to muffle every sound; the atmosphere was clear, but filled with brooding expectancy.

The three friends at the hunter's hut were early astir. Roderick, despite the fact that fortune had at last smiled and crowned with success the prolonged quest for his father's lost mine, was strangely oppressed. Buell Hampton, too, was grave and inclined to silence. But Grant Jones was gay and happy, singing blithely during the preparations for breakfast.

On the previous night he had received the story of the find with exultant delight. With such a rich mining claim all the ambitions of his life were about to be realized. He would buy out his financial partners in the *Dillon Doublejack* and publish it as a daily newspaper—hang the expense, the country would grow and with it the circulation, and he would be in possession of the field against all-comers. Then again he would acquire the *Encampment Herald* although keeping on the brilliant Earle Clemens as editor; also start another paper at Rawlins, and in a little time run a whole string of journals, like some of the big newspaper men whose names were known throughout the nation. Listening to these glowing plans as they drank their morning coffee around the campfire, Roderick and the Major could not but admire the boyish gaiety of this sanguine spirit.

"I'm going to propose to Dorothy tomorrow," exclaimed Grant by way of grand finale to his program of great expectations, "and the Reverend Stephen Grannon will marry us before the week is out We'll spend our honeymoon in Chicago so that I can buy some new printing presses and things. Then we'll be back in time to bring out a grand mid-winter number that will make all Wyoming sit up and take notice. By gad, boys, it's great to be a newspaper editor."

"Better to be a newspaper proprietor," laughed Roderick.

"Or both combined," suggested the Major.

"There you've hit it," cried Grant. "And that's just the luck that has come my way at last—thanks to you, Roderick, old scout, and to you, Major, as well."

"No, no," protested Buell Hampton. "With your happy disposition and great capacity for work, success was bound to be yours, my dear fellow. The manner of its coming is a mere detail."

"That's the way a good friend cloaks good deeds," replied Grant. "However, we'll let it go at that. Pass the frying pan please; this bacon's just fine." Plans for the day were carefully discussed. The man in charge of the burros had not been taken into their confidence; as a member of the expedition he would be properly looked after later on, but meanwhile strict secrecy was the only wise policy until the location papers had been properly filed at the county seat, Rawlins. This filing would undoubtedly be the signal for a rush of all the miners and prospectors within a hundred miles of the little treasure valley among the hills.

"Yes, there will be a regular stampede," remarked the Major— "provided the snow holds off," he added with a glance at the grey canopy of cloud overhead.

"I think we are in for another storm," said Grant, gazing around. "If so, the whole country will be sealed up until the spring."

"Which is not the worst thing that might happen," commented Buell Hampton.

"Would certainly give us ample time to make all our

arrangements for the future," concurred Roderick.

It was agreed that they would take with them that morning the sacks in which the provisions had been brought up, and bring back as much gold as they could carry. For a moment Grant and Roderick discussed the advisability of leaving their guns behind. But there were outlaws among the mountains, and it was deemed prudent to carry the weapons.

All preparations were now completed, and a start was made, the stableman being left in charge of the camp with instructions to have a good fire of embers ready for the brisket of venison they would return with about the noontide hour.

Buell Hampton led the way at a swinging gait,
Roderick followed, then came Grant Jones singing lustily:

"As I was coming down the road,
Tired team and a heavy load,
I cracked my whip and the leader sprang
And the off horse stepped on the wagon tongue."

A little way down the hill Grant called a halt He had discovered on the light dusting of overnight snow the tracks of a big bear, and for the moment everything else was forgotten. Bear-hunting to him was of more immediate interest than gold-hunting, and but for the restraining hand of Buell Hampton the ardent young sportsman would have started on the trail.

"Let's stop a while," he pleaded. "Just look at those pads. A great big cinnamon bear—a regular whale."

"No, no," said the Major decisively, again glancing at the sky. "We must press on."

"I'd like a hug all right," laughed Roderick, "but not from a cinnamon bear in a snowdrift."

"Gee, but I'm sorry I left my dogs at Dillon," remarked Grant regretfully. "The last thing I said to Scotty Meisch was to look after the dogs even if the printing press burned. There's no friend like a good dog, Major."

"Rather a doubtful compliment," replied Buell Hampton with a smile.

"Present company always excepted," laughed the editor adroitly. "Well, well; we must let Mr. Bruin go this time. Lead on, Macduff, lead on."

And again as he fell into Indian file he sang his song.

The lilt and the words of that song, the picture of the stalwart figure in the pride of young manhood carolling gaily while marching along through the brushwood and down the timbered hillside, were des-tined never to fade from the memory of Roderick Warfield. With a sob in his heart he would recall the scene many and many a time in the days to come.

Meanwhile at the camp fire in Hidden Valley, Grady and Bud Bledsoe were also afoot. They had awaked from their half drunken slumber, chilled to the very marrow of their bones. Even the sight of the heap of nuggets could not at first restore warmth to their hearts. There was no whiskey left in the flask—not a drain. Their teeth chattering, they piled fresh brush on the camp fire, and then a half-rotted tree stump that soon burst into flame. Then when warmth at last crept through their frames, they too made their plans for the day.

Buell Hampton and Roderick Warfield might come back. Perhaps they had camped all night in the mountain cave. In any case it would be safer to leave the canyon by the other way—by the trail along which Roderick must have entered and which was quite clearly defined in the snow as it led up the gorge. Yes; they would clear out in that direction, and Bud Bledsoe, who knew every track among the mountains, further proposed that they would then cross the range and take the west road to Rawlins. With a price on his head he himself could not enter the town—although a little later some of the new-found gold would square all that, for the present he must lie low. But he would guide Grady on the way, and the latter would get into Rawlins first and file the location papers without anyone at Encampment knowing that he had made the trip.

"That's the dope," cried Bud Bledsoe, as he jumped to his feet and began stuffing his pockets to their fullest capacity with the big and little slugs of gold. Grady followed his example. Then both men took up their guns, Bledsoe also the light but strong hair lariat which was his constant companion whether he was on horse or foot, and began making their way up the canyon, following the well-trodden path through the snow along which Buell Hampton and Roderick had retraced their footsteps the evening before.

It was a couple of hours later when the Major, Grant Jones, and Roderick emerged from the grotto.

"Good heavens!" exclaimed the Major. "Look there!" And with extended arm he pointed to the ascending smoke of the camp fire higher up the valley.

With the caution of deerstalkers they ascended by the stream. They found that the camp fire was abandoned. The half-gnawed bones, the empty whiskey flask, the remnant heap of nuggets, the hollows on the sand where the two men had slept—all helped to tell the tale. The names on the substituted location papers completed the story—W. B. Grady's name and those of some dummies to hold the ground, illegally but to hold it all the same. Bud Bledsoe, the outlaw, had not ventured to affix his own name, but the big whiskey bottle left little doubt as to who had been Grady's companion in the canyon overnight.

The miscreants had departed—the tracks of two men were clearly shown at a little distance from those left by Roderick and the Major. They had ascended the gorge.

"We have them trapped like coyotes," declared the Major, emphatically.

"I'm not so sure about that," remarked Grant Jones. "If there is one man in this region who knows the mountain trails and mountain craft it is Bud Bledsoe. He'll get out of a box canyon where you or I would either break our necks to a certainty or remain like helpless frogs at the bottom of a well. Then I've got another idea—a fancy, perhaps, but I—don't—just—know."

He spoke slowly, an interval between each word, conning the chances while he prolonged his sentence.

"What's your idea?" asked Roderick. But the Major waited in silence.

At last Grant's face lighted up.

"Yes, by jingo," he cried, "that may be their plan. If they can get over the range on to the Ferris-Haggerty road they may make Rawlins by the western route. That's why they may have gone up the canyon instead of returning by the cave. For they came in by the cave; it is you they followed yesterday, Major, into the valley. The tracks show that."

"I have already satisfied myself on that point," replied Buell Hampton. "I have no doubt, since we balked Bledsoe in his previous attempt, that he has been on my tracks ever since, determined to find out where I got the rich ore. But it surprises me that a man in Grady's position should have descended to be the associate of such a notorious highwayman."

"Oh, moral turpitude makes strange bedfellows," said Grant, pointing to the depressions where the two claim-jumpers had slept "But there is no use in indulging in conjectures at the present time. I've a proposal to make."

"Let us hear it," said the Major.

"Luckily I brought my skis with me, strapped to one of the burros. Didn't know when they might come handy amid all this snow. Well, I'll go back to the hut, and I'll cut across the range, and will intercept these damned robbers, if that's their game, to a certainty."

"Rather risky," remarked Buell Hampton. "Feels like more snow." And he sniffed the ambient air.

"Oh, I'll be all right. And you've got to take risks too. I'll give Roderick my rifle, Major, and you take your own. You can follow the trail of these men, and if they have got out of the canyon, then you can get out the same way too. If so, we'll all meet on the range above. Roderick, you know where the Dillon Trail crosses the Ferris-Haggerty Road?"

Roderick nodded assent.

"Well, we can't miss each other if we all make for that point. And if you don't arrive by noon, I'll go right on to Rawlins by the western road, and lodge our location papers. I'll know you have Bledsoe and Grady trapped and are holding the ground."

"Sounds feasible," said Roderick. "But first of all we've got to tear down these fraudulent location notices and put our own up again." He pointed to one of the corner stakes. "Just look—these claim-jumpers came provided with regular printed forms."

"Well, go ahead with that right now," said Grant. "No doubt the papers have been changed too down on the Major's ground. When you're through with that job, follow the trail up the canyon. Now I'm off for my skis, and then for the road over the hills. Good-by. Take care of yourselves. Good-by."

And down the valley they heard his voice singing the song of the mountain trail:

"As I was coming down the road,
Tired team and a heavy load,
I cracked my whip and the leader sprung
And the off horse stepped on the wagon tongue."

Then his figure disappeared round a bend, and all again was still.

But Bledsoe and Grady had taken their time in ascending the canyon. But at last they reached the impasse that had brought Buell Hampton and Roderick to a halt the previous evening and caused them to retrace their steps as the tracks revealed. Just as they were discussing whether it might not be necessary for them also to turn back, a deer dashed wildly past them on the narrow bench where they stood—so close that they might have almost touched it with an outstretched hand.

Grady jumped back, frightened by the sudden bound of the swiftly speeding animal.

"Do you know what that means?" asked Bledsoe quietly.

273

"We started the deer, I suppose," stammered Grady.

"No. But someone else did—lower down the gorge. We are being trailed, boss. We've got to get out of this hole in double-quick time or chance being shot down from behind a rock."

"This wall is impossible," exclaimed Grady, his frightened face gazing up the cliff.

Bledsoe was surveying the situation.

"Wait a minute," he said at last. Then he swung his lariat, the noose of which, going straight to its mark, caught a projecting tree stump full fifty feet above.

"If you can make that," he added, as he pulled the rope tight, "there's a ledge running right around and up—see?" He pointed with his finger, tracing a line along the rocky wall. "Now up you go. I'll hold the rope. It's dead easy."

Grady dropped his rifle, and with both hands began to climb. Weighted with the gold in his pockets, he made the ascent slowly and laboriously. But at last he gained the ledge, and scrambling now on hands and knees as he moved further upward and onward he speedily disappeared over the rim of the cliff.

On Bledsoe's lips was a smile of cold contempt.

"Hell!" he muttered. "I wanted him to pull up the junk first. However, I'll manage, I guess."

He proceeded to tie to the riata his own and Grady's rifle. Then he swung himself aloft.

But he was not half way up when a rifle bullet flattened itself on the rock not a foot from his head.

"Hands up!" came a voice from below.

"By God, ain't they up now?" muttered the outlaw grimly, as he jerked himself to a higher foothold. A few more springs and he was standing on the ledge. Then, when a second bullet knocked off his hat, he ducked and scurried along the narrow footway almost as quickly as Grady had done, and was gone from the view of the two riflemen lower down the canyon.

"Come on," exclaimed Roderick. "They don't seem to have any guns. We'll get them yet."

Buell Hampton followed to the foot of the cliff. The rifles tied to the lariat showed that the fugitives were in truth disarmed, so far at least as long-distance weapons were concerned. The Major carefully hid the rifles in a clump of brushwood.

They were now prepared to follow, but caution had to be used, for Bud Bledsoe no doubt had a brace of revolvers at his belt. Roderick climbed up the rope first, while Buell Hampton, with his Springfield raised, kept watch for the slightest sign of an enemy above. But the fugitives had not lingered. Roderick, from the edge of the cliff, called on the Major to make the ascent, and a few minutes later they stood side by side.

High up on the snow-clad face of the mountain were the fleeing figures of Grady and Bledsoe. Yes, they were making in the direction of the Ferris-Haggerty Road. Grant would certainly intercept them, while Roderick and the Major stalked the quarry from the rear.

"I intend to get that thousand-dollar reward for Bud Bledsoe's hide," laughed Roderick, slipping a cartridge into the chamber of his rifle.

"We must not shoot to kill," replied the Major. "It will be sufficient that they surrender. We have them at our mercy. Come along."

He advanced a few paces, then paused.

"But there," he murmured, "I do not like this snow." He held out his hand, and a first soft feathery flake settled on his palm.

"Oh, well be all right," cried Roderick. "Besides we've got to help Grant."

They trudged along, walking zig-zag up the hill to lessen the incline, but always keeping close to the trail of the men they were pursuing. On the plateau above the snow lay deeper, and at places they were knee-deep in the drift, their feet breaking through the thin encrusting surface which frost had hardened.

"It is a pity we have not web snowshoes or skis," remarked Buell Hampton when they had paused to draw breath. "We could make so much better time."

"Well, the other fellows are no better equipped than ourselves," replied Roderick, philosophically. "But, by jingo, it's snowing some now."

Yes, the feathery flakes were all around them, not blindingly thick as yet, but certain precursors of the coming storm. The trail was still quite clear although the fugitives were no longer in sight.

An hour passed, two hours, three hours—and hunters and hunted still plodded on. Roderick felt no misgivings, for he could tell from the lie of the hills that they were making steadily for the junction of the Ferris-Haggerty Road with the track over the range to Dillon, where Grant Jones would now be waiting. But at last the snow began to fall more thickly, and the encircling mountains came to be no longer visible. Even the guiding footprints were becoming filled up and difficult to follow.

All at once Buell Hampton stopped.

"These men have lost their way," he exclaimed.

"They are going round in a circle. Look here—they have crossed their own track."

The evidence was unmistakable.

"Then what are we to do?" asked Roderick. "I suppose we hardly know where we are ourselves now," he added, looking uneasily around.

"I have my pocket compass—luckily I never travel without it in the mountains. But I think it is prudent that we should lose no further time in making for Encampment."

"And Grant Jones?"

"He can look after himself. He is on skis, and knows every foot of the Dillon trail."

"Then Grady and Bledsoe?"

"Their fate is in other hands. If we follow them any longer we will undoubtedly be caught in the storm ourselves." He held a hand aloft. "See, the wind is rising. There will be heavy drifting before long." Roderick now felt the swirl of driven snow on his cheeks. Yes, the wind had risen.

"But we'll endeavor to save them," continued Buell Hampton.

"Perhaps, as they are circling round, they are not far away from this spot even now. We will try at all events."

And raising both hands to form a voice trumpet, he uttered a loud: "Hallo I hallo!"

But no answer came. Again he shouted, again and yet again, turning round in all directions. Everything remained silent and still.

The Major now glanced at his compass, and took his bearings.

"Come," was all he said, as he led the way through the loose crisp snow that crunched and cheeped beneath their feet.

Half an hour later the storm by some strange vagary abated. The wind was blowing stronger, but it seemed to be driving the snow-laden clouds up into the higher mountain elevations. All of a sudden a penetrating shaft of sunshine flashed through the dancing snow-flakes, then the flakes themselves ceased to fall, and the sun was shining on the virgin mantle of white that enveloped range and peaks as far as the eye could see.

Roderick glanced down the mountain side. Almost beneath his feet was Conchshell Ranch—he could see the home on the little knoll amid the clustering pine trees. For the moment he was thinking of Gail. But the hand of Buell Hampton had clutched his shoulder.

"Look!"

And Roderick looked—away in the direction of Cow Creek Canyon, a mighty gash in the flank of the mountains nearly a thousand feet deep and more than half a mile across. Standing out, clear and distinct in the bright sunshine, were the tall twin towers on either side of the gorge, supporting the great steel cable which bridged the chasm and carried the long string of iron buckets bringing ore from the Ferris-Haggerty mine, fourteen miles distant, down into the smelter at Encampment. Roderick at his first glance saw that the aerial cars, despite the recent snow-storm, were still crawling across the deep canyon, for all the world like huge spiders on a strand of gossamer.

But as his eyes swept the landscape he beheld outlined on the white expanse of snow the figures of three men. One, standing fully a hundred yards away from the other two and lower down the hill, was the gorilla-like form of Bud Bledsoe. The others were Grady and Grant Jones on his skis.

And as Roderick looked, before he could even utter a cry, these two figures clutched at each other. For a moment they swayed to and fro, then Grant seemed to fling his man away from him.

Almost at the same instant, just as a picture might be blotted from a screen by cutting off the light, both figures had vanished! Then, like steam shot from a geyser, there ascended high into mid-air a great cloud of powdered snow, and to the watchers' ears came a deep boom resembling the prolonged and muffled roar of thunder or big artillery.

"Good God! A snow slide!" gasped Buell Hampton.

Roderick was stricken dumb. He stood rigid, frozen with horror. He needed no one to tell him that Grant Jones had gone over the rim of the canyon, down a thousand feet, smothered under a million tons of snow.

CHAPTER XXXIV.

THE PASSING OF GRANT JONES

EARLY the following morning several hundred searchers were at the scene of the snow slide in Cow Creek Canyon. Every precaution was taken not to have anyone walk along near the rim of the gorge a thousand feet above. There were still hundreds of thousands of tons of snow on the narrow plateau at the top, which any disturbance, even no greater than a stone thrown by the hands of a child, might start moving. If another slide should occur it would overwhelm and crush the intrepid searchers below.

A systematic probing of the snow with long iron rods had been begun at once and kept up perseveringly until three o'clock in the afternoon. Then one of the searchers touched clothing or something with his rod. The snow was quickly shoveled aside, and at a depth of about seven feet the body of Grant Jones was found lying flat upon his back with his right arm stretched out above his head, the left doubled under him. The face was quite natural—it wore a peaceful smile. None of his clothing had been disturbed or torn—even his cap and his skis were in place. The poor fellow had simply been crushed to death or smothered by the many tons of snow.

Immediately a makeshift sled was constructed by strapping two skis together sideways. On this the body was taken up the steep hills by a cautiously selected route to Battle, three and a half miles away, and thence on to Encampment, twelve miles farther, the improvised sled being drawn all the way by strong and willing men of the hills. Accompanying the remains were Roderick Warfield, Jim Rankin, Boney Earnest, and other

279

faithful friends, while following came a great cortege of miners, mill hands, and mountaineers.

It was midnight before the mournful procession reached town. And awaiting it even at that late hour was a dense crowd, standing with bared heads and tear-stained faces. For in all the hill country the name of Grant Jones was a household word. His buoyant good-nature was recognized by everyone, and probably he did not have an enemy in all southern Wyoming where his brief manhood life had been spent. Fully a thousand people, of both sexes, of all classes and all ages, formed the escort of the little funeral sled on its last stage to the undertaker's establishment. Here the body was received by Major Buell Hampton and the Reverend Stephen Grannon. It had been the Major's duty that day to seek out the clergyman and bring him down in a sledge from the hills to administer the last sad rites for their dear dead friend.

Next day the search was resumed for Grady's remains. Bud Bledsoe it was known had escaped—the Major had seen him running downhill after the disaster and others had tracked his footprints, to lose them in a clump of timber. So there was only one more body to be recovered. The task of probing with the long iron rods went on for several hours. The searchers knew the necessity of working both carefully and with speed, for another snow slide was imminent. And at last it came, toward the noon hour. But warning had been passed along, so that no lives were sacrificed, the only result being to pile a veritable mountain of snow over the spot where Grady's body presumably lay. The search was abandoned, without regret on anyone's part; in the spring the avalanche would give up its dead; until then the mortal remains of the unpopular and disgraced capitalist could well remain in their temporary sepulchre of snow, "unwept, unhonored, and unsung."

But for Grant Jones there was public mourning, deep, sincere, and solemn. Toward evening the whole town of Encampment seemed to be wending their way to the little church where the Reverend Stephen Gran-non was to preach the funeral sermon.

280

And these are the words which the venerable Flockmaster spoke to the hushed and sorrowing congregation.

"My friends, our hearts today commune with the battalions who have 'crossed over.' Love broods above the sleeping dust in a service of tears. The past is a dream—the future a mystery. Sometimes the tides of dissolution creep upon us silently. Again they are as stormy seas and rough breakers that sweep all with reckless cruelty into oblivion. But whether the parting be one way or the other, in peacefulness or in the savagery of a storm, to loving hearts it is ever a tragedy.

"The grief which is ours today is as old as the ages. It brings us into fellowship with the centuries. We know now why Eve wept for Abel and David lamented Absalom. Death is the most ancient sculptor in the world. Ever since men lived and died, death has made each grave a gallery and filled it with a silent statue. Death hides faults and magnifies virtues. Death conceals the failings of those who have passed while lovingly and enduringly chiselling their noble traits of character.

"Centuries of philosophy have not succeeded in reconciling men to the sorrows of dissolution. Death makes us all equal with a mutual sorrow. We cannot forget our friend who rests here in his final sleep. In happy symbolism his shroud was whitest snow, and love thrills our hearts with sympathetic memory. Such love is the kindest service of the soul.

"Affection for those who have departed has built the mausoleums of the world and makes every monument an altar of grief. Whether the hope of immortality is a revelation or an intuition is not under consideration today. Each man believeth for himself. We know that primitive man away back in Egypt buried his dead on the banks of the Nile and thought of immortality. We know that love throughout the ages has touched the heart with its wings, and hope from the beginning to the end whispers to us that 'if a man die he shall live again.' I believe that the doctrine of evolution gives a potent hope of immortality. Evolution takes the mud of the lake and makes a water lily—the hollow reed in the hand of the savage grows into a modern flute—the rude marks of primitive man in the stone age become poems and anthems in our own age. If mist can become stars—if dust can become worlds—if the immortality of biology is a truism—if love can come from sensations, if the angel of the brain can spring into being from simple cells, why then cannot the soul endure forever although undergoing transitions in the course of its divine development?

"I believe in the immortality of the soul. I believe in the religion of humanity. Yes, on the far away rim of eternity, Faith seeks a beckoning hand and the human heart pulses anew with inspiration and unfaltering belief in the immortality of the soul. Let us believe there are songs sung and harps touched and kisses given and greetings exchanged in that other world. It is better that all other words should turn to ashes upon the lips of man rather than the word immortality. Our hearts once filled with this belief—this great truth—then every tear becomes a jewel, the darkest night flees before the breaking dawn and every hope turns into reality.

"Before us, my friends, lies the dust of the dead—Grant Jones. Away from home—away from father and mother, brother and sister—far up in these hills where the shoulders of the mountains are clothed with treacherous banks of sliding snow—he was here seeking to carve out a destiny for himself, in the morning of early manhood. The Kismet of his life, clothed in mystery, caused him to lay down his tools and leave to others his but partially accomplished mission. He was journeying upward toward life's mountain-crest—already the clouds were below him and the stars about him. For do we not know from his gifted writings that this man held communion with the gods? His heart beat full of loftiest hope. And then—even before high twelve—he fell asleep. He is gone; but a myriad of memories of his achievements gather thick about us. We see him as he was, and this vision will abide with us throughout the years.

"He was a student and a scholar. He read books that had souls in them—he read books that converse with the hearts of men and speak to them of an exalted life—a life that unfolds an ethical and a higher duty incumbent upon the children of men. He knew much about the literature of his day—was acquainted with the great authors through their writings. Keats was his favorite poet, Victor Hugo his favorite prose author and 'Les Misérables' his favorite book. Music had a thrilling charm for him. To his heart it was the language of the eternal. He heard songs in the rocks of towering cliffs, in primeval forests, in deep gorges, in night winds, in browned grasses and in tempestuous storms and in the pebbled mountain brooks.

"We need have no fear for his future, my friends—with him all is well. A heroic soul, a matchless man, cannot be lost. His heart was a fountain of love. Virtue was his motto—hope his star—love his guide. Farewell, Grant, farewell. When with the silent boatman we too shall cross the river of death and steal away into the infinite, we believe that you will be standing there in the rosy dawn of eternity to welcome us, to renew the sweet ties of love and friendship that here on earth have bound our hearts to yours."

Thus spoke the Reverend Stephen Grannon, the Flockmaster of the Hills.

THE TREASURE OF HIDDEN VALLEY

CHAPTER XXXV.

A CALL TO SAN FRANCISCO

DOROTHY mourned for Grant Jones—for days she wept and would not be consoled. Roderick had not seen her since the disaster; when he had called at the ranch Barbara had brought a message from her room that she dared not trust herself yet to speak to anyone, least of all to the one whom she knew to have been Grant's closest and dearest friend.

Roderick had now taken apartments in the Bonhomme Hotel—it would have been too heartrending an experience to return to the shack where everything was associated with the memory of his lost comrade. It had been his painful task to pack the books, the little ornaments, the trophies of the chase, the other odds and ends of sacred relics, and send them back East to the old folks at home. He had known it to have been Grant's own wish that, when death should come, his body should rest among the hills of Wyoming. So when a simple headstone had been placed on the grave in God's acre at Encampment, the last sad duty had been performed. Grief was now deadened. The sweet pleasures of fond reminiscence remained, the richest legacy that man can leave behind him.

Buell Hampton and Roderick never met without speaking of Grant, without recalling some pleasant episode in their association, some brilliant or thoughtful contribution he had made to their past conversations. With the aid of fragments of torn paper that had been clutched in the dead man's left hand, the hand that had been doubled under him when the body was found, they had pieced together the story of that fateful encounter

284

with Grady. The latter, bent on discovering and jumping Buell Hampton's secret mine, had carried into the mountains the proper declaration papers in printed forms, with only the blanks to be filled in—name, date, exact location, etc. Grant must have become aware that these papers were all ready signed in Grady's pocket—perhaps in defiance the claim-jumper had flaunted them in his face. For the struggle had been for the possession of these documents, the torn quarters of which were still in Grant's hand when the fatal dislodgement of snow had taken place. The full infamy of Grady's long contrived plot was revealed. Righteously indeed had he gone to his doom.

A week had passed when Roderick found a letter on the breakfast table at his hotel. It was from Barbara Shields.

"My dear Mr. Warfield:—

"I write to tell you that we are going to California—to spend the winter in Los Angeles. We are all sorrow-stricken over the great calamity up in the hills, and Dorothy—the poor dear girl is simply stunned. I have known for a long while that she was very fond of Grant, but I had no idea of the depths of her feelings.

"Papa says Mama and I must start at once and endeavor to cheer up Dorothy and help her forget as much as possible the sadness of this terrible affair.

"Mr. Bragdon called last night, and is to be our escort to the coast. We shall probably return about the first of May. Please accept this as an affectionate good-by for the time being from us all.

"With cordial good wishes,

"Sincerely your friend,

Barbara."

Meanwhile snow had been descending off and on day after day, until now the whole of the mountain country was effectively sealed. Evidently a rigorous winter had set in, and it would be many months before Hidden Valley would be again accessible. Roderick was not sorry—the very mention of gold and mining had become distasteful to his ears. Even when with the Major, they, never now spoke about the secret canyon and its hoarded treasures—in subtle sympathy with each other's feelings the subject was tabooed for the present Bud Bledsoe had disappeared from the district, no doubt temporarily enriched by the nuggets with which he had filled his pockets. In the spring most likely he would return and rally his gang of mountain outlaws. But until then there need be no worry about the snow-enshrouded claims, the location papers for which had been now duly registered at the county seat in the names of their proper owners.

Buell Hampton had his books and his work for the poor wherewith to occupy his mind. Roderick found his consolation at the smelter. Early and late now he worked there, learning the practical operations from Boney Earnest, mastering the business details with the aid of a trustworthy old clerk whose services had been retained as secretary. Boney, having been made the choice of his brother foremen in accordance with the new plan of operations, was duly confirmed in his position of general manager, while Roderick, formally elected vice-president by the board, held the salaried and responsible post of managing-director.

Major Hampton withdrew himself more and more into the seclusion of his library; he rarely came to the smelter plant; he left everything in Roderick's hands once he had become satisfied of the young man's aptitude for the work; he was content to read the managing director's weekly report showing steady progress all along the line—increased output, decreased operating costs, large reductions in waste and breakages, in a word the all-round benefits resulting from friendly cooperation between capital and labor, no longer treating each other as enemies, but pulling together in happy conjunction and for mutual advantage.

Another circumstance contributing to the general harmony of the community was the departure of W. Henry Carlisle, the deposed attorney of the smelter company. One of Senator Greed's hirelings, Carlisle had been rewarded by that master of political jobbery with a judgeship in Alaska. Thus was the whole country made to pay the price of shameful underhand services that had tainted the very atmosphere and might well have caused the man in the moon to hold his nose when crossing the state of Wyoming.

However, Carlisle's going put an end to much bitterness and squabbling in Encampment, and now month succeeded month in peaceful routine. As both smelter and mine were now working Sundays as well as week days, Roderick could rarely take a day off—or at least he would not allow himself a day off.

However, along with Major Buell Hampton he was the guest of Mr. Shields for Christmas Day dinner, and learned the latest news of the exiles in California; that mother and daughters were well, Dorothy something like her old happy self if chastened with a sorrow that would always leave its memory, and all thoroughly enjoying the unaccustomed luxury of a winter of warmth and perpetual sunshine. There was another item in Mr. Shields' budget. Whitley Adams had spent a month in the capital of the southwest, had brought along his big touring car, and had given the girls no end of a good time.

"What took him to Los Angeles?' asked Roderick.

"Oh, important banking business, Barbara says," replied Mr. Shields quite innocently.

Roderick smiled. "Would Dorothy be consoled," he asked himself. The enterprising youth certainly deserved the prize; Roderick recalled the mirthful warning sent to dear old Grant in the latter's dilatory courting days about the tempting peach and the risk of a plundering hand. Indeed Whitley and Grant had been wonderfully akin in their boyish good-nature and irrepressible enthusiasm. With Grant gone, it seemed quite natural that Whitley and Dorothy should be drawn together. Roderick could wish no greater happiness for Dorothy, no better luck for his old college chum. Such was the train of his musing the while Buell Hampton and their host were discussing the wonderful growth and unbounded future of Los Angeles, the beautiful city of garden homes and cultured family life.

For New Year's Day Roderick was invited to the Holdens' place, and spent a delightful afternoon and evening. Gail sang and played, and the General seemed to be mightily interested in all the wonderful results being achieved at the smelter under the new régime. Gail listened somewhat distrait, but when the conversation about ores and fluxes and cupola furnaces and all that sort of thing seemed likely to be indefinitely prolonged she stole back to her piano and began singing to herself, soft and low.

And presently, while the General meandered on in a disquisition about refractory ores, Roderick was no longer paying attention. He was listening to the warbling of a thrush in the forest, and his straining ears caught the words of the song— "Just a-Wearyin' for You." A thrill ran through his nerves. He excused himself to the General, and crossed over to the piano. Gail instantly changed her song; by a skillful transition she was humming now, "Ye Banks and Braes o' Bonnie Dhon." But their eyes met, and she blushed deeply.

During the following weeks Roderick thought much and often about the beautiful Gail Holden, and occasionally now he would relax from business duties to enjoy a gallop with her on a sunny afternoon over the foothill ranges. They talked on many themes, and, although words of love were as yet unspoken, there came to them the quiet sense of happiness in companionship, of interest in each other's thoughts and undertakings, of mutual understanding that they were already closer and dearer to each other than friendship alone could make them.

Spring was now rapidly approaching. The meadowlarks were singing, and the grass beginning to grow green in the valleys and foothills, the wild flowers to paint the slopes and dells in vivid colors. General Holden had several days before gone to San Francisco, to visit his brother there in regard to some family business. Gail had been unable to accompany her father; she had declared that the little ranch at this season required all her attention. To comfort her in her loneliness Roderick had promised to go riding with her for an hour or two every afternoon. This pleasant duty had been properly fulfilled for several days, and one afternoon, with Badger ready saddled in front of his office, the young vice-president of the smelter company was just clearing up a few items of business at his desk before mounting and taking the road for the Conchshell Ranch.

A telegram was laid at his hand. He opened it casually, talking the while with Boney Earnest. But when he saw the name on the slip of paper, he started erect. The message was from Gail, and had come from Rawlins: "My father is in hospital, having met with a street accident in San Francisco. Have just had time to catch the afternoon train at Rawlins. My address will be the Palace Hotel. Will telegraph news about father on arrival."

"Good God!" exclaimed Roderick. "She has taken that journey alone. And no one to help her in her trouble and sorrow."

There was no alternative—he could but wait with all the patience he could command for the next day's overland. For he had instantly resolved to follow Gail. Like a flash had come the revelation how deeply he loved the girl; it had only needed the presence of tribulation to cause the long-smouldering spark of the fire divine in his heart to leap into flame—to make him realize that, come weal, come woe, his place now was by her side.

That afternoon he made all his preparations for departure. The evening he spent with Buell Hampton, and frankly told his friend of his great love for Gail. The Major listened sympathetically.

"All the world loves a lover," he said, a kindly glow upon his face. "Humanity demands, conscience approves, and good people everywhere applaud the genial and glowing warmth of honest love of man for maid. And I commend the choice of your heart, Roderick, for surely nowhere can be found a finer woman than Gail Holden. Go in and win, and may good luck follow you. For friendship's sake, too, I think it highly proper you should proceed at once to San Francisco and look after General Holden. I hope he is not dangerously hurt."

"I have no other information except this telegram," replied Roderick. "But I'll surely wire you from San Francisco."

Jim Rankin drove the stage next morning. Roderick took his accustomed place on the box seat, and listened to Jim's accustomed flow of language on all the local topics of interest. But during the long drive of fifty miles there was only one little part of the one-sided conversation that Roderick ever remembered.

"Yes, siree," Jim said, "all the folks is readin' books these days. I myself have took the craze—I've got a book about the horse out of our new libr'y an' I'll be dog-busted if I ever knew the critter had so many bones. Tom Sun is readin' about wool growin' in Australia, and is already figgerin' on gettin' over Tasmanian merino blood for his flocks. And I'm danged if old Wren the saloon-keeper ain't got stuck with a volume on temperance. 'Ten Bar-Rooms in One Night'. no, by gunnies, that's not it—'Ten Nights in a Bar-Room'—now I've got it right Guess it will do him a power o' good too. Then all the young fellers have started goin' to night classes. I tell you the Reverend Grannon with his schools an' his libr'ies is just workin' wonders. An' who do you think is his right hand man, or boy, or devil—call him which you like?"

"Who?" asked Roderick vaguely.

"Scotty Meisch, that little tad of a cow-puncher you and poor old Grant Jones took up and made a printer's devil of. Well, the parson got his hooks in him and tells me he's turned out to be a first-class organizer—that's his word. It's Scotty who goes around, starts each new lib'iy, and sets the machin'ry goin' smooth an' proper. It's a case of a round peg in a round hole, although who the hell would have thought it?"

Roderick was pleased to hear this good news of Scotty Meisch, but, returning to his thoughts about Gail, failed to follow Jim as the latter switched off into another line of "unbosomings."

He was glad to be alone at last and in the drawing room of the Pullman car which he had reserved by telegraph.

CHAPTER XXXVI.

IN THE CITY THAT NEVER SLEEPS

AFTER a tedious and delayed trip of three days and nights Roderick's train steamed onto the mole at Oakland. During the last night he had refused to have the berth in his drawing room made down, and had lounged and dozed in his seat, occasionally peering out of the car window. The hour was late—almost three o'clock in the morning. The train should have arrived at seven o'clock the evening before.

There was the usual scramble of disembarking, red-capped porters pressing forward to carry hand baggage from the train to the ferryboat.

"Last boat to San Francisco will leave in five minutes," was shouted from somewhere, and Roderick found himself with his valise in hand being pushed along with the throng of passengers who had just alighted from the train. Once on the ferryboat, he climbed to the upper deck and went well forward for the view. The waters of the bay were illumed with a half-crescent moon. Far across, six miles away, was San Francisco with its innumerable lights along the waterfront and on the slopes of her hills. To the right were Alcatras Island and the lighthouse.

Then the sharp ping-ping of bells sounded and the great wheels of the boat began to turn. Roderick was filled with the excitement of an impatient lover. "Gail, Gail, Gail," his throbbing heart kept thrumming. Would he be able to find her? San Francisco was a strange city to Gail as well as to himself. She had been on the train ahead of him, and might by this time have left the Palace Hotel, the address her telegram had given. But he had learned from one of the porters that Gail's train had been greatly delayed and would not have arrived before eleven o'clock the previous night. He reasoned that she would perforce have gone to the hotel at such a late hour, and would wait until morning to hunt up the hospital where her father was being cared for.

The boat had hardly touched the slip and the apron been lowered than he bounded forward, hastened through the ferryhouse and came out into the open where he was greeted by the tumultuous calls of a hundred solicitous cab-drivers. Roderick did not stand on the order of things, but climbing into the first vehicle that offered directed to be taken to the Palace Hotel.

Arriving at the hotel Roderick paid his fare while the door porter took possession of his grips. Glancing at a huge clock just over the cashier's desk, he noticed the hour was three-thirty a. m. Taking the pen handed to him by the rooming clerk, he signed his name on the register, and then let his eyes glance backward over the names of recent arrivals. Ah, there was the signature of Gail Holden. Fortune was favoring him and he breathed a silent prayer of thankfulness that he had overtaken her.

Yes, he would serve her. He would help her. She should see and she should know without his telling her, that nothing else mattered if he could only be with her, near her and permitted to relieve her of all troubles and difficulties.

"Show the gentleman to his room," said the night clerk and bowed to Roderick with a cordial good night.

As Roderick turned and followed the boy to the elevator, he realized that he was not sleepy—indeed that he was nervously alert and wide awake. After the boy had brought a pitcher of ice-water to the room, received his tip and departed, Roderick sat down to think it all over. But what was the use? "I cannot see her until perhaps eight o'clock in the morning. However, I will be on the outlook and in waiting when she is ready for breakfast. And then—" his heart was beating fast "I certainly am terribly upset," he acknowledged to himself.

Taking up his hat, he went out, locked the door, rang for the elevator and a minute later was out on the street. He was still wearing his costume of the mountains—coat, shirt, trousers, and puttees, all of khaki, with a broad-brimmed sombrero to match. A little way up Market Street he noticed a florist's establishment. Great bouquets of California roses were in the windows, chrysanthemums and jars of violets.

He walked on, deciding to provide himself later on with a floral offering wherewith to decorate the breakfast table. He had often heard San Francisco described as a city that turned night into day, and the truth of the remark impressed him. Jolly crowds were going along the streets singing in roistering fashion—everyone seemed to be good-natured—the cafés were open, the saloon doors swung both ways and were evidently ready for all-comers. When he came to Tate's restaurant, he went down the broad marble steps and found—notwithstanding the lateness or rather earliness of the hour—several hundred people still around the supper tables. The scene had the appearance of a merry banquet where everyone was talking at the same time. An air of joviality pervaded the place. The great fountain was throwing up glittering columns of water through colored lights as varied as the tints of a rainbow. The splash of the waters, the cool spray, the wealth of ferns and flowers surrounding this sunken garden in the center of a great dining room—the soft strains of the orchestra, all combined to fill Roderick with wonder that was almost awe. He sank into a chair at a vacant little table near the fountain and endeavored to comprehend it all He was fresh from the brown hills, from the gray and purple sage and the desert cacti, from the very heart of nature, so utterly different to this spectacle of a bacchanalian civilization.

The wilderness waif soon discovered that he would be de trop unless he responded to the urgent inquiries of the waiter as to what he would have to drink.

"A bottle of White Rock to begin with," ordered Rodcrick.

As he was sipping the cold and refreshing water it occurred to him that he had not tasted food since breakfast the day before in the dining car of the train. Yes, he would have something to eat and he motioned to the waiter.

After giving his order he had to wait a long time, and the longer he waited the hungrier he became. Presently a generous steak was placed before him. Potatoes *au gratin,* olives, asparagus, and French peas made up the side dishes, and a steaming pot of coffee completed a sumptuous meal.

When he had paid his check he discovered it was almost five o'clock in the morning, and as he mounted the marble stairway he laughingly told himself he wouldn't have much of an appetite at seven or eight o'clock when he came to sit down at the breakfast table with Gail Holden. Gaining the sidewalk he found that darkness was shading into dawn.

Instead of returning by way of Market Street, Roderick lit a cigar and turning to the right walked up a cross street toward the St. Francis Hotel. In front was a beautiful little park; shrubbery and flowers lined the winding walks, while here and there large shade trees gave an added touch of rural charm.

He seated himself on one of the iron benches, took out his watch and counted up the number of minutes until, probably, he would see the object of his heart's desire. How slow the time was going. He heard the laughter of a banqueting party over at the Poodle Dog, although at the time he did not know the place by name.

"Yes," he murmured, "San Francisco is certainly in a class by itself. This is the land where there is no night."

The contrast between the scenes in this gay city and the quiet hill life away up among the crags, the deep canyons and snow-clad peaks of southern Wyoming was indeed remarkable.

It was the morning of April eighteen, 1906, and the night had almost ended. There was a suggestion of purple on the eastern horizon—the forerunner of coming day. The crescent moon was hanging high above Mt. Tamalpais.

The town clock tolled the hour of five and still Roderick waited. Presently he was filled with a strange foreboding, a sense of oppression, that he was unable to analyze. He wondered if it presaged refusal of the great love surging in his heart for Gail Holden, the fair rider of the ranges, the sweet singer of the hills. An indescribable agitation seized him.

The minutes went slowly by. His impatience increased. He looked again at his watch and it was only a quarter after five. The city was wrapped in slumber.

Then suddenly and without warning Roderick was roughly thrown from his seat and sent sprawling onto the grass among the shrubbery. He heard an angry growling like the roar from some rudely awakened Goliath of destruction deep down in earth's inner chambers of mystery—a roar of wrath and madness and resistless power. The ground was trembling, reeling, upheaving, shaking and splitting open into yawning fissures, while hideous noises were all around. Buildings about the park were being rent asunder and were falling into shapeless heaps of ruin.

Struggling to his feet, his first impulse was to hasten to the hotel and protect Gail. As he arose and started to run he was again thrown to earth. The bushes whipped the turf as if swished to and fro by an unseat hand. For a moment Roderick was stunned into inaction—stricken with the paralysis of unspeakable fear.

CHAPTER XXXVII.

RODERICK RESCUES GAIL

IT WAS but a few seconds until Roderick was again on his feet Hurriedly taking his bearings, he started off through the little park in the direction of the Palace Hotel. In the uncertain morning dawn the people from innumerable bedrooms above the stores were pouring into the streets. They were scantily attired, most of them simply in their night garments, and all were dazed and stunned with a terrible fright Before Roderick had reached Market Street the thoroughfare was almost blocked by this frantic and half-clothed mass of humanity. His powerful athletic frame and his football experience stood him in good stead, although here roughness had to be exchanged for greatest gentleness. He was very persistent, however, in his determination to reach the hotel in time if possible to be of assistance to Gail.

Less than ten feet in front of where he was crowding his way through the throng of people a portion of a cornice came tumbling down from far above. A wailing cry went up from the unfortunates pinned beneath. Roderick leaped quickly forward and with the strength of a Hercules began to heave aside the great blocks of stone. Others recognized his leadership, instantly obeyed his commands and lent their united strength in helping to release three men who had been caught under debris. The cries of the injured were piteous. Indifferent to the danger of falling bricks and mortar Roderick caught up one poor fellow in his arms and carried him as if he were a babe into a receding doorway.

"My legs, my legs," the victim moaned. "They're broken— they're broken."

Quickly removing his coat Roderick placed it beneath the man's head for a pillow, and leaving others to guard, he hastened back to the scene of the tragedy, only to find that the spark of life had now gone out from the other two bodies pitifully maimed and crushed.

He pushed his way into the middle of the street amid the surging mob, and again turned his steps toward the Palace Hotel. At last he found himself near to the entrance of the great hostelry. But everyone was seeking to escape and rushing to the street in riotous disorder. By dint of indefatigable efforts he managed to get within the gateway and then to the large trysting room across the hall from the hotel office. A group of women were endeavoring to revive a poor sufferer who evidently had fainted. Approaching, he saw blood coursing down the fair face of the unfortunate.

"My God!" he exclaimed. "It is Gail."

An instant later he had gently pushed the helpers aside and gathered the girl in his strong arms. Moving backwards, forcing a passage step by step with the determination of one who acts intuitively in a crisis, he managed to gain the open. He hoped the air would restore Gail to consciousness.

Crossing to the other side of the street where the throng was less dense he started toward a high hill that rose up far away. It was covered with residences, and if he could once reach that vantage point with his charge he felt sure it would be an asylum of safety. The distance was considerable and presently the way became steep. But he was unconscious of any weight in the burden he carried. His only thought was to get Gail away from the burning, falling buildings—away from the central part of the city which was now a fiery pit wrapped in sheets of devouring flame.

Finally attaining the eminence—it was Nob Hill although he did not know the name—he found the porches and front lawns of the beautiful houses filled with frightened people viewing the scene in awe and amazement. Formalities were forgotten; solicitude and helpful kindness reigned supreme among all the people of the stricken city.

He called to a little group huddled on the front porch of their home. "Here is a lady," Roderick explained, "who has been injured and fainted. Will you please get water and help to revive her?"

In hurried eagerness to assist they quickly brought a cot to the porch and upon this Roderick gently placed the still unconscious girl. Her face was deathly white, and a great red gash was discovered across one side of her head, from which the blood was trickling down the marble cheek. The wound was bandaged by tender hands and the face laved with cooling water. After a little Gail opened her eyes and asked piteously: "Where am I? Where am I?"

"You are safe," said Roderick as he knelt by her side.

"Oh, is it you, Mr. Warfield? How glad—how glad I am to see you. Where am I?"

"In San Francisco. Don't you remember?"

"Yes, yes, I remember now," she replied weakly and lifted one hand to her aching head. "But papa?—where is my father?"

"I am going to look for him now. You are with kind people and they will care for you. Rest quietly and be patient until I return."

Her dark blue eyes looked helplessly up into his for a moment; then he turned and was gone.

Roderick rushed down the hill, back to the scene of devastation where he might be useful in helping to save human life, determined also in his heart to find General Holden. But where was he? In some hospital, as Gail's telegram had told.

He was debating with himself whether he should return to seek some directions from Gail. But just then the surging, swaying crowd pushed him irresistibly back, then swept him away along Market Street. The Palace Hotel was on fire. Policemen and firemen were thrusting the people away from the known danger line.

Just then he heard a voice crying out in heart-rending anguish: "My little girl', my little girl." It was a frantic mother weeping and looking far up to the seventh story of a building she evidently had just left. There leaning out of a window was a curly haired tot of a child, perhaps not more than four years old, laughing and throwing kisses toward her mama, all unconscious of danger.

"I came down," sobbed the weeping mother to those around, "to see what had happened. The stairway is now on fire, and I cannot return. Will no one, oh Lord, will no one save my little girl?"

Roderick looked up to where the woman was pointing and saw the child.

"My God!" he exclaimed, "smoke is coming out of the next window." He noticed that the adjoining building was already a mass of fire. At a glance he took in the situation.

"Hold on a minute," he shouted. "I will try."

There was an outside fire escape that led from the top story down to the first floor. Roderick made a leap, caught hold of the awning braces, pulled himself up with muscles of steel, and grasped the lowermost rung of the escape. A moment later he was making his way up the narrow iron ladder, pushing through the aperture at each floor, with almost superhuman swiftness. When he reached the window he lifted the child in his arms and hastily started on the downward journey.

"Hold tight, little girl," was all Roderick said as he felt the confiding clasp of her tiny arms about his neck.

Many of the people below besides the almost frenzied mother were watching the heroic deed with bated breath. Just then a cry of terror went up. The great wall of a burning building across the street was toppling outward and a moment later collapsed, burying many unhappy victims beneath the avalanche of broken brick and mortar.

Whether the little girl's mother had been caught by the falling wall or not Roderick had no means of determining. A choking cloud of dust, ash, soot and smoke enveloped him in stifling darkness; he could hardly breathe. The very air was heated and suffocating. But down and down he went with his little burden clinging tightly to him. Arriving at the awnings he swung himself over, secured a momentary foothold, then grasped the braces with his hands and dropped to the littered sidewalk below.

The mother of the girl was nowhere to be seen. He turned down the street to get away from the horrible sight of the dead and the piteous cries of the dying. He had scarcely reached the next corner when the child, who was mutely clinging to him as if indeed she knew he was her savior, released her arms and called out gleefully: "Oh, there's mama, mama, mama." Then the mother stood before him, weeping now for joy, and through her tears Roderick saw a face of radiance and a smile of gratitude that time or eternity would never erase from his memory.

Nothing mattered now—her little girl was safe in her arms. "I don't know who you are, sir," she exclaimed, "but I owe to you the life of my child, and may the good God bless you."

But this was no time for thanks. Roderick was looking upward.

"Come quickly," he shouted, "come this way—hasten." And he pulled them down a side street and away from another skyscraper that was trembling and wavering as if about to fall.

They turned, and ran along a street that was still free from fire and led toward the St. Francis Hotel and the little park fronting it where Roderick had sat at dawn. Carefully he guided the woman's steps, keeping to the middle of the street, for the sidewalk was encumbered with debris and threatened by partly dislodged brickwork above. Here and there the roadway was rumpled and rough as a washboard by reason of the earthquake, while at places were great gaping fissures where the earth had been split open many feet deep. But soon they were in the open square, and mother and child were safe. Knowing this, Roderick allowed them to pass on—to pass out of his life without even the asking or the giving of names.

For there was other work to his hand; he hurried back to the last crossing. There under the fallen débris, was a woman obviously of refinement and wealth whose life had been vanquished without warning. One hand was extended above the wreckage. It was shapely and encircled with a bracelet, while a single diamond solitaire ring adorned her finger—perhaps a betrothal ring. Two human ghouls—not men—had whipped out their ready knives and were in the very act of severing the finger to obtain the jewel. It was these brutes that Roderick had come back to face.

Like a flash he leaped forward and with a well directed sledge-hammer blow felled one of these would-be robbers of the dead. Then he grappled with the second scoundrel. The man in his grip was none other than the outlaw, Bud Bledsoe!

With knife already open and in his hand the inhuman wretch slashed Roderick's cheek, and the red blood spurted down his face and neck. Roderick loosed his hold and stepped back a pace—the next gash of this kind might easily be a fatal one. But not for one instant did he lose his presence of mind or nerve. As the cowardly miscreant advanced, cruel murder in his eyes, Roderick by a swift swing of his right parried the upraised hand that held the knife, and then, seizing the opening, he delivered with his left a smashing uppercut. Bledsoe reeled for a moment like a drunken man, then sank to the ground a huddled heap, and finally rolled over kicking convulsively and quite insensible.

The knockout had been effected quickly and well—like a butcher would fell a bullock.

Already the devastated city was under martial law, and three or four soldiers coming hurriedly up just then, and having seen from the opposite corner the hellish attempt of the two wretches to despoil the dead, shot them instantly, Bledsoe where he lay writhing, the other as he staggered dazed-like to his feet.

Roderick wiped the blood from his face, and thanked the soldiers. "Good for you, young fellow," cried one of them as they continued on their way.

His wound forgotten, Roderick again looked round to see where he could render the most efficient service.

The night came on, and he was still at work, rescuing and helping. He had been recognized by the Citizens' Committee of Safety and now wore a badge that gave him the freedom of the streets. In all his goings and comings he was ever looking for General Holden, and he also made numerous trips to Nob Hill, searching for the house where he had left Gail. But he could never find the place again, for the raging fire was fast obliterating all guiding landmarks.

Thus for two days—terrible days, pitiful days—for two nights—terrible nights, pitiful nights—Roderick drifted with the bands of rescuers, doing deeds of valor and of helpfulness for others less strong than himself. His face was black with soot and clotted with blood, his coat he had parted with at the beginning of the disaster, the rest of his clothing was tattered and torn, his sombrero had disappeared, when and how he had not the faintest notion.

The fire had now burned out its center circle and was eating away at the rim in every direction. Roderick suddenly remembered he had tasted no food since his early breakfast at Tate's an hour before the earthquake crash. The pangs of hunger had begun to make themselves felt, and he concluded to turn his steps toward the outer fire line and endeavor to find something to eat.

As he walked along from house to house he found them all deserted. Some of the household goods were scattered about the lawns, while boxes, trunks, and bulky packages were piled on the sidewalks. Presently he found a basket which contained a single loaf of bread. This he ate ravenously, and counted it the greatest feast he had ever had in his life. He ate as he hurried along, thinking of Gail and General Holden—wishing he might divide the bread with them.

The roar of consuming, crackling flames, the deep intonations of intermittent dynamite explosions, and the occasional wail of human beings in distress, rose and fell like a funeral dirge.

His feet intuitively turned back to the burned district. There might yet be more work for him to do.

He determined to pick his way across the ruins, and ascending the hill opposite make another desperate effort to find Gail. After a fatiguing climb over hot embers and around the twisted steel skeletons of burned-out buildings he finally stood on the rim of the hill above the saucer-shaped valley of flames. Only charred and smoking ruins were about him. The beautiful residential district had like the business sections below, been swept with the fires of destruction.

Where was Gail? Was she safe? Was she dead? Would he ever find her? These were some of the questions that kept him in agonizing incertitude.

There was a weird uncanny attraction about this great amphitheatre of flame—an attraction like that of a lodestone; and he feared lest Gail had left her refuge in a vain search for her father and met with another serious accident. Roderick had visited all the unburned hospitals, but no trace of General Holden had he been able to find. The quest for both must be resumed; so down the hill he trudged again.

Ashes and burning cinders were falling like huge flakes of snow. Once more Roderick was in the midst of a throng of people—gaunt and hollow-eyed, wearied and worn-out, just staggering along. At last he recognized the little park in front of the St. Francis Hotel. Yes, he would go there, stretch himself on the grass, and rest and sleep for at least a few hours. This would make him ill the fitter for his task of searching.

Just as he was about to cross the street a dozen people shouted for him to look out; but he did not turn quickly enough to discover nor escape a burning wooden rafter that fell from the upper story of a building and struck him an ugly glancing blow on the head. Roderick dropped to the ground unconscious.

At this very moment a Red Cross automobile was passing. It stopped abruptly at the sidewalk. Two men stepped quickly down and lifted the almost lifeless body into the machine. A moment later the auto glided away down a side street in the direction of Golden Gate Park.

That night there were many in the camps of refuge around the burning city who thought about the tall, strong-muscled, square-jawed young stranger in khaki garb, while their hearts welled up with gratitude for his timely assistance and chivalrous deeds of bravery. Had they but known of the fate that had at last befallen their nameless hero, grateful thoughts would have been turned into fervent prayers.

CHAPTER XXXVIII.

THE SEARCH FOR RODERICK

THE general shock of horror caused by the San Francisco disaster was intensified at Encampment when the news ran round that three local people had been in the stricken city at the moment of the earthquake shock which had laid the business centre in ruins and prepared the way for the subsequent far-sweeping conflagration. No telegram came from either the Holdens or Roderick Warfield, and their silence, their failure to relieve the anxiety of the friends they must have known were deeply concerned about their safety, could only cause ominous conjectures as to their fate. There was no possibility of reaching them by wire, for the Palace Hotel, the only known address, had been one of the first buildings destroyed.

But Buell Hampton did not wait for telegrams to reach him. He had no sooner been apprised of the catastrophe than he was on his way to Rawlins, hiring a special conveyance on the mere off-chance that railway schedules would have been disarranged and a train might be caught at any moment. In this he showed his usual good judgment for within an hour of reaching the station he was on board a belated limited, in which he had the further good fortune to find one solitary sleeping berth unoccupied. The train was loaded with returning San Francisco people who had been absent when their homes had been swept away, anxious friends of sufferers, doctors, nurses, relief workers of every kind, newspaper men, all hurrying to the scene of sorrow and suffering.

It was on the morning of the fifth day after the earthquake that Buell Hampton, provided with a special permit, at last found himself amid the ruins of San Francisco. Many buildings were still burning or smoldering, but the area of destruction was now defined and the spread of the flames checked. With saddened heart the Major picked his way along what once had been Market Street but was now a long mound of fallen stones, bricks, and mortar lined by the skeletons of lofty iron-framed buildings. Here the work of clearing away the debris in search of victims was in progress. But any inquiries of those actively engaged in these operations were useless. Buell Hampton passed on.

Suddenly he came upon the bread line, a wonderful sight—a long row of people of all sorts and conditions, the rich, the poor, the educated, the ignorant, the well dressed, the tattered, ranged in single file and marching slowly past the commissary to receive a supply of provisions for their own famishing selves or for their destitute families. Buell Hampton scanned each face; neither General Holden nor Roderick were in the line, nor was there any sign of Gail.

Then he began a systematic visitation of the refuge camps that had been formed around the bumed-out area. The remainder of that first day he spent in Golden Gate Park. It was not until the succeeding afternoon that he found himself in the crowded tent city out on the Presidio. Here at last his patient and persistent efforts were rewarded. He caught sight of Gail seated near the door of a tiny tent-house and strode eagerly forward to greet her. In his deep emotion he folded the young girl to his breast, and she in turn clung to him in her joy of meeting at last a dear friend from home.

"Where is your father?" was the Major's first inquiry.

"He is safe. We have this little tent, and I am nursing him. His right arm was broken in the street accident, but immediately after the fire began all the hospital patients were removed to open places, and here I found him, thank God, the very first evening. You see, my uncle's house was burned. He is quartered across the bay at Oakland."

"Your head is bandaged, Gail. Were you badly hurt?"

"Oh, that was nothing," she replied, pulling off the narrow band of linen that encircled her brow. "Just a little scalp wound when I fell, and it is quite healed now. But, oh, I remember so little about the terrible disaster—how I got out of the Palace Hotel at all."

"And Roderick—where is Roderick?" asked Buell Hampton.

Gail's eyes opened wide—with wonder, then with fear.

"Roderick, Roderick!" she exclaimed in a trembling voice. "Then it was not a dream?"

"What dream?"

"That it was he who carried me out of the hotel building and to the veranda of the house where he laid me on a cot and kind friends bathed my wound."

"No dream, this. It was Roderick for certain. He followed you on the next train to San Francisco—intending to go straight to the Palace Hotel."

"Followed me? Why did he follow me?"

"To render you help when your father was hurt—because he loves you—of course, you must have divined how deeply he loves you."

The color rose slowly to Gail's face. But there was fear still in her eyes. She pressed her clasped hands to her breast.

"Then where is he now?" she asked in a tense whisper.

"That is what I want to know—I have been seeking both you and him. When did you meet last?"

"Five days ago. After saving me he rushed straight away to seek for Papa. I came to believe that it was all a dream. For I have not seen him since. Oh, he must have been hurt—he may have been killed." And burying her face in her hands she burst into tears.

Buell Hampton laid a kindly hand on her shoulder. "Come, my dear, we can do no good by giving way to weeping. I have been through many of the refuge camps, and I shall go right on searching now. You see there are thousands of people in these Presidio grounds. He may be within a stone's throw of us here at this very moment."

"Oh, let me help you." With a hand she dashed away her tears, and stood before him now, calm and resolute. "I will come with you right now. I need no hat or anything."

"But your father?"

"He is all right He is resting quite peacefully. Just spare one moment, please. Come in and shake hands. He will be so happy to see you."

She led the way to the tent door and parted the awning. Buell Hampton entered and warmly greeted General Holden. But he told him he could not linger, for Roderick must be found.

During the remaining hours of daylight the Major and Gail searched along row after row of tents. But Roderick remained undiscovered—no one had ever heard his name or could remember having seen anyone answering to the description given. Reluctantly Buell Hampton quitted the quest and led Gail back to her own place of refuge.

"I am sleeping at Berkeley," he explained. "It is best that we should both have our night's rest. But I shall be back here for you soon after daybreak, and if you can engage someone to watch by your father we shall search together all day long. Will that suit, you, Gail?"

"Oh, you are so kind taking me," she replied, resting her hands on his shoulders, tears of gratitude in the eyes that looked up into his. "It would break my heart not to be with you."

"I would not rob you of love's sweet duty," he replied as he stooped and gently kissed her on the brow.

Another day went by, but still their efforts were unrewarded. On the following morning they started for the Seal House, to search the many improvised hospitals which they had learned were located there. The first place they entered was an immense tent with two or three hundred cots ranged in crowded rows.

As Buell Hampton and Gail walked down the long central aisle, each took one side to scan the physiognomies of the poor sufferers, some moaning in delirium, others with quiet pale faces that lighted up to return the smile of sympathy and encouragement Presently, the Major who was walking a few feet in advance heard an exclamation of joy, and turning quickly saw Gail Holden kneeling at the side of a cot There was a bewildered look on the face of the patient—a lean drawn face, pallid beneath the tan, the chin stubbled with a beard of a few days' growth, the forehead swathed in bandages, one cheek scored with a healing scar. Gail had taken one of his hands in both her own. He looked from Gail to Major Hampton and then from the Major back to Gail.

"Is this a vision?" he asked feebly, as if doubting his senses.

"Roderick, my dear fellow, is it really you?" exclaimed the Major, as he bent down over him. "For days we have been hunting for you. And now we've found your hotel"—he glanced around with a little smile—"we don't propose to lose sight of you again."

Loosening his hand from Gail's and taking both of hers in his own and smiling feebly, Roderick said: "Really, Gail, I hardly know yet whether you are actually here or I am dreaming. You looked pretty white that day I carried you from the hotel."

"There is no dream about me, Roderick," replied Gail brightly. "We are going to take care of you, Major Hampton and myself, just as you so kindly looked after poor little me."

At this moment a nurse approached: "So your friends have found you, Mr. Warfield?" she said with a cheerful smile.

"Yes," replied Roderick, "the very best friends I have in all the world." As he spoke Gail felt the gentle pressure of his hand.

"Is this your ward?" inquired the Major of the nurse.

"Yes, I have had charge of it ever since this makeshift hospital was put up."

"Well, how is the patient, our friend Mr. Warfield?"

"He had received a pretty ugly cut—a falling piece of wood or something of that sort—on the top and side of his head—a sort of glancing bruise. But he is getting on very well now. We have his fever under control. For a number of days he was very flighty and talked a great deal about Major Hampton."

"I am honored," said the Major, bowing.

"Oh, you are Major Hampton?"

"Yes," said Gail, "Major Buell Hampton is Mr. Warfield's best friend—that is, one of the best." And she looked quickly at Roderick.

"How fortunate that you have come when he is convalescing. But tell me," asked the nurse, "who is Gail? In his delirium he talked a great deal about her."

Roderick's face flushed, and Gail with rising color immediately changed the subject by asking: "How soon would it be safe to have the patient removed?"

"Oh, perhaps tomorrow or the next day. The doctor says he is now quite out of danger—the fever is practically gone."

At Roderick's request he was propped up on his little white iron hospital cot, chairs were brought, and until far on in the afternoon Gail and the Major sat on either side, conversing in quiet, subdued tones, relating incidents in the terrible disaster, planning for their early return to Wyoming just as soon as Gail's father and Roderick himself could stand the journey.

A couple of days later Buell Hampton and Gail arrived at the hospital in an automobile, and carried Roderick away to a yacht anchored in the bay that had been placed at their disposal. Here Roderick found General Holden already installed in a comfortable deck chair, and he was introduced by Gail to her Uncle Edward, a hale old gentleman bearing a striking resemblance to his brother. The General looked fit even if he did carry his right arm in a sling, Roderick although weak from loss of blood was able to walk, and both could well congratulate each other on their providential escape.

"We are not going to talk about these awful times," said the General as he gave Roderick his left hand and returned the cordial pressure. "But I have to thank you for saving our dear Gail. We all fully realize that without your brave and timely help we would not have her with us today."

"Nonsense," protested Roderick. "Somebody else would have done what I did. I was just happy and lucky in having

311

the privilege."

"God bless you!" murmured the father, again pressing the hand which he had not yet relinquished.

"And so say I," exclaimed the uncle. "We could not do without our little Gail." And he patted her cheek affectionately.

There followed a week of blissful rest and happy companionship, at the end of which it would have been a hollow mockery to pretend in the case of either invalid that any more nursing or lolling in long chairs was required. Railroad accommodations were secured for the morrow.

CHAPTER XXXIX.

REUNIONS

TEN days before the departure from San Francisco telegrams had been sent in all directions giving forth the glad tidings that General Holden and Gail, Roderick and Buell Hampton, were safe and would soon be on their homeward way to Wyoming. Among those thus notified had been the Shields family at Los Angeles and Allen Miller at Keokuk. But it was a great surprise to find Whitley Adams waiting the arrival of the morning train at Rawlins with his big Sixty Horse Power automobile, and bearing the news that Mrs. Shields, Barbara and Dorothy had returned, while also Uncle Allen and Aunt Lois had come to Encampment so that appropriate welcome might be given to those who had recently come through such terrible and harrowing experiences. Jim Rankin and Tom Sun were also on the platform to exchange hand-grips with Roderick and the Major.

After the first glad salutations Whitley pointed to his car, and announced that he was going to drive the party over to Encampment.

"Sorry to be starting in opposition to the regular stage," he said with a sly little wink in Roderick's direction. "But you see Mr. Rankin's horses are hardly good enough for the occasion."

Jim drew himself up and pointed to his old Concord stage coach standing by, all ready for the road.

"The dangnationest finest pair uv roan leaders and span uv blacks at the wheel that ever had lines over 'em in this part of the country," he declared sturdily. "Just wait a bit, young man. 'Fore we're many miles on the road I make free to prognosticate you'll be under the bed-springs uv that new fangled wagon uv yours and my hosses will be whizzing past you like a streak uv greased lightnin'. How would a little bet uv ten or twenty dollars suit you?"

"Oh, bankers never gamble," replied Whitley with undisturbed gravity. "Well, you'll follow with the luggage, Mr. Rankin, and no doubt we'll have the pleasure of seeing you again sometime tomorrow. Come away, Miss Holden. Luncheon is to be waiting at my hotel in Encampment in a couple of hours."

"Blame his skin," muttered Jim when the big automobile had whirled away. But Tom Sun was convulsed with laughter.

"He got your dander fairly riz, Jim," he chuckled.

Jim's visage expanded into a broad grin.

"Guess that's just what he was arter. But ain't he the most sassy cock-a-whoop little cuss anyhow?"

"Shall I help you with the luggage?" laughed Tom Sun.

"Oh, you just quit the foolin' game, Tom. Don't come nachural from you. Besides I might be gettin' a heap peevish and kind o' awkward with my artillery. Suppose we lubricate?"

So the old cronies crossed over to the Wren saloon, where a brace of cocktails soon restored Jim's ruffled dignity.

Meanwhile the automobile was speeding along.

Roderick was on the driver's seat beside Whitley, and absorbing the news.

"Oh, I just insisted on your Uncle Allen coming along," Whitley was telling him. "And Aunt Lois, too. My old folks will arrive at the end of the week. Meantime Aunt Lois is helping me with my trousseau."

"Your trousseau!"

"Yes—socks and things. You see it's all fixed up between me and dear Dorothy. Oh, she's the best girl ever—you'll remember I said that from the first, Rod, my boy." His face became grave, and his voice took a humble tone. "Of course I know I can never, fill the place of Grant Jones, and I told her that. But I'll do my best to make her happy, and I think she cares enough for me to

THE TREASURE OF HIDDEN VALLEY

let me try."

Roderick pressed the hand next him resting on the steering wheel.

"I'm sure you'll be very happy, both of you," he said; "and I congratulate you, Whitley, old fellow, from the bottom of my heart."

Whitley looked round and was his gay, light-hearted self once again.

"Thanks, old chap. Well, Barbara and Ben Bragdon are also ready. We're only waiting for you and Gail."

Roderick's face reddened.

"You're mighty kind but rather premature, I'm afraid."

"Oh, fudge and nonsense! We're all agreed the thing's settled, or as good as settled. Great guns anyone with half an eye could have told it, to see you handing her out of the train a little while ago."

"Really, Whitley."

"There now, just forget all that. So when talking matters over with Bragdon and our dear twins I suggested that we might as well ring the wedding bells for six as for two at a time—may come cheaper with the Reverend Grannon, you know, if we hand it to him wholesale."

Roderick no longer attempted to protest, and Whitley rambled on: "But, say, old fellow, your Uncle Allen has one on you. He declares that Gail Holden is just the very girl he intended for you right from the beginning—the young lady about whom you kicked when you had that row in the banker's room a year and a half ago—Great Scott, how time does fly!"

"Impossible," exclaimed Roderick in profound amazement

"The very same," replied Whitley. "The little tot of a girl with whom you had that desperate love affair down the river years and years ago—oh, quite a pretty story; your uncle told it to me with no end of charming details. And now he is mighty proud, I can tell you, over his own foresight and sagacity in picking just the right girl for you at the very start."

"He said that, did he?" queried Roderick with a grim smile.

"Yes, and that if you had followed his advice you could have had her then, without running away from home and facing all sorts of hardships and dangers."

"No, sir," exclaimed Roderick firmly. "Gail Holden is not that sort of girl. Uncle Allen forgets that she had to be won—or rather has to be won," he added, correcting himself when he caught the smile on Whitley's countenance.

"Well, you won't forget," laughed Whitley, "that I stood out of the contest and left the way clear for you. Lucky, though, that the College Widow took the bit between her teeth and bolted, eh, old man?"

"Hush!" whispered Roderick, throwing a warning glance over his shoulder.

"What are you two boys talking about?" asked Gail, with a bright smile from her seat at the back of the tonneau.

"Old college days," laughed Whitley, as he changed the clutch for a stiff up-grade.

Arriving at Encampment, they found Allen Miller walking nervously up and down the platform in front of the hotel. The red blood in Roderick's veins surged like fierce hammer strokes, with eagerness to once more grasp the hand of his old guardian.

He hastily excused himself, jumped from the auto and grasped the extended hand of his old guardian. He was soon led away by his uncle Allen, to the parlors of the hotel, to meet his Aunt Lois.

"Oh, I am so glad you brought Roderick here, Allen; for I just knew that I would get all fussed up and cry.

"There, there, Aunt Lois," said Roderick cheerily, after embracing her warmly, "we are not going to be separated any more,—or, if we are, it will not be for long at any one time. I know the way back to old Keokuk," said Roderick, laughing and hugging his dear aunt Lois again, "and you and Uncle Allen now know the road out to the Wyoming hills."

"I declare, Lois," said Uncle Allen, "you and Roderick act like a couple of school children." He laughed rather loudly as he said this, to hide his own agitation; but it was noticed that his eyes were filled with tears, which he hastily brushed away.

It was a happy luncheon party at the Bonhomme Hotel, Whitley playing the host to perfection, his guests, besides the new arrivals, being the whole Shields family, Banker Allen Miller and his wife, and the young state senator, Ben Bragdon. And early in the proceedings Gail to her surprise learned that Roderick was no other than her little boy lover on the river steamer *Diamond Joe* some fifteen years ago, and blushed in sweet confusion when Allen Miller in radiant good humor joked about coming events casting their shadows before. Roderick went to her rescue and promptly switched the topic of conversation.

Toward the close of the meal Buell Hampton was expounding to the banker a great irrigation scheme he had in view—to bring into Encampment Valley the waters of French Creek and Bear Creek, the former by a tunnel through the Hunter Range, the latter by a siphon under the Great Platte River, whereby a hundred thousand acres of rich valley lands, now wilderness because waterless, could be brought into profitable agricultural bearing.

"So you are going to drive us cattle men off the face of the country," laughed Mr. Shields.

"Better happy homes than roaming herds," replied Buell Hampton. "What nobler work could we take in hand?" he asked. "The smelter and the mine are running themselves now. Let us then see what we can do to make the desert blossom like the rose. Mr. Miller, Mr. Shields, myself—we can all help with capital. Mr. Bragdon, there is a life's work for you in this enterprise."

"Lawyers always come in for fat pickings," laughed Whitley Adams.

"General Holden," continued the Major, "I am sure will want to join in too. Then Roderick—"

He paused and glanced in his young friend's direction.

"Oh, I'm prepared to turn in all the gold from my mine," exclaimed Roderick enthusiastically.

Indeed Buell Hampton had kindled the spirit of enthusiasm

all round. The project was as good as launched—the dream of a generation of pioneers within sight of realization.

When coffee was being served on the veranda, the Major drew Roderick aside. They were seated alone at a little table.

"Roderick, my boy," Buell Hampton began, "I want to see you tonight at my home—all alone. Come about eight o'clock. I have several matters of importance to communicate. During the afternoon I'll be busy—I have some banking business to transact, besides I wish an hour or two with your uncle before my talk with you tonight. I am sorry to leave such a happy gathering, but am sure"—this with a gentle glance in Gail's direction—"that the time will not hang heavily on your hands. Until eight o'clock then;" and with a tap on Roderick's shoulder the Major crossed over and spoke a few words to Allen Miller, the two taking their departure a few moments later.

Roderick was mystified—less by Buell Hampton's actual words than by his grave look and manner.

Meanwhile Gail had risen and entered the drawing room that opened by French windows off the veranda, and the sound of her voice at the piano broke him from his momentary reverie. He rose and joined her.

CHAPTER XL.

BUELL HAMPTON'S GOOD-BY

RODERICK was prompt to the minute in keeping his appointment. He found the Major seated before a bright log-fire, and his first glance around the old familiar room showed the progress of some unusual preparations. The open lid of a traveling trunk revealed clothing and books already packed; the violin in its case rested on the centre table.

Buell Hampton interpreted his visitor's look of wonderment.

"Yes, Roderick," he said with a smile that was both tender and serious, "I am going away. But let us take things in their order. Sit down here, and let us smoke our pipes together in the old way—perhaps it may be for the last time in each other's company."

"Oh, don't say that, my dear Major," protested Roderick, in accents of real concern.

But Buell Hampton motioned him to his seat, and passed over the humidor. For a minute or two they smoked in silence. At last the Major spoke.

"Roderick, I have news that will greatly surprise you. I had a telegram from Boney Earnest just before we left San Francisco. I said nothing to you, for I did not wish with needless haste to disturb your happiness."

"Not about Gail?" asked Roderick, his face paling.

"No, no. This has nothing to do with Gail—at least it only affects her indirectly. You spoke today at lunch time about turning in the profits of your gold mine into the Encampment Valley irrigation scheme. I want to put you right on this mining matter first. Boney Earnest's telegram showed that neither you

319

nor I have a gold mine any longer. Hidden Valley has disappeared. Our claims are under five hundred feet of water."

"How could this have happened?"

"You have read in the newspapers that the cosmic disturbances of the San Francisco earthquake extended entirely across the continent. Indeed the shocks were felt distinctly in New York, Philadelphia, Boston, and other Atlantic points. Well, a number of prospectors have been up among the mountains getting ready to stake around our claims, and they report that three miles above Spirit Falls a vast new lake has been formed, completely filling the canyon."

"The shake brought down the grotto cavern, I suppose."

"And sealed it, damming back the river. That is undoubtedly what has happened. So Roderick, my dear fellow, you have to forget that gold. But of course you know that all I have is yours to share."

"No, no, Major," exclaimed Roderick, laying a hand on his friend's shoulder. "Besides your all too generous gift at Denver, I have my salary from the smelter company, and I'm going to chip in to the limit of my power for the advancement of that glorious irrigation scheme of yours. I did without the mine before. Thank God I can do without it now. My dear father's letter served its purpose—it brought me to Wyoming, and although I have no right to say so just yet I do believe that it has won for me Gail Holden's love."

"I am sure of it," remarked Buell Hampton quietly. "She has loved you for a long time—you were all in all to her before you followed to San Francisco, as the poor girl's anguish showed during those days when we both thought that you had perished."

"Then, Major," cried Roderick, the light of great joy illuminating his countenance, "if I have won Gail Holden's love I have won greater treasure than the treasure of Hidden Valley— greater treasure than all the gold claims in the world."

"Spoken like a man," replied Buell Hampton as he gripped Roderick's hand. The latter continued, his face all aglow:

"Everything has come out right When my Unde Allen refused to help me in my New York ventures he really saved me from cruel and accursed Wall Street where more hearts have been broken and lives of good promise wrecked than on all the battlefields of the world. When he handed me my father's letter, he took me out of that selfish inferno and sent me here into the sweet pure air of the western mountains, among men like you, the Reverend Stephen Grannon, Ben Bragdon, Boney Earnest, and good old Jim Rankin too, besides our dear dead comrade Grant Jones. Here I have the life worth living, which is the life compounded of work and love. Love without work is cloying, work without love is soul-deadening, but love and work combined can make of earth a heaven."

"And now you speak like a philosopher," said Buell Hampton approvingly.

"Which shows that I have been sitting at your feet. Major, for a year past not altogether in vain," laughed Roderick. "From every point of view I owe you debts that can never be repaid."

"Then let me improve this occasion by just one thought, Roderick. It is in individual unselfishness that lies the future happiness of mankind. The age of competition has passed, the age of combination for profit is passing, the age of emulation in unselfishness is about to dawn. The elimination of selfishness will lead to the elimination of poverty; then indeed will the regeneration of our social system be begun. Think that thought, Roderick, my dear fellow, when I am gone."

It was ever thus that Buell Hampton sought to sow the tiny grain of mustard seed in fertile soil.

"But why should you go away, Major?" asked Roderick protestingly.

"Because duty calls me—my work for humanity demands. But we shall come to that presently. For the moment I want to recall one of our conversations in this room—in the early days of our friendship. Do you remember when I gave it as my opinion that it would be conducive to the happiness of mankind if there was no abnormal individual wealth in the world?"

"That a quarter of a million dollars was ample for the richest man in the world—I remember every word, Major."

"Well, Roderick, today I have transferred to your credit in your Unde Allen's bank precisely this sum."

"Major, Major, I could never accept such a gift."

"Just hear me patiently, please. The sum is quite rightfully yours. It is really only a small fraction of what your father's claim might have produced for you had I taken you earlier into my full confidence and so helped you to the location of the rich sandbar with its nuggets of gold. Moreover, you know me well enough to understand that I count wealth as only a trust in my hands—a trust for the good of humanity. And I feel that, in equipping such a man as yourself, a man whom I have tested out and tried in a dozen different ways without your knowing it—in equipping you with a sufficient competency I really help to discharge my trust, for I invest you with the power to do unmeasured good to all around you. I need not expatiate on such a theme; you have heard my views many times. In sharing my wealth with you, Roderick, I simply bring you in as an efficient helper for the uplift of humanity. It therefore becomes your duty to accept the trust I hand over to you, cheerfully and wishing you Godspeed with every good work to which you set your hand."

"Then, Major, I can but accept the responsibility. I need not tell you that I shall always try to prove myself worthy of such a trust."

"I have yet another burden to place on your shoulders. The balance of the wealth at my present disposal I have also handed over to you—as my personal trustee. At this moment I do not know when and in what amount I shall require money for the task I am about to undertake. Later on you will hear from me. Meanwhile Allen Miller knows that my initial investment will be equal to his own in the valley irrigation scheme. You, Roderick, as my trustee may contribute further sums at your absolute discretion; if the work requires help at any stage, use no stinting hand irrespective of financial returns for me, because with me the thing that counts mainly is the happiness and prosperity of this town, its people, and the surrounding valley lands."

"But, Major, can't you remain with us and do these things yourself?"

"No; the call is preemptory. And if perchance you should never hear from me again, Roderick, continue, I beg of you, to use my money for the good of humanity. Count it as your own, use it as your own. I lay down no hard and fast rules to guide you. Give to the poor—give to those in distress—pay off the usurer's mortgage and stop excessive interest that makes slaves of the poor family struggling to own a little thatched cottage. Give wherever your heart is touched—give because it is God's way and God is prompting you by touching your heart."

Roderick listened in silence, deeply moved. He saw that Buell Hampton's mind was made up—that no pleading or remonstrance could alter the decision at which he had arrived. The Major had now risen from his chair; there was a softness in the rich full tones of his voice, a look of half pain in his eyes, as he went on: "But remember, although we may be parted, our friendship abides—its influences endure. Friendship, my dear Roderick, is elemental—without commencement and without end—a discovery. From the beginning of furthest antiquity, the pathway of the centuries have been lined with tablet-stones pronouncing its virtues. Friendship is the same yesterday, today, tomorrow and forever. It is an attraction of personalities and its power is unseen and as subtle as the lode-stone. It is the motive that impels great deeds of bravery in behalf of humanity. It speaks to the hearts of those who can hear its accents of truth and wisdom, and contributes to the highest ideals of honor, to the development of the sublimest qualities of the soul. It is the genius of greatness; the handmaiden of humanity. I have sometimes thought that if we could place in our own souls a harp so delicately attuned that as every gale of passion, of hope, of sorrow, of love and of joy swept gently over the chords, then we would hear in the low plaintive whisperings the melody of friendship's sweetest note—that quivers and weeps and laughs on the shore line of immortality."

"Your friendship, Major," said Roderick fervently, "will always be one of the most deeply cherished things in my life. But I cannot reconcile myself to the thought that we should part."

Buell Hampton laid a hand upon the young man's shoulder.

"Duty calls—the two little words are enough, although it grieves me sore to think that most likely we shall never meet again. Your work is here—your usefulness lies here. But as for me, my mission in the hills is finished. I am going to a far away country—not a new one, because there are many in squalor and poverty where duty leads me. There I will begin again my labors for the lowly and the poor—for those who are carrying an unjust portion of life's burdens. There is no lasting pleasure in living, my dear Roderick, unless we help hasten the age of humanity's betterment. Good-by," concluded the Major, smiling into Roderick's eyes and pressing his hand warmly—"good-by."

Almost dazed by the suddenness of the parting Roderick Warfield found himself out in the darkness of the night He was stunned by the thought that he had gripped his dear friend's hand perhaps for the last time—that there had gone out of his life the one man whom above all others he honored and loved.

Thus passed Buell Hampton from among the people of the hills. None of his intimates in or around Encampment ever saw him again.

CHAPTER XLI.

UNDER THE BIG PINE

ON the following afternoon Roderick saddled his pony Badger and rode over to the Conchshell ranch. The Holdens received the news of Buell Hampton's mysterious departure with deep regret; the Major had become very dear to their hearts, how dear they only fully realized now that he was gone.

It was toward evening when Gail proposed that they go riding in the woods. The invitation delighted Roderick, and Fleetfoot and Badger were speedily got ready.

"Let us follow the old timber road to the south," Roderick suggested. "I want to show you, only a few miles from here, a beautiful lake."

"I know of no such lake," she replied.

"Yet it is less than five miles away, and we shall christen it Spirit Lake, if you like the name, for it lies above Spirit Falls."

"You are dreaming. There is no such lake."

"I will show it to you. Come along."

Upward and onward he led her over the range. And when they gained the summit, there at their feet lay the great new lake about which Buell Hampton had told him, fully seven miles long and two miles wide, and not less than six or seven hundred feet deep as Roderick knew, for he had gathered nuggets of gold on the floor of the little canyon now submerged beneath the placid blue waters.

Gail gazed in silent admiration. At last she exclaimed: "Spirit Lake! It is well named. It is more like a dream than reality."

He helped her from the saddle. They tethered their mounts

325

in western fashion by throwing the reins over the horses' heads. They were standing under the branches of a big pine, and again they gazed over the waters. At the lower end of the lake was a most wonderful waterfall, dashing sheer down some four hundred feet into Spirit River.

For several minutes they continued to gaze in enraptured silence on the scene of tranquil beauty. Toward the east the forest was darkly purple—to the west, across the waters, the hills were silhouetted in splendid grandeur against a magnificent sunset. The whole range seemed clothed in a robe of finest tapestry. The sun was rapidly approaching the rim of the western horizon.

The afterglow of the red sunset marked paths of rippling gold on the waters. Vague violet shadows of dusk were merging over all. Nature was singing the lyric of its soul into things—crooning lake and mountains and forest-clad slopes to slumber.

It was Gail who at last broke the spell.

"Oh, how beautiful, how supremely beautiful," she murmured.

"Well, it is the earthquake that has wrought all this wonderful change," explained Roderick'. "And now, dear Gail, I have a story to tell you."

And, seating her on the turf by his side, under the big pine, where the waters lapped at their very feet, he proceeded to relate the whole romantic story of his father's lost find—his own lost claim. By the time the narrative was ended the sun had set behind the hills. Roderick rose, and giving his hands, helped Gail to her feet.

"So all this wonderful treasure of Hidden Valley lies beneath these waters," she exclaimed.

"Yes, but for me the real treasure is here by my side."

As he spoke these words his arm stole around her waist. She did not appear to notice his half timid embrace as together they stood viewing the panorama of a dying day. Presently he drew her closer.

"The day and the night blend," he whispered softly as if fearful of disturbing the picture. "Shall not our lives, sweetheart," asked

Roderick with vibrant voice, "likewise blend forever and forever?"

Gail half turning lifted her slender hands to Roderick's cheeks and he quickly clasped her tightly in his strong arms and kissed her madly on lips, eyes and silken hair.

"Roderick, my lover—my king," said Gail through pearly tears of joy.

"My little Gail," whispered Roderick, exultantly, "my sweetheart—my queen."

Slowly the light of day vanished. The sounds of night began walking abroad in the world. Dusk wrapped these lovers in its mantle. The day slept and night brooded over forest, lake and hills.

In a little while they lifted the bridle reins of their mounts and turning walked arm in arm down the old timber road toward Conchshell ranch.

They halted in the darkness and Roderick said: "Do you mind, dear, if I smoke?"

"Certainly not," was her cheery reply.

He bit the cigar and struck a match. The fight reflected on Gail's radiant face. "Wonderful," he ejaculated as he tossed the match away, laughing softly. He had quite forgotten to light his cigar.

"Why, what did you see, Roderick, you silly fellow, that is so wonderful?"

"I saw," said Roderick, "the dearest little woman in the wide, wide world—my mountain song girl—who is going to be kissed with all the pent-up passion of a 'grizzly' in just one-half second."

AFTERWORD

Into the warp and woof of my story of the West, "The Treasure of Hidden Valley," there have been woven a few incidents of the great calamity that some years ago befell the city of San Francisco. Perhaps some of my readers will care to peruse a more detailed description of that tragic happening.

W. G. E.

IT was on April 18, 1906, that San Francisco was shaken by a terrible earthquake which in its final effects resulted in the city being cremated into cinders and gray ashes.

The trembling, gyrating, shaking and swaying vibrations, the swiftly following outbursts of fire, the cries of those pinned beneath fallen débris and of the thousands who were seeking to escape by fleeing into the parks and toward the open country, produced the wildest pandemonium.

While there was no wind, yet a hundred fires originating at different points quickly grew into sheets of towering flame and spread to adjacent buildings, burning with demoniacal fierceness as if possessed by some unseen mysterious power, pouring forth red hot smoke until the prostrate city was melted into ruin by the intense heat of a veritable hell.

The night of April 17 and 18 had almost ended in San Francisco. It had been like many another night in that cosmopolitan city. Pleasure-seekers were legion,—negligent, care-free, wrapped in the outward show of things—part of it good—part of it not so good—some of it downright wicked as in Ancient Pompeii.

328

Yet the hour was late—or early, whichever you will—even for San Francisco. The clock in the city hall had resounded forth five strokes. Peaceful folk were in the realm of dreams that precede awakening. The roistering hundreds of a drunken night had gathered in places of vice and were sleeping away the liquor fumes. The streets were almost deserted.

The great printing presses that had been reverberating with the thunders of a Jove, gathering and recording the news from the four quarters of the earth, had paused and all was still. Here and there morning papers were on the streets and the preliminary work was in progress of sending them forth to the front doorsteps of the homes of rich and poor, from one end of the city to the other. Then, without warning, just eighteen minutes after the city clock had tolled its five strokes, one of the greatest news items and tragedies of the world's history was enacted. An historical milestone of the centuries was on that eventful morning chiseled on the shore line of the Pacific Coast.

Suddenly from the womb of sleeping silence, from far below the earth's crust, just as the dawn of a new day began purpling the eastern sky, there came forth a rumbling and muttering of unearthly noises like the collapsing of palaces of glass or the clanking of giant chains. It came from beneath the entire city and was borne upward and abroad on the startled wings of a mysterious fear. It was a shrieking, grinding confusion of subterranean thunder, like the booming of heavy artillery in battle. It was deafening in its dreadfulness, and drove terror to the heart of the hardiest. It sounded to the affrighted people as if two mighty armies of lusty giants of the underworld were grappling in mortal combat and in their ferocious anger were unwittingly breaking the earth's fragile shell into yawning cracks and criss-cross fissures. Mount Tamalpais was fluttering like the wings of a snared pigeon.

In the space of seconds, the whole populace awoke, excepting those who had answered the last call; for some there were, pinned under falling walls, who were overtaken by swift death in the very act of awakening.

The uncounted number that were crushed to death and had life's door closed to them forever, no one will ever know. In the forty-eight seconds that followed the beginning of the deep guttural bellowing of hideous noises from somewhere below the earth's surface, buildings rocked and heaved and twisted, while heavy objects of household furniture were tumbled across rooms from one corner to the other and the occupants helplessly tossed from their beds.

Such an awakening, such lamentations, such cursing, such prayers, and then into the debris-littered streets the multitude began pouring forth, half-clothed, wild and panic-stricken.

The stunning shock, like a succession of startled heart-beats, lasted twelve seconds less than one minute, but those who experienced the ordeal say it seemed an eternity—forty-eight seconds—terrible seconds—of sickening, swaying suspense. A heaving earth, jerking, pulsing to and fro in mad frenzy, while countless buildings were swaying and keeping time to a wild hissing noise like the noise of boiling, blubbering fat in a rendering caldron.

It was the dawn of a new day abounding in hideous noises— detonations of falling masonry, the crash of crumbling, crushing walls, the shrieks of maimed and helpless victims—and all the people stupefied with a terrible fear, women weeping in hysterical fright and everyone expectant of they knew not what, unable to think coherently or reason, yet their voices filling the stricken city with cries and moans of heart-rending terror and lamentation. And all the while there came up from somewhere an unearthly threatening roar that awed the multitude into unnatural submissive bewilderment.

At the end of eight and forty seconds the frantically tossed earth quieted—became normal and was still. Some of the buildings righted and were quiescent, and a moment of silence followed, except for the crowing of cocks, the whinnying of frightened horses and the whining of cowering dogs. This condition, however, was only of momentary duration.

Almost immediately the streets became a wild scene of turmoil as the half-clothed, half-crazed men, women and children went rushing up and down in every direction, they knew not why nor where. Doors were broken open to allow egress, shutters were slammed, windows were hastily raised, and like a myriad of ants the rest of the people who until now had been penned up, struggled forth into open ways—thinly clad, some almost naked, trembling, gazing about awe-stricken, looking each at his fellow, indifferent to the destruction going on about them, each filled with prayerful thankfulness for life. Then, like a rehearsed orchestra of many voices, there arose, seemingly in unison, a chorus of heart-piercing wails and calls from thousands of throats for loved ernes—loved ones lost who could not answer.

In the pale light of that April dawn, this vast army of survivors, while chilled with outward cold, shivered also with an unspeakable inward dread.

Along the streets of proud San Francisco in every direction were huge masses of bricks, cornices, fallen ragged chimneys and walls, tumbled together in complex dykes of débris like the winrows of a hay field and interspersed with the dead and dying bodies of man and horse alike, vanquished in life's uneven contest.

A little later in the vicinity of the ten-million-dollar courthouse, crowds of frightened people gathered, attracted perhaps by the terrific thundering of the mammoth stone slabs and concrete sides and columns of the structure, as, in their loosened condition from the steel skeleton, they kept crashing down upon the street in riotous disorder.

Every block in the city held its tragedy, its silent evidence of a mighty internal upheaving of Goliath strength. There were hundreds of dead, while others lay maimed in tortured suffering, buried under wreckage, pinned down by the giant hands of the Angel of Destruction. The unfortunates still living were fastened like insects caught in traps, helpless, but hoping for relief, awaiting the unwritten chapter that was yet to come.

The great earthquake of San Francisco had spent its force—its rude results lay in careless disheveled evidence on every hand—and now the nerve-strained, half-crazed and bewildered people caught the sound of fire bells clanging hurriedly into nearer distances.

The fire hose and the corps of hook and ladder men came rushing with all speed, drawn by frenzied horses, hastily turning street corners and dashing around fallen walls while the automatic fire bells were cutting the air in metallic, staccato beats of wildest alarm. Soon the throbbing of the fire engines began and false hope sprung rife in the hearts of the people. Those running south on Market Street paused in bewilderment, not knowing which way to go, for fire calls and flames were evident, not in one location nor two, but in hundreds at widely separated places throughout the erstwhile magnificent metropolis of the Occident.

Black columns of smoke began rising from ominous red furnace flames beneath, and curled lazily into the balm of the upper air, indifferent to the wails of the helpless unfortunates maimed and pinned beneath the wrecked buildings of a demolished and burning city.

The murky smoke like mourning crape hung mutely above, while beneath its canopy life's sacrificial offering lay prostrate, the dying and the dead. The consuming flames spread quickly, and the horror of the hopeless condition of the injured was soon apparent, while the sobs and cries of the doomed victims became maddening because of the very impotency to succor them.

The suddenness of it all did not give time for the rescuers. Then too, the smoke-blinded and half-choked people in the crowded, congested streets were stampeding toward the open country—to Golden Gate Park and the Presidio. Many of the trapped victims, well and strong, might have escaped but could not exert normal power to shake off the fetters that held them down under fallen wreckage too heavy for their hampered strength. It was a veritable bedlam, some cursing, some praying, most all crying loudly as if in crazed pain for assistance.

The first paroxysm passed, the poor unfortunates seemingly became more patient, believing that relief would surely come. The crackling flames mounted higher and came alarmingly nearer. Finally, as the conflagration with a hurried sweep began to envelop these pinioned human beings, they shrieked in agony like lost souls in terrible anguish at a most horrible and certain death. Their voices rose with the rising of the flames until at last the piteous cries were hushed perforce, and only the crackling sound of burning wood and the forked tongues of raging red fire greeted the sun, that morning of April 18, as it climbed above the eastern mountains and looked upon the scene of woeful destruction.

Is it any wonder that strong men wept? Is it to be marveled at that those separated from friends and relatives grew bewildered, frantic and crazed with grief and fear, and that chaos reigned supreme?

Gradually amid the whirl of emotions there stepped forth men who until now had been stunned into silence and temporarily bereft of reason. The first staggering shock passed, they became possessed in a measure with calmness and courage. They girded their belts afresh and although many of them began by cursing the heartless, cruel fire and the terribleness of it all, they quickly and determinedly turned to the stupendous work of endeavoring to subdue its ravages.

Then a new terror raised its ghostly head and held the people in a grip of deepest despair. The earthquake had broken the supplying water mains, and presently the city was without water and the fire engines and other fire-fighting apparatus were worthless junk. It was a grievous blow to momentarily raised hopes and courageous resolution.

The flames raged on with the fleetness of race horses, eating out the heart of the city, burning it into cinders, and cremating the flesh and bone of fallen victims.

Dynamite was brought into use, gunny sacks and bedding of all sorts were saturated with water from barrels and tanks. Grappling hooks and human hands made up the armament of puny defense against the over-powering and masterful flames of annihilation.

Against these feeble weapons, the grim demon of fire planned an attack of certain devastation. It was as if his Satanic Majesty with all his imps were in their ruthless cunning directing a fiendish work that would permit no record but death to the unfortunate, no record to the proud city but gaunt-ribbed skeleton buildings, red hot cinders and blackened ash heaps.

Overturned stoves in a thousand houses throughout the residential districts had early started a multitude of fires and split the fire-fighters into many divisions, and therefore into less effective units in their futile efforts even partially to check the mighty master—the devouring tempest of fire that crackled and sported in its insatiable greed.

There was still to follow yet another misfortune, an execrable crime—that of wicked inhuman incendiarism. At places flames burst forth kindled by the hands of a coterie of merciless ghouls. These inhuman devils added to the calamities heaped upon their fellows by setting fire to unburned dwellings whose owners had fled. There was neither necessity nor reason for their dastardly acts. With sponges soaked in kerosene, they did this damnable work—indulging dreams perhaps of greater loot, greed and avarice in their cruel eyes, blackest hell in their debauched hearts.

In the beginning of this losing fight with terrors of the fire king, seemingly unconquerable, only one ray of hope was discernible—there was no wind from ocean or bay in San Francisco that April morning. The clouds that filled the heavens with ominous blackness were only stifling smoke from the burning buildings below.

High above the crimson snake-tongued flames the black smoke hung like a pall, silent and motionless, while fringing it around far away in every direction was the clear blue sky, serene, unfathomable.

As the heroic work of fighting the fire demon progressed, it was soon discovered that the police were insufficient. Crowds of ghouls were pressing the firemen, while robbery, rapine and murder ran riot. Human blood that day was easily spilled. For the sake of pelf and plunder, life was cheap.

The boldness of this lawless condition brought about its own remedy. Strong men arose in their might. Under able leadership they quickly formed a committee of safety. The National Guard was sent to help them.

General Fred Funston of the U. S. Army telegraphed to the Secretary of War for authority, and within three hours was hurrying United States troops into the burning city, and immediately placed it under martial law. The crowds were quickly driven back by the soldiers, fire lines were established, government troops, guards and police all bent nobly to the task of endeavoring to subdue the flames. Buildings were dynamited to shut off the fire's progress, insubordinate as well as predatory ruffians were shot down without mercy, and thus was order brought out of chaos. But as the hours went by, despite all efforts, the gormandizing flames consumed acres and acres of buildings.

Every wandering automobile was pressed into service and loaded with dynamite. Thus for hour after hour the losing fight with the merciless flames went on.

As the fire burnt its way south on Market Street, the isolated centers crept toward each other with ever widening circles of flame. While there was no breeze to fan them on, yet the flames seemed possessed of some invisible means of progression—an unseen spirit of continued expansion lurked within. The buildings were like so much dry timber, igniting without direct contact of spark or flame, only from the tremendous heat that was generated. Sweeping on and on the different conflagrations at last came together—joined in greater strength, flared up hundreds of feet high, until it looked as if the entire city was one vast molten lake of undulating waves of fire.

The roar of the flames could be heard far beyond the confines of the city—the immense columns and clouds of black smoke continued to sweep upward, until high aloft they spread out into the great canopy as if in shame they fain would hide from angels above the terrible destruction being wrought in this fiery pit below.

As the hours went by, the exodus of people continued. The fascination of it all held the multitudes spell-bound. They for a time were forgetful of hunger, but moved on, this way and that as the burning districts compelled them to go. The public parks began to fill with refugees. The Presidio and the hills overlooking the city were blackened with throngs of people shivering from cold and beginning to suffer the pangs of hunger, the rich and the poor touching shoulders, condoling one with the other in lamentations. This surging mass of famishing humanity were clothed, or partially clothed, in strange and ridiculous costumes.

Household goods littered the outlying streets. Most of the wayfarers who reached the country had little luggage. Many had carried some useless article nearest at hand, selected in their hurry without thought of its value or utility.

One woman held a bird cage under her arm—empty, with the door swinging open. Another carried a carving knife in one hand and a feather-bedecked hat of gaudiness in the other. One man was seen dragging an old leather-bound trunk by a rope—investigation proved the trunk to be without contents.

Notwithstanding the people had lost their all, and in most cases were famishing, yet the great mass were good-natured and tolerant, the strong helping the weak. The chivalry of the West and its rugged manhood abided in their midst There was a common brotherhood in the ranks of these homeless human beings. Distinctions between rich and poor were obliterated—they were all fellow refugees.

No street cars were running in the city. Market Street, into which the greater number of street car railroad tracks converged, was littered with fallen buildings, useless hose and fire fighting apparatus, twisted beams, cinders, heaps of hot ashes and charred bodies of the dead.

It was about eleven o'clock in the morning of the first day of this terrible devastation that the famous Palace Hotel had finally been emptied of its last guest. The rooms throughout were bestrewn with fallen plaster from ceiling and walls, but otherwise, strange to narrate, the structure had suffered but little damage from the earthquake while all around were collapsed and fallen buildings.

At the Mission Street side of the building and on the roof the employees had fought bravely to save this noted hostelry. But as the noon hour approached they gave up all hope. Hurrying through the rooms of the departed guests in an endeavor to save, if possible, abandoned luggage, they gossiped about the "yellow streak," as they called it, of a world-noted singer—a guest of the hotel—who had been frightened almost to death by the earthquake and developed evidence of rankest selfishness in his mad efforts to save himself.

Then in sadder tones they talked of the impending and inevitable destruction of the magnificent hotel, where most of them had been employed for years. As the heat from the on-sweeping flames began to be unbearable, they hurried away one by one until the famous caravansary was finally deserted by man and in full possession of the ruthless devouring flames.

Great crowds stood on Montgomery Street near the site of the Union Trust Building and watched the burning of the Palace Hotel. Held back by the soldiers in mournful silence, the mass of people watched the angry flames leaping from roof and windows. Soon the fire spread to the Grand Hotel across the street. The flames shot up higher, and then when their task of destruction was finally finished, gradually sank down until nothing but roofless, windowless, bare bleak walls, gaunt, blackened and charred, were left—a grim ghost of the old hotel that boasted of a million guests during its gorgeous days of usefulness, and around which twined a thousand memories of the golden days of the Argonauts of California.

Half a block away a newspaper building had been blown up by dynamite—a similar attempt with the Monadnock Building failed of its purpose.

When night finally fell, those on the north side of Market Street rejoiced greatly, for it seemed that the fire, at least in the down-town business district, had burned itself into submission. So said a well-known milliner for men, as he ate a huge steak at a famous resort on the ocean shore and indulged heavily in champagne in celebration of the saving of his premises. He celebrated a day too soon—the following morning his business house was in ashes.

To the few who were care-free in the sense that they had not lost relatives or friends, the panorama of the fire when darkness came on will never be forgotten because of the wonderful pyrotechnic display—the magnificent yet appalling splendor and beauty of the burning city.

The scene was set as by a wonder-hand of stagecraft. The fire was raging fiercely in an immense pit—topographically the lowest part of the city. Around this pit the rising ground, like a Greek amphitheatre, stretched up toward the Sutro Estate and Ricon Hill on the one side and toward California Street, Nob and Telegraph Hills on the other. To the east was Alcatraz like a sentinel in the waters; across the Bay the cities of Alameda, Oakland and Berkeley. On every vantage point the people gathered—on the heights of Alcatraz and on the roofs of buildings in the trans-bay cities. In silence they gazed at the awe-inspiring drama of destruction that was being enacted before them.

With the advance of night, the towering flames in this vast sweep of many miles of a circular fire line presented a scene that defies description. The general color effect was of a deep blood red, while the smoke as a background to the picture belched up in rolling black volumes, with here and there long forks of flashing fire shooting above the deep crimson glow of the mighty furnace.

Before the roaring billows of flame the tallest buildings were as tinder wood in their helplessness. The Call Building, lifting its head high above its neighbors, was like an ignited match-box set on end. The living flaming wall behind overtopped it as a giant does a pigmy.

Nine o'clock! Ten o'clock! Midnight!—and those who watched and waited and slept not, with nothing but excitement to stay their hunger, saw in the lurid light that by a flank movement the fire had unexpectedly crept far up Montgomery Street from the Ferry. The trade winds were stirring. The fire, in its pulsing undulations, presented the lure and the sensuous poetry of death. It barred all trespassing on the one side and burnt its way through on the other. It was seen that the entire banking district was doomed. Alas, the feeble protests of feeble men! It was a wild outlaw, untamed and untamable fire, that defied all human interference.

And Chinatown—the world-noted Chinatown of San Francisco—what of that? It too had gone the way of annihilation. They say brutality was practiced, and it is whispered to this day that those in charge of dynamiting the Chinatown section of the city were careless and did not warn the inmates of opium dens—it is said they blew up many buildings that held within them, or in the grottoes beneath, innumerable inmates. Whether or not this is true no one can positively say. If true, there is some excuse. The Chinese dwellings were honey-combed underground with dark and devious passages, and it was perhaps impossible, for lack of time and dearth of knowledge how to penetrate these hidden recesses, to warn the drugged dreamers.

In this district the fire raged as if possessed by a million devils. Over the city's tenderloin on the edge of Chinatown, it swept with a flame of reckless wrath and purification. Buildings whose very timbers were steeped in vice and immorality burned into ashes of cleanliness. The haunts of the lustful, the wine-bibber and the dope-fiend were consumed in a fashion horrible, terrible, pitiless and final.

The city was burned into scrap iron of contortioned steel beams, ragged chimneys half broken and heaps of blackened cinder. As the hours went by it seemed the fire continually found new fuel to feed upon in its savagery and madness. The accumulation of days and years of human labor crumbled into nothingness. Thousands, then hundreds of thousands, then millions, until the enormous total reached $600,000,000 of wealth that was melted away in this fiery crucible!

Egypt, cursed by Moses and weeping for its firstborn, was in no more pitiable plight than this calamity-visited city of San Francisco shaken by earthquake shock, then swept by fire.

Four and one-half miles one way the fire travelled, then four and one-half miles the other it burned its devastating way. Behind it in its path of ruin were only cracked granite walls, twisted steel girders, crumbling and broken cornices; before it, a scattering field of a few untouched buildings yet to conquer.

A Nero with an evil eye on a city's undoing, and the power of a wicked tyrant to fulfill his sordid wish, could have been no more ruthless in his dastardly heartless methods of destruction.

When the fire was finally ended the buildings that had been burned, if placed in a row, would have extended for two hundred miles in a straight line.

Never in the world's history has there been such a fire. The burning of ancient London was child's play beside it. Chicago's fire was a mere bagatelle. Never has the world read, never had the world dreamed, of such a conflagration. In days to come, grandfathers will tell of it to their grandchildren, nodding their sage old heads to emphasize the horror of it all, relating to the young people who gather about their knees, how great buildings supposed to be fire-proof crumpled up before the swirling sheets of melting flame and the entire city became a prey to the all-devouring conqueror. And this is the tragic story of proud San Francisco, cosmic-tossed and fire-beleaguered capital of the Occident.

www.ingramcontent.com/pod-product-compliance
Lightning Source LLC
Chambersburg PA
CBHW031153050726
47495CB00019B/1667